FOR LOVE OR MONEY

"Damn it all!" He swung round and lunged toward her. Catching her wrists, he fell with her onto the bed with a great creak of springs. He landed on top of her. His thigh pressed down between her legs, his face only inches above hers. "Listen to me and listen good. This is why little girls shouldn't be riding around with outlaw gangs."

She turned her head away. "Give me my money and I'll leave."

He rolled to his side, carefully lifting his leg off her. Propping himself up on one elbow, he put a hand on her chin and gently tipped it back. His voice was soft and slightly thick. "You'll leave because it's the best thing for you."

"You'd like that, wouldn't you?" she yelled. "You want all the money for yourself. You won't have to be bothered with me. You—"

His fingers crushed her shoulders. His eyes blazed at her. "Aw, hell."

He kissed her. This time his arms cradled her, one big hand at the back of her head, turning her to fit their mouths together. The kiss went on and on. She could sense he was kindling his passion. His chest heaved as if he were drowning.

"You're a fool," he murmured into her mouth. His heart pounded against her breast. "Stop me . . ."

MY OUTLAW

Rachel Davis

Zebra Books
Kensington Publishing Corp.

http://www.zebrabooks.com

For Jim
For all our love through all our yesterdays—
"Today itself's too late!"

Chapter One

Chariton River Crossing
The Chicago, Rock Island, & Pacific Railroad
November, 1874

Mary Carolyn Ross could feel the earth vibrating.

The tremors had begun beneath her boots, where they manifested themselves in a faint tingling in the soles of her feet. To be absolutely sure, she hunkered down to put one gloved hand flat on the ground.

Yes. Oh, yes. Oh, God. It's coming.

Her teeth began to chatter. She clenched her jaw and cocked her ear toward the west. She couldn't hear anything but the chirping of crickets in the darkness around her, the croaking of frogs from the pools beneath the water tank.

Rising, she burrowed her chin more deeply in the collar and shoved her hand back into the pocket of her coat. Beneath her fingers the well-worn paper crackled. There it was—comfort and inspiration and courage, all in a small much-read volume. How she wished it would provide a little warmth.

White mist rose around her, but otherwise the night was dark as pitch. No moon. No stars. Thick clouds had rolled in the day before. The rain had fallen intermittently. Bleak November was giving way to December.

As a result she was perfectly miserable. Her throat was already feeling scratchy. Her nose was cold. Her left foot ached from the icy wetness that had seeped inside her leaky boot. This outlaw game had drawbacks she hadn't counted on.

It's not too late, a voice whispered inside her head. *It's not too late.*

Another voice inside her head broke in sternly. It is too late, Mary Carolyn. You're going to do this. You have to. You'll hate yourself forever if you don't.

The vibration became more pronounced. It turned to a rumble like distant thunder. Through the trees a light shone. Bright. Brighter. So bright it was like a blast in her eyes outlining the dark trunks in fiery yellow. The rumble became a roar shattering all nature. The headlight grew bigger than the moon, had there been a moon to compare it to. The light ran past her, racing down a pair of gleaming parallel streaks of silver.

Steam hissed. The roar divided itself into the strokes of individual pistons and the clacking of steel wheels already rolling slowly along steel rails.

The headlight split and flashed on either side of the tree trunk that shielded her from view. The girl who called herself Buster when she wanted to be very brave pressed her hands against her cheeks and stared through the light, mesmerized. The noise filled her head. She slid her hands up over her ears.

The cowcatcher rolled past first like a monster's iron teeth. The Cyclops eye glared above it. Between them was the boiler, a huge black vault of steam so hot it could cook a man's flesh from his limbs. Beneath it rolled the great driving wheels with their connecting rods to the other wheels. On the back of the giant, their faces lighted by spill from the fire door, rode its masters—an insignificant engineer and fireman. At their backs rolled the coal tender, a big gold Number 6 gleaming faintly on its side.

It's not too late. It's not too late, the wheels seemed to say. Mary Carolyn's teeth chattered so violently that they shook her whole body.

"Shut up!" The voice, Buster's, growled at the silly weak girl.

Steam hissed as the rest of the stock rolled by in the darkness—stock cars distinguishable by lines of darkness seen through black slats; boxcars, one empty with its doors open and gaping; flatcars of logs bound for the lumber mill; the express car with its light showing through a grille in the sliding door; and the Pullman car—a steel hotel with beds and porters for the richer, more fortunate members of the traveling public.

After it, came the faintly lighted coaches where people could ride all night for less than a dollar. A few passengers looked as if they might be awake, sitting upright. Most were slumped to one side or the other. Probably others were stretched out on the benches, invisible to the watcher in the dark.

From the steam belly came a short, sharp whistle, adding its urgent new note to the turbulence of the night.

Mary Carolyn started to her feet. The train was almost stopped. The engine rolled abreast of the water tank to take on coal and water. Refueled, it would roll down the gentle slope from the plain to cross the bridge over the Chariton River.

The brakeman gripped his wheel and applied the brakes. The wheels squealed as steel skidded along steel. Sparks flew into the night. The cars shuddered as, one by one through the line, they fought their couplings. Last came the private car, as far away from the noise and smoke of the engine as could be. It slid past her followed by the lighted caboose. A small crew was already swinging down from it and moving up the line to check the cars.

Now comes the tricky part. Mary Carolyn waited until they had moved past her hiding place.

She pulled a black neckerchief up to cover the bottom half of her face and tugged her hat down over her eyes. Then like a shadow she darted to the private car. One gloved hand caught the brass handrail to swing up onto its platform. Then she gasped in dismay. She wasn't tall enough. Not by half. Not only had the steps been turned up, but a wire gate had been secured across the opening.

Alongside the train in the darkness ahead, one man shouted

to another. She shrank back against the side of the car. Had she been seen?

The engine rolled forward again. It jerked her off her feet tearing the handrail from her grasp. Off balance, she slammed face down into the gravel on the roadbed. Her chin hit with enough force to click her teeth together and drive the breath from her lungs. She could feel her blood beneath the handkerchief mask.

Stunned, she almost gave up then and there. She felt as if she'd been hit with a giant fist. *You can't do this,* Mary Carolyn thought. *Can't. Shouldn't. Mustn't.*

"Up you go," Buster whispered. "You just need to practice this part."

Damning her insidious other self, Mary Carolyn hauled herself to her feet and staggered after the train. The caboose had no gate. Still it was going to be a long step. The train was still rolling when she caught its handrail with both hands and swung her feet off the ground.

Her boots banged against the iron steps, but couldn't find a hold. Her toes dragged through the gravel. Her arms at full stretch felt as if they were being wrenched from their sockets. She was just about to let go when dread of being thrown again when the train stopped made her make one more effort. The engine slid again, the cars jolted forward and then backward. This action gave her enough impetus to throw one knee up onto the step.

Scrambling frantically, straining, bucking upward, she worked her way onto the platform. For a few seconds she crouched there, counting her bruises, breathing hard.

Robbing trains was going to be tough work, she decided. She had already worked up a sweat, as well as being knocked for a loop. She managed a tiny trace of a smile. At least she was mastering some of the outlaw expressions. Sucking in a deep breath, she faced the door of the private car. Another locked gate barred her way, but she took only a few seconds to climb to the rail of the caboose, step across, and swing down. The door of the private car was directly in front of her.

Don't let it be locked. Please God.

She took another deep breath. Everything was suddenly very still. The night had taken on a hundred eyes, watching her. She reached for the handle. It turned smoothly, silently. She leaned her shoulder against the door.

And pushed herself into Stygian darkness fouled by rank cigar smoke.

Clell Miller closed his eyes. His mouth partially concealed by a flowing mustache was clamped tight. His jaw was set. A nighthawk twittered softly as it swooped by somewhere in the dark sky. From the other side of the tracks a bird of a different feather made a distinctive whistle. Clell's eyes flew open. With a groan he pursed his lips and answered with the same sound. The train's crew walked past him with lanterns swinging.

Minutes later, a burly form rose from the ditch at the roadbed and clubbed the brakeman as he checked the express car. The man went down without a sound, his body sliding headfirst into the ditch. On the other side of the train another figure rose. Unfortunately, his quarry turned to look back. The first blow from the blackjack fell on his shoulder.

The crewman let out a cry, half of pain, half of surprise, before the upswing of the lead fishing sinkers packed loosely into a heavy sock caught him in the jaw and sent him sprawling backward.

"Harry?" an uncertain voice called from up ahead. "You all right?" When Harry didn't answer, the caller warily put his back to the coach. "Harry? Hey!"

Clell heard another scuffle followed by a thud. On both sides of the train, the crew was being overwhelmed by the men rising from the roadbed. Most of those targeted fell without a sound. A couple who resisted were quickly dispatched by reinforcements. Not a shot was fired. Not a minute wasted. Again the nighthawk whistled.

With a sigh, Clell swung himself up onto the platform at the back of the coach as the rest of the gang swarmed onto the platforms of the other coaches, the Pullman, and the express car.

* * *

Inside the private car, Mary Carolyn waited a full minute. Her eyes strained desperately to adjust to the tomblike darkness. She had never counted on it being so dark. The night that had concealed her so efficiently now hid her quarry.

Remember, she counseled, herself, you know how it's arranged. The parlor was at one end with its table and comfortable chairs. The bedroom and bath were at the other. Then she had a frightening thought. At which end was she? Which end had been coupled onto the train first?

She didn't know. There was no help for it. She had to strike a match.

Feeling about her until she found a surface, she drew her pistol and laid it at the ready. Then she pulled the box of matches out of her pocket. She turned her back. Her hand was shaking so badly that she dropped one. She broke another. A third flamed up with a terrible scratching sound, but died immediately. At last the fourth attempt produced a light.

A groan, a grunt, a sleepy voice, "What the hell . . . ?"

Instantly, she crushed the flame in her gloved hand.

She spun around. Her hand fumbled for the pistol, found it, then brought it up to aim it toward the sound. Her legs were shaking. Her body was cold as ice. Her blood roared in her ears. Her heart pounded so hard that it shook her chest. She brought up her other hand to steady the gun. She was doing it. She was going to rob a man.

In the darkness only a few feet from her, she heard another match being scratched against a striker. Clothing rustled. A body thumped as it turned heavily.

She tightened her grip on the pistol. Nervously, she checked the black handkerchief. The fabric seemed to be in place.

A glow appeared behind the bedcurtains in an alcove.

"Who's there?" The voice was stronger this time.

She dared not wait for her victim to reach for any weapon he might have taken to bed with him. Guided by the glow, she darted across the carpeted floor and swept the curtain back.

By the light of a small paraffin lamp, DeGraffen Somervell

blinked up at her. His thick gray hair bushed out all over his skull. He blinked and belched. "Who the hell are you?"

Then his eyes crossed as he looked into the bore of the pistol only a couple of inches from his nose. He sucked in a frightened breath.

"Roll out," she commanded, then cursed herself mentally. She had forgotten to pitch her voice low. She tried again. "Roll out of that bed, Somervell." Thank heaven for her natural huskiness. She dropped her chin and deepened her voice still more.

His eyes flew to her face, narrowing, trying to guess what she looked like beneath the mask, trying to take the measure of his assailant. Then they scanned her figure. "I'll do no such thing."

"Come on." She stabbed the pistol closer, making him snap his head back. "Come on. Roll out and crawl to the safe."

This time he swallowed. His eyes flickered uncertainly, then skittered to the small hammock secured beneath the window.

Through the netting she could see black leather and the gleam of a pearl handle above it. "Forget it," she warned. "You'd be dead before you could get that popgun out of the holster. Now roll!"

Still he hesitated. Despite her gun almost touching his chest, he leaned toward her, his eyes locking with hers, staring.

"Roll! Goddammit!" Her voice was so loud it startled her, but it did the trick. At the same moment she jerked the gun up. It hit him in the mouth.

With a blistering curse he rolled.

Buster knew a moment of sweet triumph. This robbery was going to go off just like the books. He was doing what she told him. "Popgun" had been a good word. It had sounded rough and dangerous as if she thought his weapon was useless. She stepped back out of his way. "Now crawl. And remember this pistol is pointed at the back of your head."

He crawled, his white nightshirt catching under his knees, tripping him. More curses spewing forth. He took a clumsy fall on his face. The soles of his feet and the backs of his hairy legs flashed pink.

Quelling a hysterical giggle, she lifted the paraffin lamp from its bracket and followed him. Once the safe was open, she tossed him a gunnysack. "Fill it up." She stabbed the gun at him. "Every last dollar."

"Open up." Cole Younger knocked with his gun butt on the door of the express car.

A young face appeared at the grilled window. Cole raised the brakeman's lantern and his own gun, a .44 Colt percussion with a hair trigger. "Open up or get perforated."

When the messenger hesitated, Cole thumbed the hammer back. "Your choice, rube. If you want to die for the Chicago, Rock Island, I'll personally see you get your wish."

After a moment's hesitation, the door slid back. The messenger stood silhouetted in the light. His hands reached for the ceiling. Cole grinned at his brother Bob and then hoisted his big body into the car. The messenger stood aside, his face white as chalk. Bob followed Cole.

Cole eased the hammer down and jabbed his gun into his holster. He strode to the safe, gesturing for the messenger to follow. With his big hand he indicated the solid black and green box with the steel dial. "Open it."

The messenger gulped. His eyes flickered toward the safe, then dropped. "I can't."

Bob Younger's gun prodded his kidney. "You want me to open you?"

"Honest," the youth started to protest.

Lips peeled back from his teeth in a mockery of a grin, Cole drew his gun. He stabbed it into the man's face. "Open it."

Two guns were too much. The man nodded weakly. Cole smiled as he let the barrel drop. "Mighty wise of you. Get to doin' it."

The engineer and firemen stared into Frank James's double-barreled .12-gauge sure that the slightest false move would mean they would be cut to pieces.

The black mask and the steely stare over it did their work. Cautiously, they backed away only to be herded back toward the throttle by the sight of Jim Younger's six-gun trained on them as he climbed up from the other side of the track. Frank motioned to the fireman. "Shovel in some more coal."

The fireman looked at the engineer, who nodded shortly. "Do it, Burt. The passengers'll be better off if we take 'em out of here."

"That's wise," Frank agreed judiciously. "Run it a few miles. We'll be long gone with our pistols and shotguns. You can back it up and pick up your crew. Nobody'll get hurt. You'll still make your schedule. It'll be just like a bad dream."

Ducking his head, the fireman unhitched the fire door and slung a couple of shovelfuls of coal into its fiery maw.

Frank leaned his head out the side to listen for the nighthawk's signal.

His resentment smoldering, Clell waited on the platform of the passenger coach while Jesse James waited on the platform at the other end of it. Clell pulled his hat down tight over his forehead and pulled his neckerchief up to his eyes. He had purposefully worn a bulky coat to conceal his build. Maybe altogether with the darkness and the element of surprise, no passenger would get a good description of him. With a sigh he drew his gun and forced the coach door open.

At the same time Jesse James turned the lamp up at his end of the coach. The flame wavered, then brightened. The passengers nearest stirred and blinked blearily.

Grinning broadly and aiming a gun at each side of the aisle, Jesse announced in a loud voice, "Wake up, everybody. Stand up and turn out your pockets."

The grunts and groans of people disturbed in their sleep turned to confused turmoil as men tried to make sense of the situation.

"You heard me," Jesse barked. "Everybody up. Turn out your pockets. And put everything you got in Clell's basket."

At the back of the car, Clell gritted his teeth, knowing full well why Jesse had called him by name. He caught up the broad white-oak basket the porter used to sell food to the passengers. As he passed down the aisle, he could only pray that they were making too much noise or were too befuddled by sleep to remember much that was said.

At that minute a burly drummer yelled, "Jesse James! My Gawd, it's Jesse James."

A woman screamed. The exclamations turned to pandemonium as the very name of the famous outlaw blazed through the coach.

Jesse bowed low, his blue eyes blinking furiously. His teeth flashed in a pleased smile. How he loved to play the part of King of the Outlaws! "You caught the brass ring. Now turn out your pockets, gents, and we'll let you be on your way. Do it fast. We haven't got all night."

With Jesse aiming a gun at them at the same time Clell thrust the basket in front of them, they ceased to resist. Half-blind, still drowsy, they couldn't think. Likewise, the sight of a pair of gun muzzles trained on them constituted a powerful incentive. Cursing and whining, the passengers flung handfuls of coins and bills into the basket.

"Rings and pocket watches too," Jesse called. He pushed a gun into the belly of a tall man whose suspenders held up a pair of much faded pants with a yellow stripe down each side. "You too, yellowleg." The epithet ran through the car, reminding one and all on this train bound for Chicago that Jesse James hated Yankees almost as much as he hated the railroad.

Frowning fearsomely, the ex-soldier pulled a poke out of his hip pocket.

Jesse's smile broadened. "Thank you kindly, one and all."

In a couple of minutes, Clell brought the loot to the front of the car. "Let's go."

A quick glance at the contents made Jesse's affable expression disappear. "Not enough," he called. "Let's do it over, fellas. Dig deep."

"These are just farmers," Clell protested under his breath.

"Let 'em go on. They don't have a pot—or a window to throw it out of."

Jesse waved him away with his pistols and stared at each one as Clell approached. On his second tour, the pickings increased. A half-dozen leather pokes, some snap purses, and a couple of fat leather wallets joined the other loot. Back at his end of the car, he emptied the basket into a sack. "Ready, Jesse."

"Thanks, folks." Jesse holstered one of his pistols and tipped his hat politely. His dark hair was glossy with bay rum. He looked more like a pleasant gentleman than a train robber. "It's been a real pleasure. You've been more than generous. But now, we got to be going. And I don't want any of you to do anything foolish like run out on that platform and start shooting. That'd be just plain murder—on our part, not yours. Just think of it this way. You can tell your grandchildren you were held up by Jesse James."

The preacher's son turned outlaw opened the door behind him. Clell ducked out the door at the other end of the coach. Leaning out from the platform, he whistled the nighthawk signal and waved the brakeman's lantern.

"Good night, gentlemen." With a final bow Jesse James was gone.

To her horror, Mary Carolyn realized that once she had her victim's money stuffed in her sack and the straps passed over her head and shoulder, she didn't know how to get out of the car and off the train. She wanted to be a robber but not a murderer. She couldn't shoot him. Even though he deserved it. She couldn't knock him in the head. Not with him staring at her. She just couldn't bring herself to hurt him.

The man crouched on the floor in front of the open safe, his eyes blazing at her. Suddenly, his expression changed. His body seemed to lift. He was gathering his energy around him. "Can't figure what to do next, can you?" he jeered. "I'll tell you what. Drop that money and run, and I'll forget this ever happened."

Mary Carolyn was sorely tempted, but Buster Ross puffed

out her chest. "Not on your life, mister. You just settle back down there."

But he didn't. Instead he leaned forward, his eyes narrowing. She fought an urge to touch her mask to see if it were still in place. "I know you," he said slowly. "Don't I?"

She took a step backward, then caught herself. "Sure you do," she jeered. "I'm Jesse James. Er . . . I'd be long gone right now, only I'm waiting. I'm waiting for . . . er . . . for my brother. He'll be along in a second."

Her victim chuckled in disbelief. "So you're Jesse James. You don't look much like your wanted posters. In fact you look like—"

"It's true," she interrupted desperately. "Any minute now—"

The car beneath her feet jerked forward. With a squeal, she staggered backward barely managing to catch herself. Her victim dived for her and caught her ankle. They rolled back and forth on the floor. The car jerked again. Slowly, slowly the big wheels underneath them began to turn.

Blind panic gripped her. She twisted and rolled, scrabbling at the floor, trying to crawl toward the door. She was going to be caught. Oh, God! She was going to be caught on her first job.

"Come here, you." Her victim got both hands around her ankle.

"Leggo! Leggo! Leggo!" Her free leg, flailing wildly, accidentally kicked him in the face.

Somervell let out a gurgling shriek and clapped both hands to his nose where her boot heel had connected. Blood dripped over his fingers.

"Oh, I'm sorry. I'm sorry. I didn't mean . . ." Mary Carolyn scrambled around, clutching the gun in both hands. Her victim huddled on the floor bleeding and moaning. "I didn't mean for you to get hurt."

Suddenly, she realized the muzzle of her gun was pointed at the floor. She was making so many mistakes. The gun swung wildly until she finally got it trained on him. No matter how many times she had read about outlaws committing robberies, everything in real life was so different. She was going to have to practice. "You shouldn't have tried to stop a desperate fella like me."

Somervell paid no attention. The train jerked and shuddered all along its length. The wheels rolled faster. Its speed increased. Mary Carolyn looked around her fearfully. She must get off. Very much faster and she wouldn't be able to jump. She'd be trapped here.

Shakily, she climbed to her feet and backed toward the door. "I . . . I hope you're not badly hurt. Er . . . good-bye."

She pushed the door open and stepped out into the night. The noise of the train seemed unnaturally loud. The huffing of the engine, the clacking of the wheels. The vibration scared her too. The wind caught her hat and blew it back off her face as she climbed to the top of the rail. The distance between the two cars seemed enormous now that the train was moving.

She reached her foot across the gap. Too far! Oh, too far. She couldn't reach it. The wind blew the smoke back to her. The car swayed. She let go, teetered, then threw herself at the caboose platform.

She stepped on the railing, stumbled, but managed to keep her feet. Both arms wrapped around the platform frame. She hung there shivering for a moment before scrambling down.

She had to hurry. She had to get off before . . .

She fumbled and found the handrail. Taking a deep breath, she swung herself off the edge. Her feet would have dragged the ground if she hadn't kept her knees bent. The train was moving faster. Faster. Her full weight was held on her arms.

Please, God, don't let me die.

Closing her eyes, she let go.

Clell Miller hit the ground at a roll that brought him back to his feet. He turned to flee, the sack of loot in hand, when out of nowhere a body slammed into him. It hit so hard that it knocked him flat. The breath whooshed from his lungs. Then they were tumbling across the roadbed. His forehead and then the back of his head hit the gravel. At last he came to a halt on his back. Stars flashed across his vision.

"Uh-uh-uh . . ."

Someone had jumped off the train and now lay on top of him grunting—someone who was trying without much success to draw breath into his lungs. Clell knew because he was trying to suck air into his lungs too. He failed. He tried again. His ribs hurt on both sides of his breastbone when he finally did get them expanded. He didn't even have the strength to curse as he shoved the body off him.

It was curiously light to have dealt him such a blow. His hands moved, felt slender contours, breasts. What the hell! A female! Then he found a bag. Coins. Heavy coins that clinked together. Gold. And rectangular packages that bent and crackled. Paper money. He managed a rictus of a grin. Nothing else in the world felt like U.S. silver and gold certificates.

Suddenly, he knew as if he had been sent a message that something else had happened on that train. He found his voice as he rolled over on his hands and knees. "What did you do, girl?"

"Uh-uh-uh—ow—*ow!*"

He climbed to his feet, dragging her up with him. Her breath wheezed in and out of her lungs.

At that moment Billy Chadwell came galloping out of the darkness. "Here y' go, Clell," he called. "Climb aboard."

"Much obliged." The reins slapped across Clell's chest as Chadwell swept on by, leading a half-dozen horses for the rest of the gang. Clell let go of his captive to wrap the reins around his hand and control the skittish mount. While he was occupied, she sank to her knees and tried to scramble away.

"No you don't." He caught her arm and jerked her upright again. Jesse had somehow overlooked the private car. Fortunately, this girl had robbed it. Too bad she'd crashed into him.

She flailed about despite his grip on her, and she kicked at his legs.

"Quit that." He shook her hard. The sack flopped between them. He let go of her to grasp it. "Give me that."

"No!" She spun away and tried to run, but the strap was

over her shoulder and under her arm. He used it to haul her back against him and tried to pull it away from her.

"Let go," she squealed. "Let go. It's mine."

"The hell it is. You stole it." He tried to tear it off her, but she was fighting too hard. Her hands slapped at his head and shoulders. Her boots kicked at his legs. He had all he could do to protect himself.

"Come on, Clell." Jesse's voice boomed out of the night.

The train was moving slowly. Slowly. Not picking up speed at all. Shots rang out as the passengers began to fire from the windows of the coaches. Unfortunately, with the lights on, they couldn't see a blasted thing. Their shots fell nowhere near the men who had robbed them.

Clell swung up into the saddle. The girl dug in her heels and pulled back, but he was too strong for her. Willy-nilly, he dragged her up with him. As she shrieked and pummeled his shoulders, he reined the startled horse around to take out after the rest of the gang.

They were trotting off at an angle to the train. He was way behind the others because of the hellcat he'd picked up. The engineer hadn't opened the engine up. In fact, it was slowing. It crossed Clell's mind that he could vanish into the night. He had the loot he had collected. Plus the sack his passenger had picked up.

He could run for it.

"Lemme go! Darn you!" A hard blow struck him in the stomach, below the belt. It doubled him over her struggling body.

"Ow! Quit that! Damn *you*, girl!" He thumped her on the back.

The girl redoubled her efforts, which were considerable, because she had managed to find the stirrup, her toe having gained a purchase there by the simple expedient of covering his boot. She was standing, fighting, mad as a hornet. The stream of mild expletives flowing from her lips would have made him smile under ordinary circumstances.

"Lady," he warned her grimly as the horse slowed to a

walk. "The minute we get out of range, you are in for big trouble."

At that instant, a .22 popped in the darkness. Its smaller charge of powder was easily distinguishable from the larger caliber sidearms most men preferred if they carried weapons at all.

The girl cried out. Her body slammed against him, stiffened, then collapsed across his saddle.

"What the hell?"

Chapter Two

Scattering like quail, the members of the gang spurred their horses away from the train and into the thick darkness. According to plan, they made no effort to stay together. A large band of men galloping through the countryside made too much noise and consequently attracted too much attention even in the dead of night. They knew that within minutes the telegraph would carry the news of the holdup to the railroad headquarters and from there to the U.S. Marshals and the Pinkertons.

Sooner or later the gang would all come together at Chesnut's Crossing in Iowa, just north of the state line and the town of Unionville, Missouri.

With his horse carrying double, Clell fell behind. He knew his passenger was still alive because she kept wriggling and moaning. Once she tried to struggle upright, but he slapped her sharply on the bottom. As a single concession to her comfort, he eased himself back over the cantle and pulled her down off the horn, so she lay belly down in the seat of the saddle.

Whether she was hurting or not was of small concern. Every one of them had taken a bullet at one time or another and had kept on riding. During the War he himself had been wounded fighting for the Confederacy. Early on, he had come to expect it. When it happened, he accepted it.

But shortly after Lee surrendered, he had taken two slugs riding away from a bank. Those bullets, the subsequent agony of having them dug out by clumsy hands, as well as the long bout with fever that followed, had severely dampened his enthusiasm for robbery. He had grown to dread the raids, the frightened, angry citizens shooting at them and the hard riding that followed. Moreover, his share of the loot was often pitifully little for the amount of effort involved.

Jesse, to the contrary, seemed to thrive on the adventure and the danger. The wilder, the better for Jesse James. He took particular pleasure in telling people that he was robbing them.

Clell Miller never opened his mouth. He always wore a mask and tried to bring in the horses. Yet somehow his name had come to be listed as one of the notorious gang. At last, he'd resolved to leave the life altogether. One day during a particularly wild raid, Clell hadn't joined them at the agreed meeting place. Foolishly, he'd hoped they'd think he was dead. Unfortunately, Jesse had tracked him down. And now he was at it all over again.

Clell slowed his horse to a trot that bounced the girl around until she wailed in protest. He had to put his hand on her backside to keep her from falling out the saddle. It was a thin backside. Hard and bony as a boy's. And twisting.

"For God's sake," came a weak complaint, laced with sobs. "Can't you just put me down? I swear I'll walk."

They were several miles from the site of the robbery now. He slowed the horse to ease her situation. "We're almost there," he told her. "Just rest easy."

Over her shoulder she spat what he guessed was the strongest cuss word she knew.

He chuckled and swatted her, but gently. Just like her rear, her vocabulary had a lot of room to grow.

"I want a pursuit launched tonight. I know I shot one of them. That'll slow them down."

DeGraffen Somervell, president of the Citizens Mercantile and Industrial Bank of Chicago, had tucked his nightshirt into his trousers and his bare feet into his shoes. Now he raged at the conductor and the rest of the train crew, who fell back before his wrath. His thick gray hair ruffled out around his face like the fur of an outraged wolf. His nose was swollen to twice its size and purple. His chin and shirt were spattered with dried blood.

"My property has been stolen. I had a right to protection, the same as these folks." He waved his arm to encompass a hoard of angry passengers who growled in chorus behind him.

"We got to stay with the train," the conductor insisted. "It ain't our job—"

"But they're getting away," Somervell interrupted. "With my money, my bank's money, and their money." He gestured to the other passengers. "It was Jesse James. He robbed me himself." He knew for a fact that the thief had not been Jesse. He had been robbed by an amateur. He could see the eyes of the robber above the handkerchief's edge. Disturbingly familiar. Young eyes, a young voice, and a young slender body. But more than that he would have to study long and hard to remember. For now it served his purpose to call the fellow Jesse James. Besides, if this robber proved not to be someone he knew, he didn't want anyone to know that a shirttail kid had got the drop on him. Wounded pride drove him to raise his voice. "Think, you idiot! You'll get a ten-thousand-dollar reward for Jesse James."

"A bullet is what I'll get," the conductor contradicted somberly. He threw up his hands. "All right. All right. There's three horses at the water tank. If you want to take 'em, you're welcome to them." With that he turned away.

"Who's with me?" Somervell called.

No one answered for a minute. Then a burly man with a yellow stripe down the side of his britches stepped up. "I'm with you," he snarled. "I ain't got nothing else to do but get my money and my watch back."

Another followed him.

In a short time the three were saddled and away.

* * *

Mary Carolyn moaned, while her tough, hard self Buster cursed. In the darkness neither made any impression on the man balancing her across his saddle. The train robbery had been bound for disaster. All the signs were there from the beginning. She should have stopped trying when she'd found the locked gate on the private car, she told herself. Instead, she'd bulled her way in.

Now here she was in this sorry state. She wanted to cry. In the dime novels, the hero was always wounded in the shoulder. Why had she been shot in the rear end? How did he ignore his wound and continue riding on strong and brave to rescue the heroine?

How did she end up like this? Shot, bleeding, a burning ache spreading down her thigh, her head hanging down over a galloping horse whose rider could not keep his hands off her fanny.

She was going to puke if she didn't get to sit up soon.

"I'm going to puke," she shouted back over her shoulder.

He patted her again. "I doubt it. Probably just get a case of the dry heaves. Unless you ate just before the robbery, your stomach's empty."

The horse stumbled. Her captor jerked up its head, then allowed it to slow and stop altogether. "Ginger's about worn out. We're going to have to walk, or at least you are." He shifted his grip to her belt. "I'm going to let you down now. Don't try to run away. Unless you want to give me what you stole off that private car."

Groaning with relief, she let him lower her onto her feet. As soon as her weight rested on her legs, she realized she couldn't have run away if she'd wanted to. High on her left thigh was a broad circle of fiery hot pain. When his horse sidled, she reached out blindly, her hands finding rough cloth, clutching to keep from falling. She could feel blood trickling down her leg. Red streaks barred her vision.

Then the rider hoisted his body over the cantle and clicked his tongue against his teeth. The horse started forward.

"Wait," she cried. "Wait. I can't walk. I guess you'll have to go on without me." One part of her hoped he would, the other hoped against hope that he wouldn't.

The horse stopped. The outlaw looked down at her. Dawn was breaking. The sky was streaked with pink and orange. The earth had turned to palest gray, with rocks and bushes darker against it.

She looked up at him, her vision clearing. She still couldn't see his face very well. He was tall in the saddle, three or four feet above her. His buff hat, pulled low over his forehead, left his features in darkness. His bulky coat hid the shape of his body.

When she gave up the search, she dropped her eyes to find her hands were wrapped around his thigh. She could feel a blush starting. Beneath the corduroy pantleg it was almost too warm and hard as a fence post. His hand, the hand he had swatted her with, rested just above her own. It was almost twice as big as one of hers, with long fingers.

In a daze of pain, mixed with nearly equal parts of exhaustion and embarrassment, she stared at his right hand. The little finger on it curled in under the fourth finger as if it had been broken. It was like a symbol for his toughness. Thigh, hand, fingers all revealed his strength, his power. She gulped. No wonder she hadn't been able to get away from him.

She looked up again. A blush heated her cheek. Some of the pain and exhaustion faded as she stared at the outlaw of her dreams. The Robin Hood hero of the dime novels come to life. He was The Outcast of the Border. He was The Mustang Hunter. He was The Avenger.

From beneath a flat-brimmed hat, a shock of yellow hair waved over his high forehead. His eyes were blue steel, set deep in a face that was all bones and angles. His nose was straight, and the yellow mustache on his upper lip curled down around the sides of his generous mouth. If she hadn't been in such pain and discomfort, she would have sighed in admiration. As it was, she couldn't tear her eyes away.

Just then, the sun's first rays broke over the horizon to shine full in her face. She blinked and squinted. It was he who heaved an exaggerated sigh. "Well, I'm bound to say. You're sure the homeliest mutt I've had follow me home in a long time."

His pronouncement shocked her out of her daze. Mary Carolyn's feelings were hurt. But when she would have put her hand to her face, Buster forced it back down. "You're no bargain yourself," she sneered. Instead, she lifted her scratched and bruised chin in what she hoped was a show of bravado. "Listen! Why don't you just ride on? I'll go off by myself and won't be a bother to you anymore. You don't want me around."

"You got that right." He crossed his hands over the horn and eased his weight in the saddle. "But before I take off, why don't you pass up that sack you're toting?"

She clutched at it. "Not on your life. I worked hard for this."

"It doesn't take much to rob a private car," he observed. Besides a long blond moustache and a shock of blond hair, his chin and cheeks sprouted blond bristles that glistened in the sun like gold dust. Again, she thought how much he looked like a romantic outlaw-hero in a dime novel. His voice was a liquid Southern drawl that sent shivers down her spine despite the fierce burning in her thigh. Squinting even tighter against the sun, she still couldn't tell whether or not he was smiling.

She tilted her chin even higher, then wished she hadn't, for the skin pulled. She took her hand off his thigh to touch the pumpknot. Her fingers found a scab formed. She had forgotten about the fall. She had in fact taken two falls. She wondered what would have happened to her on the rocky roadbed if she hadn't been thrown into him.

"It wasn't easy," she said at last.

He gave a short bark of laughter as if she had said something not very funny at all. "Hardest way in the world to make money." Then one long finger pointed to her bruise. "How'd you come by that?"

Buster Ross tossed her short-cropped brown hair. She had slicked it down with hair oil like a boy's, but the wind and riding hanging upside down had displaced it. Curled in dark fishhooks, it fell back onto her face, tangling with her eyelashes.

"The guy I was robbing took a swing at me," she lied. "But I knocked him down and he did what I told him after that."

Again the short bark of laughter. "Oh, you knocked him down, did you?"

"That's right."

She waited for him to commend her strength, but he merely said, "Too bad you didn't knock him out. He's probably the one who shot you."

"Him! Not likely." Still, his comment alarmed her. She remembered the gun by Somervell's bed, but, surely, he hadn't been the only man shooting. "How'd you figure that?"

Her outlaw pulled the makings of a cigarette from his breast pocket and expertly rolled one.

Fascinated, she watched him, resolving that she would learn to do that too. When he put it in his mouth and lighted it, one blue steel eye squinted against the rising smoke. It looked so evil. Like Simon Girty or Joaquin Murietta.

She had almost forgotten her question when he said, "He's the only one that had a dark car to shoot out of. He's the only one who could see us."

She still didn't understand. "But . . . but . . . in the dark?"

"Hell, but you're green. How old are you, girl?"

"Old enough." She was blushing again. She hoped he couldn't see it. He would think she was a little girl.

"Uh-huh." He looked positively devilish when he took the cigarette out and blew a trail of smoke past his cheek. "You could have gotten one of us killed. Don't you know enough to turn on the lights? That way the passengers can't see to shoot when the train pulls away."

She gazed up at him with a combination of awe and chagrin. "I never thought of that."

He gave a short bark of laughter that seemed to say she hadn't thought of a lot of things. "Time to be moving." He tossed the cigarette away and motioned with his hand. "Now just hand up that sack and I'll be on my way."

She took a step backward on her left foot and almost fell. Sharp pains shot all the way up her spine, and perspiration sprang out on her skin. She was really hurt. Desperately, she clutched the sack to her. "No. I stole this. It's mine."

"You wouldn't have got away with it if we hadn't stopped the train."

Her words all but tripped over themselves in her haste to defend herself. "Oh, no, you don't. I know all about it. The train stops there every time it comes through, twice a week. It takes on water and coal. You didn't have anything to do with that."

"We took care of the crew and held up the engineer and fireman. If we hadn't, you'd have been caught by one of them. Or"—he held up his hand to stop her protest—"you'd have been killed when you jumped off."

"Well, I almost was." Mary Carolyn was beginning to feel very light-headed. She hadn't had anything to eat in hours. She hadn't had any sleep. Her bruises ached. Every joint in her arms and shoulders felt wrenched and twisted. Most urgent was the steady throbbing in the back of her thigh. She had been shot, and her wound had not been tended. She swallowed. "The train was rolling pretty fast."

His shook his head slightly. His face was ruddy now with the morning sun shining full on it. Perhaps he wasn't quite so handsome as the drawings of outlaws in the dime novels. Still he had good strong features. Then his mouth twisted. "We were all off the train. The idea is to escape, not stand around and wait for someone to shoot us."

He was right about that as well as plenty of other things. "Who are you?"

He leaned down until his face hung only a foot above hers. His steel blue eyes narrowed like a villain's. A fierce frown creased his forehead. Malice edged his deep voice. "We're the James gang."

Mary Carolyn's mouth dropped open. Eagerly she looked around her. Then her eyes narrowed. She pressed her hand against her pocket satisfying herself that the book was there. "You! Not much, you're not!"

He heaved an exasperated sigh. "I'm not going to argue with you. Give me that sack."

Mary Carolyn clapped her arm across it, but she didn't retreat. He was trying to frighten her, but she wasn't going to let him. She had staked her whole life on this robbery. She had pulled it off. Sort of. "Not on your life."

Beneath the mustache, his teeth showed in a thin smile that sent shivers through her.

Her eyes flickered. She clutched the sack tighter against her side. "You can't have it."

He chuckled low in his throat.

She willed her wounded leg to take her weight. One step back. Another. A mist seemed to be spreading over her eyes. She couldn't run away. Her only chance was to stall and bluff, the way the heroes did when they were outnumbered. She remembered a phrase. She took another step back on her bad leg. "You'd better back off, fella. If you really are the James gang, I reckon Jesse'll want to meet me."

She didn't know whether she'd managed to get the last words out. Her lips felt stiff and numb, her sight had faded. When her legs turned to water, the world went black.

She was some sort of crazy girl. Clell was sure of that. Heaving a disgusted sigh, he stepped off Ginger and pulled the roan's bit from her mouth. "Have a feed, girl," he said, patting her rump. "But don't wander too far."

Immediately, the mare dropped her head and began chomping at the dry brown grass. Clell knelt beside the girl. He thought he'd never seen a more homely mug. Her hair looked like it had been hacked off with a knife, and it was so matted with oil that he couldn't be sure what color it was. Her face was thin, with sharp cheekbones, and it was so dirty he couldn't tell what her skin was like. Her chin was disfigured by a pump-knot and a scab. Her mouth hung slack.

When he bent over her, her sunken eyes popped open. They were bloodshot from lack of sleep. Her head rolled from side to side. "Don't," she whispered. "Don't you dare . . ." Her hands clutched feebly at the strap of her sack. "It's mine."

He grunted. Blood stained her left leg from just below the

hipbone to the knee. Lifting her by the shoulder, he pulled the sack off over her head. It was surprisingly heavy.

"No. No," she protested feebly. Her voice broke. She made a soft snubbing sound in her throat. "You skunk. I stole that. It's mine."

He lowered her gently and looked inside the sack. A low whistle escaped him. She had stolen a lot of money. Probably it was more money than had been taken by the rest of the gang in the last two robberies. She might have as many as several thousand dollars there.

A burst of inspiration set his hands a-tremble. With what he had from the coach, it was enough to disappear forever. He could go east to New York or south to Florida. He could hop a boat to Puerto Rico or Brazil. He had heard lots of Rebs had made it down to Brazil where they were starting new lives.

He pulled out one of the packages of certificates. Gold certificates, a thick wad of them, made his eyes gleam. Immediately, he upped the estimate. She had stolen more than a few thousand. With so much money he could do anything, go anywhere.

He fanned his thumb over the end of the package.

A gun prodded his belly. He froze. Her eyes were open wide and their expression meant business. Mentally he cursed himself. He should have pulled her sidearm and tossed it long before this. He let out his breath in a shuddering sigh and closed his eyes, waiting for the bullet. The angle and range of it would tear his guts out. She might be a girl with a slug in her leg, but a gun made her as big as anybody.

"Put that back in the sack," she whispered.

He opened his eyes. Women. Tenderhearted amateurs. He almost smiled, but with a hole in his belly just a finger's twitch away, he obeyed.

"Now." Her voice was so weak he needed to lean forward to catch what she said next. "You've got three choices. And frankly, I don't care which one you make. You can swear you'll take me to Jesse James, or you can get on your horse and ride off and leave me . . . or you can take my bullet in your belly."

Her voice wavered at the last. She wasn't sure she could

pull the trigger even to wound him. She wasn't a ruthless outlaw yet. And anyway, Jesse was more like a Robin Hood. She probably couldn't shoot anybody if he just acted calm and did what she said. At this point whatever she wanted, he'd do. A belly wound was a mean way to die. By the look of her, he wouldn't be in danger very long.

He looked at her quizzically. Then shrugged. "Suit yourself. I'll take you to meet Jesse."

"Good. Thank you. I appreciate ..." She slumped back, appearing to lose consciousness for a moment.

In an almost lazy motion, he wrapped his hand around the gun. One quick motion pointed it away from him and twisted it out of her hand.

She let out a pained cry and made a futile grab to retrieve it.

"Unh-uh." He rose smoothly and tucked the gun into his belt. "Maybe you can have it back later. For now I'm going to rest my horse and take a nap. I don't know about you, but I've been up all night."

"But"—she watched him silently—"shouldn't we ... ? Shouldn't you ... ?"

Ignoring her obvious desolation, he dropped the money sack at the foot of an oak tree and lowered himself gingerly. Without once glancing in her direction, he stretched out, pillowed his head on the loot and pulled his hat over his eyes.

Mary Carolyn stared in helpless frustration. He had gone instantly to sleep. She was sure of it. She bit her lip. Weary resentment welled in her. He was so strong, so sure of himself. He had disarmed her with no effort and now could put her completely out of his mind. A hardened outlaw could do that.

On the other hand, perhaps he was pretending to sleep, giving her a chance to escape. She glanced toward the horse. It had moved away, eating as it went. The tack jingled faintly as it cropped the tough prairie grass. She supposed she could steal his horse and escape.

Not much! Not without her money!

She looked at him again. Perhaps he would keep his word and take her to Jesse James. Besides, where would she go? Slightly rolling open country dotted with trees stretched to every horizon. She had no idea whether she was in Iowa or Missouri. She didn't know the towns.

She lowered her head to her chest and shivered in the weak sunlight. Mary Carolyn badly wanted to cry. Buster was determined not to.

Gradually, the burning pain in her hip separated itself from the aches that throbbed in the rest of her body. She had been shot. She should do something about that while he was asleep. Squinching her eyes shut, she rolled over on her right side.

Slowly, she opened them and twisted around.

What she could see of her hip and thigh didn't look so bad. Well, maybe pretty bad. A dark reddish brown stain discolored the side of her denims down past the knee. She pulled at the fabric until she found the hole. Mouth screwed up against the pain, she touched it with her finger. Her finger wouldn't go through it. So much blood to come out of such a small hole. That it was small had to be good for her. Maybe it would heal up of its own accord. She had heard tales from soldiers who claimed they still carried bullets from the Civil War in their bodies.

Clenching her teeth, she ran her fingers over her leg. The denim was too thick for her to feel very much. Only by the center of the pain could she know that she had a very small hole in her thigh, just beneath her buttock. Because it was so small, maybe she could take care of it herself.

She *would* take care of it herself. She cast a calculating glance at her outlaw under the tree. He seemed to be sleeping soundly. The horse had moved farther off so that even the noise of its feeding didn't disturb the peace.

She looked around furtively. She was quite alone. Unbuttoning her pants she tried to lower them on one side. No good. She couldn't get them low enough to see anything. She lifted her hips and worried her pants down to mid thigh. By the time she had them down, she was sweating with pain. Her mother had told her she always went about things the hard way. She should have stood up and pushed—

"Need any help?" Her outlaw had raised his hat and his head, and was staring at her.

Squeaking in alarm, she tried to wrestle her pants back up, but the task was too much for her. Hot blood stung her cheeks. Her embarrassment was exceeded only by her pain. "No," she snapped. "And cover your face back up. I'll do fine."

He didn't move. His gaze moved over her body, from her red face bedewed with perspiration to the bloody union suit stuck to her hip. "I think you need some help."

"No, I don't." She could feel the tremors in all her limbs. Oh, heavens, was she going to pass out? She felt so queer. Instead of hot, she felt cold. Threatening darkness made her fall limply back. Taking in deep breaths, she stared upward at the sky between the bare branches of the oak tree.

"I don't need any help," she insisted stubbornly when she was pretty sure she wasn't going to faint. But her voice shook and on the last words. It lost all its timbre and ended in a whisper. "Just go back to sleep."

She heard him move. She felt his booted feet strike the earth. Then he was standing over her looking down. "You're shot in the butt, girl," he observed laconically as he hunkered down beside her. "Unless you're some kind of contortionist like in a freak show, you can't do a thing about it. I can help you, or I can leave you alone, but if you leave that bullet in there, you could get blood poisoning and die."

She gulped. Before her tough, courageous, train-robber self could do anything about it, her sissy, cowardly, female self opened her mouth to beg. "Could you take me to a doctor?"

He laughed.

She added rude and unsympathetic to her catalogue of his faults. He was not at all like a character in a novel. When she finally met Jesse James, she was going to give him the lowdown on this member of his gang.

"Folks with bullet holes in their butts don't generally go to doctors." He put his hand on her waist. Despite her pain, ripples of apprehension radiated through her. His hand was so big. She wanted to move, but she was flat on the ground, not sure whether she was going to faint or puke. She couldn't resist when he gently rolled her over. She craned her neck to look from him to the wound and back again.

His face was serious, even though he'd just laughed. Then he caught ahold of the tough cotton of her union suit and ripped it apart.

She cried out, startled by the suddenness and the violence. She had never deliberately torn a piece of cloth in her life. The warm sun filtered down on the back of her thigh.

He sank back on his haunches, his long, strong hands hanging between his knees. "Doesn't look too bad," he remarked conversationally. "Looks like about a .22. The hole could hide under a dime. In fact, you'd probably be all right just to leave it in there if we knew for sure what the slug was made of." He met her anxious eyes. "But if it's lead, you'll get blood poisoning sure."

She waited to be sure he had said all he was going to say. Then she looked around desperately. "Is there a doctor anywhere around?"

With a malicious grin, he raised a hand to shade his eyes and scanned the horizon. "I don't see a one."

"But you know where one is?" she insisted desperately. "You could take me to him?" She was begging now.

He dropped his hand. "Yeah, I could do that. 'Course, I'd have to drop you off at the back of the doctor's office and ride on quick. And I'd have to take that money with me. Besides having to report all gunshot wounds, you can be sure the news has spread for miles around. Every place that has a telegraph knows about the Chicago, Rock Island being robbed. Every doc's probably heard that one of the gang was wounded. I admit you don't look much like a train robber, but whoever you get to fix you up just might be a little suspicious about how you happened to be carrying so much money." He looked pointedly at her awful hair and dirty face. "Specially with you looking so down at the heels and all."

She paid no attention to his sarcasm. Instead she slumped back, pressing one grimy fist to her mouth. He was right. She had read about such things. Heroes were always getting bullets cut out of them. They just gritted their teeth and grinned through the pain. Sometimes heroines endured pain, too—but not from bullet wounds! Of course, being a train robber, she wasn't a heroine. She sighed. "I guess you'd better cut it out."

Clell quickly made his preparations to remove the bullet. From his saddlebags he took a small case of surgeon's instruments. Relics of his War days, he had used them more than once to dig bullets out of his companions. When a few of Quantrill's raiders had changed into the James gang, he had needed the little kit more than ever. Not even a drunken sawbones rode with Jesse and his boys.

Besides the surgeon's scalpel, probe, and forceps were two small silver flasks. One contained alcohol; the other, whiskey. He unscrewed the whiskey and held it out to his patient.

"Have a drink."

Her face was glistening with perspiration, its blood vessels so constricted with terror, she looked like a corpse. He'd seen it all before. Her voice quavered. "No, thank you. It would make me sick."

She looked so pitiful, he almost felt sorry for her. Almost. But he'd long ago stopped feeling sorry for fools.

"Suit yourself." He lifted the whiskey to his mouth to take a drink.

"Don't," she cried. "Please don't drink and then operate on me."

He grinned. "Why not? I'll need something to steady me down when the blood starts spouting."

Her face turned white as chalk. Even her lips went white. She made an attempt to lick them, but her mouth was so dry, she couldn't manage it.

Laying the instruments down on a blanket beside her, he opened the second flask. "Now here's what I'm going to do," he told her. "This flask contains alcohol. I'm going to pour it onto this cloth and wash your skin around the hole. It'll sting some, but that's good. Just keep ahold of that idea. It'll sting, but that's good.''

She didn't move. Didn't quiver.

"Now, turn over on your stomach."

She cast him a pleading look, her eyes wide. He stared back, mocking her look. "Go ahead. It'll be all over before you know it."

She rolled over, face down, her cheek pressed to the grass. One fist remained clenched against her mouth.

He soaked the cloth and washed away the dried blood. Her skin was very white and fine grained. Exposed to the light of the sun, she didn't look quite so bony as he had first imagined. That taut little rear didn't belong to any child.

When the alcohol ran into the wound, she sucked in her breath. Her buttocks clenched. The bare skin beneath his hand flinched.

When he had finished, he cleaned the probe and the forceps. He left the scalpel in the case. With any luck he wouldn't need it. The size of the charge behind the bullet practically guaranteed that it would be no more than a couple of inches beneath the skin. If he could get it out without cutting, it would heal swiftly and leave a scar the size of a dime. Not that anybody would ever see it. He didn't know who she really was or where she had come from, but any girl as homely as she was and set on the outlaw trail, couldn't count on getting married.

He cleared his throat. "Now. I want you to put your hands behind you and clasp them real tight."

Alarmed, she pushed up. "Why?"

He pushed his hand into the small of her back. "For that very reason. I don't want you crawling out from under me when I get started."

"Oh, I won't," she promised. "I'll hold still."

"Sure you will," he scoffed. "I've seen grown men get up and run off. Now just do as I tell you and I won't tie you up."

She put her head down again, this time facing him. Her eyes met his. "You don't have to tie me up."

"Then put you hands behind you." He sighed in exasperation when she hesitated. "Do you want this done? It's no skin off my nose if you die of blood poisoning. But let me tell you, I've seen it happened and it's a mean way to go.''

Slowly, she locked her wrists together over the small of her back.

"Good. Now I'm going to put my knee right here." He knelt with his leg across her buttocks. He waited a moment for her to adjust to his weight. "You all right?"

Between clenched teeth she grated. "Just do it."

He bent over her thigh.

Her flesh had already begun to close. The slenderness of her body and the hardness of the big thigh muscles meant that this wasn't going to be easy. As the probe entered the wound, blood welled around it.

She tensed and caught her breath. A high keening sound escaped between her clenched teeth.

Down the probe went. He watched while a full two inches entered her leg.

She was making little whimpering noises with every breath. Her hands were clasped so tightly at the wrists that the knuckles showed white.

He touched the bullet.

She cried out.

"That's it. That's it," he told her triumphantly. "Hold still now. I've got it. Don't jump around and make me lose it.

"No." Her voice was a mere breath. She shuddered when he picked up the forceps.

"Now this is going to hurt the most," he told her. "If you want to scream, cry, cuss, go right ahead. Piss in your pants, puke, faint. Just don't move. It'll only make it hurt worse. You understand."

She nodded.

He aligned the forceps exactly with the probe.

Mary Carolyn wished she could faint. Another keening cry burst from between her clenched teeth. Nothing in her life had ever hurt so badly. She'd had no idea that any human being could hurt this much and not die. The pain built and built, and when she thought it was more than she could possibly bear, it became more intense.

"Good girl," she heard from somewhere behind her. "Hold still. I can feel it. Just a lit-tle more."

"Stop," she whimpered. "Stop, stop, stop." The pain turned to flaming agony. She couldn't bear it. Panic swelled within her, choking her throat, cutting off her breathing. He was killing her. Her heart was beating so fast it was going to burst. In some dim recess of her mind, she acknowledged that he had been right. If her hands had been at her sides, she would have pushed herself up and crawled away. Even now, she doubted she could keep her hands clasped. Oh, why hadn't he tied her? She couldn't stand this. It hurt so bad that all she could think of was escape. Against her will her hands unclasped. Her fingers clawed at the dried grasses beside her.

"Don't," he grated. "Don't give up. I've almost got it."

His voice sounded harsh as if he were taxing himself to the utmost.

She set her teeth so hard that sharp pains stabbed her jaws. Tears spouted from her eyes and fell into the dried grass.

"Got it!" Instantly, his weight fell away from her buttocks. He rolled off her into the grass. Miraculously, the pain eased. It still hurt like the very devil, but by comparison that was nothing.

She opened her palms and pressed them flat on the ground beside her waist. She tried to find the strength to move, but pain had drained her. Feebly, she slid one hand along the ground. When she got it to her face, she swiped at the tears. Gradually, her heartbeat slowed.

She became aware of his moving. Her eyes opened wearily. "What do you do now?"

His voice had resumed its deep, steady timbre when he said, "It was a .22 all right. Want to see it?"

Mary Carolyn would have shuddered and hidden her face, but Buster turned her upper body slowly. Her tear-swollen eyes opened wide. *"That's it?* That's all of it!"

The thing was about the size of a bean. In a flash she remembered the pearl-handled weapon that had been in the netting of

Somervell's bed. She should have taken it from him. She supposed that disarming the victim was one of the main rules of train robbery.

"That's it." He still held the thing tight in the tiny jaws of the forceps. He turned it for her to see. The instrument as well as the bullet were streaked with blood.

She swallowed hard. "But it hurt so bad."

With a flick of his wrist he flung it away and began to wash his instruments in alcohol. "Something smaller than that will hurt nearly as bad. It's the force that does it. And little popguns like that don't have much power. A hit by a .45 would nearly blow your leg off."

She glanced at the gun he wore on his hip. Then she looked after the bullet he had discarded. She had to ask. "Was it lead?"

His steel blue eyes caught and held. "Oh, yes."

He had saved her life. She felt a funny stirring deep within her, then wiped at the corners of her eyes with her dirty hand.

He carefully put the instruments away in the little case. From his saddlebags he took another oilcloth pouch. When he unrolled it, she saw he had a thick strip of gauze. "Now for the last part."

She nodded. "I really appreciate this."

"Don't mention it."

"You've been awfully good to mee-ee-ee!" When he had finished pouring alcohol over the wound, she was screaming and sweating again.

"Now you can be sure you won't get blood poisoning." Laughing, he gave her rear a pat.

She couldn't stand to be laughed at. She wiped her cheeks with the back of her hand. "You caught me by surprise. I wouldn't have hollered if you'd warned me."

"Sure you wouldn't." He was grinning as he made a pad and passed another strip of gauze under her leg to hold it in place. He tied it off and tucked the ends neatly. "You want me to pull your pants up for you?"

She clutched at them. "I can do it myself. I wouldn't want to put you to the trouble."

"Glad to hear it." He rose and stored his kit in his saddlebags while she finally succeeded in wrestling the heavy denims up and fastening them around her waist. "Well, I guess that about takes care of you except for one little problem."

She looked up at him. The sun was directly overhead, a blinding light around his head. She shaded her eyes. "Another problem."

"Yep." He set his teeth in his lower lip and whistled. "Here, Ginger!" The roan mare threw up her head with a jingle of tack. Obediently, she came to him. He tightened her girth and put the bridle back in her mouth. "I'm about ready to leave. But I don't guess you're going with me."

She struggled up to her good hip. "I am too."

His blond eyebrows rose. "How're you going to ride?"

Chapter Three

Her mouth tightened. She stared up at the hard saddle and back down at her thigh. All she could see was the dark stain on her pants. But the wound still hurt like blazes. To ride on it would be agony.

Her outlaw strolled away to the foot of the tree and picked up her gunnysack.

She couldn't bear it. Not only was he leaving her. He was stealing her money. She had held up the train, stolen the money at gunpoint, and been wounded in the getaway. She had bled for the contents of that sack, had suffered the agony of having the bullet cut out.

"That's my money," she whispered.

He thrust his head and arm under the knotted straps and settled the sack comfortably on his hip. Then he pulled her gun out of his belt, emptied the bullets out and tossed them away.

"That's my money," she said again, more loudly. She tried to sit up, but her arms trembled and she fell back. "My bullets and my gun."

Hunkering down beside her, he laid the gun beyond her reach. "You can have it back. Just crawl over and get it. I'm counting on you taking a few minutes to load up. That's in case you have any more rounds. By then I'll be out of sight.''

She struggled up again. This time she made it to a sitting position and pulled her good leg up.

"Don't try it." His voice held a note of concern. He put one hand on her chest, but she batted it away.

"I can ride," she insisted stubbornly. "You have to take me with you."

His long fingers splayed out across her chest, each one exerting pressure holding her down. She fell back, took a deep breath, and fought again. He studied her for a minute. "What's your name?"

"Ma—Buster Ross!"

He chuckled. "Buster Ross, is it? And how old did you say you were, Buster?"

"Seven—" She caught herself too late. "None of your damn business."

"That old, huh?" He was laughing at her again. He had been laughing at her all morning, maybe all night, maybe since before he'd found out she was a girl. She could feel her face turning red. She would show him. She swung the injured left leg around. The pain made her break out in a cold sweat, but she could stand it. She was tough. "I'm not hurting much." Her voice sounded shrill and quavery, like that of a child about to cry. She hated it. "I can ride."

He pushed her harder. At last she slumped back.

He leaned above her again. She could see the growth of prickly golden beard on his face, the dark circles under his eyes, the lines around his mouth. He had ridden all night, holding her in the saddle. Without him, she might have been captured. Or even killed trying to get away.

He had taken a short rest and then pulled himself together to take out the bullet and bandage her. She owed him a lot. But not a whole sack full of money. He couldn't ride off and leave her. He had to wait until she could gather enough strength to come with him. If only she didn't feel so sick and weak . . . He had to wait for her. The next words were dragged out of her against her will. "I want to thank you for all you've done for me."

His golden eyebrows shot up. He looked as if he couldn't believe her. Then he nodded shortly. "Forget it."

Suddenly, she became aware of how she must look. If he looked bad, what must she look like? She raised a hand with the idea of running it through her hair, perhaps tidying it a bit. Her hand was so dirty she wrinkled her nose at it. Every crease in her palm was rimed with grime. Every nail was tipped with filth. She clenched her fist and let it drop to her side.

"The outlaw trail is dirty work." He grinned so faintly that the corners of his mustache didn't even move. Then his face turned bleak. As with a curtain drawn across a window, the humor disappeared. "What's more it's dangerous as hell. Listen to me, Buster. If you've got a lick of sense in that stupid little head of yours, you'll roll over here in the soft grass and sleep for a couple or three hours."

She opened her mouth to protest, but he put the tips of three long fingers over it. They smelled of alcohol and whiskey. Above them, she stared at him, pleading with her eyes. The cracks and crevices in his face looked a hundred feet deep and a hundred years old.

"You roll over and get some sleep. When it gets to be about four o'clock in the afternoon, you'll get up and walk, limp, crawl—whatever it takes to get over that little rise yonder." He pointed with the hand that had silenced her protest. "You'll be looking down on a right pretty farm. Belongs to a woman named Violie Bishop. She's the salt of the earth. Lost her husband and two sons in the War. She takes in any and all comers and doesn't ask any questions."

"No." Mary Carolyn caught at his hand and clung to it as he drew it back. He pulled her up with him until pain caught her and she had to let go. Despite everything, she wouldn't stop pleading. "Take me with you. I can keep up. How much farther on were you going to meet Jesse James? I can make it. If I sit sideways in the saddle—"

His hand slipped into the gunnysack and drew out a handful of silver certificates. Peeling off a half-dozen, he rolled them in a tight wad and stuck them in her breast pocket. "Since you're a member of the James gang, we always divide evenly. That's your share."

"Damn you. That's my money. You didn't even know that private car was back there. You wouldn't have gotten it at all."

Ignoring her, he climbed to his feet. She heard his knees crack and pop. "Ginger. Come here, girl."

"No!" Mary Carolyn fell back. "You're a liar. A darned liar. You're not a member of the James gang." She thrust a hand into her pocket and pulled out her precious book. "You're not!" She thrust it up for him to see. "You're not!"

He took the book from her. A grin broke over his tired features. *"The James Boys at Cracker Neck,"* he read. "Well, I'll be. So that's where you're getting all this stuff."

"That's right. You're not in that book, I'll bet. Tell me your name."

Shaking his head, he dropped the book back onto her stomach. The mare had walked up to him and put her head in his hands. He patted her, straightened her forelock, and then swung up on her. From a long way down Mary Carolyn looked up in helpless fury. "You're already showing signs of a fever. Maybe you ought to crawl while you've still got the strength to make it."

"D-damn you!"

He reined the mare away.

"Yes. Damn you! You skunk! Stealing from a wounded girl." She struggled to her knees, bracing herself on one hand. Her whole body shook with fury. *"Damn you!* At least tell me your name, so I'll know who I'm shooting when I come after you."

He rode on.

"Tell me, you coward! You skunk! You—you robber!"

He laughed. Reining in his horse at the top of the rise, he looked back down at her. "Clell Miller's the name," he called out. "And when you ask around for me, you'll discover I've been dead for nigh on to ten years."

With that, the roan carried him over the horizon.

* * *

From the porch of Henry Chesnut's general store, Jesse greeted Clell with a cheer. "I knew you'd make it, old son."

Clell stepped down and looped Ginger's reins over the hitching post. "I'm here."

"What took you so long?" Cole Younger struck a match off his boot and held it to a fat black cigar. He puffed diligently, the smoke rising around him. His cold eyes never left Clell's face. "We was just getting ready to send out a search party."

"Why, thank you, Cole." Clell mounted the steps until he was even with Jesse's burly cousin. "I didn't have any idea you cared so much about me."

Cole lifted the cigar from his mouth and spat a scrap of tobacco in the direction of Clell's boot. "I always think the whole world and then some of the fellow who's carrying the take from a railroad car full of passengers."

"That relieves my mind. I was thinking you were about to turn human." Clell patted the saddlebags he'd slung over his shoulder. He raised his voice. "Draw me a cold beer, Henry. I'm spittin' cotton."

He strode on into the store. Jesse grinned at Cole. "I told you so," he said. "He's back to stay."

With a sour shrug Cole continued his smoke. The others tramped into the store to divide the rest of the loot.

Frank James followed more slowly. "He's a good man, Cole," he observed in passing. "He's too honest to ride off with more than his share."

"Too lily-livered," Cole muttered around the cigar.

Inside the store all of them including the storekeeper gathered round. With avid eyes they watched Jesse divide the contents of Clell's sack. "I guessed this was about the best part," Jesse crowed. "There were a couple of high rollers 'bout midway back in the car and some drummers with real fat purses."

The haul from their coach alone was close to three hundred dollars. Billy Chadwell laughed excitedly as the stack of paper money and coins mounted in front of him.

Clell was less impressed. Split seven ways ways but with

bigger portions to Jesse, Frank, and Cole—and ten dollars to Henry for the use of his store—it was hardly worth the trouble to reach over and get it. The rest of the take from the express car, the Pullman, and the other coach totaled nearly two thousand, with the largest take from the safe. They had broken the law and risked their lives for money that they could have earned in a few months' time and been safe in their beds at night.

Henry Chesnut drew a bucket of beer, and his guests dropped into chairs around the poker table. Jesse shuffled the cards, Cole cut, and the deal began. Clell slipped his share back into his saddlebags. Yawning for effect, he made his way toward the ladder to the loft where Chesnut kept shabby cots to flop on.

"Who was that fellow you was wrestling with?" Billy Chadwell asked suddenly.

Frank and Cole glanced up, but Jesse continued the deal.

"Just some 'bo." Clell had been expecting the question. Not by the flicker of an eyelid, did he betray his amazing adventure with Buster Ross. "The poor kid was scared out of his wits. He ran off."

He pulled the ladder down from the ceiling as Jesse anted up. The others followed his lead, and the card-playing began in earnest.

Upstairs, stretched out on the shuck mattress, Clell laced his fingers together behind his head and tried to plan. Exhaustion must have affected his mind because he couldn't get that girl out of it. Ugly as homemade sin, she was still as gritty as any man he'd ever encountered. Near passed out on the ground, she'd pulled a gun on him. She'd held still for him to take that bullet out as well as the bravest men he'd ever seen. He hoped she'd made it to Violie's farm. He grinned. She'd come after him in a few days. He could count on it.

His thoughts turned to the gunnysack of money buried under the big oak half a mile back up the trail.

It was more money than he could expect to earn in eight or ten years at farming or ranching, but not more than he could expect to earn if he left dirt poor western Missouri and went north to Chicago or east to New York. It was his escape, his start at a new life.

He was no longer a seventeen-year-old kid, riding after slick-talking William Clarke Quantrill and setting fire to a whole town before he knew what he was about. Moreover, he was no longer swayed by Jesse James's raving and ranting about revenge. He'd heard it all before.

"Confederate dollars aren't worth a Chinaman's whisker," Jesse had said. "Steal Yankee dollars from the bank so we won't lose the farm," he'd said.

The War had been over for ten years, for heaven's sake.

Stealing from the railroad was another part of Jesse's story. The railroads stole from the farmers. The James gang had a right to take it back. But Clell knew that was another excuse. Jesse didn't like living safe at home as Mr. Howard with his wife Zerelda and their baby.

Clell cursed softly. What was he doing here? If he'd gotten a decent job ten years ago, he'd be ahead now. He could have burned his Confederate money and earned Yankee dollars. Instead he'd stolen them and started down the outlaw trail.

And nothing lay ahead for him with Jesse and Cole but riding, robbing, shooting, and being shot at. Eventually, he'd be shot and killed. They all would. If not by the people they were robbing, or lawmen sent to apprehend them, then by traitors in their midst. Every time some young hothead came slipping around begging to join, they all watched their backs for months. The reward on Jesse's head was already in the thousands.

Tomorrow, the gang would ride back toward Kansas City. This time, Clell resolved he would find a way to leave them and go where they could never find him. He would come back for the money and be gone. He closed his eyes. It all sounded so very, very easy.

He thought again of the girl. He hadn't divided the money fairly. She had stolen it. She had taken the bullet. His conscience nagged him. Perhaps he should go back to Violie's farm. At least he owed her a bit more. She'd been really down-at-the-heels.

He shook his head. She was a silly little thing. Her and her silly book. She wasn't his responsibility. Moreover, she wasn't the first shirttail kid lured into trouble by the myth of Jesse James. Hopefully, she'd suffered enough to learn a real lesson before she ruined her young life. He'd probably done her a favor by taking the money away from her.

His eyes closed. He saw her thin face, pale, dirty, tear streaked. Her eyes burned with righteous anger and probably a spot of fever. Growing up was hell.

Mary Carolyn awoke in darkness, and the twinkle of stars overhead. She'd snuggled deeper beneath the quilt. Her breath fogged before her nose in the cold clear air. Somewhere a cow lowed. Below her she heard a faint scratching sound. Some night creature was passing beneath the porch where she lay.

She was curiously unconcerned for the minute. Her body was relatively free of pain. The ache in her thigh had subsided to a bearable level. She was warm, and her body was healing. Even yesterday and the day before seemed a long time ago. She had limped up the lane and collapsed on the porch. She hadn't known when Violie Bishop found her and spread a quilt over her.

As the sun was setting, the sweet-faced woman had awakened her long enough to guide her to a cot set up against the wall. Mary Carolyn had gone right back to sleep even before her hostess had finished tucking another quilt in around her.

Clell's eyes flew open.

He heard the scrape and thud of heavy boots. Curses. A heavy object thudded against the floor. Then window glass shattered.

"Damn! Pinkertons!" Jesse yelled. "Hellfire and damnation! Frank! Cole!"

"Sons of bitches!" Cole's big .44 Colt percussion thundered. "Henry Chesnut! You bastard!"

"Twarn't me!" Henry yelled back. "Goldarn it. You know—"

Gunshots came from every side drowning out the old man's protests. Clell rolled off the bed and crawled to the window. Easing his head up, he was able to see the situation. One man held the horses of the others in a culvert a couple of hundred yards away. Clell could count at least ten horses.

He shook his head. They were badly outnumbered.

Below, the hail of gunshots increased in volume as Jesse pulled the ladder down. "Clell!" he yelled. "How many?"

"Ten ... twelve." He scooted crabwise across the floor. Jesse lay on his side. Blood trickled down his temple. "Are you hit?"

"Hit!" The outlaw cursed violently. "Hell, I'm riddled. A couple of the sons of bitches are using buckshot."

Clell crawled back to the window. He could see two men crouched behind a rain barrel at the side of the livery stable. Silver badges glinted off their breasts. Jesse was wrong about Pinkertons. They looked like local law enforcement. The gang should never have stopped till they got across the Missouri border.

As he watched, one man gathered himself for a run. If he made it across the yard, the eaves would protect him and he could shoot in a window. Clell threw two shots at the pair. The first man screamed and spun away as Clell's bullet ripped through the toe of his boot. The other jumped back and crouched. He looked up. His eyes met Clell's.

Instantly, Clell ducked back from the window. *Stupid! Stupid! Stupid!* He hadn't pulled up his neckerchief. Now at least one of them had had a good look at him. With a sense of locking the barn door on an empty stall, he pulled up his bandanna and ducked low beneath the sill. Taking a deep breath, he stuck his head and his gun around the window on the other side.

Whatever he was, the lawman was no inexperienced rube. His gun rested on the rain barrel, trained on the window. His eyes met Clell's again just as they both squeezed off their shots.

White hot lead ripped through Clell's neckerchief and laid

a trail of fire beneath his cheekbone. If he hadn't pulled up the neckerchief, the chances were good the marksman would have shot him in the face. He saw the other man's hat jump from his head, saw blood spurt from a scalp wound, watched the man flop over backward.

With a mirthless smile, Clell ducked back out of sight again. Pulling cartridges from his gunbelt he reloaded. Then he leaned his head back against the wall. Ambushed. Surrounded. *Christ! And damn Henry Chesnut to hell!* They were all going to be killed.

"Clell!" Jesse yelled. "Which way do we go?"

Dropping on all fours, he crawled to the ladder. "Through the livery stable. They had two boys by the rain barrel, but they've both got other things on their minds now."

Jesse's white-toothed grin flashed. "You're the best, Clell!"

He scuttled to Frank, who passed the news on to Jim. "The livery stable," he called low to Cole. "Clell's cleared 'em out for us."

Cole caught the storekeeper by the scruff of the neck. "You're leadin', Henry."

"I didn't have anything to do with this," the old man screamed. "I've always been square with you boys. Don't!"

Cole pushed him ahead of them to the back door.

"Shoot out the front!" Jesse called. "Everybody. Make them think we're coming out."

Cole's brother Jim flung the door open, then slammed it again. "Fire! They're bringing fire. Those bastards are trying to burn us out."

"Oh, Lord! They're going to burn my store," Henry Chesnut screamed at Jesse. "I didn't have anything to do with 'em. I swear."

Jesse wavered. His blue eyes blinked furiously. "Henry—"

"Cover us," Cole snarled. "Come on, Henry. You don't want to burn up, do you?" He pushed the old man before him down the back steps and propelled him toward the livery stable.

One after another in quick order, the gang followed. Clell came halfway down the ladder, then stopped. A half-formed thought bloomed. Darting back up, he pulled the ladder up after him. He could smell the smoke. The store would go up like tinder. His chances of escape were small, but so were the rest of the gang's.

From the window he watched them dash across the space. Pushing Henry before him, Cole made the livery stable. The pair disappeared from view. Jesse came next, running like a deer. Clell could see bloody streams down the side of his face. They dyed the shoulder of his white shirt both back and front.

Frank came next. He ran hunched over clutching his side. Billy Chadwell caught the older man under the shoulder and dragged him along. As they disappeared into the livery stable, the smoke began to sift up through the floor by the front windows.

Clell coughed. The heat rose all around him. The timing was the most important thing here. Would the James gang get on their horses and break out of the back of the livery stable in time to draw the posse away before Chesnut's store became a furnace? Or would he pass out from the smoke and burn to death while they were still in the stable?

Coughing again, he strode across to the pitcher on the shaving stand. A couple of inches of water stood in the bottom of it. He poured it over his face, soaking his neckerchief and his shirtfront. He threw a look at his saddlebags hanging over the iron bedstead. With a shrug he detoured to catch them up and sling them over his shoulder.

He got back to the window in time to see the break. Smoke was billowing out of the store now. The outlaws rode into it, their forms concealed by it. Four abreast, Jesse and Frank and the Youngers charged out of the stable. Crowding behind them, came Billy Chadwell, his young face white, and the new kid. Clell didn't even know his name. How many were wounded, how many unscathed, he couldn't tell. As they rode past, Clell could swear that Jesse shot a look at the window, just as the smoke billowed up in a great black cloud.

As they galloped around the edge of the livery stable, the posse poured after them, running, firing, throwing shots haphazardly at the fleeing gang. Two men in suits and bowler hats led the charge. Clell nodded his head. Pinkertons. Jesse had called it right after all.

The floor smoked beneath his boots. In the store below, the crackle and roar built to a crescendo. A series of gunshots, like firecrackers, sent the posse running behind the livery stable for protection. The fire had reached Henry Chesnut's ammunition.

Clell couldn't stand the heat any longer. He tumbled out the window and flattened himself on the roof. It was like lying on a stove. Tiny streams of smoke rose all around him from between the cedar shingles. At any minute they could flash into flames. A couple of shells spanged through the far end of the roof. If the fire didn't get him, the ammunition would.

He raised his head. He could see clearly the Pinkerton man leading the horses at a full gallop toward the stable. If he could see the man, the man could see him. He flattened himself again. Smoke seared his lungs. He coughed so hard his convulsions nearly threw him off the roof.

The rest of the posse met the rider in the open in full view of Clell. The horses shied and kicked, smelling the fire, rearing every time a stray round of ammunition exploded in the inferno of Henry's store. Mounting up seemed to take forever.

Somewhere Clell found the courage to lie still, praying that no one would look in his direction. Praying that if they did, they wouldn't notice him. Praying that if they noticed him, they would think he was dead.

After what seemed an eternity, the men were all in the saddle including the one he had shot. At last they galloped off after the outlaws.

Clell rolled to the edge of the roof and dropped off. Flames shot out of the loft window. The blast of heat from Chesnut's store drove him, staggering, back across the yard. The backs of his knees struck the horse trough. Letting his momentum do the work, he twisted and slid headfirst into its blessed coolness.

"You say Clell Miller told you to come to me?" Violie Bishop ladled beans onto a plate and set a wedge of cornbread beside them.

Mary Carolyn nodded. Her mouth was watering so hard, she was practically slobbering. She hadn't recognized she was hungry. Every time she moved, her thigh felt as if it would collapse under her. Her body ached in places she didn't know she had. When she'd stripped down in the outhouse, she'd discovered that each hipbone had a bruise the size of a man's fist. Where had they come from? Then she knew. They were souvenirs of being toted face down across Clell Miller's saddle.

No doubt about it. The outlaw trail was a tough life.

At last Violie set the plate in front of her. The first bite tasted like heaven. The second was better than the one before. Her stomach rumbled in appreciation. She reached for the wedge of cornbread. The sight of her filthy hand brought all the memories rushing back. For a minute they took her appetite away. She clenched her fist and put down her fork. ''Please, ma'am, I forgot to wash my hands.''

Violie smiled her approval. ''You sure did. I wasn't going to say a word because your backbone must have been peeking through your belly button, but I've got some nice warm water here on the back of the stove.'' Like a little bird she flitted across the kitchen, carrying the kettle to the wash table.

Hurting, partly from memory, as ghost pains shot through her limbs, Mary Carolyn limped after her. As she scrubbed her hands with a brush, she could see Clell Miller clearly. Her outlaw helping her and then riding away and leaving her bereft. She held out her hands for Violie to pour more warm water over.

She would eat and thank the woman profusely, and then she would see about leaving. When she sat back down to the table, she was not only cleansed but resolved.

''Eat it all, child. You can eat the whole pot if you want.'' Violie Bishop smiled. Blond hair had faded to the delicate white of cornsilk on her head. Her eyes were faded blue. Her face had a colorless sameness about it. Only her smile lived.

Mary Carolyn smiled in return. ''Thank you, ma'am.''

They sat together in companionable silence, then Violie cleared her throat softly. ''Now about Clell Miller . . .''

Mary Carolyn nodded with a smile as if he were the most

wonderful person in the world. "He helped me," she said between bites of beans. "He did everything he could for me"— *including rob me*—"and then he directed me to you."

Two spots of color shone in the old lady's cheeks. "What did he look like?"

Mary Carolyn did not hesitate. "Tall, blond, blue eyes. I imagine most women would think he was handsome."

Violie nodded again. She picked at an imaginary spot on the oak table that had been scrubbed so many times it was almost white. "I don't suppose you noticed his hands."

Mary Carolyn nodded. "He has a crooked little finger on the right one."

Violie raised a hand to her mouth. Her eyes were shining with the beginnings of tears. "Bless God and Jesus and all the angels. Then he's not dead."

Mary Carolyn didn't know what to say. Clell had warned her that he'd been dead ten years. She stared fixedly at her plate.

Violie rose and walked to the door. "Bless Jesus," she whispered. "Not dead. Not dead."

He's still a thief, Buster Ross told herself stubbornly. I was an outlaw, and he stole from me . . .

She kept her eyes down. The cornbread crumbled in her fingers. She laid it down and took a drink of coffee. "Er . . . I'm supposed to catch up with him," she said in her sweetest Mary Carolyn voice. "He sent me to you because he had to meet Jesse—Jesse James, that is—somewhere down the road. He told me the name of the place, but I've forgotten. I think the fever drove it right out of my head."

She raised her eyes pleadingly. Violie was still staring out across the field. "Do you have any idea where I'm supposed to meet up with them? I don't want to put them in danger by keeping them waiting."

The old woman wrapped her arms around her thin frame. The words seemed to come from a long way off across the years. "I 'spect they'd wait for you at Chesnut's Crossing north of Lineville. That's where they used to meet with my Jakey and Bax."

Buster clenched her jaw to keep back the shout of triumph that bubbled up in her throat. Mr. Clell Miller thought he'd seen the last of her. Not much! She'd show him. She'd show them all. She couldn't wait to meet Jesse James.

Clell dropped down on his knees beside Henry Chesnut. The old man was slumped down in the stall. The pumpknot on his temple was rising fast and trickling blood down into his shirt collar. His eyes were barely open, his breathing was harsh. Clell delivered himself of a fervent curse on the heads of Jesse and more especially Cole Younger.

They had no excuse for knocking Henry out.

The poor old man had lost his store. The Pinkertons heading up that posse had showed no compunction about burning everything. They had burned the work of the old man's lifetime, the hope for his declining years—because he had given aid and comfort to Jesse James and his gang.

It was 1864 all over again. Clell closed his eyes against the memory of another old man hanging from the rafters of his own porch because he'd given Jesse James and his gang a place to sleep, his barn.

The acrid gray smoke drifted into the stable. The old structure might catch at any minute. Clell left Henry to get Ginger. The mare's stall was empty. Damn Cole Younger! Clell was as sure as he was of tomorrow that the outlaw had stolen her.

He froze. This was his chance to let it all go. Disappear. If he didn't show up, the gang would believe he had burned to death in Chesnut's store. It was his chance to disappear again with more money than—

"Clell, boy, help me. Please."

He swung his head in the old man's direction. Damn! Someone knew he was alive. He considered running out. Maybe Henry would forget. Unfortunately, if Buster Ross—or whatever her name was—actually caught up with Jesse James and demanded her share of that money, the jig would be up. He didn't want to be looking over his shoulder for the rest of his life. The best thing to do was to ride with Jesse for a decent amount of time. If the girl showed up, he'd get rid of her somehow. If she didn't, he'd leave one night. They might look for him for a while, but the Pinkertons were on their trail. They'd be too busy to come after him. He thought of that gunnysack stuffed with money. It could take him clear to China.

Clell went back and slipped his hands under Henry's bony shoulders. He'd stay to help Henry and then he'd catch up to the gang. After that he'd ride off forever—on Ginger.

Chapter Four

With her hat pulled down to her eyebrows and her coat collar turned up around her ears, Mary Carolyn skirted the remains of Chesnut's store. Stray wisps of smoke still rose from the piles of blackened timber. Miraculously, the stable still stood untouched. From it came the sound of hammering.

Inside was an old man. A broad white bandage wrapped his forehead. Beneath it, one eye was swollen almost shut, but he set a nail to a two-by-four and drove it in with a forceful hand.

"Hello."

He looked over his shoulder. With a tight smile, he stuck the hammer through his belt loop. As he came toward her, he wiped his hands on the seat of his pants. "What can I do for you, young fella. As you see, I've had a fire. Not much left, but everything I've got's for sale."

An array of canned goods, some touched by fire; a miscellany of foodstuffs, obviously fresh; hardware, also scorched but otherwise in good condition; and a large selection of rider's tack from the stable constituted the inventory.

Mary Carolyn needed every penny she had, but his plight touched her heart. She picked out a can of Pet Milk, stained by the smoke but not pumped, and a couple of apples. "What happened?"

"Goddam Pinkertons." Henry's face reddened. "Set fire to my place. But they won't get away with it. It ain't like it was during the War with them damn jayhawks. No sirree bobtail! I've already got ahold of my lawyer. I'm suing them for everything I've lost plus bodily harm." He pointed to his head. "Think they can just ride roughshod over law-abiding folk. I'll show them."

She counted out her coins. "Why'd they burn your place?"

Henry puffed out his chest. "I'm a business man. I rent the upstairs rooms to whoever can pay for them. The Waldorf don't ask whether a man's wanted or not. Neither do I."

A chill scudded down her spine. If Clell was dead, she'd never see a penny of that money. "Was anybody hurt?"

"Hell, yes. I'm hurt. Damn near everything I got went up in smoke." He touched his head. "If you don't count this here tap on the bean, nobody inside was hurt. It all burned for nothing." He bared his snaggleteeth in a wolfish grin. " 'Course a couple of the posse got drilled pretty good."

She took a deep breath and put her hand on her pistol. "I sure wish I'd been here. Sounds like the gang could have used another gun."

Henry's good eye narrowed. He studied her closely. "You're a mite young to be part of a gang."

She thought fast, then deepened her voice. "They don't need nobody old to hold the horses and such."

He still looked unconvinced.

She needed to get on her way before he looked at her too closely. Even with her face smeared with dirt and her hair hanging in her eyes, he might suspect that she was a girl. "Which way did they go?"

"South, like always." Henry took up his hammer and returned to his shelves. "They were headed for Kansas City, but they'll stop in just north of there probably."

"Much obliged." She put her purchases in her saddlebags except for one of the apples. As she rode off, she imagined catching up to Clell and getting her money back. She'd show him she wasn't one to give up. She sank her teeth into the apple with a vengeance.

Well after midnight more than two weeks after the Chicago, Rock Island holdup, Jesse led the gang through the tiny Missouri hamlet of Kearney to the home of his stepfather, Dr. Reuben Samuel. They had doubled back and ridden west, then south, then east. When the Iowa deputies had had to turn back, the Pinkertons had still chased them hard for a spell. They were all just about worn slick before they finally lost them. They had been shot at on numerous occasions, but nobody had been winged or even grazed. At least no one was in need of Dr. Samuel's services.

The only real problem was that they had run several of their horses into the ground and had to make "trades" with farmers along the way.

Above all things Jesse hated to do that. When they had to, his brother Frank always pitched a fit. In fact, Jesse was sure Frank would walk rather than steal another man's horse and leave a windbroken, run-down nag in its place.

On the other hand, Cole didn't seem to mind stealing from his own people. Jesse glanced uneasily at the bulky form riding point in the moonlight. Cole did the actual "trading." So far he hadn't killed anybody, but he'd broken one farmer's jaw.

The house at Kearney stood silent and dark, but the night sounds—the chirping of crickets, the croaks of bullfrogs, the trill of the nighthawks darting across the pale moon after insects—testified that no large troop of men lay close in ambush.

"Step down and come on in," Jesse invited, suiting his action to his words. "I'll roust out Papa Samuel. He'll brew us a pot of coffee."

Wearily, the gang stepped down, sure of a welcome at the Samuel farm. The place had been Jesse's father's. Robert James, the minister of the New Hope Methodist Church, had caught gold fever. Leaving his wife and sons, he had gone to California long before the War. He had never been heard of again.

His wife had remarried, and her new husband, a minister too as well as a doctor, had moved into her home. Someday the farm would be Jesse's and Frank's if they lived long enough to inherit it.

A figure stepped out of the shadows of the porch. " 'Bout time you fellas got here. And you sure as hell better have my mare in good condition.''

"Clell." Jesse sprang up the steps and wrung his hand. "Frank, it's Clell."

"Thank God." Frank joined his brother to pat Clell on the back and shake his other hand. "The last glimpse we caught of you, that building was about to go."

"More lives than a damn cat," Cole Younger muttered. He looped the reins over the roan's saddle and slid down. He hated the thought of giving up the smooth-stepping mare. He had trouble finding mounts big enough to carry his weight for a long run. To Clell he said, "She's here. I was just keeping the saddle warm for you."

"Much obliged." Clell stepped down and took Ginger's reins. He patted the big mare who whickered and nuzzled him in greeting. "Glad to see you took care of my saddle too."

Cole snarled something unintelligible. Jostling Clell aside, he mounted the steps and stomped into the house.

"Sure is good you made it, Clell," Billy Chadwell said half apologetically. One by one, the rest of the gang handed the boy their horses. He led them away in the direction of the Samuel barn.

Clell watched him go. Absently, he ran a hand over the mare's side. Then he cursed softly. "God damn him, Ginger. You've had a rough time."

The mare blew a roller threw her nose and nuzzled him. While he arranged her forelock, his fingers traced the long fresh scabs and gouges where Cole's spurs had raked her. In all likelihood, she'd carry those scars for the rest of her life. How he wished he could get on her back and ride away forever!

* * *

Clell cupped his hands around the stoneware mug, his crooked little finger slipped in under his ring finger. Face solemn, he leaned forward, willing Jesse James to take him seriously. "We've got to split up the gang," he insisted. "We're too big. If it was just the Iowa posse, it'd be different. But there were Pinkertons with them. They aren't going to quit."

"They got licked good and proper," Jesse shot back. "Hell! You drilled two of 'em yourself. And they never touched a one of us. They'll think twice before they tackle us again." He laughed, his blue eyes blinking furiously as they flashed around the circle of men. "Hell, we rode out of that stable like in the old days. All we needed was a bugle to sound the charge. They scattered like quail."

Billy Chadwell laughed loudly and thumped the shoulder of the newest and youngest member of the gang. Jim Pool was a quiet young man. People would never have taken him for an outlaw unless they looked into his eyes. Then the coldness made them shudder. He nodded slowly. His smile didn't even quiver his blond mustache.

The rest of the gang rumbled softly in what seemed to be agreement with Jesse.

Clell had argued with him for over an hour. Always in love with danger, Jesse still rejoiced in the riding through and hiding in the Missouri countryside. He liked to imagine that they were continuing the work of Quantrill, fighting for the Confederacy and terrorizing the scalawags. Every wild gallop was like a cavalry charge. Clell had realized long ago that excitement acted like a drug on Jesse. James did not want to disband the gang.

Moreover, here in his mother's kitchen, with the big iron range casting its comfortable heat, Jesse felt right with the world. An iron stockpot simmered ever so gently, filling the kitchen with a rich meaty smell. A couple of apple pies, richly seasoned with cinnamon and nutmeg, had been set to cool on the window ledge. The fact that he was wanted for robbery with a sizable reward on his head and that every lawman's hand was against him didn't bother him. At twenty-eight he was still an overgrown boy, still playing at war over a decade after the guns had ceased.

"Maybe it wouldn't hurt to lie low just for a few months, Jess." Frank James knew his little brother. He had been there when Quantrill had burned Lawrence, Kansas. A quietness sat on his spirit. A thoughtful man, he read the classics. He was also intensely loyal to his brilliant brother. Still he looked inquiringly at Clell and then around at the others. "We've got plenty of cash. Why not lay off and enjoy some of it? Take a trip or something?"

"We ain't got near enough." Cole Younger shook his shaggy head. He was Jesse's cousin, but he bore little resemblance to the James brothers. Where they were thin and wiry, he was brawny. The spirit that flamed in Jesse and the steadfastness that was part and parcel of Frank were absent from Cole. Men wouldn't follow him through love or allegiance. He led them because he was beyond fear and absolutely ruthless toward his enemies. "Something else must have gone on with that train," Cole growled. "Pinkerton wouldn't have been after us for the handful of change we took off those farmers. Ain't I right, fellas?"

The other members of the gang looked at him blankly. They sat around the edges of the room, their backs to the wall, dumbly following the conversation that would decide the course of their lives.

Clell struggled to keep his expression from betraying him. Cole was guessing. He'd been in the express car. He couldn't have any idea of the private car or the other robber. Buster Ross was recuperating at Violie Bishop's farm in Iowa or already limping back to where she came from, her tail between her legs. He cleared his throat. "Is that right, Cole? How much did you say you got out of that express car?"

The question fell like a cannonball in their midst. Men straightened and gaped at Clell. Then, slowly, they turned their eyes to Cole.

The big man half rose. "What'd you say?"

The gang, including Jesse and Frank, looked back at Clell, who sat still as as stone.

The first lesson he'd had learned in the War was never wait for the other fellow to attack. Attack him first. Drive him back. Undercut him. Destroy his confidence. He directed his most piercing stare at Cole Younger. "Just that if there was something important on that train, it had to've been in the express car."

As one, all eyes returned to Cole.

His broad face turned red. His lips pulled back from his teeth in a wolf's snarl. The chair tipped over backward as he lunged to his feet. "You son-of-a-bitch—"

Clell pushed back his chair and came up with his hand on his gun. Men scrambled to get out of the line of fire. When Cole hesitated, Frank put his hand on Clell's shoulder. Jesse caught Cole's gun arm. "Settle down. He doesn't mean anything."

Death looked out from beneath Younger's brows. Another instant and he would draw his gun. Then one of them would die. "He's calling me a thief."

After a moment's silence Jesse laughed in his most charming way. "Well, hell, Cole, you are a thief."

Cole shot his cousin a fierce look, but Frank laughed too. Cole's brother Jim chuckled. Billy Chadwell caught the joke and laughed right out loud.

The tension eased. Cole grinned a bit sheepishly. Clell let his arm slowly relax. Jesse clapped him on the back. He bent over and picked up the chair. "Sit down now, both of you, and let's decide—"

They heard a knock at the front door. Instantly, they were on the alert. Hands closed over gun butts. They heard Mrs. Samuel's footsteps across the parlor floor, heard the front door open.

"I'm looking for Jesse James."

The voice was young, feminine. It sliced through Clell like a knife. *Good God!* She had found him.

"This is the Samuel farm," Jesse's mother replied. She didn't hold with lying, but she had become adept at telling the truth without telling anything of importance.

"Yes, ma'am," came the clear voice. "But I'm a friend of his, and I know he'll be glad to see me."

A slow grin spread over Jesse's face. He looked around at the men. "Must be another one," he boasted. Climbing to his feet, he ran a hand over his slicked-back hair. "I tell you, it's a wonder to me how women just flock after—"

Clell sprang to his feet and pushed past him. "Buster!" he called. He led the way down the hall into the parlor. Her face and hands were clean, but the rest of her from the scruffy hat on her chopped-off hair to the run-over boots was just the same. She was still the homeliest mutt he'd ever dragged home. "Sweetheart."

In three long strides he crossed the room and swept her into his arms.

"Hey—"

His mouth came down hard on hers.

Mary Carolyn's eyes went wide. Her fists clenched. In effect Clell Miller had wrapped her up as surely as if he had tossed a lasso over her. His big arms held hers at her sides while his tongue drove into her open mouth. She breathed in through her nose. She couldn't believe her senses, but his scent was just as she remembered. She would have recognized him in the dark. It was male, mixed with the smoke of campfires clinging to his clothes and the odor of the horse he rode and the woods he rode through.

Waves of emotion swept her. First surprise, then fear, then something different, something more powerful than either of those.

He kissed her as no one had ever kissed her. Hot and frightening. A total kiss with touch and taste and scent involved. His tongue forced its way into her mouth. She was too shocked by the very idea of a man's tongue in her mouth to try to figure out what he tasted like. His arms held her tight against him. She could feel the beating of his heart and the crushing strength of his chest as he breathed. Everything about him was alive and male. Her outlaw. This was what Viola Vennond had felt when the masked bandit had kissed her.

Mary Carolyn almost swooned. She had expected him to be angry. She had expected him to order her to leave immediately. She had been prepared to argue. To fight if necessary. She had come determined to tell Jesse James that she—not Clell Miller—had stolen that money. She had planned to demand that she be given a fair share.

She had not expected her outlaw to kiss her.

All thoughts of her mission were driven from her mind. Sudden heat flamed in her loins. She couldn't explain it. The tips of her breasts tingled. She moaned around the hot tongue that slid back and forth between her teeth and along her own tongue. She clutched at his shoulders.

He made a small surprised sound. She could feel his muscles strain beneath her hands. Without thought, she sucked at his tongue. Then he was trying to pull back.

Her feet left the floor. She had never been so aware of her small size. He was holding her the way a child would a doll, but it felt wonderful. She gave a little squirm.

He pulled his tongue out of her mouth and raised his head. Their faces were only inches apart. She could feel his heart thundering against her breast. "Buster, you little dickens." He sounded a little breathless. Something flashed in his eyes as he stared at her. He gave his head a shake. "You just wouldn't stay put, would you?"

"Er . . . no. That is . . . No."

He set her on her feet, steadying her with a broad arm around her shoulders. Suddenly, she blushed red with embarrassment.

Three tall strangers had entered the room and now stared at her with broad grins on their faces. Behind them in the doorway, other men were clustered, looking in. They too were grinning. The woman who had introduced herself as Mrs. Samuel stood to one side, her arms folded tightly underneath her bosom. Her mouth was stitched tight with disapproval.

Mary Carolyn couldn't blame her. She would never have believed that a man—even an outlaw—would kiss a girl in front of others. Especially not the way he'd kissed her. Maybe the books were truer to life than she imagined. But she didn't want these people to think she was fast. She was a good girl even if she had decided to become an outlaw. She tipped her head back to glare up at him. For the first time she saw he had an angry red burn across one cheek. Where had that come from?

He grinned down at her and chucked her under the chin in the friendliest way imaginable. "Now, Buster, don't look at me like that. These folks'll forgive you. And me too for that matter." Still keeping an arm around her, he led her up to the woman. "Mrs. Samuel, I'd like you to meet Buster. Buster, shake hands with Mrs. Zerelda James Samuel."

Mary Carolyn looked at the lady's stern face. Buster wasn't the proper sort of name to use when she was introduced to someone like that. Mindful of her manners, she held out her hand obediently. "My name's Mary Carolyn, Mrs. Samuel. And I'm pleased to meet you. Buster's a nickname they called me at the—at school . . . when I was younger. You know how things like that . . . er . . . stick sometimes."

Mrs. Samuel looked at Mary Carolyn's callused little hand. For an instant, Mary Carolyn thought she wasn't going to take it. Then the older woman smiled stiffly. "Miss . . . er. . . ."

Clell squeezed her shoulder hard. "And these are my friends." He led her in front of a handsome man with bright blue eyes and a broad smile. "This is Jesse James."

Buster could not help herself. She stood in front of the most famous outlaw in the whole United States. The "Bandit King," the dime novels were calling him. She was scared to death. She shrank back against Clell's chest. Clell squeezed her shoulder again. "Pleased to meet you," she mumbled.

"And Frank James," Clell went on.

His eyes were kind. He looked more like a schoolteacher than a famous outlaw. He inclined his head in a formal way rather than trying to take her hand. "Pleased to make your acquaintance."

She relaxed a little. "Thank you."

"And this is Cole Younger." The change in Clell's tone made her glance up at him again. He didn't like this man. She would have to think about the why of this later. For now, she nodded to Cole. "Hello."

Cole snorted. "Well, who the hell is this, Clell? The way you were kissing her, she sure ain't no stranger."

She could feel her stomach clench. What would Clell tell them? What had he told them? Suddenly, she was very afraid she had stepped into a lion's den. Still and all, she deserved a share of that money. She cleared her throat and tried to step away from Clell.

Her outlaw dropped his arm from her shoulder to her waist and hugged her tighter against him. "Well, I didn't want her around here, but she was just bound and determined to come. She's another reason why I want us to split up for a while. This little girl is my wife, folks. Mary Carolyn Miller is her name from now on."

With an outraged gasp, she tried to twist away. Somehow, his hand had fastened on her wrist. She spun away from him. He jerked her back. She crashed against his chest. "I know I made you promise not to tell, sweetheart—"

His steel blue eyes glinted, promising terrible punishment.

She cast a swift glance over her shoulder. They were grinning at her, all right. Like wolves. Instead of pushing away from him, she was afraid she should be pushing toward him.

"—but listen here. I want to spend some time with you. And I don't want them to think bad of you." He looked up. "You won't, will you, boys?"

Behind her the "boys" all rumbled their assurances.

"And Jesse and Cole are wanting to plan another job right away."

He splayed his long fingers over her back. Her breasts flattened against his chest. He was so tall she had to tilt her head back at a sharp angle to look him in the eye. She caught him staring down into her face. The steel blue eyes moved over her. By a trick of light, his expression appeared to alter slightly. Then he gave his head a slight shake. As if he were her lover and she a beautiful woman, he dropped a light kiss on her mouth.

Suddenly, she was confused. She knew that he wasn't glad

to see her, yet the kiss seemed so real, affectionate like a father's or a brother's. But that couldn't be. Still, she didn't want to fight him anymore.

He kissed her again, the same light brush of lips, then raised his head, and smiled at the gawking men. His mouth thinned, leaving the smile without humor.

Like a flash of lightning, the reason came to her. He was playing a game and willing her to play along. He wanted her to pretend to be his wife. She felt stupid beyond belief. She should have caught on immediately. And the reason he was doing this must be the money—her money. Her eyes widened and then narrowed. She could not suppress a superior smile. When he saw it, a faint flicker of doubt swept across his face.

So! He had not told the James gang about the money.

She could tell them! She could push her way out of the circle of his arm. Perhaps she should strike him and call him a liar. It would be like a scene in a novel where the heroine reveals all to defeat the villain. She could tell them that she had stolen a great sack of silver and gold certificates as well as gold and silver coins from the safe of the private car. She could tell them, furthermore, that he had stolen the loot from her. She could tell them . . .

Except that somehow things were all mixed up. She wasn't sure who was the villain and who was the hero of this adventure.

She looked into the handsome face of Jesse James. His eyes were glittery and without warmth like a rattlesnake's. He had several scabs on the side of his head. And Cole Younger's mouth was mean and unsmiling. A lifetime of ruthlessness showed in its deep lines. A white scar seared a line across his cheekbone, aimed at a notch in his ear. He might have been the most evil and desperate villain in a dime novel.

Suddenly, she could feel chills chasing themselves up and down her spine. More than a little frightened, she cast her lot with the devil she thought she knew rather than the devils she didn't. She hung her head like an embarrassed girl. "You didn't have to tell them, Clell."

She could feel the breath he had been holding slide out of his lungs. He squeezed her waist. "That's all right, honey. I

sure wouldn't want Jesse's mother to think bad about you."
He looked hopefully at Mrs. Samuel, who had relaxed slightly.
"I shouldn't have kissed her like that, but I was just so glad
to see her."

Mary Carolyn looked up. "He's really good to me," she
pleaded. "He's been real worried about me. I've been sick
some."

Mrs. Samuel relaxed completely. "Well, I can understand
that. You sure don't look too good even now." She held out
her hand. "Why don't you come with me? You can wash up
a little."

"That's not necessary," Clell began. "I can take her down
to the creek."

"I wouldn't hear of it." Jesse's mother motioned to Clell's
"wife."

Mary Carolyn cast a pleased look over her shoulder as she
stepped out of her "husband's" grasp.

Mrs. Samuel led her down the hall. "Clell's a good boy.
I'm so glad to meet his bride." She emphasized the last word.
She cast a sidelong glance at Mary Carolyn. "It's time all the
boys were settling down. Jesse's finally married Zee. You know
she's my godchild. She was named Zerelda for me. And Frank's
made peace with Annie's father. It's good you've come. You'll
be another good influence. I've told Jesse time and again that
I won't have his little brother exposed to anything immoral.
Archie's only nine and he just about idolizes Jesse and Frank."

Mary Carolyn scarcely heard her. The farther she got into
outlawry, the more exciting it became. She and her outlaw were
acting together now to trick other outlaws. It was all very
exciting.

On the other hand, what did that say for the honor among
thieves the dime novels always talked about? The inevitable
answer to that question sobered her. Evidently Clell Miller had
no honor. As an outlaw, he didn't have to be careful about
that.

* * *

In the parlor the outlaws gathered around to clap Clell on the back and congratulate him. Frank produced a box of cigars, and they all lighted up.

Puffing away in the corner with the new man Jim Pool, Cole Younger blew a long stream of blue smoke into the air. "There must be more to her than meets the eye," he opined. "She sure ain't long on looks, and she's gimpy to boot."

The new man blinked once. "They were talking to each other."

Cole looked at him speculatively. "That so. And what were they saying?"

"I'm not sure." Jim Pool rose. "But I mean to watch them. I'll find out."

Mrs. Samuel proved to be a kind and gentle person. She was not at all the sort that Mary Carolyn would have expected to be the mother of the two most famous outlaws in the United States. She seemed to think that her lone female guest needed to be entertained and kept away from the men in the parlor.

Buster would have given anything to join the gang and listen to their arguments which went on and on. Their deep voices rose and fell. Once in a while someone—always the same person—would curse.

At that point Mrs. Samuel would tighten her mouth in disapproval.

The entire thing came to an abrupt halt when Reverend Samuel came home. Everybody except the James brothers, the Younger brothers, and Clell excused themselves and went out to bed down in the barn.

Mary Carolyn waited uncertainly.

"We'd like you two to stay to supper." Mrs. Samuel said graciously. "I've known Clell since he was a baby child. He's like my own. His mother was my best friend when Reverend

James went to the gold fields. We never saw him again. It was hard for Jesse and Frank losing their father like that. I often think if he'd stayed here where he belonged . . .''

She let her voice trail off.

Mary Carolyn could certainly sympathize with any boy who was raised without a father. "I don't know any of Clell's people," she said. "I'd like to stay and hear more about them."

"How long have you and Clell been married?" Jesse's mother asked.

Mary Carolyn realized that she should have been prepared for that question. Indeed, she should already have made up the answer. Too late, she stammered and stuttered. Finally, she tucked her head down and thrust her fists into her pockets. "Just a few days," she whispered. "We were married just before the . . . er . . . before he had to go meet Jesse."

"Ah."

While Mrs. Samuel fixed dinner, Mary Carolyn and Clell were never left alone. He pulled her down to sit beside him while Reverend Samuel held forth, mostly on the wages of sin and the blessedness and happiness of the godly, upstanding life. The reverend then spent several minutes on the sanctity of marriage and beamed with approval at Clell, with disapproval at her.

"Why is he smiling whenever he looks at you and frowning when he looks at me?" she whispered to her outlaw.

"Because you're wearing pants. Brother Samuel doesn't hold with women wearing men's dress. I think it looks great. 'Specially since I've seen what's underneath." He tugged at the corner of his blond mustache in an exaggerated leer like a villain in a melodrama.

"Oh." Blushing, she pulled her legs tight together at the knees. She looked around her to see if anyone else was staring at her.

Jesse and the Youngers were leaning back in their chairs.

Their faces were blank as the minister's words went in one ear and out the other. Frank was sitting a bit straighter. His expression was serious. Once in a while, he would interject a word or two.

Mary Carolyn leaned against Clell. "I don't ordinarily wear these except when I need to ride. How does he expect me to ride?"

"In a buggy."

The meal was a modest affair. If Jesse James had stolen thousands of Yankee dollars, his parents didn't seem to have any of it. The food was humble—biscuits and sausage gravy, home-canned green beans, home-canned tomatoes, and pickles, both sweet and sour. For dessert they ate the two apple pies with sweet cream spooned over them.

No one talked at the table after the Reverend Samuel asked the blessing. Mary Carolyn had a chance to look around her and to let the unfamiliarity sink in. The table was crowded. Besides the preacher and his wife at the head and the foot, there were Jesse and Frank and their little half brother Archie, also Cole and Jim Younger.

She sat at one corner, the table leg between her knees. Her plate and Clell's almost touched. Their shoulders did. She could feel the movements of warm hard muscles beneath his wool shirt. His nearness was unsettling. She forced her thoughts into another direction.

The outlaw life wasn't what she had expected it to be. Certainly it wasn't lonely nights on the trail with the stars above and mournful howls of the timberwolves coming from the nearest hills. It was more like the life of ordinary people.

She couldn't believe that Jesse and Frank had wives somewhere. Did they also have children? Likewise, where was the sheriff of Kearney, Missouri? Why wasn't he here to arrest them? Where was the U.S. Marshal for this state? Where were the lawmen from nearby Kansas City? How could Jesse and Frank and their cousins sit peacefully at their mother's table when they had prices on their heads? Why weren't people trying to collect them?

She began to make a mental list of things she was going to ask Clell when she had some time alone with him. She also wondered when they were leaving. That should be a safe enough question. She looked around her. The silence was peaceful in a way. Not like the cold silence at the long table where she had eaten until she had made up her mind to rob the train.

She would save the question about leaving for later. He probably wouldn't want to tell her, or if he did, he would probably lie about it. He was probably planning to slip off in the middle of the night.

She was going to have to keep a close watch on him. Otherwise, he would ride off and pick up their money—she thought of it as theirs—and steal it all. She set her fork down, touched the napkin to her mouth. "That pie was so good." She smiled at Mrs. Samuel. "I can't remember when I've had a piece of pie that tasted so good."

Her hostess beamed. "The apples come from our own orchard."

"With God's blessing," Reverend Samuel added sternly. He rose, the signal that the meal was over.

Darkness had fallen. Jesse picked up the lamp from his end of the table and carried it back into the parlor. Mary Carolyn rose and began collecting the plates, but her hostess shook her head.

She motioned to Clell and put her arm around Mary Carolyn's shoulders. "The Reverend and I have a plan for you," she said softly. They bent their heads to her. "We want you to take our bed for the night."

Clell's eyes widened, then he grinned. Mary Carolyn turned white and then red again. "Oh, no. We couldn't take your bed." She looked up at him, urging him to agree with her. "It wouldn't be proper. Would it, Clell?"

He kept on grinning.

"Clell!"

"That's the nicest thing you've ever done for me, Aunt Zee. And you've done a lot of wonderful things." He put a big hand on the side of Mary Carolyn's face and tipped her head gently onto his shoulder. "We're much obliged. You can just bet we'll make good use of it, won't we, sweetheart?"

Both women blushed, for very different reasons.

Chapter Five

Buster had had more than two hours for her anger to build while she waited for Clell to join her in the Samuel's bedroom. Through the thin walls, she had heard the outlaws laughing and talking. An almost constant rumble of masculine voices had come from the parlor. She had distinctly heard the men say good night to each other. The thud of boots and heavy shoes followed, the squeak and click of doors. Then she had heard footsteps coming to her door.

Mary Carolyn had shivered and clasped her hands together until her brave other self forced her in a different direction. Buster doubled her hands into fists and gathered herself for a fight. This adventure was all too real. In the dime novels, the heroine frequently had to face the outlaw and dare him to do his worst. But he always acted like a gentleman. Why in *Myrtle, the Child of the Prairie,* he had offered up his life rather than dishonor her.

Excitement set goose bumps to rising on her arms. This fight would be between Clell Miller and her. Of course, she was almost sure she had the upper hand. He hadn't told the other members of the gang about the loot. To her that meant he didn't

intend to divide it with them. She had met up with a real outlaw.
He stole from everybody.

She was still gathering her courage when he came in without
knocking, his saddlebags hanging from his arm. His expression
was a little sheepish, his shoulders hunched like those of a little
boy who's done wrong and knows he's going to get a licking.
Dimly, she wondered how he'd ever become a thief with a face
that easy to read. She met him in the center of the room with
her fiercest expression.

"Where'd you hide my money? Tell me, you skunk!"

He blinked. Clearly, he hadn't expected her to ask that question. His expression hardened. She didn't even see him move,
so quick was he. The saddlebags dropped with a thump. His
arm looped around her body. His big hand clapped across her
mouth. "Keep your voice down," he whispered. "These walls
are thin."

A prisoner in his iron grasp, she didn't know whether to be
afraid that someone could hear her or that someone couldn't.

"You heard me coming, didn't you?" He eased the pressure
of his hand.

She nodded. Her lips moved over the hard calluses on his
palm. The lamplight leached all the blue out of his eyes, leaving
them gray and glittery like a gunbarrel.

He inclined his head until his forehead almost touched hers.
"Then they can hear whatever we do or say."

She squirmed in protest. Somehow she always seemed to
end up being manhandled by this man. Here she was, in his
arms again, pressed against him, bent back over his arm. Her
meager breasts were crushed against his chest.

She sucked air into her lungs and with it the smell of soap.
She didn't know why that reassured her so much. The fact that
her outlaw washed his hands didn't mean he was any better or
any worse than Cole Younger, for instance.

He squeezed her a little tighter, his expression severe. "Are
you going to keep you voice down?"

She nodded again.

Slowly, he removed his hand from her mouth, but kept it

raised and ready to clamp down again. Seconds passed. They stared into each other's eyes.

Then he relaxed and let her go. Stepping back, he ran a hand over the lower part of his face. His expression was bleak. Barely above a whisper, he told her, "You're crazy, you know that?"

She shook her head adamantly. "I'm not!"

He pointed one long finger at her. "Anyone who'd just knock on the door of a stranger's house and ask for Jesse James is crazy."

She had caught up to him. He wasn't going to order her around or insult her. She batted at his hand. "I'll have you know—"

"Sshhh!" He caught her by the arm. "Keep you voice down. If Cole Younger gets the least bit suspicious about why you're here, we'll be cut to pieces and then murdered. That man is meaner than a rattlesnake."

She eyed him narrowly. Of course, she didn't want him killed. She owed him too much for that. Furthermore, she liked him when she wasn't mad at him. She just wanted her money. She wanted him to give it to her. "Not me," she boasted, though she kept her voice down. Their faces were only inches apart. "All that hogwash you were spouting about the James gang and how they always divided everything. You told me that since I happened to rob the train at the same time you all did, what I took was part of the loot. Part of the loot! Hah! Not much!"

"Sshh!" He raised his hand again.

Instantly, she lowered her voice until it had no timbre at all. "Part of the loot, my eye! You didn't tell them about it. If I tell them, they'll kill you. But not me. I didn't keep the money a secret from them."

"I . . . I had some trouble." With an exhausted sigh, he untied his neckerchief and draped it over the back of the chair. "I got separated from the gang."

Her eyes flew to the saddlebags. "Is that where it is? Is that why you brought your stuff in here?"

She took a quick step in their direction, but he caught her arm and hauled her back. "That's just my clothes and things."

She looked at him skeptically. "Sure it is."

"It is," he insisted.

She nodded her head so vigorously that her hair flopped down into her eyes. "I knew it. I knew it. That's why you kissed me, wasn't it? You didn't want me to mention the money."

He let the corner of his mouth quirk in a smile. "Well, it sure wasn't because I was glad to see you turning up like a bad penny. Or was struck with your beauty."

"I know that." Equal parts of anger and hurt swept over her. They drove heat into her face. She knew what she looked like, but he didn't have to say so. She fought the urge to smooth her hair back into some sort of order. "You didn't want me to give you away. That's why you grabbed me and kissed me. It wasn't a kiss at all. Well, that's fine with me. I wouldn't want to be kissed by someone as old as you."

The half-smile disappeared instantly. His eyebrows drew together in a fierce frown. "Old!"

She grinned at the shock he registered. He couldn't help a glance across the room to the washstand mirror. Any man with a handsome handlebar mustache was bound to be vain. And he probably didn't like to be reminded that he was getting old.

"Well, sure," she said, turning the knife. "You're probably thirty-four or thirty-five. Right? You probably thought you'd keep it for your old age. So, tell me. You hid it somewhere, didn't you? Somewhere back along the trail. It's *my* money. Tell me where you hid it, you skunk."

He stared down into her face. She couldn't read the expression in his eyes. Then, with a shake of his head, he left her. Unfastening his gunbelt, he hung it over the bedpost before he dropped down on the bed. The bedsprings creaked loudly. Crooking one long leg over the knee of the other, he began to tug at the toe of his boot.

She had expected him to argue with her. "What are you doing?"

He let the boot fall with a loud thump. It toppled over, but he reached for it and set it upright. He had a hole in his sock, worn into it by the toenail of his long second toe. He pulled off the sock and draped it over the side of his boot. His bare foot was long and narrow. How could it look so naked? It was only a man's foot.

"What are you doing?" she repeated. Her voice broke with alarm. "Answer me. You mustn't just get ready for bed easy as you please. You stole that money right off my body. I want it back."

"That's what outlaws do," he said softly. "We steal. We steal from good people and bad people. It doesn't make any difference to us." He pulled off the other boot and sock, and placed them neatly beside the first. Then he stood up. With unnecessary force he snapped the tip of his belt out of the buckle. The tongue scraped out of the punch hole. The leather creaked.

She jumped back. "Don't get undressed. Stop. Stop," she demanded in a voice that trembled with uncertainty. "You . . . you . . . tell me—"

"You're a nag," he whispered.

Her eyes flew from his hands busy with the buttons of his fly, to his face, then back to his pants. Her throat was dry. She could feel her scalp crawl in fearful anticipation. Before her startled eyes he dropped his pants.

She cried out and cowered back in shock. This *never* happened to the heroines in the dime novels. *Never.*

Still staring at her, he unbuttoned his shirt and pulled it off too. A tall flat figure clad in long woolen underwear, he hung his shirt on the peg beside the bed. "I suggest you get undressed and climb into the bed on the other side."

"What? I'll do no such thing. You can forget that, mister. I'm not . . ."

He leaned down to pick his pants up off the floor.

She relaxed a little. He was decently covered in his long-handles even though he wore them unbuttoned almost to his waist. Through the opening, she could see the plane of his chest and the whorls of dark gold hair that covered his pale skin. He should have looked smaller now that most of his clothing was gone, but he looked bigger than ever. And intensely male.

He stretched his arms wide above his head and rolled his shoulders. He was big. She'd never been around a man so big.

He tilted his head to one side and then the other. A small smile twitched the corners of his mustache. "If you have any sense at all, you'll strip in a hurry. My guess is that Jesse and some of the boys are planning an old-fashioned shivaree right now."

She stared at him blankly. *A shivaree?*

Then right before her eyes, he undid the last two buttons on his longhandles and stepped out of them.

Hot blood rampaged through her body. Her eyes flew to the dark whorls of golden hair at the top of his thighs and the male part of him hanging there. She knew what it was. Knew what it was for. She didn't know, nor did she want to know, how he'd use it.

Whimpering in fear, she spun around. Her hands flew to her face to hide her blushes. She had seen a man naked before, but he had not known she had seen him. She had been so much younger then. Clell's nakedness was an entirely different matter. She had been kissed by Clell and handled by him. The sight of his body, all six foot of it and covered with silky dark gold hair made her insides tremble. She clutched her middle. Her breasts tingled. Heat pooled in her belly.

"Hurry," he said softly. Behind her, the springs creaked.

Fearfully, she threw a glance over her shoulder. He was in bed, the covers pulled up to his waist, the most terrible part of him modestly hidden. Her eyes must have been enormous because when she looked into his face, he mocked her, widening his eyes as hers must be. He laughed.

The laugh steadied her. It triggered her fury. "Oo-oo-ooh. You're no gentleman."

"And you're no lady. Quick. Strip down and climb in."

"No. No!"

She would have said it again, but they both heard the thud of boots on the porch, a man's deep laughter.

His eyes met hers, challenged her. The unspoken I-told-you-so hung in the air between them. Suddenly, she believed him utterly. They were seconds away from disaster. She darted to the other side of the bed.

"Close your eyes," she commanded. Her fingers flew over

her clothing, tearing buttons out of the buttonholes, careless of whether he looked or not.

He remained sitting where he was. His eyes were on the door. Out of the corner of her eye, she saw he had drawn his gun.

The footsteps came closer. She could hear several men chuckling now. Giggling. They were giggling like bad boys. The James gang of thieves and killers.

She stripped her coat, vest, and shirt down to her waist in one movement. Beneath it she wore only a chemise. The long knit underwear that he had cut off her when he'd removed the bullet, had been too ragged and too badly cut up to mend. The thin lawn garment that Violie had given her took a second to untie. When she shrugged it off her shoulders, it fell about her waist.

The door shook on its hinges from the thunderous knocking. Someone must be using a gun butt. All the anger left her. They were going to come in and see her. She couldn't get undressed in time. She was so embarrassed she wanted to die. She looked at Clell for help.

"It'll be all right," he said softly. "Cross your arms over your breasts and just stand there."

"Oh, no," she murmured. "Please." She could feel the tears starting down her cheeks, but she was too frightened not to obey.

The door burst open. Jesse and Cole catapulted into the room. The others crowded in behind them, then stopped short at the scene they had interrupted.

Clell Miller sat naked upright in bed, his gun drawn, pointed at them. His young bride stood naked to the waist beside the bed. Obviously she was in the act of undressing for him. She stared at the unwelcome visitors in horror. Her arms crossed over her breasts; her hands clutched at her slender shoulders. The lamplight shone on the paths of tears trickling down her cheeks.

Their lascivious grins faded. They looked at each other sheepishly. Someone cleared his throat.

"Aw, hell," Billy Chadwell blurted out. "Beggin' your pardon, ma'am.'' He backed away through the door and thudded back down the hall.

Without a word the rest of the gang followed him. Their footsteps were much lighter as if they were tiptoeing so as not to disturb the newlyweds further.

Only Jesse and Cole remained in the room. ''Looks like we got here a bit too early.'' Jesse backed toward the door. ''I sure do apologize, ma'am . . . er . . . Mary Carolyn. We were just having a little fun. Joshing ol' Clell here. He's waited so long to get married, we thought he'd never get the job done.'' He paused and glanced sheepishly at Clell. ''Looks like we should've waited till morning. Come on, Cole.''

But Cole Younger smiled sourly. His eyes crawled over Mary Carolyn. She imagined she could feel them like the prickly legs of insects. He looked at her everywhere—the curve of her waist, her navel, the center of her body where her breasts swelled on either side of her arms. ''I'm kinda beginning to see what you married her for, Clell. I thought you'd lost your mind.''

''Cole,'' Jesse called from the door. ''Come on.''

''Hell, I mighta wanted her myself if she hadn't looked so homely in the face. I guess that gimp leg don't matter in bed neither.''

Mary Carolyn wanted to cry in earnest. She knew she was no prize. But she shouldn't have to stand here and take these insults from Cole Younger. She threw a desperate look at Clell.

He thumbed the hammer back on his pistol. It clicked ominously adding to the tension in the room. ''Get the hell out.''

Cole's expression darkened. His hand covered his gun butt.

''Cole.'' Jesse came back and caught his arm. ''We made a mistake. Let's just get out and forget it.''

''He drew down on me!''

''Hell! He'd've been within his rights to've drilled the both of us.'' With a scuffle of boots and a slam of the door, Jesse and Cole were gone.

Mary Carolyn sank to her knees. Suddenly released, her body hurt all over from the strain she had put on every muscle. The bedsprings creaked again. She heard the pad of bare feet. A

leg covered with golden hair appeared beside her. A warm
hand covered her naked back.

"Come on," he whispered. "Stand up." Another hand
clasped her waist. He lifted her to her feet and guided her to
the bed.

Still weeping, still in shock, she allowed him to pull the straps
of her chemise up onto her shoulders. Swiftly and efficiently, he
pulled off her boots. He unfastened her belt and pulled down
her pants.

The chemise which reached to mid thigh was sheer cotton
as were the drawers underneath it. She was almost paralyzed
with embarrassment. Then he lifted her in his arms and swung
her over the bed. He held her for a moment before laying her
on down. Hot color suffusing her face, she met his eyes.

His steel blue stare told her nothing, but his words were
heavy with warning. "Being an outlaw is a bad life, Mary
Carolyn. I'll bet you didn't read about any of this in that crazy
book you're carrying around. And being a member of the James
gang is just about as close to hell as you can come before you
die and go there."

He laid her down, then went around the foot of the bed and
got in on his side. The bed was narrow. The springs were old.
His greater weight tipped her toward him. Before she knew
how she got there, she was in his arms.

"Now, you listen to me," he said softly. His voice came
from above her. His chin touched the top of her head. As he
talked it bumped her lightly. "What happened tonight is just
the beginning. If you don't ride back home to your mama
tomorrow morning at first light, you'll be stark naked in front
of them from now on."

"No," she whispered. "Not without my share of that
money."

"Yes," he argued. "Hell, girl. Don't you see. We'll be
expected to do it because we can't help ourselves. We're married and so much in love." Sarcasm made his voice flat.

She had stopped trembling. The heat from his body wrapped
around her. Suddenly, his hand moved to cover her breast. She
gasped.

"That sounds good," he complimented her in the same sarcastic tone. "They'll like that. But they'll want you to moan, louder and louder. They'll like to hear me grunt and groan on top of you too."

Not from her, she vowed. She wouldn't groan and take on. She would simply tell him in a firm voice to stop that nonsense. "Please stop."

Oh, lord. Her voice was quavering. She let out a shuddering breath. "Stop that this instant."

"Not much chance that I will. We'll be riding and hiding for weeks sometimes. Why even you will look pretty good after a while." His hand squeezed her breast. His thumb rasped across her nipple which had appeared as if by magic through the fabric.

"Stop that." She slapped at his hand.

He paid no more attention than if she had been a child playing pat-a-cake. In a normal tone at odds with the disturbing things he was doing to her body, he explained as if what he did with his hands was the most logical thing in the world. "If you travel with me, this is what I'll want to do. And why shouldn't I? You asked to come along. You followed me here. I'm a man. You're masquerading as my wife."

"You stole my money," she protested lamely.

"And I'm not going to go get it until I'm damn good and ready."

She tried to pull away, but he tightened his hold. The oddly terrifying thing was that he wasn't really holding her. She could have fought her way out of his arms, if only she had dug down deep for the strength. His hand moved to her other breast and created the same storm of pleasure. She moaned again, despite pressing her lips together hard and vowing she wouldn't.

"Do you want your money more than you want your virtue?" He slid his body down a little in the bed. One arm was under her neck, the other across her chest between her breasts. His lips moved against her ear. His warm breath filled it, sending ripples of pleasure all through her body.

She didn't want to reveal them. She wanted to lie still and cold, but her hips shifted involuntarily.

"Do you want your money more than you want your virtue?" he asked again, something like a sneer tinging his voice. He slid his thigh across the tops of hers. The hard muscles tensed and knotted across her mound. "Maybe that's it. You're not much to look at, but maybe you're all hot for it?" he suggested. His whisper swirled the breath round in her ear. "I can sure oblige you, sweetheart. Who knows? Maybe you'll get to like me so much you'll forget all about the money?"

"Huh! Not much!" She tried to work up a terrible fury at his suggestions. She tried to shake her head, but his fingers slid around her neck, kneading the nape, making her shiver. Chills ran up and down her spine. She shivered again and had to clench her teeth to keep them from chattering.

He nibbled at the corner of her mouth. "I say yes. I say your body wants me to take it."

"No. No."

His hand slid down her chest, fingers first, straight as an arrow between her breasts, across her belly. They slid between her thighs. The oft-washed chemise did nothing to conceal her. Through it she could feel every ridge and callus of his hard fingertips. Her own heat and excitement dampened it. His middle finger parted her, touched the throbbing center of her. She arched and twisted.

"I could roll over on top of you right now." He reared up. His chest pressed tight against her shoulder. His face was inches from hers. "I could spread your legs." His knee nudged between hers. His fingers moved, slid back and forth, stroked her. The fine cotton was simply another texture to torment her.

She was woman enough to know that in an another minute, she wouldn't be able to stop him. He would do as he said and she would welcome him. This was the searing, overpowering passion the dime novels mentioned before the lights went out. She was so hot and wet. Her blood pounded in her ears. She was breathless.

"No-o-o-o." She tore herself out of his embrace. Rolling over, she drew her knees up against her chest and wrapped her arms around them. In a tight ball, she teetered on the edge of the bed.

He caught her and pulled her back against him. "Easy does it. Easy. Easy."

She pushed and clawed at his hands. She kicked backward with her bare feet. Then suddenly, she collapsed. Covering her face with her hands, she began to weep.

He released her. "Hey. Take it easy. I didn't mean to make you cry."

He pulled the covers up over them both and held her until the storm passed. In less than a minute she was able to stifle her sobs. Within two, she was dabbing at her eyes with the corner of the sheet. "I'm fine now."

"That's good." But he didn't let go of her.

Buster felt compelled to make an excuse. "I . . . er . . . I couldn't help crying," she told him, making her voice a little bit deeper. "I'm just tired from all that riding. When I get tired, sometimes I just can't help it. Ordinarily, I'm not silly like that." She tried to straighten her legs, then stopped when her feet came in contact with his naked thighs.

He didn't say anything. His hands were on her body, but they no longer moved to create those frightening, disturbing sensations. They were like a friend's hands, like a brother's would be (if she had ever had a brother).

Against her will, she began to doze. She didn't dare relax in his arms, yet how could she help herself. She was exhausted in every way. She tried to shrug away from him.

"Easy." His voice was a breath of sound against the shell of her ear. "You can go to sleep. No need to be afraid. And in the morning, you can go home."

"No," she said sternly, but a yawn took the edge off the denial.

"Sure you can." His hand came up to stroke her hair. "This isn't what you thought it would be."

She was too tired to argue. She merely shook her head.

They lay in easy silence. She could feel herself drifting away, floating in warmth, protected . . . enclosed . . . safe . . .

"Why are you doing this?" he whispered. "What in hell are you doing here?"

She couldn't think of an answer. Certainly, she wasn't going to tell him the long story of her life. He probably wouldn't believe her anyway. Her last conscious thought was that his whispered words were meant more for himself than for her.

"Did you find any trace of her?"

Roger Somervell stared out the window into the icy, gray weather. Lake Michigan was creating another winter storm of sleet and snow. Coming off the great lake, it turned Chicago into the most miserable place in the midwestern United States. Roger hunched his narrow shoulders as a particularly powerful blast rattled the window. He turned away, leaving a moist gray circle where his breath had fogged the glass.

His father's office was scarcely warmer. From the outside the Citizens Mercantile and Industrial Bank of Chicago resembled a prison more than a bank. It only needed a high gray wall around it to complete the picture. A gray marble structure with black bars across every window, it was chilly even in summer. Now it was like an icehouse.

Roger moved closer to the radiator and clasped his hands behind his back. "She's gone. No one had the least idea where she went. She ran away from the school with a year and a half tuition still paid for."

DeGraffen Somervell nodded. "She's a fool. I should have thought she'd have sense enough to know when she's well off. She's probably taken a slave's job somewhere. Still, there was something about the son-of-a-bitch who held me up. I had this eerie feeling that he was kin to . . ." He shook his head. "And then I realized it could be a women. It could have been her. I couldn't be absolutely sure. Something about the eyes. Of course, I could be wrong entirely. Probably am. He was probably male, some prissy fairy trying to act big." He shrugged. "Nevertheless—"

"Nevertheless, you want me to find my dear bastard of a stepsister and discover what she is about." Roger crossed to the desk and accepted the photograph his father held out to him. He glanced at it, then laughed. "This must be half a dozen years old."

"It's seven actually. She was ten when it was taken. Her mother wasn't aware I knew about it—or her for that matter. If there was any maternal feeling, Madeleine concealed it well. The child was sent off to school. Tuition paid for eight years before we ever married. No records were kept. I don't suppose I saw the child more than a couple of dozen times."

He looked at the photograph. "But she looks like her mother. Particularly around the eyes. Yes, there's something about her, around the eyes. And those eyes over the bandanna."

He handed the photograph back to his son with a sniff. "When I took the occasion to visit the school, awful place that it was, I took care that she didn't see me. But I saw her. She didn't look like that then. And I'm sure she doesn't look like that now."

"It won't be a lot of use." Roger stared at photograph. The child in it was solemn faced. Long dark hair had been brushed in waves over her shoulder. She sat upright on a big curved chair. Obviously it had been taken in a photographer's studio. "I don't even remember my stepmother very clearly. If you'll remember I was sent away to school, too."

His father's eyebrows rose at the sarcastic tone of the remark. He cleared his throat and shuffled through the papers on his desk. "It was the proper place for you. You got an excellent education, and you learned to be a man."

"Without any of the loving kindness and family feelings that so hinder you, Father." Roger's face remained impassive.

Somervell rose abruptly. He came round the desk in a rush. His right hand clamped on his son's shoulder. His thumb pressed Roger's adam's apple. "Do you want this job, or not?" he snarled. "I'm perfectly willing to pay the Pinkertons to take care of this as well as to recover my money. Since I'm inclined to believe the two may be related, they may not even charge me for this bit of work."

Roger remained upright, his eyes burning. His father's hand tightened on his throat. "I want it."

"Good." Somervell shoved with all his strength. His son staggered back a couple of steps, gagging from the sharp pressure on his throat. "Find out where she is. If she's leading 'the

upright life and pure'"—sarcasm dripped from his voice—
"leave her alone. Go away and don't let her see you. No sense
stirring up old longings."

"And if she's not?"

Somervell rubbed his right arm at the elbow. He had set his
rheumatism to hurting by shoving Roger. He didn't like to
be reminded of it. It was another sign that his powers were
diminishing. To cover the infirmity, he crossed to the radiator
and turned up the heat. "If she's not, you may use your own
best judgment. I just don't want to see her again ever. Nor to
hear of her. Even an illegitimate offspring can ask embarrassing
questions."

Roger stared at his father. "You must have lost a lot of
money."

"*We*, Roger. Don't be stupid. *We* lost a lot of money. You
know you're my only heir." DeGraffen strode back behind his
desk and opened his humidor. He made a ritual of selecting a
cigar, rolling it next to his ear to test the tightness, clipping off
the end, striking off a match, lighting it with much puffing and
sucking. When it was smoking to his satisfaction, he sat back
down and regarded his son through the haze he had created.
"My heir," he said again. Was there a note of contempt in his
voice? "All this will be yours someday. It's your job to protect
it."

Roger said nothing. The health of his father was a sore spot
with him. The man had outlived two wives and a couple of
mistresses. He couldn't be expected to die before the end of
the century. "I'll remember."

He raised a hand to his throat. "I'll need some money to
make the necessary trips."

At this juncture his father made no effort to conceal a look
of utter contempt. Roger shrugged blandly. He knew how his
father hated—more than anything—to spend money.

Chapter Six

Between slitted eyelids, Clell observed his "wife's" slender
back. He had felt her inch her way off the mattress, had heard
her breathe as she crept to the washstand on silent feet.

Now she stood there, a wet cloth in her hand, trying to wash
herself silently. With her back to him, she had turned her
chemise down to the waist. Evidently when he'd cut off her
underwear, he'd damaged it beyond repair. Or perhaps it had
been too badly stained to clean. He wondered about the wound.
Had he done a good job of closing it?

He couldn't see the back of her thigh through the chemise
and drawers which reached to her knees. She got around well
for someone who had been shot a couple of weeks ago. She
looked good too. Like a flower, her slender body rose out of
the clothing. Below that roll the curves of her neat little rear
showed faintly pink beneath the layers of thin material. A dark
shadow marked their division. He had had his hands on that
flesh, he remembered. He had spanked it a couple of times. He
resisted the very real need to shift his weight as his thoughts
led him into dangerous territory.

She washed herself thoroughly, sponging around her neck,
across her back as far as she could reach, under her arms. The

mirror reflected her rubbing the cloth over her chest and rib cage.

When she was finished, she hung the cloth on the rail, cupped her breasts in both hands, and stared at them in the mirror. What she was thinking, he could only imagine as she tilted her head to first one side and then the other. What he was thinking, as his heartbeat stepped up a notch, was that he hadn't really paid them enough attention when they were bared last night. Damn Cole and Jesse anyway! The cold wash water made her nipples hard. And the sight of them made him hard.

With a sigh, his "wife" shook her head. Then she leaned forward and splashed water on her face, careless of the greasy short-cropped hair that fell over her forehead. When it got in her way, she shoved it back impatiently, It stood up in spikes like scalded chicken feathers. She was sure a homely little mutt.

With the water still dripping from her chin, she leaned forward. Using the sliver of soap, she lathered her hands and washed the grime off her face.

He allowed himself to open his eyes a little more. Her skin wasn't half bad when it was clean. It was pale as any lady's. Her brown eyes, lashes, and brows looked pretty good when they weren't peeking out from behind the chopped-off hair. In fact, if something were done about that hair . . .

He forgot himself and shifted on the bed. The springs creaked loudly. Her eyes met his in the mirror. She gasped and began to struggle with the chemise.

"Turn your back!"

The show was over. He obliged by rolling over and sitting up as if he didn't care one way or the other. He reached for his own underwear. "No need to get all het up. You woke me up with all that splashing around."

He heard her stumbling against the furniture and guessed she was trying to tug on her pants. She was panting when she said, "I'm sorry. I didn't mean to wake you up. I just wanted to get dressed before you woke up. No. Don't get up. Wait! I'll be out of here in just a minute."

He thought about teasing her, then decided against doing so.

He settled back on the bed. "How's the leg? I noticed you were limping some."

She buckled her belt. "It's fine. I forget about it most of the time. You did a good job. Thank you."

He grunted a response. Then, "Are you heading out?"

"Out?" She stared at him, buttoning her buttons without looking. "I'm getting out of this room."

"No. I mean heading on back home where you came from?"

The question galvanized her. Her chin came up. Her body loosened like a boy's. She finished doing up her buttons and swaggered to the bedpost. Clenching her jaw, she managed to conceal her slight limp. Snatching down her floppy hat, she clapped it on her head. She gave him a cocky smile. "Not much!"

She wasn't his "wife" anymore. Nor was she Mary Carolyn. Before his eyes she'd changed into that strange contradictory character Buster. Boot heels thudding as hard as her legs would bring them down, she swaggered to the door.

"I think I'll go hunt up Jesse and the boys and ask if I can join the gang."

"Wait. Mary Carolyn. Don't be a fool!" He threw back the covers, but the door slammed behind her.

"I don't think that's such a good idea," Jesse opined. "I sure wouldn't let Zee come with me, even if she wanted to. Which she doesn't. She doesn't hold with any of this. Frank's Annie pretends she doesn't know anything about what he does for a living."

"But—"

He held up his hand. "I know that little fly-up-the-crick Myra Belle Shirley used to ride around with Cole some. But that was right after the War. Things was looser then. And she got pregnant pretty soon. Had to go back home I guess. You're a lady, Mary Carolyn. You're Clell's wife. You need to wait for him at home."

"We don't have a home yet. And I want to be with him," she pleaded. "I have to be with him. I . . ." She reached into her pocket as she looked up into the outlaw leader's handsome face. He would swear her eyes had tears in them again. "I want to be a good wife to him."

She pulled a small paperback book out her pocket. "Zerelda came to rescue you when you were trapped by Sheriff Timberlake's posse in Cracker Neck."

He frowned as she passed him the book, but when he turned it and read the title, his face broke into a grin. *"The James Boys at Cracker Neck.* Well, Hell. Where'd you get this?"

"In Chicago. Er . . . that is"—she shrugged—"someone gave it to me." She hurried on. "If Zerelda can be there for you, why can't I be with Clell? I want to do more than just cook and keep house for him. I want to be by his side, just like your wife wants to be by yours. If he gets shot, I want to be there to take care of him. Please, Jesse. Please say I can."

The outlaw looked around helplessly. He handed the book back to her, even though he wanted to read it himself. He didn't know what the book said, but Zee Mimms had never rescued him. She kept as far away from his outlaw dealings as she could and was always nagging at him to quit.

Clell's wife evidently had the wrong idea. Unfortunately, she'd caught him alone in the stable, taking care of his horse's split hoof. He had always been soft around women. He looked at her kindly. She looked just about the same as when she'd ridden in yesterday afternoon, except her face was a little cleaner and she didn't look quite so scared.

But he carried in his mind the picture of her standing beside his friend's bed with her arms crossed over her naked breasts and a pair of tears trickling down her cheeks.

"He's so good to me." Mary Carolyn tugged down her sleeve and scrubbed the edge of it across her cheek. "I—I know I'm not much to look at, but I love him so. I'd take care of you too. I want you to know that."

The tears made her eyes shine. They were just about the prettiest he'd seen in a month of Sundays. On the whole she wasn't much to look at, but there were some good parts. He blinked rapidly. "I sure hope that's not necessary. I try to take good care of my boys. I don't lead them where they might get hurt.''

He'd said the wrong thing. She smiled a bright smile. It lighted up her face. *Dang! If she wasn't getting prettier by the minute.* ''Then there wouldn't be any reason why I couldn't go with Clell. You'd keep us safe.'' She thrust the book back in her pocket and took both Jesse's hands and shook them gratefully. ''Oh, thank you, thank you. You're wonderful. You're the kindest man.''

''Mary Carolyn . . .''

She hop-skip-jumped back toward the house.

The president of the Mercantile and Industrial Bank of Chicago described the robbery of his private coach to no less a personage than Allan Pinkerton himself. The ''Eye'' was getting way too old to make the train ride from New York to Chicago, but the amount of money stolen and the importance of the victim had demanded a concession.

''The James Gang will be my number-one priority,'' Pinkerton agreed.

''They should have been apprehended long ago,'' Somervell remarked sourly.

The great detective's face remained impassive. ''We are for hire. If the Chicago, Rock Island is willing to pay our price, we can have a guard force available for every train that runs.'' He met Somervell's eyes squarely. ''You could have hired a guard to accompany you. In the future, I strongly recommend that you do so. You can rest easy in your car, even though the rest of the train is carried off lock, stock, and barrel.''

He handed Somervell the agency's card. It was an unnecessary gesture, but it underlined his meaning. It displayed the famous open eye and the motto under it: ''We never sleep.''

An angry flush stained Somervell's cheeks. He pretended to inspect the card and then carefully stored it in his breast pocket. ''This money is a considerable sum, over fifty thousand dollars.''

Pinkerton nodded. He had already seen the federal marshal's report.

"I had just settled my late wife's estate. The money was to have been placed in trust for her stepson Roger. He's naturally upset about the loss and even more upset about my danger."

Pinkerton nodded again. He took out the pocket notebook, made famous by Scotland Yard detectives and now an essential part of police work. "What person or persons knew you were carrying the money?"

Somervell ground his teeth. He had already castigated himself a thousand times. He had traveled by train in a private car hitched next to the caboose where the conductor, brakeman, and most of the rest of crew rode. An alarm from him would have brought them on the run. He had been confident that he would travel without incident. To be certain, he had placed the money in his safe. Nothing could possibly have happened.

Therefore, he had made no effort to be discreet as to when and where and how he carried the money. All sorts of people in Chicago knew where he was going. As many others in St. Joseph knew about the various transactions. Some knew everything about them. Embarrassed, he muttered as much to Pinkerton.

"Anyone you suspect?"

For a minute he was tempted to tell about the strange feeling of recognition, the feeling that he somehow knew the robber. Then he changed his mind. He would sound like a fool if he told Pinkerton he thought that a seventeen-year-old girl might have robbed him. Slowly, he shook his head. "No doubt it was a member of the James Gang. They were all over the train. And there must have been ten or twelve of them."

Pinkerton did not write down that last observation. The report had said six and a seventh holding the horses. Moreover most of the gang didn't even bother with masks. Two of his men had ridden with the posse at the request of the Iowa sheriff. But once the James gang had crossed into Missouri, they'd refused to pursue them where they had no juridiction. Federal marshals were spread too thinly to do the proper work. The Jameses and the Youngers simply rode back across the state line into Missouri and hid out with their kin. "This could be expensive."

"I'm prepared to offer a tenth of the recovered fifty thousand dollars." Somervell's mouth snapped to like a bear trap.

Pinkerton's eyes gleamed. Five thousand dollars was a substantial sum. But more important to him was this golden opportunity. He could extend the agency's influence into Missouri, a state full of Southern sympathizers, where his men had never been welcomed. Although the state itself was poor, great wealth poured through it on the way West. St. Louis, Kansas City, and St. Joseph were all potential headquarters for Pinkerton branches.

He rose and extended his hand. "We'll get them. I'll have your money back—and the James boys in jail within ninety days."

Clell was fit to be tied. He kicked a heavy oaken bucket clear across the barn. Mary Carolyn jumped and ducked behind a stall. She hoped none of the people in and about the farmhouse had heard that clatter. The less attention she and her outlaw drew to themselves the better.

"How'd you do it?" he yelled. "How'd you get Jesse to let you come along?"

She stuck out her chin. "I don't know what you're yelling about. I just asked him nicely."

He doubled up his fist and brandished it in her face. "Don't give me that. You didn't just ask him nicely. He's his mother's son. He doesn't believe in girls putting on pants and riding with outlaws." He went so far as to tap her on the chin. "Come on. What'd you tell him?"

She jerked her head back out of the way. The only time she'd ever seen a man this angry before, she'd gotten the beating of her life. And then she'd been locked in the cellar and kept on bread and water for a week. The memory skittered over her skin like ice. Somehow, she didn't think Clell would hit her. She wrapped her arms around the four-by-four at the end of the partition. "I told him I wanted to be around to help you if you got wounded."

Clell's blue eyes flashed. "Try again. He's dug bullets of me himself."

"But I really do want to help you," she protested. "You helped me. You dug a bullet out of me and bandaged me."

Clell thrust his face into her own. "And stole your damn money." He whispered. "Did you hint to him that that's what this was all about?"

"No. Of course not. I wouldn't tell him about that." She began to feel better. He was really angry, but he wasn't going to hit her. She was good at judging people. They passed a point of anger, then they began to cool off. Clell was beginning to cool off.

"I know you didn't, but what did you do? Damn it! Tell me."

She shook her head. Not for anything in the world would she tell him she could cry when she wanted to. It wasn't much of a trick. And she only used it when nothing else would work. But she found it worked pretty well. "I showed him the book. His book. You know. The one about the James boys. Honestly, I didn't do anything else. He just looked at it and then he agreed that I could be like Zerelda. That's Zee. His wife."

"I know who his wife is," Clell growled.

"He probably felt sorry for me. After all, I'm a homely mutt. Right? I told him I'd hold the horses."

Clell cursed and spun around. Another bucket blocked his path. He aimed a kick at it, then thought better of it. He strode away to the end of the shedrow, then back again. He pointed his finger at her. "You aren't coming with us. Get that through your head."

She remained stubbornly silent.

He charged back down the floor and caught her by the shoulders. "Listen, you little fool." He gave her a shake. "Do you think I'm here because I want to be?" Shake. "The gang thought I was dead not too long after the War." Shake. "I didn't want to come back to this life, but Jesse's a hard man to say no to." He let her go and spun away. "Especially when he lets your boss know about your past."

He turned back to her. "There's nothing great or wonderful about Jesse James," he said bleakly. "The smartest thing for you to do would be to get on your horse and ride out of here."

"Not without that money." She planted herself in front of him. Head up, legs spread wide, thumbs hooked into her pants in a boyish posture, she faced him. "When you go get it, I'll be with you to collect my share."

"Then be damned to you." He brushed by her, knocking her off balance, and strode out of the stable.

The gang was restless as a pack of wild dogs. They hadn't pulled a job in over a month now. They were irritable. Playing poker for each other's share of the same money had brought about several explosions. For more than a week, Cole Younger had been snarling and snapping at everyone in sight.

One night Jesse called them together in the stable long after the Samuels had gone to bed.

"We need to do one more big job before Christmas." Jesse's eyes blinked and shifted around the circle. His brother Frank made no sign either of assent or denial.

Cole Younger nodded with satisfaction. "Now you're talkin'."

Billy Chadwell cuffed Jim Pool on the shoulder. "What'd I tell you? We can spend Christmas in St. Louie at the Silver Garter."

Around the circle everyone smiled at his youthful enthusiasm and at the prospect of having fresh money to throw around at a whorehouse.

Only Clell laced his fingers together between his knees. Glumly, he stared at the barn floor. His breath fogged before him. Since the Chicago, Rock Island robbery, light snow had fallen three times. Although as yet none had remained on the ground more than a few hours, they could be riding around in a blizzard. "It's easy for a posse to track us in snow," he reminded them. "Six or seven horses cut a mighty wide swath."

One and all, they scowled at him. A little snow wasn't going to bother them.

Jesse scowled blackest of all. He wanted everyone to think his plans were perfect from beginning to end. "The sheriff'll have trouble getting a posse together if it's snowing. Posses don't like to ride in the cold."

"Jess is right," Bob Younger agreed. "Farmers and ribbon clerks get froze mighty quick with sleet hitting them in the face."

"And so do we." Clell argued.

They couldn't argue with him. Frank nodded sagely. He had been wounded in the robbery of a bank in southern Missouri several years back. The sheriff had chased them into Arkansas. A blizzard had caught them unprepared. If they hadn't found a cousin to spend the night with, he might very well be dead.

"You afraid of a little cold weather?"

All eyes turned to look at the man who had asked the question. Jim Pool seldom spoke. He kept his own council and let Billy Chadwell stomp around and create the fuss. His hooded eyes reminded Clell of a snake's.

Once he would have taken offense at any man who hinted that he might be afraid of anything. Now Clell no longer cared. He was probably eight or nine years older than Pool, but he felt about a hundred. "When you've had your cheek freeze to a rock while someone digs a bullet out of your back, it'll make you think some."

Jim Pool sneered and spat a stream of tobacco into the dirt.

But Frank James's deep voice slid between them. "I'll surely testify to that. Cold weather takes its toll on man and beast."

A couple of mutters could be heard from the darkness, but no one wanted to argue with Jesse's older brother.

Jesse rose hastily. The nail keg he had been sitting on toppled over and rolled into the darkness. His color was up. Jesse enjoyed arguments because he usually won them. If he couldn't make his opponents see his side, then he could always draw his gun. To his way of thinking, the Colt wasn't called a Peacemaker for nothing. He turned to Frank. "Now, nobody's going to get shot if we plan this right. We pick a big fat bank. One we haven't hit before. Someplace up north of here.''

"We were just up north. We stirred them up pretty good just last month. They're bound to be jumpy." Clell continued, inexorably pointing out the obvious problems.

"Goddammit." Cole Younger slammed his fist into the wall. "We robbed a goddam train. They won't be lookin' for us at a bank.''

One and all, they scowled at Clell. They had already made up their minds.

He shrugged. "Where'll it be?"

Jesse grinned in relief. He moved to set the nail keg upright and closer to the lantern. Frank and Clell exchanged resigned looks. Jesse's older brother's expression seemed to say, *One more thing to be gotten through.*

The town of Ottumwa had a bank that was just bulging with silver certificates, Jesse told them. It was a farmer's bank, with a lot of depositors, in the middle of the cornfields. A trunk-line railroad ran through it to carry the harvest to Chicago. It should be just filled with money at this time of the year.

Clell bit his tongue to keep from reminding them all that farmers usually didn't make enough to put much in the bank. His comments wouldn't do any good. But Ottumwa was in Iowa ... The germ of an idea flickered in Clell's mind. Cole hated him. If Clell agreed, Cole would disagree and vice versa. When they rode past the buried money, he could take a detour. And hightail it for Brazil. He cleared his throat and shook his head. "This isn't a good idea. It's only a few miles from where we held up the Chicago, Rock Island.''

"Right," Jesse said as if he had anticipated that argument. "We know that country. It's close to the state line."

"We can't stop at Chesnut's store anymore," Clell reminded them. "It's burned to the ground. Henry'd be within his rights to shoot us on sight if we rode near there.''

"We oughta ride by just to shoot him," Cole snarled. "I still think he called those Pinkertons down on us.''

Smiling inwardly, Clell shook his head in disgust. "Henry's an old man who just purely hates Yankees and Pinkertons. He built back after the War, and now he's probably lost everything he owned again. You can bet he wouldn't have taken a chance on them burning him out. He didn't have anything to do with them showing up. He's probably freezing to death right now.''

"Clell's right," Frank said. "We could be in trouble in that part of the state. 'Specially if we rode south for Unionville."

Jesse's blue eyes were getting stormy. He didn't like the idea of people ganging up on him. He looked at Cole, but his cousin had lost his temper. When Cole was angry, he couldn't think straight. Jesse glared at them all. "Well, we wouldn't ride south," he grated. "We'd fool them. That's what they'd expect us to do. We'd ride . . . er . . . west. Toward Council Bluffs."

Clell could feel his hopes sinking until Frank objected. "Council Bluffs is a long way away."

"I—know—that." Jesse was steaming now, spacing each word to keep from spewing them out like bullets. "I didn't say we'd ride *to* Council Bluffs. I just said we'd ride toward it. We'll turn south about the middle of the state. Then we'll go back east."

"I doubt if that bank has enough money to make it worth the effort." Clell held his breath.

"It'll be loaded." Cole sneered. "I say we hit it hard."

Jesse shot Clell a look that should have killed him where he sat.

"Sorry." Clell held up his hands in surrender.

At that moment the stable door opened. A cold draft swirled the wisps of hay around their feet. The Youngers drew their guns as did Billy Chadwell and Jim Pool.

Clell jumped to his feet. "Goddam. What are you doing here?"

Mary Carolyn closed the door and backed up against it. "I couldn't sleep."

He strode toward her to hustle her out. Playing the angry husband to the hilt, he tried to spin her around and push her out the door. "Get on back to bed. I'll be there in a minute."

For the benefit of the gang, he grinned over his shoulder. "It's a terrible life, fellows. Being married and all. They just won't leave you alone."

The boys chuckled and relaxed. She would have been out and gone if she hadn't balked on him. On the other hand, he could almost have predicted that she would. She was the stubbornest woman that God had ever created and, to his way of thinking, the strongest argument against marriage he had ever heard of.

She craned her neck to get a look at Jesse. "If you all are planning a job, I need to be in on it. You promised me I could ride with you."

Clell froze. He too looked back at Jesse. So did the other members of the gang.

Now it was Jesse's turn to look uncomfortable. His ears reddened. "I—You don't need to be in on the planning, Mrs. Miller." He gulped. "This is man's work."

While Clell stood stunned, she ducked under his arm and came to the circle. "I'll bet I could help. Someone as clever as you"—she looked up into Jesse's face—"could think of something really important for me to do. Something that would keep them from shooting at us."

Clell came back cussing. He clamped his hands down on her shoulders. "Damn it, Mary Carolyn."

She looked up at him, with her sweetest smile. He had noticed she had a smile when she wanted to use it. It did things to her face, turned up her usually sullen mouth and revealed a dimple in her right cheek. Her eyes crinkled at the corners and sparkled with light. Her face didn't look nearly so plain and homely when she smiled. If only she'd do something about that god-awful hair, besides slick it down with hair tonic.

"Mary Carolyn." His voice was softer than he had intended.

He blinked as Frank coughed. Clell hadn't realized how much time had passed since he'd put his hands on her and pulled her back against him. He looked around the circle. The faces of the gang reflected their attitudes toward him and love and marriage in general. Billy Chadwell as well as Bob and

Jim Younger looked envious. Jesse and Frank, married men themselves, were grinning. Cole Younger was scowling. Only Jim Pool maintained his icy hooded stare.

As if her shoulders were hot, Clell jerked his hands away. "She'll just be in the way," he growled. He put all his effort into catching Jesse's eye with a meaningful stare. "I know you never had any idea of really taking her along, Jess."

Jesse was slowly nodding in agreement, when Cole broke in. "I think that's a great idea, Jesse." Anything that smacked of taking advantage of someone else always pleased him. He laughed as if it were the greatest joke in the world. "We'll ride on into town behind her. Nobody'll ever suspect a thing."

For a full minute no one spoke. Clell could tell they were all thinking hard, trying to picture what Cole had said. Then Frank made a cutting motion with his hand. "Forget that right here and now. I'm not riding into town behind a woman's skirts."

"No. Wait." Jesse blinked the way he did when he became excited. He smacked his fist into the palm of his hand. "I see what Cole's talking about. It's perfect. She could go into town ahead of us and check out the bank. It'd be great. No one would ever suspect her."

"Oh, yes." Mary Carolyn sidestepped before Clell could catch her shoulders again. "I could do that. I could ride into town and pretend that I had some business there. I could talk to the banker about putting some money in the bank. Like making a deposit. I could be thinking about putting some money in escrow to buy some property."

As her words tumbled out, Clell gaped at her in amazement. Had she lost her mind? She was a homely ignorant scrap who called herself Buster. He couldn't believe that she knew anything about banking. She must be repeating something she'd heard.

He looked around him hoping to see the gang getting ready to burst out laughing. Then he gaped at them. Instead of brushing her off like a pesky horsefly, they seemed to be giving her their undivided attention. They were looking at her seriously. He had to put a period to this quicklike.

He reached out and knocked her hat off. His hand scuffed through her greasy hair. "Oh, yeah. You look like you'd have money to deposit to buy some property. They wouldn't even let you in the door except to sweep the place out."

She swung around at him, her fists doubled up. Her hair flopped in her eyes. He grinned and she faltered. Embarrassment flushed her cheeks with color. "Well, I . . . I guess I could get cleaned up if Jesse wanted me to."

She swung back around. Her hands raked back her hair. She smiled hopefully at Jess. Though everyone else was looking doubtful, Jesse nodded his head. "Why sure. I think she could get cleaned up. Put on a skirt and a hat. Then she could go in like she says, get the banker to show her around. If she could get him to open and close the vault for her to show her how safe her money would be, she might get a look at the combination."

"I have a good memory." Mary Carolyn chimed in excitedly.

The outlaw positively beamed at her. "That's great. You could see how many tellers they have behind the counter. And if they have a guard, he'd be there and she could—"

Clell felt he was living a nightmare in which everybody but him was crazy. The fool girl didn't have any idea what she was getting into. "Stop right there!" he yelled. "Just stop it. She doesn't have any idea what to do. And besides, she doesn't have a skirt." He flung his arm in her direction. "Hellfire, Jess! Take a good look at her!"

They all looked at Mary Carolyn in her filthy, ragged, shapeless coat and denim pants. Her lace-up brogans were run over at the heels and caked with mud and manure. Her hair sprouted out from her scalp in spiky points and hung over her forehead and in her eyes. A self-respecting cat would refuse to drag her anywhere. Under their critical stare, hot color welled into her cheeks.

There was a moment's awful silence. Then Jesse smiled his most beatific preacher's boy smile. "Well, hell, Clell, why don't you buy her some new clothes? You're her husband, after all.''

Cole gave a short bark of laughter. Frank nodded sagely. As one they looked at Clell.

As if she felt the turn of the tide, Mary Carolyn smiled too. She laced her fingers together in front of her like a schoolgirl reciting a piece. ''Just before he married me, he promised he'd buy me a new dress.''

Clell's ears burned as their stares became accusing. He opened his mouth, closed it, then opened it again. ''All right!'' he yelled. ''All goddam right. If that's what you all want.''

He pulled his hat down tighter on his brow and stormed out of the barn.

''Now you've really done it.'' Clell caught her by the arm as he she came out of the building. ''You fool girl. You've set yourself up to get another shot in your butt.''

She tried to twist free. ''Leggo. You're hurting me.''

''You'll think hurt, if you don't do what I tell you to,'' he promised as he dragged her down toward the creek. ''You're going to march right up to Jesse in the morning and tell him you've changed your mind. That you're too scared to go into a bank full of strangers and rob them.''

''I'm not scared. I'll do it.'' She whirled to face him. One little fist thumped him in the chest. ''I will.''

''You'll get yourself wanted by the Pinkertons,'' he countered even as he let her go. ''They put women in jail just the same as men, and don't you forget it. For the last time, robbery is dangerous business.''

For a minute he thought he'd convinced her. Then she shook her finger in his face. ''I know why you don't want me to come, Clell Miller. You don't fool me for one minute. You'd like it if I stayed here with Mrs. Samuel and waited for you. Except you wouldn't come back. You'd get separated from the gang like you did after the train robbery, except this time they'd never see you again. None of us would ever see you again.''

Her voice rose with each sentence. Alarmed, he looked back toward the house. "Keep your voice down."

She lowered it immediately. "You can't fool me the way you fool the rest of them. I knew what you were doing. You kept begging them not to rob the bank in Ottumwa 'cause you knew you'd get to ride right back by where you stashed that money."

He could feel the heat rising in his face. Desperately, he tried to change the subject. "You were listening at the door."

"Of course, I was," she admitted triumphantly. "I heard you trick them. It was so easy. You knew Cole and Jesse would be set on it if you didn't want to go. You knew it."

He was lucky it was dark. His ears were burning. That made twice in one night. But damn if she wasn't right. Though he wasn't going to let her know she was. He shook his head. "I've never heard anything so crazy in all my life. And I sure don't understand the way you think. You're crazy. And Jesse and Cole are purely crazy to go into that part of the state where we were just last month."

"I'm not crazy," she snarled. "But I do know how people think. And how they get people to do what they want. I've had to learn. I've had to." She stopped abruptly.

He stared at her. She had almost told him something that he might be able to use to get her out of his hair. "Why?"

She retreated. "None of your damn business. I'm going and that's final. You can't stop me."

They were both breathing hard, their antagonism sparking in the night. "For the last time. Get the hell out of here!"

She thrust her chin out. "No!"

"Not even if I do this?" With that he played his last card. He caught her by the shoulders and hauled her into his arms.

"Hey . . . !" Her toes scraped over the ground. Her chest smashed into his.

His mouth slammed down on hers, driving her head back on her slender neck. His tongue ravaged her. His arms wrapped round her body and cupped her buttocks.

She cried out against his mouth, making little whimpering sounds as she twisted and turned ineffectually. He didn't stop.

The idea was to frighten her thoroughly. He bent her back, catching one flailing wrist and thrusting it down between them onto his angry arousal.

He could feel her shudder as she sucked in air. He knew he was hurting her. She'd probably have bruises in the morning. But better bruises than a bullet. She mustn't be allowed to ride with them. He had to convince her to leave. The outlaw trail was twice as bad for a woman.

She moaned and thumped his chest again. He arched her back still further. One leg slipped between his. She was straddling his thigh. She struggled against him for a moment longer. Then she went limp.

When he felt her surrender, he eased his kiss. Just in time. Her clothes might be dirty and her hair a mess, but they were only what showed. What was underneath was shattering his control—a slender female shape, a hot quivering mouth, and a clean ladylike scent.

Another minute and he would be out of control. He had never committed a rape. Not even in bloody Lawrence. Moreover, he hated himself for hurting another human being, especially one as small and tender as his "wife" was proving to be. When it came to men and their matters, she had no more experience than a child. And she was so sweet. But she was hell on wheels with her tongue.

He heaved a sigh as he let her go, keeping one hand on her to steady her when she swayed. "If you don't want more treatment like that, you'll leave," he whispered. She didn't make a move. He shook her gently. "Go on. Get out while you can."

She pulled herself out of his hands and stepped back. Deliberately, she swiped the back of her hand across her swollen lips. Her eyes glittered in the dark, whether with tears or anger he couldn't tell.

"You keep your hands off me, Clell Miller, or you'll be sorry. I swear I'll tell Jesse the truth if you don't. You're a pig. You stink, and you hurt things that are littler than you. And if I have to tell Jesse to keep you from hurting me again, then I will. So, don't you dare give me any more treatment like that. But I'm going on this raid and everywhere else you go until we go get that money. After that you'll be rid of me for good."

With that she turned and ran off into the darkness.

Chapter Seven

Mary Carolyn paced along the edges of the James homestead for nearly an hour. Clell's kisses had shaken her to her very core. But perhaps not the way he had intended. Something had broken loose inside her. For what seemed like forever, she hadn't allowed herself to feel. But passion had crashed through that restraint. Passion and a tiny whisper in her mind that he didn't want her to be shot.

He was an outlaw. If he were as ruthless as he claimed to be, her claim on the money, the trouble she was causing him, her threats of blackmail could all be solved by a quick blow to the head. He hadn't done that. Instead, he had kissed her.

But that didn't mean he really cared anything about her. She must keep a tight grip on her emotions. Otherwise, she'd fall madly in love with him the way the heroines did with the heroes in the dime novels. Malaeska, the Indian wife of the white hunter, had loved her man so much she had died for him. And Clell wouldn't appreciate that. Not him. He'd probably leave her broken body lying at the foot of the cliff and ride off into the darkness to return to the outlaw trail.

Her walk had carried her back to the porch. She was not surprised to see Clell come down the steps to meet her. Obviously, he had taken the time to think as well. He didn't touch her. In fact, he seemed resigned. "I guess you've made up your mind."

"Yes."

At that moment the end of a cigar glowed in the darkness. "If he don't buy you a sackful of pretty dresses, you throw him over and come see me."

"Get the hell out of here. This conversation is private." Clell made a move to pull Mary Carolyn against his chest, but she had had enough of that to last her a lifetime. She ducked away.

Cole Younger laughed. "Looks like she wants somebody who'll show her a better time. Come on here, little lady. I'd be right happy to oblige you. A girl needs a few fancy dresses. I bet you'd be real good to look at if you was fixed up right."

When she realized who had spoken, Mary Carolyn froze. Hot color ran into her cheeks. Changing her mind, she stepped back into Clell's shadow.

His anger boiled over. He hated Cole Younger. The man was a cold-blooded killer. And more dangerous than a rattler. At least the snake gave a warning before it struck. Cole claimed he preferred to shoot a man in the back. That way his victim couldn't shoot back. The thought of someone as stupidly innocent as Mary Carolyn Ross running afoul of the most vicious of the Younger clan made Clell's skin crawl.

He acknowledged that Mary Carolyn was his responsibility. At least for the time being until he could get her on her way out of his life. He threw his arm around her shoulders. This time she went willingly enough to his side. She might be getting smarter. "I'll buy the clothes for my wife," he said. "I was going to. But I haven't exactly had the time."

"Uh-huh." Cole grunted. The cigar glowed again. Its rank smoke reached their nostrils. "Now you got the time and the excuse. Just be sure and get her something fancy. Not something like you'd buy for your wife." He said the word as if he didn't believe it. "Bankers like to see a lot of chest."

Mary Carolyn gasped. Her arms crossed over the portion of

her body Cole had named. "I thought Jesse said I was supposed to be a widow."

"Hey!" The cigar swung down in an arc to tap the ash off and went back to Cole's mouth. "You could be a grass widow. Every so often one of them comes around."

"Come on, Mary Carolyn." Clell spun her around and hurried her back toward the storeroom where they had their bedrolls stowed. After their "honeymoon" night, the Reverend Samuel had given them that small room in the barn for their privacy. Jesse and Frank slept in the house in their old room. The rest of the gang bedded down in the stalls.

Cole's laugh followed them into the icy night.

"What's a grass widow?" Mary Carolyn asked when they had closed the door behind them. The little room was hardly bigger than a box stall, but it broke the wind. Rolled up in their blankets and huddled together, they were warm enough even on the nights when the temperature fell toward zero.

"A grass widow is a woman who's gotten a divorce," Clell told her. His anger still simmered. Despite her being an awful nuisance, he didn't want her to have any dealings with Cole Younger. For that reason, he was desperate to make her understand. "You can't go through with this. I absolutely forbid it."

Hands on her hips, she thrust her chin up into his face. "You don't have any right to forbid it. We're not married, and you're not my boss."

He flung a hand at the door. "All right then. Go to Cole Younger. You heard his offer. He'll be happy to buy you some new clothes and let you ride with the James gang. You want to be an outlaw, he'll let you outlaw with him."

She backed away and lowered her chin. "I don't want to outlaw with anyone. Certainly not with Cole Younger. Tell me where my money is and I'll ride out of here tomorrow. You can tell them you convinced me not to help them or that you were scared for me and ordered me to go home."

Clell barely stifled a heartfelt curse. "If you think I'm going to let you ride out of here and pick up that money all on your own, you're crazy. Besides. What would a scrap like you do with all that money?''

"Live a good life," she countered.

The answer stopped him for a moment. It was so close to the dream he had for the money. He had to stop a minute to frame his argument. "You wouldn't even have survived the jump off the train if you hadn't fallen on me.''

Stubbornly, she turned her back on him, refusing to answer. She was sure he exaggerated, even though she could acknowledge to herself that she would have been hurt, perhaps badly if she had fallen onto the roadbed at that speed. She thought of stories she had heard of people cut in two by trains. Her mental pictures made her faintly sick.

Sensing she was not listening to his arguments against robbery, Clell tried another tack. "If you know so much about banking, you ought to get an honest job. Go to work in a bank.''

She shook her head. Really, Clell was hardheaded. He was going right on with the argument. He was stupid too. Nobody would hire a woman to work in a bank. Surely, not DeGraffen Somervell, from whom she'd gleaned those fragments of information. "I don't know anything about working in a bank. Where'd you get that idea?''

"Oh, words like 'deposit' and 'escrow.' Plus the fact you knew about vaults and safes. I'll bet even money that you come out of the Ottumwa bank with the combination in your head. You'll know where to stand to look over his shoulder while he's opening it. You sounded like you've spent some time in a bank.''

"I have not. You've got it all wrong.'' But he was right. Until that moment she had never thought how much a person told about themselves without really meaning to.

He laughed. "Don't tell such awful lies. They make you look stupid.'' he caught her chin in his hand and forced her to look at him. "For the last time, you're going to get yourself killed. No amount of money is worth dying for. Will you get the hell out of here?''

She shook her head against his hand. "No.''

"Then God help you." He dropped his hand and turned away. He did not say another word all night long.

Mrs. Haltom's boarding house in Kansas City had a feature that Clell meant to use. It had a bathroom off the back stairs. Jesse had sent him off with a couple of twenty dollar bills and one of them was going to be broken to pay for Mary Carolyn's bath.

He was going to give it to her himself, scrub every strand of that filthy hair and every inch of her body. If she fought him, if she was humiliated or frightened, then so much the better. Better to scare her now and make her ashamed than allow her to be frightened and humiliated—and worse—at the hands of Pinkertons or local sheriffs.

With that firmly in his mind, Clell followed her into the bathroom and lighted the hot water heater. Shaking the fire out of the match, he looked at her with his best imitation of Cole's lecherous grin.

She blinked, clutching the towel and washrag to her chest. "You can go now. I don't need you to watch me."

His grin turned into a leer.

She gaped at him. Even as she began to shake her head, he motioned to her to undress.

She offered a feeble smile. "I haven't been in a bathroom like this is a long time. This is really nice. I promise I'll wash."

"You sure will. Every part of you," was Clell's reply. She'll bolt now, he thought. Arms crossed in front of his chest, he set himself to laugh as she backed out of the room and out of his life.

Mary Carolyn hadn't thought of getting cleaned up when she'd volunteered to help Jesse with the bank robbery. She had hidden behind her dirty clothes and face so long that they seemed like a part of her now. She would be naked without them. But when she saw the bathroom, she was ready to give in to temptation. She hadn't seen anything so warm and spar-

kling clean in seven long, cold years. She would take a bath
there, no matter that it would knock off her disguise. She could
easily get dirty again.

She could have cried when Clell Miller continued to prove
that he wasn't a gentleman.

"I can't get undressed in front of you," she protested.

"Every part," he went on as if she hadn't spoken. "I'm not
taking you to a fancy store and buying you nice clothes to put
on, if you're dirty as a pig. The state you're in, they wouldn't
even let you try them on."

The water in the copper tubing was hot. He turned on the
tap and let it run into the bathtub. As Mary Carolyn watched,
the steam rose between them. He gestured to her. "Come on."

"No." She hugged the towels against her chest. Her heart
was pounding. "Get out. I'll do it myself."

"I'm not going to take that chance. This is costing me a
dollar." He started round the tub.

"Stay back." Dropping the towels, she shrank away, throwing up her hands to ward him off. "I tell you—"

Too late. He swept her up in his arms. They were very strong.
Strong as steel. She doubled up a fist. His blue steel eyes dared
her. She didn't strike. It wouldn't have done any good.

"Do you want me to put you down and let you undress and
step in there? Or do you want me to drop you in with your
clothes on?" His voice was gruff. A couple of quick strides
and he had her positioned over the tub. "I'll get a laugh out
of that. And you'll be all wet. Your clothes need to be washed
anyway."

Oh, how she hated bullies. She had been in their clutches
before. In this case where she was so obviously outweighed,
her only hope was to do what she was told. That way she
maintained some faint illusion that she had made the choice
for herself. In which case she might be given other choices
rather than being whipped until she did as she was told.

Escape, her other choice, had been stripped from her. Unless
she chose to leave all that money behind.

With an effort she relaxed her fist. "Put me down. I'll
undress."

His mouth sobered. He looked faintly disappointed as he set her on her feet. Without much conviction, he said, "Now you're talking sense. I'll just stand over here by the door."

She felt as if her entire body were one huge blush. Her heart was beating so hard and fast, she wondered that if didn't leap from her chest. Slowly, and in agony, she pulled off her coat. Sitting down on the bath stool, she unlaced her cracked, worn shoes and pulled them off. Her socks stank. She wondered that she could feel ashamed of them, wondered that she should be ashamed when she should be afraid.

Her fingers fumbled at the buttons of her shirt. Finally, she pulled it off. She threw a wild glance over her shoulder.

When their eyes met, he raised his eyebrows. He had folded his arms across his chest and leaned one shoulder against the wall as if he were prepared to enjoy a show.

She turned her back to him and unfastened her pants. They fell to the floor, and she stood in her chemise and drawers. She had already bared herself to the waist before the entire gang. She asked herself why this time was so much more humiliating. The answer was that her protector was now her enemy. She closed her eyes, as her fingers pushed beneath the eyelet strap. She drew in a deep breath and pushed it off her shoulders. The thin cotton garment drifted down her body and settled soundlessly on top of her pants.

She waited for some sound, some cough, some rustle of clothing, something. None came. Eyes still closed, she plucked at the ribbon on her drawers. It came untied. They joined the chemise. She wanted to die.

The air of the room was quite pleasant unless you were naked and afraid. She could almost feel the steel gray eyes gliding down her spine and over her buttocks. She began to shiver. In fact, she was sure that her whole body was covered in goose bumps. She looked down at herself. It was the first time she had seen her body in weeks. Her ribs showed. Her belly was concave. He had said more than once that outlawing was the hardest way to make a living.

Behind her she heard a smothered cough. The skin between

her shoulder blades prickled as if he might throw a knife into it. *What was she doing here?*

The money! She must keep her mind on that money.

She stepped into the tub.

The water rose to her waist, warm and soothing. She knew a moment of painful regret that she wouldn't be allowed to enjoy this. She had been a long, long time without such pleasures. She wet the flannel washcloth and raised it to her breast.

His boots thudded across the floor.

She closed her eyes and set her teeth, but she was sure he could hear them chattering. She prayed that tears didn't leak beneath her lashes. She drew her knees up tight against her chest and draped the washrag across them. He really couldn't see anything except her shoulders and the bare expanse of her back. She didn't dare look up at him. If she didn't see the expression on his face, she could better bear the humiliation.

He was standing beside her, looking down at her. After a short, painful silence, his voice came from directly above her head. It sounded funny. "Let's start with your hair."

His command destroyed the last shreds of her composure. Her hands flew to her head. Somehow that hair had been her greatest protection. She knew how bad it looked. A beautiful, desirable woman had long beautiful hair either hanging down her back or swept up in curls and rolls. Short-cropped hair slathered in bay rum turned most men away. "Oh, no, I can't wash my hair."

"Sure you can."

"No! Listen!"

Too late. His palm came down on the top of her head. He pushed her under the water.

She kicked and splashed, forgetting that she was trying to hide her body from him. In the act of protesting, she lost her air. She shrieked at him to let her go before he drowned her, but he wouldn't stop. She found his wrist and clawed at it. She rolled halfway over in the tub, sending water everywhere in her efforts to get away.

From above her she heard him laugh. Murderous rage flashed

through her. She yowled in fury. Suddenly, his hand was gone. She clawed her way to the surface.

He was waiting for her with a handful of liquid soap from the jar. He slapped it onto her scalp and began to rub vigorously.

"Ow-woo-ow!" The stuff ran into her eyes and mouth. "Damn you! Stop! That—"

"You'd better keep everything closed," he growled. "This'll sure sting if it gets in your eyes."

It was stinging like fire already. "I hate you." Then she had to spit as the stuff slid into her mouth. She was crying now, but the tears were from the lye in the soap. "I'll kill you! Swear to God, I'll—"

He pushed her under again.

This time he did not have to push far. She was already sprawled half in, half out of the tub. Her legs were spread wide, hooked over the sides. The water was higher also. He had left the tap on.

When she clawed at his wrist again, he slapped his other hand down on her belly. The contact froze her. She remembered where she was and in what condition. The fear came flooding back.

For several seconds she lay trembling under his hands. The big palm and the splayed fingers covered her small belly. The thumb pressed her hip bone. The long third and fourth fingers slid into the hair at the top of her thighs.

Thereafter, she lay like a statue, with soapy tears streaming down her face as he washed the rest of her body with embarrassing thoroughness. She promised herself, she would let him kill her rather than reveal how his hands were driving her crazy.

When he allowed her up, he washed her hair again. She sat with closed eyes, her teeth clamped over her lower lip. At last, he stood back. "Can you finish it? Or do you want me to rinse you all over?"

She shook her head. Her eyes were still tightly closed. He was a monster. She hoped he would think her face was red from the heat of the water, rather than the effort to keep her body from writhing. Her jaw ached from being clamped. It clicked when she unhinged it. "I'll finish."

He put her saddlebags beside her. "Change into something fairly clean."

She opened her eyes as he bent over. To her dismay she realized their faces were close. How well was he able to read her emotions?

As their eyes met, a red stain spread quickly over his cheekbones. She felt a rush of satisfaction. He was not unmoved by all of this. Some strong emotion was working on him. Good. She hoped he was embarrassed too.

Hastily, he straightened. "Maybe Cole Younger was right," he muttered. "You are going to be a pretty thing once you're cleaned up."

Clell tilted his head back against the bathroom door and closed his eyes. If that didn't scare her away nothing would. It had certainly scared him. His body was aching. Lust rampaged through him in shuddering waves. Damn her for coming into his life anyway!

He couldn't remember the last time he'd had a woman. He had lost his taste for whores a couple of years ago. The thought that they might come to him from the likes of Cole Younger made his skin crawl. Furthermore, he hadn't looked to court himself a wife until he could get completely free of the James gang. Just about the time he had thought himself safe, Jesse had found him.

Now his body was sending him agonizing signals that it had been denied too long.

He tried not think about that beautiful body. When that failed, he tried to find fault with it. She was much too thin, much too small. But her skin was like satin. As the dirt and hair tonic floated away, his desire mounted.

He shook his head as memory overwhelmed him.

He had forgotten what a young girl looked and felt like. Ironically, a young girl had given him the only real experience of his warped and lonely life. His first experience—he couldn't call it love—had been with Esther Woodson, Jesse's cousin.

The preacher's daughter. With the war all around them, he had wanted one thing. He had not wanted to die a boy.

They had both been green as grass. He had been inept, fumbling. He knew that now. He had hurt her, and he had been ashamed of himself because he had. But for him, a raw boy nearly sure he was going to his death, her body had been heaven.

Opening his eyes, he tried to bring the whitewashed walls and worn backstairs of Mrs. Haltom's boarding house into focus. He hadn't eased his ache. He'd only made it worse. Damn Mary Carolyn "Buster" Ross anyway! This was her fault. He spun around and pounded on the door.

"You dressed yet?"

The handle rattled. She came out with her head high. He gaped.

He choked. "My God, Buster. Your hair's blond."

"Why don't you just give this up, girl?" Clell asked for about the hundredth time. "You can't pass yourself off as a rich woman wanting to look at a bank vault any more than a sow's ear can get picked over a silk purse. You're making a dern fool of youself."

He kept dragging his feet, letting her lead the way down the sidewalk. The couple of times she had glanced over her shoulder, she had caught him staring at her hair as if he couldn't believe his eyes. She wasn't going to give up on it, though she hadn't been able to smooth it down. The way it looked was his fault. It curled up all over unless she used hair tonic, and he'd taken that away from her.

She wasn't going to give up though even if he probably was right. The more he insulted her, the more determined she became. Rich women were ugly too. She knew enough about banks to know that a banker wouldn't refuse a woman about to make a large deposit no matter what she looked like.

Her lips moved as she read the big cream-colored sign with the barn red letters in curving scrollwork. She waited for him beneath it. "As long as we're here, we might as well go in.

Jesse told you to buy me a dress whether we went through with this or not.''

With that she pushed open the double doors and entered the store.

Kansas City's Parisian Emporium was a shock after living so long in impoverished circumstances. It was almost the size of the Chicago stores her mother used to take her in when she was a child. That was before her mother had gone away and she had been sent to school. She wondered fleetingly what had happened to all the lovely clothing she had outgrown.

As they hesitated in the entryway, she realized that everywhere on the walls were boughs of greens with red velvet bows tied on them. She inhaled the scents of cedar and pine. Her eyes grew wide as the significance of all of it dawned on her. ''It must be nearly Christmas,'' she whispered.

Clell looked around him, amazed at the garlands of greenery. They draped the staircase. They hung in scallops across the front of the mezzanine. In the center of the balcony hung a large picture of a jolly, smiling Saint Nicholas surrounded by more real greenery twined with red velvet.

''Yeah. Christmas.'' He shrugged. A man with no family and no religion didn't celebrate that particular holiday. He cast a sidelong glance at her. Were her eyes moist? His voice was gruff. ''Outlaws don't even know there's such a thing.''

Memories of her mother flooded in upon her. She had thought they were so happy at that last celebration. Even with the stern-faced man hovering in the background, there had been so many gaily wrapped presents.

She forced the memories back. She couldn't think about them. She wouldn't. And her outlaw couldn't be expected to buy her a present. Even this excursion was for business. She mustn't even pretend that it was any different.

She blinked fast, then looked around her dry-eyed. Dresses arranged by sizes in more than a dozen different colors hung on racks. Underclothing of silk and lace in ecru and tearose pink as well as white was folded in glass-fronted drawers. Higher than a man's head, boxes of gloves and shoes lined the shelves, labels showing their sizes.

Mary Carolyn shook her head faintly. It was so much. She had forgotten so much. And there were so many things she'd never had time to learn about before . . . She knew a moment of desperation. She needed another woman to talk to. She needed her mother.

She thrust that thought aside and stared at the mannequin at the head of the aisle. It was dressed in what must be the latest style, a velvet jacket and plaid taffeta skirt swept up in back into an enormous bunch. The mannequin held a plaid taffeta parasol, decorated with a red-velvet bow and a sprig of holly for the season. A little hat with a bow in the same taffeta as the skirt completed the ensemble.

Unfortunately, the mannequin's hair was arranged in a pompadour style with long curls hanging down the neck. Mary Carolyn put her hand to her distressingly short hair. She surely didn't have enough to look like that mannequin.

When Clell put his arm under her elbow to lead her forward, she balked. He looked down at her, the beginnings of a grin on his handsome face.

He looked wonderful. She might have known a successful outlaw would. While he'd been giving her a bath, he'd sent his change of clothing out to be cleaned and pressed. Now he wore a black frockcoat over dark trousers. A starched white collar and shirt, with a black string tie. While she had been fussing and poking at her hair, he'd bought himself a dove gray brocade vest and had had himself barbered. His longish hair shone in the sunlight like gold. His cheeks were freshly shaven and his blond mustache was trimmed and waxed. He could have been a banker or a lawyer.

No one would ever suspect he was a train robber. She gave a little shiver of excitement.

He must have felt it. "Changed your mind?"

Before she could answer, a salesman in a black morning coat approached them. "What can I do for you, sir?"

Clell did not answer. He squeezed her arm. His steel gray eyes sized her up.

She swallowed hard. "Me. It's for me. I'd like a new dress."

The man glanced down at her as if he had just noticed her

for the first time. A hot blush rose in her cheeks as he took her in, from short curly hair to old drooping men's clothes to cracked and run-over brogans. Then his eyes met Clell's. "Are you buying for the lady, sir?"

Ordinarily, she would have kicked him in the shins, but the store would likely have what they wanted. And she did look awful. He probably didn't want to sell her anything. People would see her wearing it, and it would reflect badly on the Parisian Emporium.

Clell shrugged. "My wife's just in from the country. She needs some help deciding what to get."

Her chin came up. She flashed him an angry look. If he said much more, she'd kick *him* in the shins.

"Ah, newlyweds, are you?" The clerk smiled in a friendly way. "Mrs. Stanhope will be just what you want."

In the bare minute they were alone, Mary Carolyn caught Clell by the sleeve. "You can go somewhere else. You don't have to wait. Just give me some money. I'll buy the dress and—"

Clell shook his head. "I'll buy the dress. God knows what you'd pick out for yourself. As long as you're doing this, you might as well look as good as you can."

His tone conveyed the idea that she couldn't look anything but terrible. It hurt. She knew she wasn't pretty, but she hated it that her handsome outlaw didn't mind telling her so. Moreover, she wished she could look better. He might be friendlier to her, if she did. "Rich people are ugly too," she told him. She could speak from experience in this affair, and she consoled herself: "The banker won't care what I look like, so long as I look like I've got money."

Mary Carolyn disappeared behind a curtain after first casting him a worried look. In a few minutes, the saleslady followed her, a load of brightly colored dresses in her arms. So much for wearing black, like a widow. It wouldn't work anyway since he'd let his tongue slip and told the clerk she was his wife.

He'd let Jesse and Cole make up a new story. His part in this was buying the dress. Clell leaned back in the chair that the clerk had brought for him. The man had also brought a ten-cent cigar and had lighted it before bowing himself away.

Clell's eyebrows had risen in alarm. He wasn't used to such treatment. He would die rather than admit that this was his first experience with a big-city department store. All his purchases his whole lifelong had been from general stores in small towns. Last year he had seen a catalogue put out by a Mr. Montgomery Ward and Company of Chicago, but he hadn't been able to make head nor tails out of it.

He hoped the fellow wasn't going to be disappointed when Clell bought Mary Carolyn just the one dress and then skedaddled.

He looked around him. It was all so new, he was decidely uncomfortable. He studied the people wandering to and fro in the store. They all seemed to be busy. Clerks displayed goods for them, described their merits with bright animated faces. Instead of one cash register at the front of the store, several were located about the floor in the center of the various areas where different types of goods were displayed. One or the other of them seemed to be ringing every minute. He wondered at the money people were spending here.

A very uncomfortable thought struck him. Were any of them people he had robbed? He shifted in the chair and crossed one leg over the other. His hair prickled at the back of his neck. He fought the urge to run his hand over the spot. He would never be safe until he was completely out of the country.

Again he wished he could ride away and never be heard from again. Damn this "wife!" If he left, she'd spill the beans. Then Jesse and Cole would be chasing him for the rest of his life.

He heard voices coming from the dressing room. A protest arose. With a wry smile he recognized Mary Carolyn's voice.

Then the curtain was swept aside. Mrs. Stanhope smiled rather sourly at him. "Here she is."

Chapter Eight

He had already risen to his feet before he realized it.

Mary Carolyn Ross in a dress was a revelation to him. Even though the hair was still short and wispy, it didn't look nearly so horrible. Someone had taken a comb and some spit to it so that it curled around her cheeks and forehead instead of looking like it had been dried with a rough towel.

Cole had said she might clean up pretty good. In fact, she'd done more than clean up. For the first time he saw her dressed in a fashionable gown *à la mode*. Another credit to the saleswoman's knowledge had been the choice of a dusty rose gown. It complemented the color of his wife's skin and accentuated the natural blush in her cheeks. It made her brown eyes seem warmer. They contrasted vividly with the blond hair.

Careful there, old son, he warned himself. You slipped up and called her your wife. You'd better get your thinking cap on straight.

Studying her further, he noted with a stab of pleasure that the girl had a chest on her. Of course, he had seen her naked, but with the waist buttoned tight to push it up a bit, it threatened to knock his eyes out. Both she and Mrs. Stanhope were waiting, but he couldn't take her all in. He knew he was looking too long at her white throat and the swell of her bosom over the dress's square neckline, but she was quite a sight after months with Jesse and the boys.

As a matter of fact, the thing was more than a little low in the neckline. He could see more than just the swells of her breasts. He could see the division between them. Why the dress was practically indecent! He could already tell this wasn't going to be right for a widow.

Reluctantly, he tore his eyes away, and again he was pleasantly surprised. He knew she was thin, but clothed in the tight-fitting bodice that came to a point in front, her waist looked incredibly small. He'd bet he could span it with his hands. And his fingers itched to try.

As she walked toward him, he couldn't quite make out how the thing was fixed in back. But from the front she looked good enough to eat. The moire taffeta skirt rustled like the trees in autumn.

While he glanced around to see if anyone else was staring, Mary Carolyn stopped in front of him and turned to look at herself in the cheval mirror. He stared at the silhouette. That couldn't be her rear end. All that taffeta was stiff, but it wouldn't stand out like that without help. He frowned trying to figure out what the trick was.

"This is called a bustle." Mrs. Stanhope adjusted the cloth to better advantage.

He stared at the draped material caught up in a big bow at the back of the waist. It balanced the seductive curve of her breasts in front. His mouth felt dry. He licked his lips. Even with the hair she was damn near beautiful.

"It's the very latest Paris creation," the saleslady explained. "It came all the way here by steamboat from New Orleans. The black piping and ruching make the dress suitable for winter wear. And your wife is just the person to wear it. She looks just like the pictures in the fashion plates."

He didn't know about the fashion plates, but he knew she looked beautiful. Still, it wouldn't do to give her a big head. He cleared his throat, but his voice came out as a croak. "The . . . er . . . hair."

"Oh, that's really never been out of fashion," Mrs. Stanhope assured him with a knowing smile. "Even when everyone is letting their hair grow long, there are always some daring women who set their own style."

Clell could have hooted at that. If the saleslady had caught a glimpse of Buster Ross before he'd stuffed her head under the water, she'd have known better than to talk about style. "I guess that's right for some women, but—"

Mary Carolyn glanced over her shoulder. The look in her eyes brought him up short. She had caught that little bottom lip in her teeth. She looked like she was about to start crying on him.

"—she's a little young," he finished lamely.

She turned to face him, her hands clasped in front of her. "What do you think of the dress . . . dear?"

His eyebrows flew up. In that moment he knew he could hurt her badly. And he didn't want to hurt her anymore. She actually hoped that he would like the way she looked. He felt a surge of pity and something else. What sort of life had she led that had brought her to this moment? He managed to give her a careful smile. "I think it looks real good. Er . . . there's just one thing. Isn't that neckline a little low?"

The saleslady smiled broadly. "Every man will envy you, Mr. Miller."

He never realized there was so much to outfitting a woman. A dress was not even the half of it. He'd had to buy stuff from the skin out. Hose and shoes—she couldn't wear those brogans and men's socks. Chemise, petticoats, and drawers—her others were threadbare. A long wool coat with a Persian lamb collar— it was winter. A hat, a pair of gloves, a parasol, a shawl, a purse . . .

His head was spinning. Once that saleslady got started, she was a whirlwind. In the end he thought he was going to have to drag Mary Carolyn away from her. Even then, his arms were stacked with packages.

"You've spent your share of the money," he informed her on the walk back to the boarding house.

"Me?" She held her gloved hand out in front of her, admiring the richness and smoothness of the leather. "It was terribly expensive, wasn't it?"

"I'll say."

"Mrs. Stanhope looked shocked when you said you weren't going to buy the corset and corset-cover." She lowered her voice on the last words.

He looked her up and down. "You don't need a corset any more than my horse does."

She looked down at herself. A smile curved her mouth up at the corners.

It was a pretty mouth. Beneath those lips and that determined chin was an expanse of smooth creamy skin that made his britches tight. It made him think maybe the time had come to get her into bed. If she was his wife, she could do her part.

Yes, tonight would be the time to roll the dice for the last time. She needed to know just why it wasn't a good idea for a young girl, especially a pretty one, to be riding around the country with a bunch of outlaws.

Suddenly, he realized she wasn't with him anymore. He turned around to find her stopped in front of a store window. In the manner of every husband in the world, he rolled his eyes.

Then she smiled at him, her eyes pleading. "Do you have a nickel?"

The smile did it. "I guess. What for?"

He fished it out of his pocket. While she darted inside the store, he looked in the window. A stack of books were on display, under a sign. "Beadle's Half-Dime Library," he read aloud. And then the title of the book. *"The James Boys in the Wild West; or, The Train to No Man's Land."*

The dining room in Mrs. Haltom's boarding house contained two tables. Both were long enough to seat a dozen. The food was served on large platters and in big bowls that were passed around. Because Mary Carolyn and Clell were late, they had to sit across from each other.

The fare was simple and indifferent. Because Kansas City was a railhead, steaks were cheap. They came fried in butter and seasoned with salt and pepper. On the side was a huge bowl of mashed potatoes from the fall crop. Beside them were the ubiquitous baking powder biscuits and pan gravy. The dessert was cobbler made with canned peaches.

Mary Carolyn found she wasn't hungry. Instead she was nervous. Something was different about Clell. Ever since they'd put the boxes in their room and came down to supper, he had been looking at her strangely.

She glanced around nervously. The room was full of people, some talking, some eating noisily, smacking their lips and chewing their food with their mouths open. Some talked and ate at the same time, a disgusting combination. A man farther down the table was eating quietly, cutting his meat precisely. He looked like he didn't belong here.

She glanced back at Clell and caught him looking at her chest. He didn't look away. Instead he smiled. Just a little lift of his mouth at one corner. Not the pleasant smile she had seen only rarely. It looked almost like a sneer.

Still, it made her feel warm. The heat rose in her cheeks. She looked at him again.

This time he did smile, a real smile. "You're blushing."

She reached for the water glass and took a swallow. "I-I don't know why."

"I do." His voice was husky.

She couldn't think what to say. She set the glass down carefully and studied her hands. The beautiful black kid gloves were back in the room. Her worn little paws reminded her of what she was. Their calluses were hard as shoe leather, and their nails were whittled down with a penknife. They reminded her of how ugly she was. Even with her new clothes and her hair combed, she was still Buster.

For a couple of years now, she had been on her own, living from hand to mouth. She had imitated a tough kid with a chip on his shoulder until he had almost become her.

She couldn't believe her outlaw was thinking about her as a woman. From time to time, other men had discovered that she was a female. And sooner or later, they had moved to take advantage of her.

Some of them were content to go away when she told them no. Some got angry and called her names and went away cursing. Some tried to hurt her. The first time she'd encountered one of those, she'd punched and bitten and kicked until suddenly he'd screeched and doubled over. The kick had done it. Quite by accident, she'd hit the right spot.

Oh, she knew what to do. But she wasn't blushing about that. She didn't know why she was blushing. "If you know, you'll have to tell me."

He had finished his meal except for his coffee. Now he raised the cup and toasted her before he took a drink. "I'd rather show you."

A chill ran up her spine and prickled the hair on her scalp. Her heart stumbled, then stepped up its rhythm. She knew what he wanted to show her. It was the same thing other men had wanted. The difference was that she wanted him to.

Clell was her outlaw. He'd saved her from arrest by carrying her off on his horse. He himself would say that he did it for the money in her sack, but somehow she knew that he would have done it anyway.

He could have ridden until they got out of sight of the train, then stolen the bag and thrown her down on the road. Instead, he'd kept her with him and dug out the bullet. He wasn't all bad.

He didn't want her to go through with this robbery. Everything he had done since Jesse had decided to include her had been directed toward making her so uncomfortable that she'd quit. Under her lashes she looked up at him. She'd never seen a handsomer man.

A muscle in his jaw flickered.

He must have caught her peeking, for his steel gray gaze swept over her body. Hastily, she closed her eyes. She imagined she could still feel him. She shivered as if a goose had walked over her grave.

"Mary Carolyn." His deep voice sent another shiver through her.

She clenched her jaw and raised her head, in time to see him rising, his long, strong body unfolding, up and up. "We've had a long day. It's time to turn in."

Her eyes locked with his as he came around to pull her chair back. He held out his hand. Without a will of her own, she laid her hand in it and let him draw her to her feet.

From outside her body she watched as he tucked her arm through his. Her ears were burning. She could imagine all the other diners watching them, whispering that she was being taken up to bed, knowing what was going to happen.

Together they walked out of the dining room and up the stairs.

"I wouldn't have kept her but till the end of the month." The shopkeeper moved his quid of tobacco from one side of his jaw to the other. "She was clumsy and lazy. She broke a jar full of horehound drops. I made her pick every one of 'em up and dust 'em off and put 'em in a new jar."

"Why didn't you dismiss her on the spot?" Roger Somervell asked curiously. "If she was so clumsy and lazy, why did you want to keep her on?"

The man looked over the tops of his glasses at a shopboy down on his knees scrubbing the floor around the barrels of beans, flour, and pickles at the far end of the counter.

"I ain't no fool," he muttered out of the side of his mouth. "I can get a full month's work outta them before I get rid of 'em, and then I don't have to pay 'em."

Following the man's stare, Roger guessed that the young boy working so industriously was out of a job right after Christmas. He kept his face impassive. "So your helpers come and go. I'm surprised you remember her in the first place."

"She broke my jar," the man snarled. "I don't forget things like that. And the next day I couldn't find her. She hadn't opened up and swept out. I went up to the loft and found she'd gone and taken the blankets with her. Right off the floor she did. I was mad. Let me tell you. Them was Army blankets with lots of good left in 'em. The fellers what traded for 'em didn't know what they was worth.''

He paused to shake his head, discouraged by the cruel world he was forced to make a living in.

Roger broke in before the man could continue his cynical recital. ''Then you have no idea where—''

The man interrupted. ''Forget her. Not likely. When I got down she'd taken a dollar and thirty cents for the thirteen days she'd worked.''

''Good Lord,'' Roger said dryly. ''Imagine that. A dollar and thirty cents. Why that's ten cents a day!''

The shopkeeper nodded grimly. ''And the blankets.''

''Yes. And you don't know where she went?''

''After I told the sheriff about her, he found out she'd bought a ticket for Chicago.''

The room was dark and warm. The coals glowed through the grate of the potbellied stove. Mary Carolyn shivered, clenching her teeth to keep them from chattering.

Clell didn't light the lamp. Locking the door behind them, he drew her into his arms. His head bent to hers, his mustache brushed her cheek. Her legs grew weak as the silken hairs tickled her. She had not expected them to caress her while his lips barely nibbled at the corner of her mouth.

''Open your mouth,'' he whispered.

She hardly understood his demand, she was so overcome with the sensations racing through her. Even before his tongue touched her, she had parted her lips to pull in more air. He was holding her so tightly against him that her chest had almost no room to expand.

His tongue thrust into her mouth, gently this time, as different from his angry kisses as day and night. His superior strength and height tipped her head back on her neck. Somehow, the steel of his arms and the pressure of his kiss only made her hotter. She wanted more. Her hands clasped his shoulders.

Finding it impossible to pull him down to her, she lifted herself on tiptoe to him.

He deepened his kiss. One hand left her waist to force a way between their bodies. His fingers splayed across the tops of her breasts.

She moaned as desire that was almost pain stoked every nerve in her body to throbbing fire. She couldn't think about what was wrong or right. This man, the man of her romantic dreams, was kissing her. She never wanted that kiss to end.

Her emotion was too strong to be contained. She could feel the tears starting down her cheeks. She who never cried for pain or disappointment was crying for love.

"Here now!" He must have felt her tears for he tore himself away.

She swayed, bereft, her eyes closed, her hands reaching. She heard him strike a match, heard the scrape of the chimney. She opened her eyes.

He swung around and held the lamp aloft. "Now will you get the hell out of here?"

She shook her head. Still dazed, she stared at him. "What do you mean? What are you talking about?"

He towered over her. His chest heaved. His face was red as if he had been running. "Can't you understand plain English? I said, 'Get the hell out of here.'"

"Why?" She caught at the heavy taffeta of her skirt. "What have I done?"

"Done!" He shouted the word. "Done! You've almost gotten yourself raped. That's what you've done."

"What?" She still didn't understand what he was talking about. "I didn't—"

He set the lamp down on the table with a thud that splashed the kerosene in the well. "I want you. Don't you get that, little girl? I'm a big bad outlaw, and I want you. I want you right now, spread on my bed with my tongue in your mouth and my . . . my . . . The rest of me where it belongs."

She saw him through a haze. She couldn't think why he was so upset. As she stared at him, he cursed. Then he slammed his fist into the wall beside the door.

"Damn it all!" He swung round and lunged toward her. Catching her wrists, he fell with her onto the bed with a great creak of springs. He landed on top of her. His thigh pressed down between her legs, his face only inches above hers. "Listen to me and listen good. This is why little girls shouldn't be riding around with outlaw gangs."

At last she understood what he was doing. She felt a stab of awful pain and disappointment. He hadn't wanted her with all the passion of a lover. He was still after her money.

She stared at him, her eyes dry as dust. Then she turned her head away. Her body, so eager and vibrant, slumped. "Give me my money and I'll leave."

He rolled to his side, carefully lifting his leg off her. Propping himself up on one elbow, he studied her face. At once, she turned her head to the other side, away from him. He put a hand on her chin and gently tipped it back toward him. His voice was soft and slightly thick. "You'll leave because it's the best thing for you."

Bitterness and self-disgust made a sickening combination in her throat. "I'm sure that's true, but I need that money. I stole it. It's mine."

He swallowed hard as if he were controlling himself with great difficulty. "It's not yours. It's not mine. Hell. It probably doesn't even belong to the rich son-of-a-bitch you stole it from."

If he had loved her, she would have told him whose money it really was, but he did not. She shook her head. "It's mine."

His body twisted like a coiled spring. He caught her by the shoulders and reared up on his knees, dragging her up against him. "Do you want to be raped?" he growled. "Do you want to be passed from man to man until there's nothing left of you but a bleeding rag?"

Why should he care? He thought she was ugly and undesirable even dressed in the best that his money could buy. She shook her head, her own anger kindled. She knew she looked horrible, but she could still fight. "Who'd want me?" She twisted and struck at his chest with her fists. "Some axle grease and a pound of dirt and nobody'll even know I'm a girl. I'll just be Buster.''

He scanned her face, his eyes raking across her. His unreadable expression made her even angrier. He looked disbelieving, he looked incredulous, he looked cynical. ''You'll never be Buster again,'' he rasped. ''Cole Younger and Jesse James and all the rest of them have seen you naked to the waist. All I have to do is blink, and Cole'll have you on your back in ten minutes flat.''

The play of emotions drove her wild. ''And you'd do it, wouldn't you?'' she yelled. ''Then you can have all the money for yourself. You won't have to be bothered with me. You—''

His fingers crushed her shoulders. His face hung over hers. His eyes blazed at her. ''Aw, hell.''

He kissed her. This time his arms cradled her, one big hand closing over the back of her head and turning it to fit their mouths together. The kiss went on and on. She could sense he was kindling his passion. His chest heaved as if he were drowning.

''You're a fool,'' he murmured into her mouth. His heart pounded against her breast. ''Stop me.''

She had no wish to stop him. His kiss had reignited the fire. Every nerve flamed in instant response. For whatever reason he could find to desire her, she was desperate enough to take what he offered.

He slid to one side on the bed, pulling her down beside him. His mouth moved over her cheek, her throat, the swells of her breasts. His hands found the buttons at the back of her dress. He maneuvered the first one from its hole. The second.

She lost count. Cold air wafted over her fevered skin. Her dress came down off her shoulder. His mouth took its place, kissing her, tracing the line of her collarbone with his tongue.

His hands touched her naked breasts.

In ecstasy, she set her teeth, then exploded into a thousand excited pieces. She might have lost consciousness for a few seconds, but he was still kissing her when she regained her sense. What had happened to her? Clearly, something had occurred, but he seemed unaware of it. His attention was fixed on both her breasts. He held them in his big hands and kissed and suckled them.

She felt a warm wetness between her legs. She stiffened with embarrassment. Had she somehow lost control? Of course, she had, but had she done something she had to be embarrassed for? She raised her head to look down at the top of Clell's blond head.

She started to speak, but at that moment he pushed her dress down to her midriff. His hot breath and tongue traced a path to her navel. All thoughts of herself were swept away. She arched mindlessly. His fingers plucked and rolled her nipples while he plundered still more of her secret places.

Suddenly, he jackknifed away from her. "Stand up."

He stood her on her feet. While she swayed, staring at him, he stripped off every piece of clothing except for her silk hose and lace-up shoes. Because he moved so fast and so efficiently, she had no time to do more than stare at him. His mouth with its silky mustache glistened. Even his deeply tanned skin glowed with high color. His eyes met hers. He swept her up in his arms.

"No more chances, little girl. I told you a long time ago that I was a bad *hombre*. Now you'll just have to take what comes." This time he did not fling her on the bed. Like a dancer with his partner, he lowered her. Holding her with one arm, he freed himself from his pants and came down on top of her.

She gasped when his male hardness drove between her legs. She knew a moment of concern that he would feel she had wet herself, but the hot, slickness seemed to wait for him. Moreover, the feel of him excited her all over again. Her heart stepped up its rhythm.

He groaned. She put her arms around his back and hugged him to her.

Eyes closed, he kissed her.

She was completely surrounded by him. His weight covered her, pushing her down into the feather bed. She could taste his kisses, breathe in his scent, hear his breathing.

He lifted his head. His eyes were smoky. The steel had been overwhelmed by heat. "You're ready."

She wasn't sure what he meant, but if a body on fire and a painful ache between the legs was ready, then she was. She nodded.

His hands parted her. She felt him—hard, hot, wet—at the opening of her body. She drew in a quick breath. He put his hands on her shoulders.

And slid into her.

Only tightness. No tearing, no pain to speak of, only excitement and heat.

She let her breath out in a keening cry. It was happening again. She exploded almost before she realized she was about to. This time her knees jackknifed and clasped him hard between her thighs. Her arms clamped around him. One hand buried itself in his thick blond hair and tried to pull him down to her mouth.

But he arched away. The groan became a growl and then a cry. He collapsed, his hot face pressed into the pillow beside her, their cheeks touching.

Clell pushed himself off Mary Carolyn and braced himself against the headboard in order to stand. The intensity of his climax had left him weak-legged. He raked his hair back from his hot forehead.

She sat atop the rumpled bed, naked except for the silk stockings and shoes he had bought for her. One leg was bent at the knee and pulled up toward her waist. The other sprawled to the side. Moisture smeared her thighs and curled the dark hair at the bottom of her belly. She looked open and limp and whorish.

He would feel a whole lot better about himself if she were a whore. Unfortunately, he knew she wasn't. While his experience was a lot less vast than he would let on to Jesse and the boys, he knew a virgin when he took her. This girl hadn't known what to do. She'd only done what came naturally.

He smiled at her. She smiled back, even as her eyes drifted closed.

And what came naturally had left him replete. Satisfied to the point where he could barely stand. He pulled his clothing off and tossed it over the chair. Only as an afterthought did he pick up hers and add it to the pile. They would sort it out in the morning.

He pulled off his boots and socks, added more coals to the stove, and climbed into bed beside her. Wrapping her in his arms, he pulled the blankets up around their shoulders.

He buried his face in her short-cropped hair and inhaled deeply. She smelled of soap. He sighed and shifted his body into a comfortable position with his sex pressed between her buttocks.

He closed his eyes. A few minutes later he opened them. He rolled onto his back to stare up into the darkness. His problem had not gone away with seducing her. In fact, if anything it was worse.

If he knew her—and he was beginning to know her all too well—she would be determined to go through with her part in the raid on the Ottumwa bank. On the other hand, he was more determined than ever that she shouldn't. She was so sweet. The body she offered was so responsive that he couldn't let her go into harm's way.

She would be even more of a temptation to the gang after they saw her dressed up in that damned low-necked outfit. She looked good enough to eat. And he was very afraid that some of the men would want to. He sighed. In that moment he made up his mind to share the money with her. They could both run away. But Jesse had chased him down before, and two people would be many times easier to find than one.

He set his jaw. He was working himself into a lather when he needed to get some rest. He felt as if he were lying on a bed of nails. And the more he turned the problem around in his mind, the more complicated it became.

Hell! I've even gotten to where I like her hair.

Chapter Nine

Mary Carolyn opened her parasol on the station platform at Ottumwa. As she tilted it up, she caught sight of Clell over its rim. He wore his oldest clothes, with an old Yankee campaign hat pulled down over his face. Their eyes met without any sign of recognition as he swung down off the car ahead of her. With several days' growth of beard and dust rubbed into the creases round his eyes, he looked much older.

He had insisted on coming with her even though she had insisted that she didn't need any help. He had embarrassed her with his determination. Cole had sneered and Jesse had grinned. But he had stood like a stone wall.

Now she was glad he was there. Despite her brave front, she had to clench her jaw to keep her teeth from chattering. At the same time her stomach felt sickeningly hollow. *Was that how men felt just before they caved in?*

His eyes slid over her and then gazed around him beyond the other passengers. Imitating the walk of so many injured veterans, he hitch-stepped past her and swung off the platform. Mixed with her excitement was a sense of being alone as he slouched away down the street. Even though he was there in town with her, he was not by her side.

The whistle blew two long blasts. The engineer released the brakes. A shudder ran through the length of the train as the big wheels began to roll ever so slowly.

Mary Carolyn tucked down her head against the cold wind, then thought better of that move. She was a rich proud lady. She lifted her chin as such a person might do and marched to the end of the platform.

"Let me help you, ma'am." The young drummer with the bright blue eyes sprang to the ground and offered her his hand. She remembered he had been ogling her the whole trip.

She smiled down at him a little shyly. She wasn't used to a young man being nice to her. She was also glad of his help. The taffeta skirt caught at her ankles with every step she took. She could already see it was going to be a problem to maneuver. Even now she had to lift the skirt almost to the knee and turn sideways to come down the three rough steps to the sidewalk.

There she froze. A tall, loose-limbed man with a deputy's star on his vest pushed away from the wall of a hardware store. Oblivious to her frightened stare, he pushed aside his coat to free the butt of his revolver holstered for a cross-draw. Out of habit he tipped his hat to her before he crossed the sidewalk in front of her and stepped down into the hard-packed street. She watched him follow Clell like a hound on the scent.

"Ma'am?" the young man asked.

She stared at the drummer, barely concealing a shiver. It ran through her although she wasn't cold. She was effectively hobbled. If somebody should see through her disguise, she wouldn't be able to duck and run. She would be caught in a minute and hauled off to jail. Her jaw began to ache.

"May I escort you, ma'am?" The young man was still at her elbow.

"What?" She looked up at him in some surprise. He was still at her side.

"I'd be happy to escort you wherever you want to go." He was so earnest, his expression so transparent.

She almost looked around to see who he was admiring with

such fervor. Then she remembered and nodded. "I'd appreciate that so much, sir. I'm going to the bank."

He offered his arm. "It'd be my pleasure."

Jehu Tull reached up automatically to smooth his curly side-burns. They reached all the way down his jaw to the corners of his mouth. While his wife did not like them, they were his pride and joy. He had been told that they made him resemble William Vanderbilt, the commodore's son. He felt they gave him the air of distinction and respectability that a growing bank needed.

With a broad smile he rose and came around the desk to meet the young woman who had just walked in the door. Her clothing, her carriage, the aristocratic cast of her features all bespoke wealth. The Bank of Ottumwa was always ready to welcome new depositors.

"May I help you, madam?"

She appeared startled. Then she smiled a little tremulously. Her expression relaxed. "I'd like to speak to the president of the bank."

He actually bowed rather than give a perfunctory nod of his head. "You are, madam. I am Jehu Tull. You may have noticed my name in the window." He was proud of the gold lettering. It shone through the iron bars quite nicely. "How may I help you?"

She clutched at her parasol and looked around her nervously.

He took her discomfort for lack of confidence in his bank. "I assure you that we're extremely safe. All the latest precautions have been taken. And you'll see our guard in the corner."

She had not seen. Over her shoulder she found him, an old man half-asleep, rocked back in a chair behind the door. A shotgun lay across his knees. She smiled as if she were extremely pleased and extended her hand. Summoning all the memories of her childhood, plus the language of the dime-novel heroines, she made her voice soft and low. "I wanted to be sure. I have a grave responsibility upon my shoulders."

"The bank stands ready to advise you as well as guard your money. Come right this way." Tucking her hand in the crook of his arm, Tull led her to a chair in front of his desk. Rather than seating himself behind it, he backed up to the edge of it and leaned above her. He smiled warmly, his eyes drawn by the curve of her breasts rising out of her gown's neckline. The black piping accentuated the whiteness of her skin. He cleared his throat. "Now why don't you tell me what your problem is. I'm sure we can help you solve it."

To cover her nervousness, she took her time closing her parasol. He waited patiently while she buttoned it at the top and stood it on the floor at her knee. The she extended a gloved hand over the handle. "I am Mrs. Oliver Appleton III. My husband is attending to the estate of his dear father, Oliver Appleton II." She bowed her head a moment out of respect for the departed, then looked up expectantly. "Perhaps you've heard of his factory."

Excitement stepped up Tull's heart rate. A factory sounded very good. Very profitable. Regretfully, he shook his head.

She waved a hand. "Well, never mind. Appleton's makes, that is to say, it made farm implements. They're quite famous in Indiana and Illinois. Dear Father passed on only last week."

Tull mumbled his sympathies. She had wonderful breasts. They rose and fell when she breathed.

"My husband wants to use his father's considerable estate to relocate our own business. We want to live the quiet life, but not too quiet." She looked up to catch him staring at her. "I'm to look around from place to place to see what I like. Then Oliver will join me."

She cast a hasty glance around before she leaned forward, displaying a scrap of satin and lace in the shadowy valley. He leaned forward too. His nostrils caught the scent of *eau de toilette.* "I need to deposit a sum of money, but I have to be sure it will be safe. One hears so often of robberies."

Feeling a flush of unaccustomed heat, Tull leaned back and crossed his arms over his chest. "Never in this town. Never in this bank."

She smiled. "That's so reassuring. However, Oliver was

very specific. He wanted me to be sure that you actually had a vault. So many bankers say they have safes and things when they really only have strong boxes.''

Whoever her husband was, he was certainly a lucky man. Tull rose, eager to display the pride of the Bank of Ottumwa. ''Then you can put your fears to rest and your husband's too. We have a fine steel and iron model. It came all the way from Philadelphia by train. Why, it's so big it had to have a flatbed car all to itself. We had to use a four-mule team to drag it down the street. The back of the building was opened up and the vault bricked into the walls.''

Her eyes were shining. ''It sounds so—so impressive.''

''I assure you it can never be broken into.'' He puffed out his chest. The way he told it, the vault did sound impressive. Pleased with himself, he led her behind the three tellers' cages, where two men were working.

She smiled at them. ''This is really good of you, Mr. Tull.

''It has a combination lock as well as keys to the deposit boxes. If you wish to keep your valuables and family heirlooms with us, they'll be safe as well as your money.''

The big iron door was closed. As he began to work the combination, he caught the scent of her *eau de toilette* again. She was standing so near. Her skirt brushed against the leg of his trousers. He had heard that city wives were freer than country ones. With a flourish he turned the handle and pulled the door open. ''There you are.''

Her lips were moving. Then she smiled like a child. ''You've put to rest every one of my fears. I'm sure our money will be safe here.''

''I don't like this at all. The sheriff's a former sergeant in the mounted infantry. He's got two deputies. Neither one of them look like deadbeats or boozehounds.'' Clell's face had darkened beneath his tan. His back was itching furiously where the bullets had been dug out so long ago. He could feel the sweat in his armpits.

The trains weren't so bad. In the middle of the night, the

passengers were half-asleep, half-blind. Only by accident would a man be shot. But a fat bank in the middle of a prosperous town in broad daylight was crazy. At the first shot every man would be out on the main street and aiming at them.

"I always thought you were yellow." Cole sneered.

Clell made no effort to conceal his disgust. "I don't give a damn what you think. Some of us could get shot doing this. The only good thing I can think of is that one of them might be you."

The gang were bedded down with a James cousin whose farm was just across the Iowa-Missouri border. So long as Jesse added a little money to help pay their high taxes, his cousins were everywhere, a constant source of food and shelter.

Long after midnight the boys gathered around a hooded lantern in the barn. Clell had suggested that Mary Carolyn would be better off not attending, but she had insisted, saying that she was part of the gang now.

The idea that someone might get wounded or killed slowed the discussion for a minute, particularly among the older ones who'd been shot in the War. Frank looked thoughtfully at Clell.

Jesse's eyes were blinking furiously as he sprang to his feet and began to pace the length of the shedrow. He wanted to carry out this robbery even though he could see his brother was uncertain. He had difficulty getting the words out so great was his agitation. "We w-won't lose anyb-body if we have a plan."

"That's right." Jim Pool, the youngest member of the gang, spoke up for the first time. "We need a plan."

"We need to forget about this," Clell insisted.

Jesse came over to stand in front of his brother, but Frank leaned back against the wall, his eyes slitted. Clell looked at him too, a plea in his eyes. If Frank spoke, his word would sway them either way. But he had decided not to speak. Clell could imagine Frank's deep voice quoting Goldsmith. "Silence gives consent."

Jesse strode off again, looking from side to side, waving his hands. His voice took on a deeper tone, like a preacher exhorting the congregation not to sin. "We ride into town in twos. We come from different directions. Nobody notices us."

"I've already told you, they've got three armed lawmen within shooting distance of the bank," Clell argued. "Those men are paid to notice every stranger who comes into town. And there's a gunsmith across the street. He can open up with some big stuff if he gets wind of what's going on."

"There's a guard inside the bank with a shotgun," Mary Carolyn reminded them a bit timidly. The reality of what they were about to do was hitting home. Likewise, she was remembering the pain of her wound. Maybe it was too dangerous. "He looked me over pretty carefully too. He's behind the door."

"Which side?" Jesse said softly. All heads swung in her direction. All eyes narrowed.

She had to stop and think a minute. "Left. As you walk in."

He nodded approvingly. "Good girl. You got the real thing here, Clell. That's where they put 'em all right. Most people are right-handed. They open the door and it swings open on the right side. The bankers wouldn't want the door between the guard and the outlaws." He nodded to Jim Pool. "You can stick a Colt in his ear, can't you?"

The young outlaw's mouth quirked up. "I hope to live, I can."

Clell threw up his hands. Why couldn't she have been wrong? "You've still got three guns facing you."

"And a ten-gauge shotgun in their faces—already cocked," Jim Younger said meaningfully.

Clell heaved a deep sigh. "There's still the gunsmith."

They fell silent. The firepower of most men who made and repaired weapons was truly awesome. Moreover, these men were usually deadly shots, spending hours a day perfecting the barrels and balances on their wares. A smooth-action Sharps on the shoulder of such an expert could take them all down at full gallop, particularly when they offered the broad targets of their backs as they rode away down a long street.

"We take care of him first," Frank said. He rose from his place against the wall and stood shoulder to shoulder with his brother. "You and me, Clell. We'll ride in and hold him up. Pay for a couple of Sharps. Then when he opens the cash drawer, we stick a gun in his ear and take our money back and his too."

"That's great. Real great." All the men liked and respected Frank for his experience. The fact that he was participating was a sure sign with them that the robbery would be successful. "Good idea."

"We still can't count on everybody acting reasonably," Clell argued doggedly. "Somebody's always got to be a hero. Or someone walks in on us and pulls his gun. The first shot will bring half the men in town running. That bank doesn't have a back door. We'll have to come right out onto the main street. Not only that, the road only runs one way. The bank's a block from the railroad, but it's a long ride back down Main Street to open country. Some of us are going to get shot for sure."

The prospect of a crossfire quieted them down. Still Clell could feel the sickness rising in his throat. He didn't have much hope that this objection would stop the robbery. Jesse was set on it, and Frank was backing him. Clell could only hope to get out with a scratch or two.

Suddenly, Cole Younger heaved himself to his feet. His grin spread from ear to ear. "I got it," he announced, his voice laced with pure malice, his eyes fixed on Clell to gauge the reaction. "We take her as a hostage."

"What?"

He jerked his thumb in Mary Carolyn's direction. "Sure. She rides into town in her little buckboard to deposit her money."

"No!" Clell bawled. He came at Cole in a rush. "Not on your life."

"Hey! Cool down." Billy Chadwell dove between them and pushed Clell back.

Mary Carolyn looked from Cole to Clell. Beneath her excitement was a hint of confusion.

"I'll kill you before I'll let you do this," Clell panted. "I'll be damned if we'll ride out of town with every man shooting at us and her in the saddle."

"I can do it, Clell." She put her hand on his other arm.

Ignoring her, his eyes were hot enough to set the barn afire. Every man jack of them recognized a man close to killing. His words were sharp as nails. "She doesn't know what she's talking about."

Cole laughed in the face of Clell's rage. "Seems like the little lady is willing."

"She's my wife, and I say she doesn't go. She's not going to have her face on a wanted poster." He swung his fist at Cole's grinning face.

In the nick of time Mary Carolyn caught his arm and Cole stepped back. "Clell! I can do it. I think it's a good plan."

He turned on her. His index finger came out of the fist and stabbed right for her nose. "You don't know what you're talking about. It's a terrible plan. These sons-of-bitches are going to cover their faces, wear slickers to hide their builds, but you'll be recognized. The banker's going to remember you. When you ride off with us, he's going to try to find out where we've taken you, or if we've killed you. When no husband comes looking for you, he's going to put two and two together."

She shook her head. "Not about me. They'll be looking for a lady dressed in a silk dress with her hair put up in style. They'll never spare a glance for me."

Clell slumped back. "You could be killed."

Her answer was so low the gang had to lean forward to hear her words. "I don't care enough to worry about that."

He leaned forward then, trying to read her secret in her face. It was absolutely expressionless. Yet something spoke to him from her eyes. It tore at his heart. So young, so hopeless. A part of him wished he had never met her.

She looked around her, her face suddenly filled with false brightness. "So is it settled?"

The other men relaxed. Jesse clapped him on the back. "Great little wife you've got there, Clell."

"Uh-huh." At the word wife, he shuddered. His reaction was part nervousness, part excitement inexplicably sexual. Anticipation of danger always strung his nerves to the breaking point. Likewise, her acceptance of her death made him want to remind her of life. While the silence spread like a pool around them, he put a hand under her elbow and guided her to her feet. As their bodies came together, he could feel himself harden. "Let's go then. Let's get this mess over with."

Cole Younger wouldn't let them leave without a commitment from Clell. His voice was so loud that it startled them all. "Is she in or out?"

Frank shot his cousin a dark look. Clell looked down into Mary Carolyn's face. Her eyes glistened faintly from the shadows. He slipped his arm around her waist to give her a comforting squeeze. She never wavered.

"In," Clell called over his shoulder. "We're both way the hell in. And double-damned for it."

The night before Christmas was unseasonably warm with a quarter moon and a scattering of stars peeking in and out among the clouds.

"What's the best weather to rob in?" Mary Carolyn asked from the shelter of his arm. She could feel her nerves singing. As their arguments always did, this one had left her with a peculiar stretched feeling in her belly and her heart beating as if she had run up a flight of stairs.

He shortened his stride to match her steps. "Blizzard."

She looked up. "Why? I thought—"

"Posses don't get started near so quick, nor ride near so long. Sometimes they don't get started at all." He opened the door of the toolshed.

Mary Carolyn and Clell spread their bedrolls side by side on the rough-hewn floor. Never looking at her, Clell dropped down and tugged off his boots. He shrugged out of his coat and draped it across the blankets. Then he crawled in and pulled everything up to his chin. He stared straight upward.

She could see his face only as a pale oval in the cool blackness. After a moment's hesitation, she knelt facing him, her hands clasped between her knees. "You called me your wife." She nudged at him softly with her voice. "You were really upset because I wanted to help."

"Was I?" His voice was flat. "Don't get the wrong idea.

I'm the one who doesn't want to do this. I gave this life up once, but it found me again. I don't want to end up shot or hanged.''

Rocking nervously, she slid the palms of her hands back and forth on her thighs. ''You acted like I was something important to you. As if you didn't want me to be in danger.''

''Forget it.'' He threw one arm across his eyes. ''Go to sleep.''

''No, I can't. You argued more about me than about yourself.'' She slid over onto one hip. It brought their bodies together, hip to thigh. ''If I were killed, you'd be free and clear. You wouldn't have anybody to pester you to divide the money.''

''You're the smokescreen,'' he sneered. ''I threw you out because I hoped, surely to God, Frank James would have enough decency not to hide behind a woman. Or so I thought. It didn't work.''

The answer disappointed her even though she should have expected something like that. With a sigh, she wriggled around until she could pull her shoes off and get under the covers. She could smell the dust in the blankets. The floor was hard beneath her hips and shoulder blades. She remembered the bed at the Samuel farm. Her wedding night. What a lie! The whole of her life was a lie.

In the silence she heard a hoot of laughter from the direction of the barn. A few minutes later, a man's voice rose in anger. Fortunately, she couldn't make out the words. They were probably foul. She had discovered that outlaws used foul language more often than not.

She closed her eyes.

Beside her she felt Clell move. Slowly, smoothly, he rolled over. His hand came across her and clasped her shoulder. She opened her eyes as his lips found hers and caressed her. ''I don't want you hurt.''

She didn't know whether or not to believe him. She really didn't care. He was her handsome, tormented outlaw, wanting to give up the life, but trapped. She knew all about being trapped. Warm liquid pooled in the bottom of her belly.

His lips traced a path across her cheek to her earlobe. "You're a sweet girl, Mary Carolyn."

"Sweet!" She managed a dry chuckle. "I'm not sweet. I'm a smoke screen. You be sure you remember to call me Buster."

"With a crazy turn of mind." He went on to trace the path back again to the corner of her mouth. His hand slid off her shoulder and slipped beneath the blankets.

She squirmed. She worked her own hand out and pushed halfheartedly against his shoulder. "What are you up to?"

He kissed her again, tracing the curve of her mouth with his tongue. With his hand he covered her breast, pressing down against the nipple. "I'm up to making love to my wife."

From the moment in the barn when he had put his hand underneath her elbow and pulled her against his body, she had felt the burning desire that somehow communicated itself through his hands. Willingly, she opened her mouth. When his tongue slid between her lips, she met him with tongue and teeth. If he kissed her like that, then he must like it. She would kiss him that way. Her tongue slid over the top of his. She moved her jaw, letting the cutting edge of her teeth tantalize him.

He shivered and squeezed her breast harder than ever. The pain of it, the heat in her loins, made her arch up involuntarily. Her body was itching, aching, throbbing. Tension set her muscles to vibrating. Her desire was the first time all over again, except this time, she felt it more intensely because she knew what was coming. Anticipation drove her wild.

He was going to make love—he *was* making love to her. She didn't want him to stop. Her legs thrashed beneath the blankets. The bedroll came apart and her legs closed around him like a trap.

"Mary Carolyn." His hot breath sent shivers up her spine and curled her toes. If her legs had not been free, in that moment she would have died to free them. His voice was a deep-throated growl in her ear. "Are you sure you know what you're doing?"

Two could play at that game. She set her teeth in his earlobe. She hadn't intended to do more than touch it with her tongue, but something deep and primitive rose inside her. Before she could tamp it down, she bit him.

With a curse he ground his hips down into the cradle between her thighs. If the barrier of their clothing and a couple of heavy blankets had not been between them, he would have impaled her in one thrust and she would have welcomed him, gloried in his strength, cried out with pleasure. As it was, she champed her teeth in frustration. This time, she grazed his cheek.

"You little devil!"

He reared up and away from her. When she tried to pull him back to her, he caught her wrists and pushed her hands above her head. She tossed her head on the blankets. "I'm not a devil."

"No, ma'am, you're sure not. You're Santy Claus, come out of the dark with a whole passel of presents in a gunnysack. Just for me." He bent over her again. His breath was hot on her neck.

She gasped when he set his mouth and sucked her skin above the pulse beat. "Stop."

He chuckled deep in his throat and bit the updrawn skin. This time she cried out. Her wrists strained. Her body arched upward.

Abruptly, he was gone. Her body slid back down trembling. She opened her eyes. All six feet plus towered over her. He stood astride, his feet planted at her shoulder and her hips. In the near darkness, she heard the rustle of his clothing, heard him strip. In a few short seconds, he stooped and ripped the blankets away.

His fist gripped the front of her shirt. "Do you want to take your clothes off or do you want me to?" His voice was hoarse.

She couldn't think. Ecstasy throbbed through her. His voice drove her wild. She wanted the strength. "You do it," she whispered.

He laughed. In the darkness her clothing rustled as he pulled it off and dropped it carelessly on the floor. His body was a pale moving shape beside her. She could feel his heat. She was sure she could smell the scent of his loins. She recognized it from before. Her heartbeat accelerated. Her eyes burned trying to penetrate the darkness to see him clearly.

He went down on one knee beside her. His thigh brushed against her hand. She caught hold of the lean quadriceps muscle. It was like an iron bar sheathed in hot satin. When she flexed her fingers, he caught his breath. "I thought the money was the temptation. But I was wrong. It wasn't anything but bait. Now I've got to run from you. And I can't."

With almost dispassionate efficiency, he handled the knots, the buttons. Layers of clothing fell back. While she shuddered and whimpered and moaned, he unfastened her pants and pulled them down off her hips in one swift movement.

Her new underwear followed. Then he made a hissing sound between his teeth as he ran his hands up from her ankles to the tops of her thighs. Hot with anticipation and hard as iron, he straddled her legs and pushed higher until both hands covered her breasts.

Shivering, shuddering convulsively, she wondered how much of her he could see. She wanted her body to be as exciting to him as his was to her. She wondered how she looked to him. "Can you see me?"

"No. But I don't need to." He sank back until his buttocks almost touched her feet.

She couldn't imagine what he was doing until his breath fanned the hair at the bottom of her belly. She cried out in embarrassment and tried to sit up, but his hands on her breasts were iron hard. "What are you doing? Stop. You're not supposed to do that."

He chuckled, his lips touched her. She could feel him breathing, feel his heat. He turned his head and kissed the lips concealed in the nest of curly hair. She was sure she was going to die of shame, but instead a primal tide of pleasure swept through her. It lifted her body. Rather than try to escape his mouth, she arched upward. He chuckled again. His tongue moved.

Dear God! It was too much. She couldn't bear this tearing apart of her body again.

She convulsed a second time even before the first wave began to recede. She struck at his head and shoulders with her fists. Struck not to wound or to drive away, but to drive him onward.

He lifted his head. At the same time, his hands caught her wrists. "Easy there. Easy."

In a practiced motion his hard male member slid between her thighs. Recognizing it even in the throes of passion, she opened to it, bucked her hips upward.

He fell forward, pushing her hands above her head and pushing into her. She twisted, accommodating him as if she were born to the skill, taking him, reveling in the feel of him. Like his tongue's sliding into her mouth, he entered her with ease. And she clenched the muscles of her thighs and buttocks to hold him.

"Happy Christmas," he growled in her ear.

He was like a rod, her outlaw, invading her with his steel. Shooting great wet spurts of fire into the center of her.

His pelvis ground against hers, twisting her nether lips apart, twisting against the center of nerves concealed there and driving her higher than ever. She had not thought she could possibly feel again after the pleasure of his mouth. Now she stiffened. From the back of her head to her heels she lifted in a bow, arching up against him, seeking the same desperate release.

"Clell!" Her cry gurgled in her throat. She pushed and pushed as wave after wave of pure pleasure shuddered through her.

His own cry answered hers as the waves drew her tighter and tighter still. He covered her, shaking, as she sank into the welter of blankets.

Chapter Ten

An unseasonably bright January sun threw shadows across Mary Carolyn's face. One that bisected her eyes and another that sliced down her cheek were formed by the ribs of her parasol. The thin cloth shielded her from the direct rays but little else.

Unconsciously, she twirled it, making its ruffle flare out from the edges. While she hoped she appeared serene, her thoughts were anything but. She sat in the buggy one of the gang had rustled up for her. In this case she was sure that rustled was the correct word. She would ride into Ottumwa in it. She'd do it in spite of everything Clell had said. For three days now he'd been impassive. All the amiability that had been blooming between them was wiped away.

And she missed that. Missed the protection she had not known he provided—until he took it away.

Beneath the layers of taffeta and wool on her arms, chill bumps prickled. With her gloved hand she tugged at the skirt stretched tight over her knees. She was back in hobbles and the thought terrified her. She'd had to gather all the skirts and petticoats together over her arm just to put her foot on the buggy's step and climb over into the box. The very weight of her clothing—skirts, petticoats, bustle, waist, and enveloping shawl, even the hat and parasol—would slow her down though she'd slit the seams to the knee. She couldn't run. And more than ever she might need to do so.

She hadn't thought about the clothing when she'd volunteered to become the girl outlaw. She had just wanted to be sure that Clell didn't—

"I heard you squealin' last night."

Mary Carolyn jumped. Her parasol tilted in her hand. The words shattered her reverie and tore her into the unpleasant here and now.

"Just like a little pink piglet that was gettin' stuck."

Heart pounding, she looked down into the leering face of Cole Younger. At first she couldn't make sense of what he was saying. Then his shocking words made her blush brick red with embarrassment. For the first time since Clell had bought this dress for her, she felt uncomfortable in it. The way Cole's eyes were riveted on her bosom made her flesh crawl. The oldest of the Younger clan had walked up beside the coal-box buggy. His hand rested on the dash rail a couple of inches from her leg.

He was horrible. And she could think of nothing to say. Her words came out in a sputter. "You ... I ... th-that wasn't—"

While she looked around desperately for Clell, for Billy Chadwell, even for Jesse, Cole laid his hand on her knee. His voice oily with insinuation, he leaned toward her. "Listen, sweet eyes, if you ever decide to walk out on that four-flusher, you know where to come."

Her mouth tightened. She leaned forward to pull the whip from its socket. "For your information I won't be walking out on my husband. And if I did, I wouldn't come to you. Get your hand off."

His leer turned to a sneer that displayed nothing but contempt for her pitiful insult. "You think you can take a whip to me? Just try it. Go ahead. I'll give you first lick." He squeezed her thigh. "Then I'll take mine."

She was in trouble. But she wasn't about to sit still and be insulted, much less treated like a whore. She was a married woman for all he knew, the wife of one of the gang. Not that that made any difference to him. Nothing was sacred to Cole Younger. He was the sort of man who gave outlaws a bad name. She drew the whip back. "Take your hand off my leg. I swear I'll strike you if you don't."

He laughed. Then his expression sobered. He assumed an air of innocence as he stepped back, his arms spread wide.

She looked around. Clell came striding toward them, his face like a thundercloud. She let her arm drop and flashed him a relieved smile.

"Clell, I—"

Her outlaw didn't slow, didn't stop. Three long strides took him around the back of the buggy. His fists fastened in Cole's lapels. Their faces were inches apart. Cole must have been thirty pounds heavier, but Clell pulled the shorter man up on tiptoe.

"Hey!"

"Keep your dirty hands off my wife." Clell's teeth were bared. The words came out between them like bullets. "Don't you touch her, you hear me? Don't come near her."

"Listen. I was just—"

"Don't bother with lying. She's putting her life in danger because of your filthy plan. If you insult her again, I'm going to ram my fist down your throat."

"God damn you!" Cole tried to throw Clell's hands off. His shirt ripped. Buttons popped. He staggered back and to the side. Clell followed him. Cole sprawled back over the shaft with Clell's fist in his face. The horse neighed in alarm and lunged forward.

Mary Carolyn hauled back on the reins. "Whoa, boy. Whoa!"

"Easy does it, boys." Frank James's voice brought them all to attention.

"Get him off me, Frank." Cole called. "Damn this son-of-a—"

"Not another word. Not in front of my wife," Clell cut short the foul language.

"She's nothing but—"

"Shut up, Cole! He's right!" Frank threw an apologetic glance in Mary Carolyn's direction.

She was too busy controlling the nervous horse to react to the bad language. Besides, she had heard much worse. "Make them stop!" she yelled to Frank. "They're going to hurt each other and wreck the buggy."

The older James drew his gun. "The lady has the right idea, boys. I'd have a hard time deciding which one to put a bullet in. So why don't you save me the trouble and separate?"

Both men slowly dropped their hands and stepped apart. Cole shrugged his burly shoulders and straightened his lapels. He ran his fingers over the mutilated shirt facings. "Dang you! You tore my good shirt. I was just passing the time of day," he whined. "She got the wrong idea."

"Go on and get mounted." With his pistol Frank gestured toward the corral. "Leave these two alone."

Cole stomped off. Clell nodded shortly to Frank as he stepped to the horse's head and caught the bridle. His hand, the one with the crooked finger, went up to stroke the poll and straighten the forelock. The horse quieted instantly.

Mary Carolyn replaced the buggy whip in its socket and smiled her thanks to Frank. He smiled back as Cole came to Mary Carolyn's side. "I guess we're about ready for you to go." He holstered his pistol and pulled out his watch. "Yep. It's about time to go."

When Frank was out of hearing, Clell looked Mary Carolyn full in the face. "You can still back out."

She shook her head. Even though her jaw was clenched to keep her teeth from chattering with excitement, she wanted to do it, to pull this job. In her purse she carried the book that Clell had bought for her in Kansas City. She had already read it twice. Her outlaw adventure was about to begin.

Mary Carolyn's hands were damp and cold inside her black kid gloves. She had spotted the lanky deputy reared back in a rocking chair on the boardwalk a couple of doors down. With difficulty she pulled her stare away from him as she fumbled for the knob on the door of the bank.

Directly across the street, she caught sight of Clell and Frank James climbing down from their horses to enter the gunsmith's shop. Her outlaw "husband" paused to scan the street. He pulled his hat off his head and ran his fingers through his thick blond hair. His eyes met hers but did not stop in their survey. So slight was his movement, she might have imagined that he nodded to her.

Somewhere behind her, perhaps at the end of the street, Jesse and Cole would be riding slowly toward the bank, their weapons concealed beneath their yellow slickers. Somewhere in the saloon, Billy Chadwell and Bob Younger would be finishing a beer and sidling toward the windows to peer out.

As she looked up the street, she saw Jim Pool step off the station platform onto his horse and walk it slowly toward the bank. His eyes met hers and the dead menace in them set her to shivering all over again. To his left the lanky deputy never ceased rocking in his chair. His eyes beneath his black felt hat watched Jim's progress.

All this movement could not have taken more than a few seconds, yet it seemed like forever. At last she was able to grip the knob and turn it. As she stepped in, she was aware of the old man on her left. She had hardly noticed him before. Now she could barely keep from turning and staring hard at him. As she crossed to the teller's window, she imagined his shotgun aimed at someone stepping into the bank, intent on robbery. The outlaw would be cut down before he could take two steps.

"My dear Mrs. Appleton." With a wide smile, Jehu Tull rose from his desk. He stretched out his hand, inviting her to come behind the rail and the row of cages. "What a pleasure to see you back so soon."

She smiled, hoping that her lips didn't look as strange as they felt. They were so dry, she wondered if they might crack from the strain. "I . . . I sent a telegram to Oliver, that is, Mr. Appleton. He was favorably impressed with everything. But he sent me back to ask a few more questions. I hope you don't mind."

At her back she felt the door open. Cold air blasted across the floor, sliding under her skirts and chilling her ankles.

They were in. Jesse James and Cole Younger stood in the bank only a few feet behind her.

Panic. What was she supposed to do? Her blood began to hum through her veins. Spots of light flashed across her vision. She was trembling from head to toe. She couldn't remember what she was to do next.

"Of course not." The bank president slipped her hand over his arm. "I'm glad to help in any way I can. Just come over here to my desk."

She was supposed to go with him, but her feet wouldn't move. He looked down at her, his expression turning inquiring. "Mrs. Appleton, are you all right?"

Two shots rang out, another two, a fifth. He froze. She knew they came from across the street, knew who had fired them. Still their eyes met, hers wide and frightened.

"Stay here." He dropped her arm. She pivoted with him in time to see him step in Jesse's path. At the same instant, Jesse's gun came square in his belly.

The outlaw's blue eyes blinked rapid-fire. "We're here to make a withdrawal," he quipped. "Here's my passbook."

The old shotgun guard started to his feet. His gun whipped round. And Jim Pool stepped in through the open door. The gunsight lodged in the hollow behind the guard's earlobe. "Let that barrel drop," the young outlaw grated, "or I drop you."

All the color drained out of the old man's face. Mary Carolyn's sympathetic heart went out to him. He looked about to faint. Then Jim Pool wrenched the shotgun out of his nerveless hand and motioned him over next to the cages.

Cole Younger lunged by her and swung around behind the tellers. "Don't reach for any hide-out guns. I can drop you before you can get 'em cocked. Come on! Come on!" he yelled to them. "Fill up these bags and be quick about it."

With a grin on his face Jesse pushed Jehu Tull back toward the safe. "Open it."

The president gulped. "There's nothing in it." His lie must

have sounded weak even to his own ears. He faltered, licked his lips.

Jesse waved him aside with the gun. "That safe don't look like much. I've seen a couple like that. They all work the same."

"Hurry," Cole called. The cash drawers were empty. "Back against the wall," he pushed the muzzle of his gun into the nose of the first teller. The man fell back, stumbling over his stool and crashing to the floor. The other reached to help him. He fell too. Together they scrambled back against the wall in a tangle of legs and arms. Cole laughed out loud.

Mary Carolyn was frozen in place. She might have been an actual customer of the bank rather than a part of the outlaw gang. She couldn't think. She couldn't speak. She felt so light-headed that she actually thought she was about to faint.

Jesse spun the dials, turned the levers, and tugged the safe open.

"How'd you do that?" Tull cried. He forgot the guns pointed at him in his disbelief. "Tell me." His hands were shaking. He was reaching for Jesse's shoulders with the intent of making him reveal his secret.

Laughing like a demon, Jesse waved him back with the gun. "Hell, Mr. Jay Gould Banker, you've been suckered. All of them vaults got the same combination."

Cole passed Jesse the saddlebags and came out from behind the cages. "We need a hostage. I think that's you, sweet eyes." He grabbed Mary Carolyn by the shoulder and spun her around. "You're coming with us."

"No." She didn't have to pretend she was terrified. In that instant she knew Cole Younger was going to hurt her. "Oh, no." Her voice rose in a shrill scream.

Every man in the place growled. Only Cole's and Jim Pool's guns held them back. Jesse filled the saddlebags. He glanced regretfully at the row of safety deposit boxes. He hadn't thought about them. This wasn't as well timed as it might have been.

A rifle boomed in the street.

"Time to leave." He dodged out into the middle of the lobby and delivered a low bow. "This bank has the honor of having been robbed by Jesse James. I hope you all realize how lucky you are.''

Tull followed him, his hands at shoulder level. ''Don't take her, man. I appeal to your honor. She doesn't even live here.''

For answer Cole threw an arm around Mary Carolyn's neck and quick-marched her to the door. She could smell his sweat, acrid and strong, and his breath, stinking of whiskey and cigars. As he shoved her through the door, he chuckled deeply—and bit her earlobe.

She screamed. She couldn't help it. The pain was sharp, tearing a hole in her self-control. She wanted nothing so much as to run for her life.

Jehu Tull lunged forward and ended up with Jesse's gun in his belly. Every man in the bank strained forward. Jim Pool's guns swept across them, holding them back. With a laugh Cole pushed Mary Carolyn through the door.

Out in the street, chaos reigned. Billy and Bob had horses waiting. But they were merely silhouettes in the black cloud of smoke that obscured every thing.

''Something's on fire!'' Mary Carolyn exclaimed.

Cole chuckled in her ear. ''Not likely. Frank's set off some black powder over there in that gunshop. That old boy don't miss a trick. He's sharp as they come.''

He jerked Mary Carolyn with him. Bob Younger had maneuvered his brother's horse broadside to the boardwalk. Cole tossed the saddlebags over its withers and stepped aboard. His gun was inches from her breast. He smiled.

He was going to shoot her. She was going to die. She didn't want to die, not at the hands of this swine.

''Come on.'' Jesse came running up behind her. He swung his saddlebags over the front of his saddle. ''Come on,'' he grabbed her by the arm and pulled her with him as he sprang on his horse.

Gunshots were going off from the gunshop. Just as Jesse set her before him, Clell came charging out of the black smoke. Frank had already set spurs to his horse and ridden it at a dead run down the street.

Jim Pool snapped a couple of shots in through the door of

the bank before he leaped for his saddle. Yelling like banshees, Cole and Bob were already tearing down the street. Billy Chadwell's horse curvetted, then vanished into the smoke. Jesse wrapped an iron-hard arm around Mary Carolyn, clamping her precariously against his side. She slid her foot into his stirrup, so he wouldn't have to bear her entire weight. Clell circled his horse behind Jesse's.

Mary Carolyn felt a spurt of love as she realized what he was trying to do. He was covering their retreat. He couldn't carry her himself, but he would try his damnedest to protect her.

"Make tracks!" Jesse yelled.

At that instant Mary Carolyn caught sight of the lanky deputy with a rifle thrown to his shoulder. Like an ungainly wraith, he appeared in front of Jim Pool's horse. The animal reared as the man pulled the trigger.

Screaming, the horse crashed over backward. Jim flung himself off, falling and rolling headlong. Another man with a badge came running out of the smoke. He was coughing so hard, he could barely keep his head up. His gun bobbed up and down.

Jesse spurred his horse straight for him. Mary Carolyn screamed. Jesse's horse thudded into the man's body. He was flung backward. The horse stumbled over the downed man. Jesse hauled its head up and lashed its rump with the reins. It galloped on.

Mary Carolyn looked back over his shoulder in time to see Clell swing his roan mare in a tight circle.

"Jim!" he yelled. "Jim Pool!"

The young outlaw staggered up, arms raised. He grabbed Clell's arm and swung up behind him. Clell pulled Ginger around again and headed her back down the street. Too late. The smoke was clearing. Men lined Ottumwa's streets.

The lanky deputy rose from the side of his fallen partner and levered another shell into the chamber of his rifle.

The gunsmith knelt behind the hitching post, steadying a rifle on its crossbeam.

"Clell!" Mary Carolyn screamed.

Her outlaw bent low over Ginger's neck. Jim Pool likewise

flattened himself along Clell's back. The tall mare stretched out. Hooves sending the churned earth flying, she ran the gauntlet.

The deputy pulled off his round first, but the smoke was still swirling around him. Eyes watering and chest heaving, he tried to control the spasms in his laboring lungs. As the men flashed by, he lost the battle. His gunsight wavered and lost the bead. The shot tore over their heads.

The gunsmith had more luck. Holding his breath, he squeezed the trigger just before the smoke obscured them from view.

Clell's hat went flying. Blood splattered and he pitched forward unconscious on the horse's neck. Only Jim Pool's arms kept him from falling from the saddle.

Any doubts the gang might have had as to whether Mary Carolyn cared about her husband were dispelled at the rendezvous. Darkness had fallen as they shifted from one foot to the other around a tiny fire and slapped their arms about their sides as the temperature dropped below freezing.

As the minutes ticked off, she paced, wringing her hands, straining her eyes in the darkness. Finally, when Jesse suggested softly that they'd better ride on, she whirled on him like a tigress. Fists clenched, eyes wide and white in a face made grimy by black powder smoke, she faced down Jesse James.

"You're not going to desert him!" she snarled. "I won't let you. You left him back there in the street, but we're going to wait for him."

Hands raised in surrender, the outlaw backed away from her. "Now just calm down. We'll wait. I didn't mean . . . He'll be here in a little while." He tried to placate her. "I just thought we could find you someplace where you'd be out of the cold. But we'll wait. You just see if he doesn't come riding in here."

Frank tried to take her by the shoulders. "He'll come. Clell Miller's too smart to stop a bullet."

"Too smart. Too smart!" Mary Carolyn railed at the older James brother. "What does being smart have to do with it? Nothing. Nothing. That's nothing but a bunch of hogwash. You call yourselves the James gang. You're supposed to be noble and fine, rebel soldiers stealing from the rich to help your neighbors keep their farms. But you're just robbers. Robbers!''

She paused for breath.

The men stood in a semicircle, helpless in the face of her rage and grief.

''We have to go back for him.'' She pivoted, her eyes scanning each face. Some were sheepish, some ashamed.

All except Cole Younger. He stood slouch-hipped with one hand on his gun butt. ''I say we ride on. He took his chances just like the rest of us. Sometimes one of us doesn't make it.''

In a couple of strides, Mary Carolyn was up against him. Her teeth champed a couple of inches from his chin. ''I wouldn't have made it if you'd had your chance, would I?''

Cole stiffened, his sneer slipped for a brief second; then he shrugged. ''I was just scaring you a little.''

''I don't think so.''

The rest of the gang stared at the two. The confrontation should have been laughable. Cole Younger outweighed the girl by a more than a hundred pounds. But her anger made her fearsome. The outlaw took a step back, looking to his brothers for support.

Jim Younger, who was sweet on Zee's sister Ellie Mimms, stared at Mary Carolyn in open admiration. Bob Younger merely shrugged. Let Cole squirm his way out of this one himself.

''Somebody's coming,'' Billy Chadwell called.

Almost as one they drew their guns and scattered into the brush. Only Mary Carolyn remained beside the fire. Her face filled with hope, she strained to see through the blackness. Then with a smothered cry, she dashed forward.

''It's them,'' Billy called as the single horse plodded toward them.

Out of the blackness, Ginger appeared. Mary Carolyn immediately had her hand on Clell's thigh. Jim Pool guided the horse, the other man's body leaning back against him, head lolling, arms dangling.

''Clell,'' she cried. ''Oh, Clell.'' She caught his limp hand and pressed it to her cheek.

The others hurried up to lead the horse to the fire and help the riders down. As Frank and Billy stretched Clell out on the ground beside the fire, Mary Carolyn sank to her knees, telling herself over and over that she would not faint.

His face was streaked with dried blood that glistened in the firelight. The back of his neck and his shirt were covered with it. "My God," she whispered. "What happened?"

"He's been shot in the head," Jim Pool told her.

She closed her eyes. For the barest instant she lost consciousness. Then she rallied. He must still be alive. He must.

Jim Pool dropped down on the other side. For once the outlaw's chill reserve seemed cracked. The front of his shirt, the hands dangling between his knees were stained with Clell's blood. "Creased," he pronounced. "At least I think that's what happened."

Frank James elbowed him aside. With the demeanor of a man used to handling all sorts of wounds, he rolled Clell onto his side, exposing the back of his head to the firelight. Far from drawing back at the sight of the bloodied mass, he parted Clell's hair and examined the skin beneath. "Yep. That's what it is."

"What does that mean?" Mary Carolyn managed to swallow the vomit in her throat. To her it looked as if the whole back of Clell's head was blown away.

"It means the bullet hit him and laid open the skin along the top of his skull. It didn't go in." Frank grinned a little. " 'Cause Clell's just too hardheaded."

The others chuckled a little in relief.

Only Cole Younger sounded a sour note. "More lives than a cat."

"But the blood?" Mary Carolyn shook her head aghast. The back of Clell's coat was sticky to the waist. How could any one person lose so much blood and live? She looked around her. None of them seemed to think anything of any importance had happened.

"Anytime you get a crease, you're going to bleed," Frank reassured her. "A fellow might wake up weak. He might wake up with a powerful headache. But he'll be all right."

"They don't even get infected." Jesse put his hands on her

shoulders and tried to raise her. "Let my brother patch him up and we can move on."

She shrugged him off. "How can you even suggest this? He's wounded. He needs to rest. He needs a doctor."

Clell's eyelids fluttered. Finally, they managed to stay open. "M-mary . . . Mary . . ."

She leaned forward. "Oh, Clell, we've got to take you to a doctor."

"Do 's Jess says."

"Oh, sweetheart, we can't. You need rest." She put her hands on his cheeks, leaning far forward to kiss the side of his mouth. She could feel him shake his head.

"Nnnn."

"You need a doctor."

His eyes opened wider. Beyond the pain in them was a stern command. She clenched her teeth. In spite of his pain he wanted her to get control of herself. "We're outlaws," he whispered. "No doctors."

His head hung heavy on her hands. She lifted her anguished gaze to Frank. In the meantime, Billy had brought Frank's saddlebags.

As Mary Carolyn watched, the older man pulled out the familiar tools she had seen before. A surgeon's kit, a roll of bandage, a silver flask. "Maybe you'd better go off somewhere else," he suggested.

She shook her head. She had been shot herself. She could remember the terrible pain of having a bullet dug out of her. Somehow that had not registered with her as a common occurrence until now. Now.

"What are you going to do?" she asked Frank.

"Stitch him up," was the laconic reply.

She swallowed hard. Remembering the probe and forceps going into her leg, she could imagine the awful pain Clell was going to have to endure. He was wounded, like the heroes in the dime novels who brushed their wounds aside as unimportant.

They never had to ride in unconscious on a cold night and be sewn up by firelight. In fact, after the wound was brushed aside, they forgot it. Now she knew how ridiculous that all was.

She went down on her knees to take hold of Clell's icy hands. He opened his eyes. Their steel blue gaze was clouded with pain, but he held steady. Was it her imagination or was he drawing strength from her?

His face was deathly pale. His eyes were sunken in his head. As their gazes held, he changed her grip to his wrists. With a terrible smile, she clasped them. He wasn't going to run away.

"Sweetheart," she whispered. Then, "Go ahead," she said to Frank. She owed her outlaw every bit of strength she had and more.

Chapter Eleven

"Get away from me." Clell pushed aside Mary Carolyn's hands. He was hurting and cross as an old bear. But she took heart from his griping and complaining. He must be feeling better even if he thought he felt worse.

After Frank had set five surprisingly competent stitches and bandaged Clell's head, the gang had ridden on for the rest of the night. Much farther, Mary Carolyn thought, than a man who had been shot in the head should have ridden.

Now they were camped for the day beside a stream.

"We've got fresh water here," she pointed out in her most reasonable tone. "Your bandage needs changing. It's filthy. More important, your head wasn't washed except with a trickle of whiskey when Frank wrapped it up." She leaned forward to whisper in his ear. "I suspect it was all he had. He'd probably drunk the rest."

Their blankets were spread a little apart from the others. She was in no real danger of being overheard, but she wanted to touch him to reassure herself that he was all right.

Billy Chadwell had been stationed back on the road in a treetop. From his post, he could see the surrounding countryside and the road for over a mile. Half a mile farther on, Jesse had called a halt to rest the horses. The gang had immediately pulled their boots off and dropped down under the scrub oaks in the tiny grove. Minutes after they'd pulled their hats over their eyes they were snoring.

The hobbled horses grazed a short distance away in some farmer's cornfield. The stalks rustled as the animals tore the leaves off and even pulled up whole stalks to assuage their hunger.

Clell sat Indian fashion on his bedroll, his chin in his hands. His throbbing head made a case for all he hated about the outlaw trail and all he had tried to tell Mary Carolyn about. With a withering glare, he regarded her efforts to play the part of some dime-novel heroine.

"Damn you. It's just a crease," he snarled at her, fending off her hands. Once upon a time he might have been willing, even eager to let a silly female fuss over him. Now all he wanted was to lie down, close his eyes, and suffer in silence until his abused head began to heal itself.

"But if you get an infection—"

"Listen, Buster." He almost spat the nickname on the ground. "The part you can bandage is nothing. It's the least of my worries. What I've got going on inside my skull right now is pure hell and damnation. And a ruffle off a petticoat won't make that even a little bit better."

She flushed, glancing guiltily at the long strip of clean linen. It had indeed been stripped from her petticoat. After the robbery, her elegant clothing had been damaged irreparably. The first thing to go had been the beautiful hat, blown away in the speed of the gallop. When Jesse had set her on her horse a mile out of Ottumwa, the elegant taffeta skirt had ripped up the side seam. Trail dust filled every pleat and tuck.

She had closed her eyes when she had ripped the linen petticoat. Clell himself had paid for the outfit with his own money. At least he would get some good out of it. Except that he didn't want her help. He didn't want anything from her.

What a shame! She wanted to give him so very, very much. Instead of riding out of town with Frank James, he had stayed behind to back up Jesse and her. The last rider out was in the most danger of being shot. In all probability, he had saved her life.

He had undoubtedly saved Jim Pool's. She looked contemptuously in the direction of the young outlaw. His feet were covered with several layers of gray rags. When he had pulled his boots off, a couple of the men next to him had wrinkled their noses and cursed him.

He hadn't said a word of thanks to Clell for riding back down the street and carrying him out even though without him Pool would be dead from the lanky deputy's bullet or languishing in jail awaiting a speedy trial and a speedier hanging.

Mary Carolyn leaned forward. "Please let me help you."

Clell sighed and straightened his back. A painful inch at a time, he let his head sink back on his shoulders. With eyes closed he waited.

Her fingers felt good, he acknowledged. Cool and light. She had a gentle touch. He was probably feverish.

When she unwrapped the filthy bandage, she almost fainted at the sight of his head. The thick blond hair was matted with blood. The wound was terrible to behold. A groove nearly two inches long ran diagonally across the top of his skull. The gunsmith had missed blowing Clell's head off by less than an inch. Luck and nothing more had saved him.

The stitches Frank had set were practically hidden in the swelling bruise. She wondered if strands of hair were caught in them. She wouldn't think about that.

She swallowed hard. "This needs to be washed."

He did not open his eyes. "That'd hurt too bad. Just wrap it up."

"But you can't see this. You don't know—"

He opened his eyes. Her face, pale as a sheet except for the decidedly green cast around the mouth, hung above him. He could imagine the pain in her gut. He'd had it too many times during the early days of the War. "I know," he said quietly. "Believe me, I know."

She dropped her eyes. "I . . . I guess you do."

He waited patiently while she dipped a strip of petticoat into the free-flowing stream. Her touch as gentle as she could make it, she swabbed at the wound. "Does this hurt too badly?"

He closed his eyes. "Actually, it feels pretty good. I guess it's because it's so cold." He thought he heard her gag. "Did Frank do a pretty good job?"

"I guess so. It just looks so awful." Her voice was thick.

"Wrap it up."

Surely, something else needed to be done. Some kind of antiseptic needed to be poured on the wound. Something besides water and whiskey. But they had nothing. As she stared at the wound, spots threatened to overwhelm her vision. Considering the way she felt now, she would probably fall over in a dead faint if she didn't do as he said.

"All right." She wrapped the ruffle around and around his head, trying as best she could to cover the wound to keep the dirt out of it.

When she had finished, he shuddered. He needed to be in a warm bed, to sleep for a week and be fed nourishing foods to replace the blood he had lost. She looked around her at the bleak countryside. They were on the run from the law. They could not stop.

She helped him stretch out, pulled off his boots, and spread the blankets over them both. Then she pressed herself against him. She wanted to weep, but she sternly suppressed the emotion. Once they got out of the state of Iowa, she would get Jesse to leave them behind in some town along the way. With that thought for comfort, she fell asleep.

Jehu Tull led the posse himself. The sheriff and the deputies as well as half-a-dozen stalwart citizens whose money now rested in Jesse James's saddlebags galloped along in his wake. All the banker could think of was the frightened face of Mrs. Oliver Appleton as Cole Younger had dragged her out of the bank.

She had screamed so pitifully. He had run to get his gun from the desk drawer, but another outlaw had fired through the bank door and driven him back. Now he hated the fact that he had not protected her. He should have led her out of the way instead of letting Jesse James and his gang ride roughshod over him.

He still burned with righteous anger at the thought of the outlaw's grinning face. The entire town knew about how his bank had been robbed. His tellers had gaped openmouthed when the safe swung open.

Yes, Jehu Tull had more than one reason to capture the outlaws, and he was bound and determined to bring them to justice. Mrs. Appleton would be eternally grateful. Her husband would put his money in Tull's bank. And no outlaws would dare to try to steal from him again.

He lashed his reins across the horse's withers to step up the pace. The sheriff followed in his wake.

Clell put his arm around Mary Carolyn's shoulders and held her against him to keep himself warm. Chills skittered over the surface of his skin. He cursed softly even as he recognized what was happening. He knew all the stages of healing.

The day was colder for him than for the others because he was getting a fever in his wound. He closed his eyes and tried to ease himself into a more comfortable position. He was feeling what he had hoped never to feel again. The excruciating pain would give way to dull throbbing. Then to an ache. The fever would rise. He might be out of his head although he doubted that. The wound had bled too much to get seriously infected.

When the fever fell, it would leave him almost too weak to ride. But he would ride, holding on to the saddle horn. He would walk, lope, gallop, or run Ginger as the law dogged their trail. If he lost consciousness, Jesse or Frank would tie him in the saddle. A few miles of riding that way and his belly would be black and blue from breastbone to navel. By that time his belly would be empty, so hunger would be added to his pains.

He was getting too damned old for the outlaw trail. He calculated. A year and two months and he would be thirty years old. And what did he have to show for it? A roan mare. A stash of loot that he couldn't touch.

And a ''wife'' that wasn't. He held her a little closer. She murmured something and tilted her head up. Her lips brushed against his neck. She nuzzled him, then settled down. Her breath evened immediately. She was constantly surprising him. Just like today when she'd taken care of him.

He knew how bad wounds looked. He'd heard her gag, but his head felt much better because of her care. She was really something. She stirred and caught at him. She was undoubtedly exhausted.

He stared upward at the shifting clouds against the gray sky. There might be snow in those clouds. A good snowstorm would put paid to all of this. The posse would turn back. He thought about praying.

Dear God, he began. Then he stopped. God had nothing to do with them anymore. He hadn't been inside a church in a dozen years. God cared nothing about outlaws. On the other hand, he couldn't be sure. *Dear God!* A smile twisted his lips. *Would it be too much trouble for you to send a hell of a blizzard?*

''Posse! Posse's comin'!'' Billy's horse skidded to a halt in the midst of the gang. Its hooves tore up the ground at the edge of their blankets.

''Goddam, Bill!'' Clell yelled. ''You're gonna cripple one of us. Get that nag out of here.''

But Jesse sprang up and caught the horse's bridle. ''How many and how fast?''

''Nine or ten. I didn't count too careful. And comin' fast.'' When Jesse let go, Billy wheeled his horse back out of the grove and headed off down the trail at a fast lope.

Behind him the camp sprang alive. Men pulled on their boots while they hopped after their horses. They threw their blankets over the backs of their saddles and tied them down.

Only Clell could not get to his feet. He had pulled himself to his knees, where he swayed. One hand was propped against the trunk of the tree, the other held his head. His face glistened with sweat.

Mary Carolyn knelt in front of him, looking into his eyes. He blinked, tried to focus, got one foot under him, and groaned. She rose and dashed to catch Jesse's arm. "We can't ride on. He's too feverish."

The outlaw hurried to Clell's side and helped him to his feet. "Bring his mare, Frank."

"No." Mary Carolyn supported her outlaw on the other side. "He can't. Go on. You can't take him with you."

Frank tightened the cinches. Then he brought the roan mare and turned her left side to Clell. Jesse urged his friend forward. "That's it. Foot in the stirrup." To Mary Carolyn, he said, "We have to take him. None of my gang yet left anybody behind. Clell's tough. We'll just tie him in the saddle and—"

"Let her ride behind him. I'll take her horse." Jim Pool had the animal by the bridle and turned to climb aboard.

Jesse shot him a furious look. "Like hell you will. She'll ride her horse and lead Clell's if he can't manage on his own."

"But she's lightest," the young outlaw whined. "Wouldn't hardly make no difference to that big mare of his."

"He's right, Jess." Cole had already mounted and now reined his horse around in a circle. "Let her get up behind her husband."

But Jesse was adamant. "I said no." His steel-edged voice made both Jim and Cole retreat from the argument. "Get on your horse, Mrs. Miller. Frank and me'll take care of Clell." He put his shoulder underneath Clell's buttock. "Up you go, fella."

With his brother's help Jesse had Clell astride in a couple of seconds. Automatically, his feet slid into the stirrups. "Do you want to ride on your own," Jesse asked, "or you want me to tie you on?"

Clell's lips barely moved. "Tie."

Frank was already passing a rope under the roan's belly. Jesse looped it around Clell's waist and then around the horn.

Clell managed to straighten. He shuddered with nausea and fever. His overbright eyes met Mary Carolyn's. She had already mounted, but she looked as if she were about to cry. "Good enough," he muttered.

"Let's go!" Frank swung into his saddle. Jesse handed Mary Carolyn the reins. He slapped Ginger on the rump. "Get on outta here!"

Mary Carolyn kicked her horse into a gallop that carried them out onto the highroad. Jesse swung into the saddle, and he and Frank followed her.

"Come on. We'll get you on down the road a piece." Lips pulled back from his teeth in a wolf's snarl, Cole allowed Jim Pool to mount behind him and the two brought up the rear of the cavalcade.

They were moving too slowly, Jesse thought desperately. "Too damn slow," he called to Frank.

His brother cast an experienced eye at the grayish purple sky and smiled. "It'll be all right."

Within a half-mile snow began to drift down in great fluffy flakes. Within an hour it was snowing hard. Despite Jehu Tull's protests and his promises to double the reward, the sheriff called a halt when he could no longer see the tracks in the road.

"What's this? What's this?" DeGraffen Somervell stared at the artist's sketch on the fourth page of the Chicago *Tribune*. The likeness was crude. Nevertheless, anyone who had ever known Madeleine or her daughter Mary Carolyn would recognize the girl. He shook his head in amazement, almost sure that she was the young lady depicted there.

"Pardon, sir?" the maid asked. The plate of eggs and toast she was about to set before him bobbled slightly.

He shook his head. "Nothing, Emma. I was merely commenting on a picture in the paper. You may go."

She poured his coffee from a silver pot and set it on the tray in front of him behind the sugar and creamer. With his eyes still on the paper, he helped himself.

" 'Kidnapped by the Infamous James Gang.' "

Somervell snorted. The infamous James gang had robbed the train on which he had been traveling. He himself had been robbed by a single outlaw, slender and tall, face covered by a mask, hat pulled low over the eyes. The voice had been raspy, somewhat like a man's. However, as he remembered it, he was sure it had been forced into a lower register. Therefore, the sex of the robber was uncertain.

He laid the paper down and smoothed the creases out of the young face. The eyes looking out at him could be the ones he had seen over the top of the train robber's bandanna. He could not be certain of that. But he was certain that if he had seen beneath the mask, the sweet mouth would have been the image of her mother's. He felt a surge of longing, a painful throbbing that reminded him of all he had once cherished and all he had lost.

Further down the page he read that the search was under way for Mrs. Oliver Appleton III of Pennsylvania. The Bank of Ottumwa was offering a $100 reward for information leading to Mrs. Appleton's rescue. The article went on to state that as yet Mr. Appleton had not been located.

"Wherever he might be," the writer posited, "he is undoubtedly sick with worry over his wife's tragic disappearance."

Somervell discounted the rest of the article. With that sentence the reporter had begun speculating. Instead, he went back to Mary Carolyn's picture. She looked very mature. Much more mature than she could possibly be.

He had to think hard to remember how old she was. He guessed she must be about seventeen.

He looked again at the picture. The hat and the hairstyle were not appropriate. She should be wearing more youthful styles. She was scarcely out of short skirts after all. It seemed all too short a time since he had married her mother. Yet it seemed forever since Madeleine had died.

Staring at the picture, he finished his coffee. Laying aside his linen napkin, he folded the paper so the picture and article were uppermost and then tucked it under his arm.

Another visit to Allan Pinkerton was in order. The efforts to capture the James gang should be increased. He considered adding Mary Carolyn Ross to the list of those the Pinkertons were to find. Then he changed his mind. Roger could find her if she were to be found elsewhere. Surely, his whelp could find one small girl engaged in an innocent occupation. For the

Pinkertons he would suggest that particular note should be taken of Mrs. Oliver Appleton III.

When Roger Somervell saw the picture, he had no doubt that his father was looking at it. He felt a surge of hope. If his despised stepsister had been kidnapped in a bank robbery, perhaps she was dead. Perhaps she was even now lying in a ditch somewhere beside a road, rotting. If he really got lucky, she would be in some remote cave where she would never be found. Some cave where Jesse James and his gang were said to hide their loot.

If that were true, he wouldn't be able to find her. If she were dead, he could go home. He sighed. He had to be as sure as he could possibly be. He couldn't go home without having tried. He couldn't just report his hopes to his father. The old man wouldn't go for hopes or prayers.

He tore the picture out of the paper, folded it twice, and stuck it in his wallet. He'd have to pursue the James gang. He'd start where they were last seen—Ottumwa (ridiculous name), Iowa (another ridiculous name). Where had such names come from? Michigan born and bred, he was fairly sure of Iowa, but the other was a blank.

He took another swallow of coffee and grimaced. It tasted terrible just as the rest of the swill in this hellhole of a drummer's hotel. He looked down at the burnt offering on his plate and around him at the dining room's dingy furnishings.

With a curse he condemned Mary Carolyn Ross to hell. With any luck at all she was already there, courtesy of Jesse James.

Mary Carolyn spent the next two hours with her head twisted round on her shoulders. Along toward the end of the first hour, her arm felt as if it were being pulled from its socket. When the gang stopped a moment to confer on the best direction to take to avoid pursuit, she tied the reins to her saddle.

While they argued, she held her canteen for Clell to drink. Although she poured water into her hand and patted it onto his hot cheeks, he didn't really seem to know her. Eyes slitted against the pain, all he could do was cling to the horn. Sometimes she was sure he had lost consciousness.

She could only try to imagine his agony. She had had only one headache in her life—the result of a fall from a horse as a child of six. She had cried until she had nothing left but dry sobs. Her mother had sat by her side in a darkened room and placed cold cloths on her head. They really hadn't helped. Even when the thing had finally run its course, it still returned every afternoon for weeks. Clell had been right when he'd told her there was little anyone could do for him except let him suffer.

The gang turned west, then north again to double back on the posse. The icy wind hit them full in the face. The snow pelted their cheeks. They were not traveling fast now. She pulled Ginger forward so that the roan walked beside her bay.

"Clell. Sweetheart," she added for the benefit of the others, "how're you doing?"

He made no response. His face was pressed into Ginger's sparse mane. His eyes were closed. "Clell."

He lifted his head a couple of inches. "I'm awake, damn it to hell. I'm hurting like blazes, thank you. What else do you want?"

"Are you cold?"

He nodded slowly before letting his head fall back onto the horse's neck. "Freezing."

The single word tore at her belly. She had never felt such pity and love before. She called to Jesse. "I have to leave you now. Clell has to rest."

Almost as one, the outlaw gang swung round in the saddle to stare at her. Then they looked to their leader.

He reined his horse around and came back to Clell's side. He put his hand on the wounded man's shoulder. "You're all right, ain't you, Clell?"

No answer.

"He's not all right," Mary Carolyn protested. "Any fool can see that he's not all right. He's not riding the horse. He's tied on. He's in pain." She reached out to press her hand against his cheek. "He's running a fever. In this cold it's bound to turn to pneumonia. I've got to find some place for him to spend the night.''

Jesse did not look at her. He leaned low in the saddle until his face was level with Clell's. ''You want to stop?''

To Mary Carolyn's surprise Clell opened his eyes again. He moistened his lips. ''No. Keep going.''

''No.'' She caught hold of his shoulder. ''No. He doesn't know what he's talking about.''

''Sure he does.'' Jesse smiled and clapped him on the back. ''He's tough. He's been shot in half-a-dozen places. Nobody can go it like old Clell here. He doesn't ever give up.'' With that he reached across Clell to catch hold of her fluttering hand.

His voice turned serious. ''I promised you I'd take care of my men. And I intend to keep that promise. I don't leave anybody behind. That's why the James boys have stuck together all these years. Don't you worry about him, Mrs. Miller. We'll get across the Missouri border soon and then everything'll be different.''

Five miles farther up the road, with the snow fall beginning to slack off, Jesse's horse threw up its head and whinnied. From the clump of trees at the bend of the road ahead, another horse answered.

''Damnation!'' was all Cole had time to yell before the firing began. A half-dozen rounds whistled among them in the dusk.

''Scatter, boys!'' Jesse yelled. Putting spurs to his mount's sides he wheeled him from the road.

Like a bevy of quail, they scattered. Before Mary Carolyn could think what was happening, she was left sitting her horse in the middle of the road with Clell slumped unconscious over the saddle. Her fleeting thought was that Jesse had deserted them. It was accompanied by a fine rage. A great ''Bandit King'' he'd turned out to be. After that fine speech he had made about taking care of his men, he hadn't given the two of them a thought. And he had books written about him.

Her horse buck-jumped as a shot creased his rump. The bay came down at full gallop dragging Ginger with him. Mary

Carolyn had all she could do to keep her seat. They flashed into a clump of trees.

"Head down!" Clell roared from behind her. "Down! Down!"

His warning came just in time. An overhanging limb grabbed her hat from her head as she pressed her face into the horse's mane.

Then they were through and out into open country. Into the thickening darkness they fled.

"Pull 'em up," he called to her. "Slow 'em down."

With every thrust of his hooves, her horse was grunting under her. She sawed back on the reins. Looking behind her, she could see nothing in the darkness. That was good, she reasoned. If she couldn't see the men who shot at them, they couldn't see her.

The horses were ready to quit. Their gait slowed almost instantly, to a canter, then a bone-jarring trot, then a fast walk. She looked at Clell.

He was sitting upright in the saddle. His hands crossed over the horn. "Whoa, girl." He spoke soothingly to Ginger. The mare shuddered to a halt. Mary Carolyn's mount halted too.

With knees and voice, Clell maneuvered his mount closer to Mary Carolyn's. His first words were, "Are you all right?"

"Y-yes." Now she could begin to shake. Except she wouldn't allow herself to. She concentrated on how exciting the wild flight had been. Somehow it lost something of its glamor when people were shooting to kill you.

Clell was much taller in the saddle. She looked up to find the shadowy oval of his face. "Untie the reins."

Her hands were shaking. She had to turn her attention to something else. As she fumbled with the knot, she suddenly burst out, "What kind of heroic outlaw would leave a girl and a wounded friend on the trail to face the law?"

His hand covered hers. She could feel the heat in it. He was still feverish, but for the moment he seemed all right. "Any kind of outlaw." He kept his voice low. "Jesse James. Cole Younger. Any of them. Get it through your thick head. There's nothing heroic about being an outlaw. A soldier might—I say, might—help somebody who's been wounded, somebody he knows and likes real well. Maybe. But outlaws. Never. It's every man for himself.''

"But Jesse told me—"

"He doesn't want me to get away. I know too many places where they might hide. There's always the chance I might tell a sheriff or a marshal to try to keep from being lynched. You?" She had an impression that his big shoulders shrugged. "Who knows what he has in mind for you?"

She shivered at the thought. While he spoke, his hands were busy untying the rope that had lashed him to the saddle. He coiled it and tied it to the saddle horn.

"Should you be doing that?" she asked in alarm.

"I'm all right." He reached for her reins. "Now be quiet."

They sat still, side by side, listening. From far, far away off to the right, they heard the distant rumble of horses' hooves. But no more shots. "Come on," he whispered.

A sudden realization dawned on her. She gasped in amazement. "You're all right. You're not badly hurt. You've been faking."

He chuckled. "Oh, my headache's still with me, but I can sit a saddle without puking up my guts. And the fever's not as bad as I've had."

She still couldn't get over his deception. "Why? Why did you ride all hunched over like that and let me worry and argue and—"

"Keep your voice down. In fact, don't talk at all. You don't know who's listening here. You can be sure those deputies or whatever are looking for the entire James gang. They know we scattered. Might be a couple looking for us."

It was full dark now. He took his bearings in the starlit night. The snow that had melted during the day had crusted over in an icy film. The horses' hooves crunched noisily beneath them. "Due north," he muttered.

She thought a moment. Then she clapped her hands softly. "We're doubling back, aren't we? We're going to elude the posse. How clever. It's just like Dandy Dan of Deadwood when he was getting away from the claim-jumping sheriff. They never did catch him.''

Clell said something that sounded very much like ''fool girl.'' Then he clicked his tongue to the roan mare. Ginger started forward obediently.

''I still can't get over Jesse James,'' she said finally. ''Everybody who reads the books about him sure does get a different idea.''

They rode for a while in silence. Then Clell gave an exaggerated sigh. ''Sometimes you're just about more than a man can take.''

Chapter Twelve

"Why didn't you tell me you were tired?"

The words came from a long way off, echoing. She was being shaken. Mary Carolyn fought her way back out of the blackness until the red light of morning shone through her eyelids.

With it came memory. Numb from the knees down, so tired she could barely rally strength to keep her head up, she had watched the sky turn gray. The tall grass had made a brittle crackling sound as the horses passed through it. A faint pink had edged the horizon line. As it had grown, it had turned orange.

Now as she sprawled on the ground, the edge of the sun appeared over the horizon. It outlined Clell's figure in golden radiance. She rolled her head away. She must have gone to sleep and fallen out of the saddle. She tried to speak, but her throat was too dry to bring out more than a hoarse croak.

He slipped his hand under the back of her neck and held his canteen to her mouth. "Why didn't you ask for a drink?" His voice sounded angry. "What are you trying to do to yourself?"

She looked up into his steel blue eyes. Why was he so angry?

"I didn't want to slow us down. I didn't want them to catch us."

"Oh, for God's sake!" He sprang to his feet letting her head thump back against the ground. Spinning on his heel, he strode away.

"What's wrong?" She pushed herself back up on her elbows. The world tilted, then steadied upright. The grass beneath her was cold and damp. "I was just . . ."

He made a quick about-face and came back to her side. Dropping down on his knees, he glared at her. "You're still trying to be an outlaw."

"Well, yes."

"A bandit queen. A heroine." Rocked back on his heels, he rested his palms on his thighs. "Just tell me why?"

She flushed. He was disgusted with her when he ought to be praising her for her grit. This wasn't going as she had expected. At least she could tell him part of the reason. She lifted her chin. "I need the money. You took mine."

His eyes narrowed. "So it's the money, is it? If we go get it and divide it right now, will you quit?"

She thought about it for a full minute, ignoring his impatience. She wanted the money, of course. Of course, she did. But somehow things were different now. A small smile curved her lips. She thought about the bank. The excitement of going in by herself and tricking the banker. The wild ride down the main street with guns blazing at them out of the smoke. In the end it had been like a game. She had liked it. In fact, she had loved it.

Looking back on it, she had never felt anything like the rush of heart-stopping excitement. They had been in danger from all sides. The deputy, the guard in the bank, the banker himself, the sheriff, others that she had not seen had all been out to shoot them. Thanks to Frank's cleverness, they were away and free. Nobody had been badly hurt. It was like winning a battle against great odds.

She looked into Clell's steel blue eyes. Not even the pleasure that he gave her when they made love could equal it. She could feel heat rising in her cheeks. Quick as those thoughts organized themselves in her mind, practicality asserted itself and made her ashamed.

Clell looked gaunt and exhausted in the full light of morning. Two high spots of color shone in his cheeks. Other than that his face was pale, tinged with gray beneath his eyes and around his mouth.

She knew she must look terrible too. Still . . .

As if he couldn't bear to look at her, he swung his face toward the sunrise. Deep creases slashed down between his eyebrows. His chin and cheeks were covered with dusty bristles. He looked like an old man. "I'll be damned. You liked it."

"No, not exactly."

Mary Carolyn reached out to touch him, but he moved away. She watched while he dropped down on his side. He stared at her with furious eyes before he broke off a bit of grass and slashed it back and forth.

She had made him terribly angry. He had been angry for a long time. She still felt a little shaky. Sitting up, she pulled her legs under her Indian-style and looked at him apologetically.

How could she explain what she was feeling? She took another swallow from the canteen and cleared her throat. "There's more to it than that. It's just that I feel like I belong with the gang. They've taken me in. Jesse's mother was so nice to us on our wedding night. Even though it wasn't a real wedding night, I felt a little like a bride."

"You weren't a bride," he snapped.

"No. But everyone was nice to me." She stared at her grubby hands. The black kid gloves had been stuffed into her saddlebags with the remains of her outfit. "You don't know. It's been a long time since anyone's been nice to me."

She saw him wince. Maybe he was in pain. Or maybe what she had said irritated him. She couldn't guess what he was thinking. They sat silently, facing each other, hemmed in by the dead prairie grass. The horses tore off great mouthfuls of it. She could hear them chewing. She could hear a faint scratching in the grass somewhere nearby as some small animal went about its daily business. The whole world was waking up.

"Can you understand what I'm feeling?" Mary Carolyn asked at length.

Clell's gaze was bleak. He looked as if he was about to say something. Instead, he patted the ground beside him. "I guess we'd better take a little nap. This place is as good as any. Whoever was chasing us doesn't seem to have caught up to us yet."

Glad of the change of subject, she relaxed slightly. "You don't think it was the posse?"

He started to shake his head, then immediately raised a hand to his temple. All this hard riding and jostling around must have made his head ache much worse. Ignoring her, he pushed himself to his feet and went to fetch the bedrolls and saddlebags. He tossed Mary Carolyn hers, spread his out, and dropped down on it.

She spread hers as close to him as possible. "That was the posse, wasn't it?" she insisted.

He pulled his hat over his eyes and crossed his arms upon his chest. "I doubt it. The posse wouldn't have been able to get around us and ambush us. That was probably somebody after the reward."

"There's a reward for us?" she asked, amazed. A little thrill trickled down her spine. Of course, there was no reward for her. Probably it was only for Jesse. But she was a member of the James gang. She was worth something to somebody. This was growing more exciting by the minute.

Clell yawned widely. "Flashed over the telegraph in every direction. The James gang. Jesse and Frank. The Younger brothers. Cole, Jim, and Bob." He sighed heavily. "And the rest of us that they'll put together from descriptions."

"But how would the people who shot at us know who we were?"

"They didn't. They took a wild guess. Innocent strangers riding along that road could have been shot yesterday evening. Instead, they got lucky. There aren't many roads in Iowa. Jesse was stupid to lead us south by the most obvious one." He lifted his hat to stare out from its shadow. "Go to sleep. When we wake up, we'll find some food."

She grimaced. Her belly button was practically sitting on her backbone. "I'm awfully hungry right now."

From beneath the hat, his voice was heavy with sarcasm. "It's part of the excitement of being an outlaw. Lots of hard riding and starvation."

Somewhat beyond noon, Clell opened his eyes to the sun on his face. It was a warm yellow sun that melted the remains of yesterday's snow. Instead of an icy gale, a pleasant breeze rustled the dry prairie around them.

His next thought was that the pain in his head had subsided from a throb to a dull ache. Thank God, his skull hadn't been fractured. Carefully, he ran his fingertips over the bandage. He couldn't feel any swelling to speak of or any exceptional tenderness that would indicate an infection. He sighed. His luck hadn't run out. But it had been damned close.

He couldn't remember the bullet striking him. Perhaps the old saw was true. *You never hear the one that gets you.*

With his primary question answered, he closed his eyes, content to lie in the long grass that shut out the rest of the world. He needed to think about what to do with the body that weighed his down all along the left side. His wife, who had started by cuddling so warmly against him, now lay practically on top of him. The top of her head was pressed beneath his chin, keeping him from turning his head. His arm was asleep.

How quickly he had gotten into the habit of thinking of Mary Carolyn Ross as his wife. How quickly too he had assumed the role of protector. She needed a protector in the worst way. She was brave to the point of stupidity. She reminded him of a feist—a small dog with a great heart. Too fierce to know when she was overmatched.

She lay loose-boned, her head on his shoulder, where she did more than keep him warm. She kept him . . . What was the word he wanted? Contented. Soothed. Happy. He shook his head. He couldn't remember when he'd thought he was happy. He wondered if wives lay just so against their husbands for all their married lives.

Her breasts were pressed against his chest. Her left hand nestled inside his coat. The inside of her thigh lay across his sex. The realization teased him.

He stroked her back, tracing her spine from her shoulder blades to the tip between her buttocks. She couldn't possibly feel him through all the layers of clothing, but she squirmed and murmured. He hooked his other hand under her knee and pressed her to him.

Poor, stupid little girl. Where had she come from? More than likely she was an orphan. That remark about belonging to someone had told the tale. He had to give her credit for pluck. He didn't know anyone else who would have had the nerve to rob a private car on a train. Too much pluck. Too much fearlessness.

Feists were expendable creatures. One swipe of a bear paw, one twist of a bull's horn and they were dead. Bleeding, they would tumble through the air, yelping in agony, to land with scarcely a thud. Their noise would be cut off as if by a knife. No one cared. They had served their purpose. While the bear or bull was concentrating on them and their ferocious yapping, the powerful hunters and the bigger, more valuable hounds would move in for the kill on whichever unprotected side the giant beast would present.

The strategy had stood the test of time. Clell knew Cole Younger understood it. Frank did too. Probably Jim Pool for all his youth thought nothing about what they had allowed Mary Carolyn to do. Perhaps even Jesse didn't, although Clell really couldn't believe that Jesse would do something so callous. But then no one really knew about Jesse James. Just as no one really knew about Robin Hood.

Clell's desire for his wife had been building slowly. Now in a rush it seemed almost to overwhelm him. The pressure of her body set him afire. He pulled her knee tighter against him. His other arm locked around her. He rolled over.

"Hey! What's . . . ?" Her eyes opened wide in confusion.

He grinned down at her. "It's me," he whispered. "Everything's all right. In fact everything's . . . just . . . fine."

His last words were uttered between kisses. He kissed her

mouth and then his lips slid off the side of her jaw to rasp her
neck with his mustache. She clutched at his shoulders. He
heard her little unintelligible sounds of protest or pleasure. He
couldn't tell which.

He lifted his head to find her smiling, her eyes closed. Immediately, he kissed her again on the other side. She arched her
upper back, offering him her throat.

In that moment he realized what marriage to her might be
like. They could wake up like this for the rest of their lives.
Except she would have on a thin cotton nightgown instead of
layers and layers . . .

He began to unbutton her clothing.

"Don't!" She sounded appalled. "We can't do this. Right
out here in the middle of a field in broad daylight. Why it must
be noon!"

His fingers continued their assault. His mouth continued to
move on her naked flesh, kissing it by the inch as he peeled
back the cloth. He moved his body as well, rubbing himself
against her.

"You mustn't." She sounded breathless now. And her voice
was high as if she were really afraid. "You can't do this."

He bared her breasts. With a groan he covered one with his
whole mouth. His tongue circled the nipple already hard and
waiting for him. His teeth closed urgently on the aureole. He
could feel the skin turn pebbly beneath him.

"Don't . . . Stop . . ."

He could have cheered when he felt her hips buck upward.
She wanted this. In all his life, he'd never had a woman truly
want him. Whores might moan and take on, but they didn't
fool him. They were all staring at the ceiling and counting the
minutes and the money.

How could a man know whether he was a good lover or
not? Only if he made love to a woman and drove her out of
her mind. He changed his mouth to her other breast and began
to open the buttons on her pants.

"Clell," she moaned. "It's daylight. We're in the middle
of a field."

"God's seen it all before." He ran a hand over her belly and dived into the hot wetness between her legs.

"Clell!" She sounded as if her teeth were on edge.

Her eyes were glittering with moisture. Not tears. The moisture of excitement. He had never really noticed her eyes. They were dark brown, polished as agate. And glazed with passion. She had caught her lower lip between her teeth.

He kissed it, laving it with his tongue. "Open your mouth, sweetheart," he whispered. "Open your mouth."

She gasped. "I'll scream."

"Not yet. Lift your hips." He pushed her pants down and covered her center with his hand. She trembled against his palm.

Her mouth was open now, but her eyes didn't focus on him. Instead, they stared sightlessly upward as she listened to her body. He kissed her again, then returned to her breasts. Her rib cage rose and fell as if she had been running.

He freed himself. No need to take his time, to ease her way. She was waiting for him, eager for him.

"Hold on," he called softly. "Here I come."

What she did to hold on, he never knew. The second he touched her opening, she lunged upward. He found himself engulfed in waves of sensation. Her muscles rippled all along his length.

He pulled back to stroke her, and she cried out again between clenched teeth. "Do-o-o-n't!"

He drove into her again. "Don't what?" And again. "Don't what?"

"Don't stop! Don't stop!" Every breath was a sob of ecstasy. Her legs stiffened, lifting him up.

"God," he murmured. "Lord, god." He swayed on the saddle of her hips as her force drove him deeper. He wanted it, wanted more. He caught her by the hips and lifted her up. Her legs wrapped around his waist. She lifted herself and then dropped down, grinding her pelvis against him.

And then she flew apart in his hands. Her keening cry lifted to the heavens, her arms and legs swept wide. Her back arched.

All served to impale herself on his rod. Holding her struggling body, he exploded and collapsed on top of her.

"The trouble with Iowa is that it's so damned flat. Whoa, Ginger. Steady there, girl."

"Be careful, for heaven's sake!"

Mary Carolyn stood at the roan mare's head, stroking her face, and staring up into the gray winter sky at Clell. Her outlaw stood straight up on the back of the saddle, his toes anchored under the cantle. From that promontory he could survey the countryside.

"I think there's a road over there. Yep. For sure. Running east and west."

Mary Carolyn turned her body slightly to look in the direction he pointed. When she did, Ginger shifted her weight from one hip to the other.

"Whoa!" Clell called in alarm. "Keep her steady." Carefully, he bent at the knees and hips, then came down on his haunches and dropped astraddle of the horse.

Mary Carolyn let go of the bridle to clap delightedly. "I can't believe you did that. I've seen pictures of circus riders doing that. But I never saw anyone else do it. Let alone an outlaw."

He shot her a sour glance as he threw one long leg over the cantle and dropped to the ground. Every movement was so graceful that Mary Carolyn knew she was falling in love all over again. No one could be more handsome than her outlaw.

To prove it to herself, she reached up to kiss him. Her intention was to brush him lightly across the cheek. But he grinned and caught her and kissed her very thoroughly. Several minutes passed before they mounted and headed south toward the road.

"Where are we now?"

"Not too far from the Iowa border."

"Close to where you buried the money?"

He gave her a calculating look. "That bunch of men who

tried to ambush us ran us away from there. We're miles west of there, and lucky to be alive.''

''Are you telling me the truth?''

He lifted one dark gold eyebrow. ''I'm an outlaw. What do you think?''

She twisted her mouth. ''You're probably lying. On the other hand you could be telling me the truth because you think I'd think you were lying.''

He chuckled.

''Who are we running from then?'' she asked after they had ridden another mile.

''Everybody. With a reward out for us, everybody would like to take a shot at us.''

''What about the posse?'' She thought of the lanky deputy.

''Not them. They're all upright citizens with business to tend to. They've probably given up and gone home long ago.''

The posse from Ottumwa did not give up and go home. Or at least the sheriff and his deputies and the banker did not.

Jehu Tull had lost his soft belly. With a week's growth of beard on his cheeks, he looked tough and fit, but his good humor had completely disappeared. He was a man with a mission. His bank had been robbed. It was his duty to get the depositors' money back.

Whenever he thought of going home, he pictured his new safe swinging open on the first try by the smirking outlaw. He ground his teeth until his jaw trembled. Moreover, the thought of the hardships the lovely Mrs. Appleton was enduring spurred him so that he could not sit still when they would stop for the night. He wanted to ride on and on.

The deputized citizens flagged after three days, but four Pinkerton agents connected with the posse south of Osceola. When they produced their identification, Tull shook their hands enthusiastically. The sheriff of Ottumwa scowled.

''Are you sure it was Jesse James?'' Howard Pearcy, the leader, asked. ''We've been through every case attributed to him. He's never harmed a woman before. It's not his style.

He's polite as a preacher, makes a big show of giving them back sentimental pieces of their jewelry. They flutter their eyelashes at him and he smiles like they're special.''

"He said he was Jesse James," the banker insisted.

"Lots of men are pulling crimes all around the countryside and laying the blame on him. Two fellas in the same night last fall. One in Kansas, one in Missouri. The one in Missouri got shot and killed. Turned out to be a local boy trying to get some money for his folks."

"He fit the wanted poster." The sheriff scowled defensively. "Description was right on the button."

The Pinkerton detectives shrugged. They were used to local law enforcers resenting them. Pearcy smiled as if the lawman had asked for their help. "I'm sure it was. Now here's the plan. We want to drive Jesse James into Missouri and pursue him across the state line. Will that work for you?"

"What?" Tull appeared flabbergasted. "You don't want to catch him as soon as possible?"

The Pinkerton men exchanged glances. "We want him over the state line. Missouri's protecting him. We want to catch him there—and some of the people he's been running and hiding with. Then we'll be able to move into Missouri to show them how much they need us."

"But—but what about the bank's money? And Mrs. Appleton?" The banker couldn't believe what he was hearing.

"Oh, we'll get those back," Pearcy assured him laconically. "But what we really want is the whole gang. Jesse James needs to be put out of business permanently."

A week of hide-and-seek heading west along the Missouri border had worn the gang slick. They were all for splitting up the money and crossing the border in twos and threes. Only Jesse insisted that they stay together.

"No. Goddammit. I'm not going to go on without them." He stood toe to toe with his cousin. His eyes flashed blue fire, and his hand flicked back and forth across the butt of the weapon in his holster.

"More for us," Cole insisted hotly. "If they can't—"

If looks could kill, Jesse's would have slain Cole on the spot. "They both get a share. Hell, she ought to get two. She went in twice and did twice as much work. And Clell ought to get his and Jim Pool's."

"Now just a goddam minute—"

Jesse whirled on the newest member of his gang. He pointed an accusing finger at him. "He pulled your bacon out of the fire," he snarled. "You'd be long gone. The next shot would have taken you down. You were supposed to cover us, but you moved down too soon. You didn't do a thing but get in the way. And slow us down because you lost your horse."

Jim Pool drew his gun, but Jesse's was already aimed at his chest.

"Go ahead," the outlaw snarled. "Bring it up another inch. I'll pull the trigger before it comes two inches higher."

The sound of horse's hooves coming hard forestalled the shoot-out.

"Posse!" Bob Younger spurred his horse through camp, his yellow slicker flying straight out behind him. "Posse!"

As one they sprang into the saddle. The horses had been running for four days. Four days without grain. Four days without rest. The posse came barreling through the trees on horses furnished by the Pinkerton Detective Agency.

Still, Jesse's rawboned stud with the white face quickly overtook Bob's gelding. "West!" he yelled. "Head west. We'll cross the river."

But the posse swung wide. Their fresher mounts were quickly running almost parallel.

"We've got to head south," Frank yelled to Jesse. The brothers bent low over their horses, riding side by side. "South into Missouri where we'll be safe."

Jesse couldn't have agreed more, but he hated to be herded. The stubbornness that was part and parcel of his nature made him set his teeth and lash the stud across the withers.

"Jesse!" Frank yelled.

His brother pulled ahead. The Nodaway River was only a

mile away. The brakes were thick along its banks. He raised his arm and motioned the gang to follow him.

"It's a chase all right," Clell agreed. From the fork of a tree, he could see the riders.

Mary Carolyn and he had just made the decision to turn south at the railroad bridge over the Nodaway. They could be in Missouri in a day or two. Then they had heard the hoofbeats.

She climbed into the tree beside him. "Could it be Jesse and the gang running from a posse?"

He looked at her sharply. "It could be anybody. For any reason."

"But not likely."

As they watched, the leader of the nearer bunch lashed his big horse.

Mary Carolyn shaded her eyes against the light. "That looks like Jesse. And Frank." She dropped her hand and caught Clell's arm. "It is. It is. Oh, we've got to help them."

Clell would just as soon have let them ride on to whatever fate they could expect. Either the posse would catch up to them and there would be a surrender or a shoot-out, or they would get away in the brakes. Jesse was smart as a whip. The thickets of vegetation as well as the shallows along the river were perfect for disappearing into and lying low.

A posse would halt and make a plan before they followed the gang in. Jesse would have plenty of time to set up an ambush. Still and all—

"It's them!" Mary Carolyn wrapped her hands around his arm. "Oh, I know that's Jesse's horse. What can we do?"

He shrugged. "They don't need us. They're heading for the brakes. They'll hide out in them."

Unfortunately for Jesse's plan, the posse had seen Jesse's intent. The riders were pulling their rifles out of their saddle boots. A shot threw dirt into the nose of Jesse's horse. It shied, breaking stride, but Jesse lashed it again.

"They missed," Mary Carolyn cried. "Oh, but they were so close."

"They didn't miss by much," Clell observed dryly. "They don't want the gang to make the trees."

Suddenly, she punched him in the shoulder. "Do something. You have to. We can't let them be captured."

"They'll be all right," he insisted.

"No. They've got our share of the money." Quick as a flash, she swung down from the tree and ran to his saddle. Drawing his rifle, she brought it to him along with the saddlebags.

Cursing, he took them. Of course, he might have known his wife would be concerned about money. "What do you expect me to do?" he complained, but he had already formed a plan in his mind. "I'm not going to shoot somebody from ambush." As he spoke, he pulled a handful of shells from his saddlebags and began to feed them into the magazine. "I'm not a murderer."

She stared up at him, exasperated. "You're an outlaw," she declared. "Pull an outlaw's trick. In *Gunpowder Jim; or, The Mystery*—"

"Spare me," he groaned. He brought the rifle to his shoulder. Just as Jesse's stud plunged into the trees, Clell squeezed the trigger. The bullet spanged into the ground in front of the leader of the posse. He hauled back on the reins.

Clell jacked another shell under the hammer. He squeezed it off. And another. And another. All of them tore up the ground in the midst of the posse's horses.

The posse's mounts were milling about in disarray. A couple of men whirled their horses and headed back in the direction from which they had come.

Five riders in the forefront pulled into a knot. One gestured wildly toward the trees. The others shook their heads.

Just for good measure, Clell cocked the rifle one more time. This time he aimed high. It was taking a chance, but they'd done it to him. One man's hat went flying off. He clapped his hand to his head.

That shot decided them. With their tails between their legs, they galloped back the way they had come.

"You did it! You did it!" Mary Carolyn clambered up beside

Clell and put her arms around him. "You didn't hurt anyone and you saved our friends. Oh, you are a hero. A real hero."

He hugged her to him. He'd rather enjoyed it himself, although he wouldn't have told her for the world. He hoped he'd notched that fella's ear. It would make up for the headaches and fever from his own crease.

"You're a wonderful outlaw." She lifted her laughing face for a kiss.

They pulled apart when they heard hoof beats, horses moving steadily toward them through the brush.

In a minute they looked down into the grinning face of Jesse James. "If that don't beat all. Goldang, Clell Miller, if you're not the beatingest ... Look here, Frank. We've found our strays."

The gang gathered in a semicircle beneath the tree staring up at Mary Carolyn and Clell.

He clasped her hand. "Grab on, sweetheart."

When she had hold of him, he lowered her to the ground and then eased himself down beside her. With his rifle in the crook of his arm and his wife at his side, he faced them. "Matter of fact, we found you," Clell said. "You looked like you were in a peck of trouble."

"Hell, no," Cole began, but Jesse waved him to silence.

"You're sure right about that." Jesse offered Clell his hand. "And I can tell you right now, we'll never forget it."

Two days later in Council Bluffs, they decided to avoid Missouri completely. If the posse wanted them there, they weren't about to oblige. "I've a hankering to see Texas," Cole said. "I've got a real close friend there. I ain't seen her in years."

"We'll all go. I know what. Let's take the train." Jesse was grinning from ear to ear before Clell could protest. It was the sort of crazy thing Jesse would do. "Hell. We've got plenty of money. Nobody'll be looking for us on it."

They all stared at him as if he'd lost his mind.

He was laughing fit to be tied. "Don't you see? The whole

James gang'll be riding the train together.'' He slapped his brother on the back. "Don't you just hope somebody tries to rob it? We'll know just what to do.''

Clell looked at Mary Carolyn. Her eyes were shining. To her all this was fun. To him it was exhausting. They were getting in deeper and deeper. And the trap could spring at any moment.

Chapter Thirteen

"Black is the color of my true love's hair.
His cheeks are red as roses fair,
If he would return . . ."

The singer's hands fluttered over the piano keyboard, careless of striking a false chord. Her eyes skimmed over the men entering the Palace Saloon on Elm Street. They skipped on to a rowdy bunch sitting at a card table in a swagged alcove. Then they flashed back.

The handsome group paused in the doorway. All were bathed and barbered. The five in the front were nattily dressed in new suits and hats.

Her hands stilled as she stared into their faces. The music faltered as she forgot the words. Most of the patrons didn't noticed the lapse, for she recovered, picked up the tune, and continued to the end. Nor did they notice that she played it faster and with a lilt in her voice.

The James gang surveyed the room, their backs to the double doors. Shoulder to shoulder with Jesse stood Cole Younger. His eyes burned as the singer swung around on the stool.

Sweeping her skirts wide, she rose and came down the small stage to the steps.

Her black velvet dress was wide skirted, with tassels of black silk fringe around the deep yokes at both the bosom and the hips. A white chiffon jabot spilled down between her breasts, and white chiffon ruffles fell away from her wrists. Her hair was black too, done up in a knot at the back of her head. Only a short half-bang swept to the right relieved the severity of the style.

More than polite applause attested to her popularity. One poker player even yelled that she should play some more. She acknowledged him with a thin-lipped smile and a distracted ''Later.'' In the gaslights across the front of the small stage, her eyes glittered as they centered on the burly Missourian. She put her hands on her hips. He grinned, his lips pulling back beneath his waxed mustache.

Letting her skirts trail behind her, she descended the five steps and walked toward him. Their eyes held. Only the necessity for weaving in and out among the card tables slowed their pace.

Almost dead center in the room, they came together. His hands gripped her arms. He pulled her up to him and kissed her full on the mouth. The crowd left their card-playing and drinking long enough to give a rousing cheer. Then the woman leaned back in Cole's arms and slapped his face. Another rousing cheer. He clapped his hand to his cheek with a look of outrage. She drew back to hit him again.

Then he laughed while she tore herself out of his arms and darted away. At the foot of the stairs, he caught her. Throwing an arm around her waist, he jerked her back against him. He was still laughing and biting her neck as he half-carried her, half-dragged her up the stairs.

Laughing and winking broadly, the rest of the James gang moved as one to the polished walnut bar. The men already lining it gave way before them. Frank called for a bottle of whiskey and shots for them all.

Only Mary Carolyn continued to watch the struggling pair as Cole stood the woman on the landing. ''Isn't somebody going to help her?'' Mary Carolyn whispered to Clell. ''He's mean as a snake.''

Clell tossed off his whiskey and then reached for hers. ''If she needs any help, she'll scream bloody murder. They've got bouncers around to take care of that.''

''But—''

He tipped his hat back and studied the pair. ''I'm not sure. She looked familiar, but it's been a long time. I only saw her once before. If she's who I think she is, the last thing she needs is our help.''

The woman in black swung a powerhouse punch at Cole, who ducked and danced away down the walkway. She came after him. ''Bastard! You lying bastard!''

''She's screaming.'' Mary Carolyn looked around for the bouncers, but if they were there, she could not distinguish them from the rest of the patrons. A few were still enjoying the spectacle, but most had returned to their card-playing.

Mary Carolyn looked again at them. She couldn't forget the way Cole had grinned at her when he had dragged her out of the Ottumwa bank. She would never know if he would have killed her. Cole Younger had no gallantry like Jesse, no education or touch of civility like Frank, no kindness and gentility like Clell. He was a vicious tough. She shivered at the thought of any woman manhandled by him.

''She looks like she's doing a pretty good job of taking care of herself. Unless I'm far wrong, underneath the skirt, she's got a .22 pistol strapped to her thigh.'' Clell wandered over to the free lunch and helped himself to a boiled egg. Cracking it, he rested his elbows on the bar beside Mary Carolyn and began to peel it.

The combatants had fought their way back to the door at the end of the hall above the saloon. The black-haired woman punched Cole's heavy shoulder with her fist. He ducked under her arm and reached around her to open the door. Then he pushed her through it and slammed the door after him.

Pushing her coat back around her pistol butt, Mary Carolyn started for the stairs.

''Hey, Buster!'' Clell caught her by the seat of the pants and pulled her back. "They know each other. I'm teasing. I know who she is. She's the reason we came so far. You know we could have hidden out in Oklahoma City or Wichita. They were a whole lot closer and right on the way. We didn't have to come all the way to Dallas, Texas."

She allowed him to pull her back. "Who is she?"

"She's a fence for one thing." At her puzzled expression, he sighed. "If you're going to be an outlaw, you ought to learn a little bit about the business. She takes stolen goods, horses and cattle mostly, and sells them for the rustlers."

"Oh?"

He shook his head with exaggerated patience. As if he were explaining something to a very backward person, he spoke slowly and distinctly. "A fence deals in stolen property. Takes it back 'over the fence' into polite society, so to speak. And when she does that, she takes a cut of what she sells. That's how she makes her living. She also deals cards and sings and plays the piano. Oh, Belle is quite a gal."

Mary Carolyn looked at him with dawning wonder. "She's an outlaw. A real one."

He dropped the empty eggshell into the sawdust on the floor and cracked another. "About as real as it gets. If you want to learn the ropes, you need to talk to her. Her name's Myra Belle Shirley. But she doesn't like anyone to remember her first name."

Mary Carolyn said the name a couple of times to herself to be sure she would remember it. "I guess I should have realized that she and Cole knew each other."

Clell looked at her consideringly. The scales needed to come off Mary Carolyn's eyes. "You could say that. About five years ago, she claimed she was going to have his baby."

"So she's his wife?" She had no idea Cole Younger was married.

Clell rolled his eyes. "Miss Myra Maybelle Shirley probably wouldn't get within spittin' distance of a preacher. And Cole Younger couldn't be bothered."

"But . . . but . . . the baby—"

"I heard Cole one time say it was a girl."

"Oh." Mary Carolyn stared hard at the door beyond the railing. One part of her was supremely shocked by what Clell had told her. Another part was barely able to keep from pressing her hand against her own flat stomach. Cold chills skittered up and down her spine. She felt a rising bubble of horror. She knew absolutely nothing about babies—except where they came from. And she and Clell could have already made a baby.

Why hadn't she thought of that? What would she do if such a thing had come to pass?

The events of her own youth played themselves out in her brain. Her own mother hiding her away, teaching her three new names in the short space of four years. Finally, her world had fallen apart. She had helped her red-faced mother pack her things. She had been put into a coach and driven away alone to the convent school. To the nuns and the strangers. Still, she had not known what was going to happen until days and weeks had gone by and her mother had not come.

She had never seen her mother again. She had never again seen anyone that mattered to her. A stranger in a house of strangers, she had never made friends with anyone again. Until Clell.

A tiny voice niggled at her. In a terrible sort of way, she could understand her mother now. At least a little. Her mother had been stupid as she herself had been stupid. Stupid. Stupid. She had lost control in Clell's arms. Suppose she had a baby inside her. Her throat was dry, her tongue seemed stuck to the roof of her mouth. She reached for the bottle and poured herself a shot of whiskey. "Where is the baby?"

"Probably she's got it farmed out somewhere."

He was looking at her curiously. She wondered if her face was white. Or red. Or if she looked no different in this murky room. She couldn't sort out the odors that assailed her nose or stung her eyes. Cigar smoke, kerosene from smoking lamps, beer, whiskey, and the all-pervasive sweat from unwashed bodies.

She became aware of the noise. A couple of men had taken Myra Belle's place on the small stage. One played the piano, the other a banjo. Mary Carolyn couldn't understand the words to their song, but evidently the rest of the crowd did. They were cheering and whooping. Rebel yells erupted at several tables.

She made a double fist around the shot glass. Far from being a palace, the saloon was the ugliest place she had ever been in. The dirt floor was inches deep in sawdust. The walls were smoke stained, the ceiling blackened. Men in filthy aprons, with their sleeves rolled up and no collars, bore foaming steins of beer and glasses of whiskey to the tables, collected coins, and brought back the empties.

"Seen enough?"

She heard his voice directly in her ear. His breath too smelled like the whiskey he had just drunk.

The crowd quieted, waiting for the end of the song.

> *"And I don't want no pardon for what I was and am,*
> *I won't be reconstructed, and—"*

Every male throat opened to belch out the last words.

> *"—I do not give a damn."*

She turned her face against his chest. "Yes."

"Damn you, Cole Younger." The black-haired woman lay with her white arms stretched above her head. Her long hair swirled like a horse's mane across the pillowcase. "You split my lip."

She ran her tongue over the wound. Despite the words, her voice was hoarse with satisfaction.

Cole grunted and rolled over on his side. His big hands reached out and hauled her to him. Her breasts were small, but the hard dark nipples pointing up from the smooth rosy brown aureoles excited him. He leaned over and bit one lightly. She gasped and clutched at his hair.

He raised his head. "Put them hands back around those bedposts, Belle, or I'll tie them up there."

She bared her teeth at him, but reached above her and caught at the wrought-iron curlicues. Grinning, he moved to the other breast, and she tensed. Instead of the pain she was expecting, he licked it and suckled it. Then he took a deep breath against her stomach. He could smell the sex rising from the bed. She was steaming hot.

He'd been little Myra Belle Shirley's first man, and in six years he'd never forgotten her. He had only just had her and already he wanted her again. He hoisted himself over her. "Open up."

Her jaw set stubbornly. She sucked her thin lips in between her teeth and gripped the iron behind her. The muscles flexed in her arms. She was a hot little bitch. He could almost feel the blood rushing through her veins. A bright flush stained the pale magnolia skin between her breasts.

"Open up, Belle!"

She tossed her head. The black hair swirled on the pillow. He had to bend low to catch the whisper. "Make me."

He grinned and slapped her. Her head snapped to the side. He slapped it back the other way. Not too hard. But not too lightly. He grinned as the red stains appeared beneath her skin. Then one hand gathered her meager breast to squeeze it so the tip stood up even higher.

"Open up," he warned.

She tensed. With a snarl he bit the hard nipple. She cried out. Her legs spread wide. He slid his hands in under her buttocks and pulled her hips up to him, then lunged forward, driving himself into her as far as he could go. She screamed. A full-blooded war whoop. A rebel yell.

He pumped inside her once, twice. Her white thighs closed round him. Her calves pulled him tighter. He couldn't move except into her. At the same time he felt the sucking of her womb.

Jesus Christ! She'd learned a thing or two since he'd been away.

It was his last conscious thought before he exploded. His lust sated, he slumped forward, his head pillowed on her breasts.

He was snoring before she eeled out from under him and hurried to douche herself with vinegar.

"We can't find hide nor hair of them. I swear they've crossed out of Iowa, but where they've gone to, nobody knows. Nobody's seen them in Missouri. Leastways nobody's talking. We've got agents at some of their relatives places."

"You've let them get away." Jehu Tull sat slumped on the haybale with his hands clasped between his knees. He was as tired as he had ever been in his life. And for what? Rather than capturing the James gang when they had the chance, the Pinkertons had insisted that they needed to chase them back into Missouri. The U.S. marshal had agreed. The Ottumwa sheriff and his deputies had turned back several counties ago.

All he could think of was that he had failed Mrs. Appleton. Poor lady. He had held out hope of finding her and rescuing her until that very moment. Now he could only hope she was dead. Poor, poor dear lady. He shook his head thinking about what she must have had to endure at the hands of Jesse James and Cole Younger.

"I'll offer a three thousand dollars reward," he said solemnly. "Dead."

The agent stared at him. "Yes, sir. I'll send that over the wires. Er . . . maybe you'd better head on back, Mr. Tull. You've done all you can. From now on we'll take over. But trust us. We're true to our motto. 'We never sleep.' We'll bring them all to justice."

DeGraffen Somervell read the paper and flung it aside with a disgusted snarl. According to the reporter, the James gang had simple vanished in the storm. The gallant lawmen had been in hot pursuit when the sky began to darken and the wind to howl. Soon icy pellets of sleet had turned to snow. They had been forced to turn back.

Somervell found the account highly fanciful, especially since the winter had been quite mild. He would bet a considerable amount of money if he were a betting man, that the detectives and U.S. marshals were making excuses to cover up their own incompetence. He hoped Allan Pinkerton was smart enough to recognize the story for what it was worth.

He had heard nothing from Roger. Perhaps a "storm" had delayed him too. Or perhaps he had decided to settle down to wait somewhere until his money ran out and then return with the sad story that he had been unable to find Mary Carolyn Ross.

Somervell consulted his calendar. The next few weeks were clear of all but the usual business of the bank. The assistant manager never had a chance to earn his wage anyway. He could begin tomorrow.

Tomorrow Somervell decided he would begin to institute his own search. Beginning with the James and Younger home places near Kansas City, Missouri. He had no doubt he could gather information with ease. Invariably people who were visited by a banker inquiring into the land deeds and payments became so nervous that they divulged any information he might request.

Mary Carolyn put on her nightdress behind the screen, then climbed into bed without looking at Clell. She huddled on the edge of the mattress as far from him as she could get and pulled the covers up around her ears.

He stripped down to his underwear, blew out the lamp, and climbed in beside her. He put his hand on her hip, but she shrugged him off. "Why don't you tell me what's wrong?"

"No."

She uttered the single syllable with more force than necessary. He could picture her with her mouth drawn down tight, her fists clenched. He thought about closing his eyes and trying to go to sleep. The street below the window was noisy. Cowhands fresh from the trail drives to the railhead were blowing off steam. From a couple of dance halls in the same block of Merchants Street, the music accompanied by cheers and applause dinned in his ears. Occasionally, a gunshot would punctuate the night.

He felt her tremble. The mattress was barely an inch thick. No more than the thickness of a couple of winter quilts slung across the coil springs. She was really upset.

He was a little surprised at the wave of concern that swept over him. He admitted to himself that he had come to like her—just a little bit. He had certainly gotten used to having her around. Once he wouldn't have believed that either she or any other woman could keep up with them. But she had. And she was willing. He'd never see a woman more willing to do for them.

In fact, Jesse used her like a servant. He had only to smile that devil's smile and ask her nicely and she would fetch like a slave. Billy Chadwell hung around her with a moony look on his face. Frank complimented her looks and every so often would remind Clell that he should be careful of her. Frank liked to quote some Englishman about a wife and children being "hostages to fortune." Since both Jesse and Frank had wives that only the Youngers had seen, the quotation carried no meaning whatsoever.

A tiny snubbing sound came from the other side of the bed. Clell raised his head. It didn't come again, but he could feel the faintest vibration of the mattress. "Are you crying?"

After a brief hesitation she answered "No" in a choked voice.

"You are." He rolled over and put a hand on her shoulder. "What's the matter?"

"Nothing." She drew away from him. "I'm all right. I think I've got a cold coming on."

But he was on to her. Paying no attention to her stiffness, he pulled her over on her back and put his arms around her. "Come on, Buster. You've slept out on the ground in snow and rain, and you've never had so much as a runny nose. Don't tell me you've caught a cold now that we're staying in a warm dry hotel."

She said nothing. Like a child she scrubbed the sleeve of her nightgown across her face.

Without thinking about what he was doing, he dropped a kiss on the top of her head. There was nothing sensual in it. Some long-forgotten memory of his mother guided him to do it. "Tell me what's wrong," he urged her. "You can tell me."

"Why didn't Cole Younger marry Myra Belle if she had his baby?"

So that was it. Clell thought about his answer. "Because I don't suppose either one of them wanted to get married. Or maybe she did. She wasn't much more than fifteen at the time. But her papa was too scared to come after Cole with a shotgun. Which is what he needed to do."

"But the baby. Didn't anybody think about the baby?" She was making no attempt to hide her tears now. Her voice sounded drowned.

Her distress tugged at Clell's heart. She needed reassurance. "I imagine Belle's got it someplace where it's being taken care of."

"But you don't know that," she whispered. Her voice had a tremor in it. He could tell she was in pain. "You don't know where that baby is. It's a child now. What if no one loves it?"

His mind was working fast. What things did he know about her? What had she said? "That's not very likely. A lot of babies with no fathers were around after the War. People stepped in and took care of them."

She gave a quick shake of her head. "You don't know that. A lot of them ended up in orphanages. Those are the worst places in the world."

So that was it. He had expected as much. Lots of orphaned children after the War. He would have been one if he hadn't been old enough to take care of himself. He sought to console her. "I can't imagine Cole Younger as a father."

For a long time she didn't say anything more. He was beginning to get sleepy. "How do you feel about being a father?"

Instantly, he was alert. All thoughts of sleep fled before the awful thought that she might be about to tell him something he didn't want to know. He had to stop himself from jumping out of bed, so upset did her question make him. He closed his eyes, trying to think about her body functions. They had been together now for almost two months. He knew she'd had two monthly flows because she'd had to ask him to take her into a general store to buy a couple of yards of unbleached domestic.

She had been washing them out only last weekend. She couldn't know she was carrying a baby. She couldn't be pregnant.

His sigh of relief was audible. "I guess I can manage that when the time comes."

She took a deep breath. "What if we were having baby?"

In the cold noisy silence of the rented room, he thought and thought about her question.

He might have kept on debating all night long except he realized she was holding her breath. Under his palm, her heart was thudding against her ribs. He came to a decision. He wouldn't make love to her anymore. Then he could afford to make her a promise that would relieve her mind.

"I'd marry you."

She swallowed hard. "Would you really?"

"Hell, yes. I wouldn't want any kid of mine to grow up without a father. I may be an outlaw, but I'm man enough to take responsibility for whatever I do." He kissed her again— just to reassure her. "But you're not having a baby. So don't start shopping for a white wedding dress yet."

"How do you know?" she asked.

"Humph! For a smart girl you sure are stupid." He hiked himself up in bed, resting his shoulders against the headboard. With the air of one imparting common knowledge to the ignorant, he told her all he knew about female bodies. His facts were sketchy. Once or twice he filled in with what he was sure was just pure common sense.

After all, he was repeating sections from a conversation overheard in the back hall of a brothel in Kansas City and supplementing it with his observations of mares, cows, and bitches. His crudities brought the hot blood flowing in her cheeks, but the information he provided sufficed to relieve her mind. "So now you know that you aren't," he finished. "So you can stop worrying."

She lay so long that he was pretty sure she had gone to sleep.

He eased himself down in the bed and closed his eyes. But his mind wouldn't stop. All that talk about a woman's body had set him to thinking about it—specifically about hers.

He cursed himself for ever picking her up and stealing her money after the train robbery. He cursed her for being there, warm and breathing, beside him. He cursed her smooth white skin, her soft breasts, the long delightful slope from the tips of those breasts down over her ribs and the flat plain of her belly to the pale thicket of hair between her legs.

Damn!

He was hard and aching. He couldn't make love to her anymore. She had reminded him all too vividly of the consequences.

He had to get rid of her and soon. Maybe he could just simply give her all the money from this robbery and buy her a ticket back to wherever she had come from.

On the other hand she'd all but told him she was an orphan and didn't have any place to go or anyone to go to. *Aw, hell!* She'd stick to him like glue.

She rolled over in bed. Her buttocks rubbed against his thigh.

With a curse, he flung back the covers and sprang out of bed.

She sat bolt upright. ''What's wrong?''

''Plenty!'' he snarled. He could see her pale shape in the darkness. He was stumbling around like a drunk in a dark alley trying to pull on his pants.

''Clell?'' Her voice was soft and doubtful. ''Have I done something wrong?''

Without bothering with his socks, he crammed his feet into his boots and pulled on his coat. If he buttoned it up, he wouldn't need a shirt. ''Hell, yes, there's something wrong. I haven't been thinking worth a damn. It's bad enough having you trailing around after me. With a big belly, you'd be three times as much trouble. And then—''

''But you said I wasn't . . . er . . .''

He bent over the bed to enunciate each word clearly, his face only inches from hers. ''And I'm going to be double-damned sure you don't get that way. Until I get you out of my hair for good, I'm going to keep way far away from you.''

"Oh." She sank back on the pillows, a hot blush rising in her cheeks.

"Yeah. Oh!" He jerked the edges of the coat together across his chest. "I'm going out. I'm going to get drunk. Go to sleep. If you know what's good for you, you'll be sound asleep on your side of the bed when I get back."

He stalked out and slammed the door behind him.

A couple of doors down Merchants Street, he bought a bottle of whiskey in a saloon and retreated to a dark corner to get drunk. A half-dozen fiery shots and he was still furiously angry. He couldn't think about anything but her and that made him even angrier. With the bottle in tow, he plunged out into the street. A couple of drunken cowboys reeled toward him. One was hanging on to the other's arm and laughing.

Clell stepped in front of them. They crashed into him.

"Sorry, mister." The one who could still walk fairly straight apologized blearily. "Didn't—"

"Watch what the hell you're doing," he yelled. "If you can't hold your liquor, don't drink."

They gaped at him. The laughing one looked at his companion. "Dosh 'e wanta fight, Dobie?"

"Sure looks thataway, Mick."

Clell laughed deep in his throat. With exaggerated care he set his bottle down behind the end of the horse trough. "You're—"

He never finished the sentence. Dobie and Mick swung at him. Mick's fist missed entirely, and he sprawled on the ground. Dobie, who was soberer, caught Clell flush on the chin. His teeth almost met in the end of his tongue as he staggered back.

Recovering himself, spitting blood, growling, he barreled into Dobie and drove him back against the sidewalk. Punching and jabbing, they rolled off into the street. Staggering up, Mick joined the free-for-all. Rather than run the risk of hitting his friend, he settled for kicking Clell in the side and hip.

Dobie's short jabs under Clell's heart knocked the breath out of him. Pain ripped through him like a knife as he felt at least one rib crack. He bucked up and rolled to try to get the

Texan underneath him. Mick swung his leg and knocked Clell's elbow out from under him. He fell back helpless with Dobie pummeling his sides like a madman.

The end was never in doubt. The Texans were vicious brawlers. Moreover they were laughing. His blows became weaker. At last he covered his face with his elbows and curled into a ball. While Dobie climbed to his feet, Mick delivered another fierce kick to the tip of Clell's spine.

Laughing and congratulating themselves, they caught the nearly unconscious Clell under the arms and doused him in the horse trough. Then picking up his bottle of whiskey, they passed it between them before sauntering on down the street.

Chapter Fourteen

Dressed in her boy's clothes, Mary Carolyn faced the Dallas streets. She wouldn't go to Jesse for help in finding Clell. They were supposed to be married, practically newlyweds. What would Jesse think if he found out Clell had stormed out of their bedroom and ended up . . . ? She didn't know where her outlaw had ended up.

Sometimes she forgot he was an outlaw. Other times such as now, he was unfathomable to her. He had told her several times, he was a bad man. She just had trouble believing it. She peered around the door of the Palace Saloon. The stink of the place first thing in the morning before it had a chance to air out was enough to gag a sow. Her eyes started to water.

The only person in sight was a black swamper. He had the spittoons lined up at the end of the bar. As she watched, he emptied one and then began to polish it with a rag balled up at the end of a long stick. He stared off into space as he performed the task. She supposed it was the only way he could get through it.

Holding her breath, she stepped inside the door and stared fixedly at the six rooms upstairs. She knew Cole Younger was up there, probably snoring away. Or maybe he was up. Mary

Carolyn tried without success to pull her mind away from the picture of Cole and the saloon singer wallowing in a rumpled bed. Was Clell behind one of those doors? Was the whole gang up there?

As if Mary Carolyn's thought had called her forth, one of the doors opened. The black-haired singer Myra Belle Shirley stepped out. At first, Mary Carolyn thought she was dressed in the same dress she had worn the night before. But as the woman came down the stairs, Mary Carolyn recognized her costume as a black velvet riding habit. On her left hip a pearl-handled pistol was belted to accommodate a cross-draw. She carried a man's Stetson with a black ostrich plume attached beneath the brim.

As she came down the stairs, she caught Mary Carolyn staring at her.

"The Palace is closed until Rex gets up." Her voice was a surprise. It seemed too deep for her small body.

"I—I don't want a drink."

Belle stopped. She blinked, then scanned the figure in front of her. "You're a woman?"

"Yes, ma'am. I'm Mary Carolyn . . . Miller."

"Don't call me ma'am. I'm too young to be a ma'am. Besides, I'm not married."

"No . . . er . . . no, Miss Shirley."

The woman came to stand beside her in the doorway. Even though the day was cold, the bright sun had melted the frost. Squinting, Belle clapped her hat on her head. "I go by Belle."

"Belle."

"Didn't I see you with Jesse's bunch last night?"

Mary Carolyn was a little surprised that Belle had noticed anything but Cole. "I ride with them. I'm married to Clell Miller."

That announcement did catch the other woman's attention. "Is that so? I heard that Jesse and Frank had gotten married, but I didn't know anybody else had."

The swamper finished the spittoons and came with the bucket. They had to stand aside for him to get out the door. Both women wrinkled their noses at the noxious odor. Mary Carolyn gagged.

Belle grunted. "I don't blame you. So you came in here with Jesse. I didn't think they'd take a woman into the gang."

"I'm married to Clell," Mary Carolyn repeated. Then she added carefully, "They find things for me to do."

Belle regarded her steadily. "They must be mellowing in their old age. Why don't you come for a ride with me? You can tell me all about it."

"I don't have a horse."

"You can borrow one of mine. Come on."

Mary Carolyn took one last look around and then followed her. As she walked down the street beside Belle Shirley, she had the feeling that a fire burned inside the smaller woman. With each step, her boot heels thwacked the boards. Her ostrich plume fluttered in the breeze. Her black velvet skirt, caught up over her left arm, flowed around her like a royal gown. The people in her path cleared out of her way.

At the livery stable she called out, "Saddle Lady Grace for my friend here. You'll like her. She's got a gait like a rocking chair. I'll ride Venus."

The ostler grimaced. The two boys lounging on the hay bales looked at each other. With an air of resignation, they disappeared into the stable. The ostler went with them. In less than a minute, he returned leading a pretty black mare with four white stockings and a white race down her nose. Her dainty dishface proclaimed a touch of Arabian.

"Oh, she's beautiful," Mary Carolyn exclaimed.

Belle looked pleased. "Wait till you try her. You won't want to get off."

"Oh, is she for me?"

Belle smiled. "I like to ride a real horse."

From inside the stable came a grunt and an outraged whinny. Iron-shod hooves stomped the ground. A loud crash accompanied a splintering of wood. Mary Carolyn jumped and stared into the dark interior. Belle remained unfazed. From within, the ostler's commands were punctuated with foul curses.

Finally, he and the stableboys led out a raven black stallion.

A giant of a horse, he was fully sixteen hands high. The two stableboys kept his head under tight reins. As he came into the bright sunlight, he snorted and kicked out with his hindquarters. The ostler waited until he came down, then ducked out the door and moved in on the animal's left side to boost Belle into the saddle.

She grinned at Mary Carolyn's openmouthed amazement. "This is Venus. Not the Goddess of Love, but the planet. The evening star. Isn't he a beauty?"

Mary Carolyn could only nod.

Belle went to the horse's head. As she raised her black-gloved hand past his muzzle, he snapped. Mary Carolyn cringed, but Belle laughed and rubbed his nose. Her hand slid up the shiny black face over the perfect four-pointed white star. She caught his forelock and pulled his handsome head down. "You're a beauty, aren't you? And you know it, don't you, you vicious son-of-a-bitch? I ought to sell you for crowbait. And I will if you ever put those teeth in me."

Her deep voice gave the lie to the words. It flowed over the stallion, quieting him, until he stood perfectly still. His ears flicked forward. He nuzzled at her hand. She let the black skirt fall to the dust and produced a small apple. As soon as it left her pocket, the stud reached for it and lipped it up.

While he chewed, Belle mounted. The stable boys waited. "Let 'im go!"

On a silent count of three, they both jumped back.

"Eeeeee-haw!" Belle slapped her quirt on the blue-black shoulder. The stallion half-rose, then sprang away with all the bunched strength of his powerful hindquarters.

Mary Carolyn watched in awe as Venus tore down the Dallas street. The pair made a sight to behold. Belle sat perfectly balanced in the sidesaddle, dressed in black velvet and ostrich plumes. Almost to the end of the street, the shining black stallion kicked up his heels and buck-jumped, curvetted in a circle and tried to pull the reins out of her hand. She hit him with the quirt. He shook his head and laid his ears back. His teeth champed the bit.

Finally, he seemed convinced that the rider could not be

unseated. She turned his head away from the stable and tapped his shoulder with the quirt. Venus took off like a race horse.

Mary Carolyn dug her heels into Lady Grace's sides and galloped after in their dust.

"So tell me how you happened to meet up with Clell Miller." Belle Shirley said. They had galloped across the bridge over the Trinity River and now allowed their horses to drink from Kidd Springs, an artesian springs a couple of miles south and west of the river.

Mary Carolyn hesitated. Out of the sun, in the shade of a pair of live oaks, the January day was bitterly cold. She shivered as she tried to decide what to say. No one had asked how they happened to meet. She had not thought about a story since the James gang accepted the lie about their marriage. At length she said, "We met on a train."

Her companion raised her sooty eyebrows. "On a train, huh? Was he robbing it?"

The frank question, delivered without a trace of recrimination, made Mary Carolyn wonder if here was the one person to whom she could tell the whole truth. Better not. No one needed to know that except Clell and her. She would only embarrass herself by pouring out her heart. Moreover, this woman was a lover of Cole Younger. If he ever doubted the marriage, he would delight in tormenting them both. No, the truth would be dangerous.

She plastered a smile on her mouth. "Not that time."

Belle smiled in return. "And has he since?"

Mary Carolyn frowned. Was Belle Shirley trying to pump her for information? How much did she really know about the saloon singer? Only what Clell had told her when he admitted he hadn't seen her in years. She decided to tell Belle nothing. "Whatever Cole Younger told you is probably pretty close to the truth."

The woman in black laughed nastily. "Cole Younger would lie when the truth would do better. He'd lie to his own mother. In fact, he probably has. He's lied to me often enough. I was just wondering why he doesn't have anything good to say about you.''

Mary Carolyn could imagine some of the things Cole had said. If he had said them to make Belle jealous, nothing she could say would make any difference. She looked at the clear icy water bubbling from the nearby springs. The bright sunlight had fooled her. She should have worn her gloves.

At last Belle seemed to relax. ''I can see why he doesn't like you. Cole doesn't like anyone he can't bully. And you're closemouthed as well,'' she said approvingly. ''How old are you?''

''Seventeen.''

''A baby. But you're sure old enough to be married.''

Mary Carolyn wished the conversation were over. She should never have come in the first place. She wondered where Clell was. She looked back in the direction of the Trinity River.

''That must be what the gang keeps you around for,'' Belle ruminated. ''Are you really married to Clell?''

''Yes.'' She could deliver that lie with authority. She had said it so often, she almost believed it herself.

Belle pulled Venus's head up. Interrupted in eating a clump of dry grass, he tossed his head up and down and pulled at the rein. ''I haven't married yet.''

In a burst of inspiration to end the talk, Mary Carolyn posed a rude question. ''Why not?''

Belle must have recognized it for what it was, for she made a wry face. With a nod of acceptance, she tapped Venus's shoulder with her quirt and reined him back down the road. They rode for a few minutes at a brisk walk; then she cleared her throat. The sadness in her voice struck a chord in Mary Carolyn. ''I've never been asked. By the right person, that is.''

As they walked the horses over the bridge into Dallas, Belle pulled Venus to a halt and rested her arm on her cocked knee. With the air of one imparting the wisdom of the ages, she looked Mary Carolyn straight in the eye.

''A woman who loves an outlaw is just asking for a heap of trouble. And she has to love trouble. On the good days it's like fire in the blood, and on the bad days it's like ice. The bad days come about three hundred and sixty days a year. Married, I don't know about. But I imagine it's a whole lot of being alone and pregnant. And never knowing when you're going to open up the newspaper and read that your husband is dead or in jail or condemned to hang in Judge Parker's court.

"I sure as hell wouldn't want any of that, thank you very much. And as for romance." She snorted and looked around in a mockery of searching. "Jesse and Frank are both married. I don't see Zee and Annie having a picnic with us."

"I'm not pregnant." Mary Carolyn could feel hot blood in her cheeks. She was discussing something very personal with a stranger. But she wanted to set the record straight. Moreover, her certainty showed in her voice. The conversation last night had eased her fears.

"You won't be long in getting that way," Belle observed with vicious sarcasm. The anger in her voice was the diametrical opposite of the sadness of a few moments ago. "Loving an outlaw and riding with him doesn't last very long. That's the hell of being a woman. A few nights of paradise and we're burdened for the next nine months. Men have it all over us. Sometimes I hate every single one of them. Damn their eyes!"

Mary Carolyn reached down to pat Lady Grace's shining neck. She wondered how Belle would react if she were told she was a dime-novel temptress come to life. Her hair was raven black, her eyes flashed passionately, her complexion was somewhat olive. Mary Carolyn wondered if Belle had a bullet waiting for Cole Younger, the way Cherokee Sue did in *Wild Ivan; or, The Brotherhood of Death*.

Somehow, she doubted it. She wondered more about their child. Where was the little girl? Did she cry at night for her mother? The rude question she longed to ask was burning on her tongue. She couldn't bring herself to ask it, especially of this woman who had been kind to her. But Belle had said she wasn't married. The shame would be greater if an illegitimate baby was hidden somewhere.

All she could bring herself to say was, "I'm sorry."

Belle muttered a vile word under her breath as she kicked

Venus in the barrel. The big black trotted down the street with all his flags flying.

In front of the hotel, Mary Carolyn sawed back on her horse's reins. "Clell!"

Her outlaw had thrown one arm around one of the posts supporting the porch and balcony of their hotel. He was so badly damaged that she could only stare in shock. The side of his jaw swelled out deforming the whole side of his face. One eye was a slit in a mound of purple flesh. When he saw her, he tried to straighten.

He was in too much pain. His face contorted and he slumped back, listing to the side. A filthy hand, the knuckles swollen and scabbed over, was pressed against his ribs. His clothes were caked with mud and other things as if he had rolled in the streets.

"Did someone beat you up?" she cried and then felt like a fool. Of course, he had been beaten up. He could barely stand.

He mumbled something unintelligible.

Belle had looked over her shoulder and seen Mary Carolyn stop. Now she came cantering back down the street. She saw him and laughed. "Whooo-eee, Clell. Looks like you bit off more than you could chew."

Mary Carolyn started to climb down, but Belle caught her by the arm. "I wouldn't if I were you."

"But he's hurt. He's all bloody and swollen."

Belle surveyed him with a practiced eye. "Looks like it happened hours ago. He'd already be dead if he was going to die."

"But . . ." Mary Carolyn's own stomach was clenched in a painful knot at the sight of his condition. A vagrant breeze carried the scent of whiskey and sour vomit to her. He was filthy as a hog.

Belle obviously saw nothing to be concerned about. "Who'd you pick a fight with, big boy? Some Texas drovers?"

He managed a rictus of a grin, even though it must have pulled his face and jaw painfully. "Yeah."

Mary Carolyn looked from one to the other in amazement.

He was actually smiling. And far from showing any sympathy, Belle appeared to think Clell's pitiful condition was funny.

" 'Cause you're a son-of-a bitch."

He licked his bruised lips. The swollen eye closed. From its corner a bead of pinkish liquid trickled down his filthy cheek. "That's about the size of it."

"Need any help?"

He looked at Mary Carolyn. Something flickered in the one good eye. Then he hung his head. "No."

Mary Carolyn stopped trying to get down off her horse. Belle let go of her arm and folded her hands over her knee. "Why don't you go get a bath and a shave? Put on some clean clothes and come around when you're decent. Come, Mrs. Miller. We ladies will have breakfast in the Palace."

She turned Venus back down the street. Mary Carolyn looked at Clell a minute longer. He shook his head. The motion must have made him sick at his stomach because he tipped farther over the porch railing. Rather than wait to see whether he could control himself or not, she swung Lady Grace's head around and trotted down the street.

To her surprise, when she caught up, she found Belle was laughing. "Did you all have a fight last night?"

"Not really. No, I couldn't say we had a fight."

"Did you have a tussle?"

"No. That is, I . . ." Suddenly, Mary Carolyn realized what sort of tussle she was referring to. "No. We didn't. We just discussed"—she gulped—"having a baby."

Belle choked and then hid her mouth behind her hand. "And what did he say to that?"

"Well, he told me I couldn't be . . . er . . . going to have a baby. He explained why." Mary Carolyn knew her cheeks must be bright red. "And then he said he wouldn't . . . er . . . that is . . . anymore." She faltered to a stop.

Belle put back her head and whooped with laughter. "No wonder he acted like a jackass." She sobered. "I wish I'd had that conversation with Cole Younger when I was fifteen. But, of course, Pearl's been the light of my mother's life. And mine too. So I guess it all turned out all right."

"I don't understand." Mary Carolyn was proud of the fact that she didn't blink or stammer. Of course, Belle hadn't actually said that she had had Cole Younger's child, but the implication was pretty clear. Why wasn't she ashamed? Why wasn't her daughter being put away in some convent? Instead, Belle had actually said her mother was raising her daughter. Where was the "living death of a fallen woman" the dime novels talked about?

She longed to ask, but Belle's mind was on things other than the fact that she had revealed that she had borne a child out of wedlock. She watched as Clell staggered off down the street in the direction of the bathhouse. Belle shook her head in wonder. "He must really love you, honey. You've got him on the ropes."

Mary Carolyn didn't think she had Clell on the ropes.

The women had finished breakfast and the table had been cleared when he came in. His body was damp and smelling of bay rum. His clothing was cleaned. His hair was wet and slicked back. Still, he moved like an old man. He used his toe to pull out a chair because his hands were too swollen. He looked like he'd been through hell, but at least he didn't stink.

"Eggs, bacon, hominy?" Belle offered sweetly.

He looked at her from out of his raw face. "Coffee."

She signaled to the waiter, who came and set a mug and the pot in front of Clell. Then she smiled at Mary Carolyn. "I'll leave you two to discuss this between yourselves." She put her hand on Clell's wrist. "You've got a sweet girl here. Treat her right or you'll answer to me."

When she was out of earshot, Mary Carolyn leaned forward. "Clell, what happened?"

He tried to sip his coffee, but his mouth was so badly swollen it dribbled out of the side. Scalding hot, it burned his tender flesh. He set it down and cursed in an exhausted way.

Mary Carolyn could only imagine how much he must be hurting. "Would you like me to help you to bed?"

He nodded slowly.

"Come on." She came around to his chair and helped him out of it. With her arm around his back, she walked him down the street and up to their room. There she helped him remove his coat and hat. With a sigh he stretched out. She pulled off his boots and covered him with a couple of quilts. Then she sat down on her side of the bed.

"What are you looking at?" he mumbled.

She shook her head. "I don't know. I thought I did, but I don't know you at all."

He turned his face away. "I'm a bad man. Get the hell out of here and leave me alone."

"Soon." She took his badly swollen left hand between her own. Gently, she traced the bruises and abrasions with the tip of her finger. "Why did you do this?"

"Men just go crazy sometimes," he said after a long moment.

"Was it about the baby?"

"Hell, yes, it was about the baby. We're not married. Even though we've been playing house for two months now, we're not married." His steel blue eyes leaped out at her from the red streaked whites. "We're not married. You're not my responsibility. All you want is your money. I wish to God I'd never seen it. But I swear I'll get you up there to that tree and give it to you. You can have it all."

"You got drunk and picked a fight because there wasn't any baby, and you wished you could give me the money?"

"Oh, hell, no." He tried to sit up, but his body was so sore that it had stiffened up on him. He clenched his fists, and they hurt. He slumped back and cursed.

"Don't curse. Tell me why you did this. I want to understand." At that minute she could believe that she was almost as miserable as he was.

"I'm an outlaw with a price on my head. I'm a member of the James gang. When I'm caught—and it's just a matter of time until I will be—I'll be in jail for the rest of my life if I'm lucky. I'm not going to marry you. And that's my final word on it. And I sure don't want you to have a baby." He stared bleakly at the ceiling. "You're an outlaw too. If they catch you, they'll send you to prison. If you had a baby, who'd take care of it?''

She shuddered. ''An orphanage.''

''Smart girl.'' He stared at the roof above his head. The second-story hotel room didn't even have a ceiling. Then he looked at her. He licked his abused lips. ''But that doesn't mean I don't want to screw you to the headboard every damn time I look at you.''

She gasped at his coarseness. Embarrassment brought the blood to her cheeks at the same time self-awareness set a throbbing heat deep in her belly. She had asked, but she'd never expected him to say something like that. Outlaws in books never, never did.

A cold wind slanted the icicles off the water tower twenty miles north of Kansas City. In the dead of night, a special train consisting of an engine, a club car, a cattle car, and a caboose rolled onto a remote siding.

It had not ground to a complete stop before a dozen heavily armed men leaped down. They slid the doors back on the cattle car and pulled the ramp down. Like a trained corps, they led their horses down. Still operating without orders, they tightened the saddle girths, slipped the bits into the horses' mouths, and swung into their saddles.

Elsdon Crown, the leader, counted his men. With a wave of his hand, he turned his horse and led them away across the countryside at a fast lope. Muffled to the eyes, with greatcoats flapping, they looked like spectral horsemen on the devil's wild hunt.

At the crossroads outside of Kearney, they met their spy. Months ago he had hired on at the farm across the road from the James place. Now he made his report. With their horses' heads like spokes in a wheel, and the white fogbreath rising like a plume from the center, they planned their operation.

''They're there,'' the spy assured them in a whisper. ''They've been riding in one at a time and in pairs, but I know they're there.''

"It won't make any difference if they're not." Crown raised his voice so the men could hear. "Nothing like rousting a family out of their warm beds to throw a scare into 'em. Get 'em scared enough and they'll start complaining. The gang'll want revenge. They'll get mad and careless."

"I don't know as that's such a good idea," the spy objected. "They're good people. The old man's the town doctor and a part-time minister. There's just him and his wife and the little boy."

Crown had his speech ready for the newspapers. He practiced it in ringing tones. "The whole state has hidden outlaws and bushwhackers for years. But the new governor doesn't want it anymore. This'll send a message to everybody. We mean business, and they'd better get back on the right side of the law. Pinkerton is going to straighten out the state of Missouri. The governor wants it. The President wants it. And so does the boss. Let's get this started before we get any colder."

The last sentence stifled the spy's objections. Crown reined his horse forward, breaking the circle. Once he was in the clear, he broke into a trot. The spy joined him to lead the way. The detectives followed two by two.

Chapter Fifteen

On Saturday night Belle Shirley stood in the center of the Palace Saloon's small stage. Instead of accompanying herself, she had hired another musician to play while she sang.

In place of her habitual black velvet, she wore a low-necked white satin bodice with swagged sleeves that hung off her ivory shoulders. It fitted smoothly over her rib cage and descended to a V over her flat stomach. A black velvet skirt, the only familar garment in her costume, was overlaid with six white satin panels. Each ended in a point just below the knee from which hung a white satin tassel.

Around her neck she wore a gold locket on a white velvet ribbon. Gold hoop earrings dangled from her earlobes.

Her long black hair was braided through with white satin ribbons and coiled at the back of her head. She had added an unusual touch of artifice, for she had powdered her face and lightly rouged her cheeks and lips. For a woman who despised mirrors, she had obviously put one to good use. She smiled at the audience and bowed her head graciously as she acknowledged their welcoming applause.

The James gang occupied a large table front and center. Cole

Younger sat closest to the stage, his eyes half-closed, his face intent as Belle began to sing.

At first, Mary Carolyn had refused to come with them. Clell's voiced dislike still made her a little ill. Alone in their room she had counted her share from the Bank of Ottumwa. Back in the orphanage, she would have thought it a fortune.

Now the realities of how much money she needed to live preyed upon her mind. She could live six months, maybe even a year if she lived very frugally. But then what would she do? She was a woman. Women married, or they stayed at home and took care of their parents. Then they turned their homes into boarding houses. A few might find work in shops if they could sew. Some might become schoolteachers, but they were educated. Some with great talent and nerve might sing and play piano on the stage as Belle Shirley did.

Mary Carolyn Ross had nothing. No chance. No education beyond the ability to read and write and do simple sums. She could not sew or cook or sing. She needed the money she had stolen from the Chicago, Rock Island. She would keep out of Clell's way as much as possible and at the same time hold him to his promise.

And then they would go their separate ways. Why did the thought hurt so much? Because those cursed dime novels had misled her with a romantic dream. She had thought that her outlaw would fall in love with her. The fact of the matter was he didn't love her at all. He hated her. He cursed her. He didn't even want her near him.

And she? She didn't know. She had thought the tenderness she felt for him along with the burning passion was love. She had thought the natural ending for their lovemaking was a declaration and a proposal.

Now she sat beside him, carefully turned half away from him, as he was from her. On the table in front of her, a beer was slowly going flat. He stared at his whiskey. His bruised eyes burned in his swollen face. Every so often—too often— he took a sip.

Reluctantly, music and song brought Mary Carolyn out of her depression. Belle was singing a stanza and chorus of a popular ditty. The audience laughed appreciatively as she tapped her toe in time to the pianist's interlude.

> *"Madam, I have gold and silver.*
> *Madam, I have a house and land.*
> *Madam, I have a world of plenty.*
> *It'll be yours at your command."*

Then the smoky contralto welled again without any effort from the small body. In lilting three-quarter time Belle swayed to the music. She tilted her head and smiled at Cole Younger. For once the card games had halted, and the conversation remained at a discreet hum or ceased altogether. The Belle Shirley who sang that night sang from her heart.

> *"What care I for your gold and silver?*
> *What care I for you house and land?*
> *What care I for your world of plenty?*
> *All I want is a handsome man."*

She tilted her chin and snapped her fingers as if to send her would-be lover on his way. The gang laughed. Billy Chadwell leaned forward and poked his finger into the middle of Cole's back. The older man threw a ferocious scowl over his shoulder. Chadwell grinned and shook his finger.

Mary Carolyn leaned to whisper in Clell's ear. "Sounds like you were right."

He nodded slowly. "Sure sounds like she's sending him a message. The only question is whether he ever asked her to begin with. I'm betting he never did."

Mary Carolyn sat back. In her mind she turned over the problem of Belle Shirley and Cole Younger. If he had known her a long time ago and hadn't been able to forget her, why didn't they marry?

Likewise, if Pearl, whom Belle had spoken so lovingly of, was Cole's child, then why didn't he care? Why wasn't he stepping forward to give the child a name and a decent place in society?

Mary Carolyn shivered, and the room around her seemed to fade away. She didn't know the answer to that herself. She had never known her father. She and her mother had lived alone. Now that she thought back, her mother's life had not seemed "the living death of the fallen woman." Then her mother had sent her away. As it always did, the memory brought tears to her eyes. Why had she been sent away? At least Pearl had a grandmother who thought she was the "light of her life."

Whoops and hollers erupted from the audience when Belle's saucy song ended. Men at the bar pounded on its oak surface. Only Cole retained his scowl.

Belle caught his eye, but her expression never changed. She curtsied elaborately to the audience and signaled to the pianist. Half-a-dozen songs later she joined the gang who stumbled to their feet, pushing back their chairs noisily. Jesse bowed gallantly and offered her his chair beside Cole. With a flirtatious smile, she shook her head. Frank had already risen to fetch another one. When he returned, she took a seat between him and his brother.

Cole Younger's face was a study. In the grip of strong emotions, his skin darkened. His eyes narrowed. Then he managed a thin smile. "Champagne for the lady!" he called. "Hell! Drinks all around!"

When they were brought, Belle ordered another glass to be poured for Mary Carolyn. "Take away that stale beer," she ordered the waiter. Then she laughed and slapped the man nearest her on the shoulder. "I've got a bone to pick with you, Jesse James. She's the first lady member of your gang. How come you never asked me to join?"

He poured himself a glass of whiskey from the new bottle and watered it from the pitcher. "Well, I'm sorry about that, Belle." His handsome grin flashed around his circle. "But that was a long time ago. Times have changed. Gals have got all sorts of notions now besides having babies—"

"Watch it, Jesse." Frank's warning came just too late.

An embarrassed silence fell. High color came and went in Belle's face. Cole scowled. Jesse's eyes blinked furiously as he cursed himself. The others tucked their heads down or looked sheepishly around the circle. Only Mary Carolyn looked across the table and nodded. She put into her smile all the support, all the encouragement she could muster.

Belle smiled and nodded as if the two of them shared a secret before she said softly, ''I didn't plan to have a baby, Jesse.'' Then her voice strengthened. ''Of course, a lot of fifteen-year-old girls do. But not me. I wanted to ride with the James gang. Why should women be left behind while the men have all the fun?'' She lifted her champagne glass. Her eyes met Mary Carolyn's across the table. ''To outlaws.''

The men hesitated, trying to figure out whether or not she was mad or hurt or embarrassed.

Only Mary Carolyn understood her perfectly. She wondered what it would be like to have Belle Shirley for a friend. Her own bleak thoughts had driven her inevitably to the conclusion that men and women could never be friends. She caught up the glass of champagne that Belle had ordered for her. ''To outlaws.''

The Pinkertons walked their horses down the lane. Chased by a chilling wind, black clouds scudded across the sliver of moon. The stars shone a billion miles away, too cold to send the least bit of light.

When the men could see the white clapboard front of the house, they dismounted. Without command they fanned out, completely surrounding the silent farmstead. With luck they would be stationed inside a circle with a fifty-foot radius before their quarry knew they were there. Rifles and shotguns would be cocked, ready to mow down anyone who didn't come out with his hands up.

A faint glow showed through several windows, evidence that fires banked for the night were warming sleepers in those rooms.

When they were all in position, Elsdon Crown, the agent in charge, used a tin clicker to pass the signal around the circle. On the front porch a liver-spot coonhound's eyes opened. His ears lifted. Crown and the Pinkerton spy moved forward, dry leaves rustling under their feet. The hound's head snapped up.

Borne on the cold air, the scents of three Pinkerton agents hit him full in the face. He threw his muzzle to the stars and sent his hoarse bugle ringing to the night sky. His companion, a female, sprang to her feet and began a harsh chopping bark.

Inside the house the glow in one of the rooms became brighter. Someone had turned up a bedside lamp.

Crown cursed the spy. "You didn't mention the dogs."

The spy didn't dare to answer. He had made a stupid blunder.

The light rose and moved from one room to another. It grew brighter lower down as if someone had stirred up a fire. The silhouette of a man passed in front of the window. A slighter figure followed it. And one even smaller.

"Gabriel! Dinah!" The man's voice could be heard yelling at the hounds. Light held high, he moved into another room, coming toward the front of the house. The animals stopped their belling and scrambled to the edge of the porch. Their heads whipped from side to side. Their nostrils dilated as they located the various agents by their scents.

Intent on smoking everybody out the front door, Crown ran forward and flung a heavy object at the lighted back window. With a crash the glass shattered to smithereens. A woman screamed.

A moment later a boy's high voice cried, "I've got it, Maw!"

"Archie, get away from there."

Then the interior of the house exploded. The agents on two sides of the structure fell back as flying window glass and pieces of wood slashed toward their faces.

"Don't take what Belle Shirley says seriously."

Clell caught Mary Carolyn by the waist and pulled her off the sidewalk and into the doorway of a general store. The James gang, happy and drunk, wove its way down the street, with Belle leading them in song. After her last song at the Palace, they had moved to the Mustang, then to the Arrowhead. Now they were out on the streets again.

A wave of longing went through Mary Carolyn as one long arm squeezed her waist, the other wrapped across the front of her shoulders. She was dragged backward against his tall familiar body. She could barely stifle the desire to turn in his arms and press her mouth to his, to flatten her breasts against his chest, to grind her hips against his maleness.

She ached for him. Ached and burned for Clell Miller. And she hated him. He had taken her money and her virginity. He had taken her heart; and, just when she thought someone might care for her, he had rejected her.

"I thought she made perfect sense." Her voice was so hoarse the words came out in a growl.

"You would." His hands clenched, bruising where they gripped flesh.

"Women ought to be able to steal a few dollars for themselves. We can't do anything else to earn a living"—she paused a second letting her words sink in on him—"except whore."

He let her go. Or rather he wrenched himself away from her and stepped out into the street. His hands on his hips, he leaned back looking up at the cold stars in the Texas night sky. "You don't know what you're talking about," he threw over his shoulder. "You read those stupid dime novels and think this is a game."

In the absolute darkness of the doorway, she pressed her hands against her breasts. Beneath her clothing her nipples were aching, her breasts hard. She could feel a heat and heaviness at the juncture of her thighs. She sucked in a deep breath. He would not know. He would never know.

"The dime novels don't have anything to do with real life. You've made sure I know that." She sauntered out onto the sidewalk beside him. "I also know that there's not a thing in this whole, wide world I can do," she told him flatly. "Oh, I could be somebody's maid and clean out his dust and dirt. Or wash his filthy laundry. But I can't sing and play the piano to entertain him like Belle. I can't sew and make dresses for his wife or trim her hats."

"There's plenty you can do," he argued.

"I can steal," she agreed sweetly. "I stole a safe full of money from a train. And I helped rob a bank."

"Luck," he repeated. "You got lucky the first time. And

it's gone to your silly little head. Even getting shot in the butt didn't teach you anything. If you keep on, the next time you could get a horse shot out from under you like Jim Pool except you'll be caught and go to jail. Or you could stop a bullet like I did except it'll be an inch lower. In which case it won't matter anyway cause you'll be dead.''

She knew he was going to argue with her again. And what he said was the truth, but he didn't understand. And she wasn't going to try to make him understand. She was afraid he might pity her because she wanted him so desperately. ''Why don't you find somebody else to listen to your lecture on what it takes to be an outlaw?'' she suggested sarcastically. ''What happens to me isn't any concern of yours any longer. You and Cole Younger have had your fun. He even knows he's got a daughter, but he hasn't once asked to see her. Poor little thing. She's better off. Once you give me that money, then you don't ever need to see me again.''

He swung around to face her. Fortunately, she couldn't see his face in the shadow, but she could imagine how angry he must be from the heaviness of his breathing. ''You don't know what you're talking about. But let me tell you. If I had a way to get that money tonight, I'd ram it down your throat. I was just trying to warn you. Belle Shirley's just talking crazy because she's mad at Cole. She's trying to show him that she doesn't care, and she really does. She doesn't want to be an outlaw.''

''In your mind no one wants to be an outlaw,'' Mary Carolyn scoffed. ''I've never seen anyone so blind.'' She pointed to the reeling, swaying figures. ''Look at them. Open your eyes and look at them! Every one of the gang wants to be an outlaw. They're having the time of their lives.''

From farther up he street, the sound of raucous laughter reached their ears. Light spilled out of a door as Frank James opened it and ushered them all in ahead of him. He looked back over his shoulder and waved at Clell and Mary Carolyn.

Buster waved back, then pulled her hat down more securely on her forehead. ''Now, if you'll just get out of my way, I'll catch up to them. I was having the time of my life until you pulled me into that doorway to give me a temperance lecture.''

He looked like he wanted to grab her and drag her away. His shoulders actually flexed. Then, with an exaggerated bow, he stepped aside. She pushed past him and ran up the street. Her boot heels sounded as loud as thunderclaps in her ears.

Clell knew he had said everything badly. *But damn it all!* She was falling deeper and deeper into the outlaw trap. He knew because he'd been there himself. He'd idolized William Clarke Quantrill. He'd rushed to join him when he was just sixteen years old.

He'd taken part in the raid on Lawrence. And the nightmares had begun. At first, he'd believed all the excuses and all the lies. He'd even believed he'd get over them. But from guerrilla to outlaw was an easy slide down a very slippery slope. He'd been trapped.

And she was about to be too. She didn't realize that Belle Shirley really was as immoral as a woman could be. He didn't doubt that she was filling Mary Carolyn full of bull in the hopes she'd pass it on to Cole.

Hell! Cole was probably right not to marry her. He couldn't be sure the child was his. Clell toyed with the idea of telling Mary Carolyn that Belle'd had a second child she was keeping mum about. He didn't think she'd bothered to marry Jim Reed either.

He took a deep breath of the cold Texas air. Then he resolved, like Pontius Pilate, to wash his hands of Miss Mary Carolyn Ross. He'd take her back to get her money and then say good riddance. He'd tell Jesse he was leaving the gang because he'd had a fight with his wife. That was the one excuse Jesse just might accept.

The thought comforted him. It was the closest he'd been to truth in a long time.

* * *

The cold morning light revealed the aftermath of the Pinkerton raid in horrifying detail. The shots and the explosion had brought the neighbors at first light. Dr. Samuel had already dispatched a hired hand for the county sheriff. The man made it his business to stop at every farm along the way.

From four miles away in Kearney, people came to view the carnage. Friends and neighbors as well as the entire congregation of the Methodist Church of Kearney, where Dr. Samuel sometimes preached, had gathered on the front porch and under the trees.

"You get off a-here," Deacon Robertson ordered the agents, brandishing his walking stick. "You ain't welcome here."

"We came to arrest Jesse James," Crown insisted doggedly.

"He ain't here," Robertson snarled, making his stick sing in the air as he drove the agents back. "He ain't never been here. This is a God-fearing household. These are God-fearing people."

At the mention of her outlaw son, Zerelda James Samuel began to weep and wail.

Crown hunched his shoulders as the woman's grief, and anger crashed over him. He couldn't blame her. He himself had seen the charred ruin of the kitchen. The interior of the farmhouse had been wet down to keep the fire from spreading. It stank of smoke and kerosene.

But why, in God's name, hadn't the good women taken her away to one of their homes? No one expected her to stay here. On the front porch her neighbors had set up a bed from which the doctor tended her mutilated arm.

He was just about to offer that a couple of his agents would be glad to move her when one of his men came running with news that made his blood chill.

A reporter from the *Kansas City Times* had just driven up in a buggy. He and his photographer had had to tie their horses at the neighbor's farm. The lane was crowded with vehicles and horses and people.

Crown saw them coming. One had his notebook out and was scribbling furiously as he walked. The other was burdened by his photography equipment. Crown rushed to meet them to try to head them off with an explanation.

The irony of the situation was that he himself had notified them. He had told them they would be able to report the capture and arrest of the James gang. Instead, they were going to find quite another story. The thought of Allan Pinkerton's reaction to the story and photographs made Crown sweat.

"Archie, my poor Archie," Zerelda James Samuel called, her voice strong but hoarse, as the two men approached. The women from Dr. Samuel's Missionary Society tried to console her. With much weeping and praying, they had washed and dressed the stark, cold body of her last son.

Archie Samuel, Jesse's half brother, had been wrapped in a black and white "tree of life" quilt and laid out on a door at the other end of the porch. Bare to the world was his little face, all twisted in a rigor of death. A fragment from the grenade had blown a jagged hole in his neck.

The reporter began to talk to the men gathered around.

"Looks like Vicksburg in that there kitchen," one man opined grimly. "Poor little boy. That grenade sure got him."

"Hellsfire! I was in St. Louis the day when that Yankee bastard Lyon had his men kill all them unarmed civilians. I didn't see nothing that was no worse than this." A second man wearing an old Confederate kepi crossed his arms over his chest and glared at the Pinkerton agents.

They ranged along the rail fence beyond the front yard and off the property. All the people spoke in carrying tones intended for their ears. The agents could see the glares and stares and the fingers pointing at them. Cold, frustrated, and wishing fervently they were someplace else, they arranged themselves so that they guarded each other's backs.

"It wasn't a grenade," Crown hurried to deny. "It was a flare. I don't know what happened. It was supposed to make the inside of the room light enough to see." He willed the reporter to understand and believe him. "That's so we wouldn't shoot anybody by mistake, don't you know? I swear to God I don't know how this happened. It was just an accident."

The man from the *Times* dutifully wrote down the explanation while the newspaper photographer set up his camera and took their picture. While Crown ground his teeth, the photographer also took a picture of Mrs. Samuel as she knelt by Archie's side, the white bandages on her arm prominently displayed. Then he disappeared into the house to take a picture of the kitchen.

"It was a goddam grenade." One farmer spat tobacco at their feet. He loped away and came back with a squirrel rifle. When a couple of his friends saw him, they left and returned with theirs.

Dr. Samuel came out on the porch and lifted his arms. "Let us pray."

The friends and neighbors gathered in the yard and bowed their heads.

The reporter scribbled frantically. The photographer moved his tripod to another spot and took a picture of what amounted to a prayer service.

A gig came tearing down the road and was almost wrecked before the driver could get it stopped. He and his companion jumped out.

"It's Jones from the *Kansas City Star*," the reporter told his photographer. "We need to get on out of here and file our story."

Crown's shoulders slumped. He had not contacted the *Star*. The news must be going out all over the country.

At the end of the prayer, Zerelda asked to be stood on her feet. Supporting her among them, the women from the Missionary Society helped her. Her face was white as her hair, her eyes a blazing blue and red rimmed. Her right arm was swathed in bandages. Her blood had seeped through the cotton.

She came to the edge of the porch, her eyes fixed on the Pinkerton men. "My sons are good boys. All my sons were good boys. If it hadn't been for you all, my boys never would've broke the law. They were just trying to save this farm for me—a poor widow woman—and others for their friends." She pointed her left hand at them. "You're the thieves and murderers here. You. And you." She pointed at Crown. "God knows what you did."

Another tray of flash powder exploded as the *Star* got its picture. Both the *Star* and the *Times* took everything she said word for word.

With that Zerelda collapsed and her friends carried her back to her bed. Her husband gathered with his churchmen, his own eyes red from weeping, his face stern as the Day of Judgment.

The Pinkertons climbed on their horses and rode back down the lane accompanied by the scorn and curses of outraged Missourians.

Clell Miller choked on his coffee. He read the story on page one of the *Dallas Times Herald* for the second time. And then the third. A wave of sorrow swept over him, accompanied by a sense of the utter waste, the utter futility of the outlaw life. Eyes misting, he read the second paragraph of the story over and over. He swiped at his eyes.

"What's wrong?" Not until Mary Carolyn squeezed his wrist did he realize she had asked the same question a couple of times.

Passing her the paper, he squeezed the bridge of his nose tightly between his thumb and forefinger.

"Oh, no," she whispered appalled. "What are we going to do?"

"I'll take care of it." Clell took the paper back from her and tucking it underneath his arm, he rose and climbed the stairs to the James brothers' room. At the door he sucked in his breath and looked around.

Mary Carolyn had followed him to the foot of the stairs and stood staring up at him. Her eyes sparkled with tears.

He shook his head to her. Then, without knocking, he went in.

"Jess. Frank. I've got real bad news."

The night that he heard about the attack on his family and the death of his half brother, Jesse shot up the Palace Saloon. Cole and Frank finally had to corner him and wrestle him down before he killed someone. The bill for the broken glass and furniture amounted to over two hundred dollars.

Early the next day, the train bound for Oklahoma City and Wichita with connections to Kansas City pulled into the station. The James brothers and their cousins the Youngers waited on the platform to climb aboard. They were bound for Missouri as fast as the Missouri Pacific could carry them. The rest of the gang was to work its way back upcountry and wait for orders.

"Take it easy, Jesse," Clell said as he shook the outlaw's hand.

The only answer was a white-lipped smile.

"She'll be fine." Mary Carolyn placed a gentle kiss on Jesse's cheek and hugged Frank. Frank nodded, but Jesse did not acknowledge her in any way. She might have laid her lips to a stone, so frozen were his features. The look out of his blue eyes was frightening. The last vestige of the Methodist minister's son was gone forever.

Clell and Mary Carolyn stood on the station platform to wave them off. As the last notes of the whistle trailed away, Clell's steel blue eyes focused on a man farther on down the platform. He might have been a drummer with an unusual case of samples. Or he might have been a Pinkerton agent with a long narrow box of arms. At that minute he looked in Clell's direction.

Clell forced his eyes not to engage the other man's. Instead, he let his gaze slide idly on to the other passengers most of whom had gotten their bearings and were moving on.

Mary Carolyn put a hand on his arm. "Is something wrong?"

The station platform, under the eyes of the stranger, was not the place to tell her what he suspected. Moreover, he might be wrong. Clell heaved a deep sigh. "When I said I wanted to get away from the gang, I didn't mean for it to happen this way."

"It's the worst thing I've ever heard of," Mary Carolyn agreed. "What kind of law officers would throw bombs into the homes of innocent people?"

"Pinkerton agents," Clell told her. His eyes flickered to the back of the man who had stepped down off the platform and was striding away in the direction of the hotel. "They don't have to live among the families of the people they come to arrest. They don't even have to live in the same state with them. And the rewards are getting bigger all the time."

Mary Carolyn wiped at her eyes. Hastily, she turned away and walked to the end of the platform. "Those dear, dear good people. They welcomed us into their homes. She and the doctor gave up their b-bed for us to have a wedding night."

Clell came with her and put an arm around her. "It's pretty bad, but this had been about to happen for a long time. Jesse doesn't hide who he is when he's robbing. In fact, he brags about it. And everybody knows where his farmhouse is. They even know that he stays there from time to time. In a way the Samuels might have been lucky. It could have been a gang of bounty hunters. They'd have set the house on fire and shot everybody who came out."

Mary Carolyn pulled her handkerchief from her coat pocket and wiped at her face. She hated to walk down the street sobbing, but she couldn't be strong at a time like this. She remembered Jesse's handsome little brother dogging his older brothers' footsteps the entire time the gang had been there. The thought of him in the cold ground made her ill.

She took another step or two, crying blindly, before Clell pulled her in between two buildings and held her against his chest. "Sshhsshh, sweetheart. You'll make yourself sick. You're not helping them one bit."

"That poor little boy—"

"I know. I know. Hush now."

"He was just a b-baby. Nine years old."

Clell rubbed her back. At last she lifted her face. She could imagine what she looked like. Crying always made her nose and eyes swell and left red blotches on her cheekbones.

Clell kissed the tip of her nose. His eyes narrowed. Over her shoulder he caught a glimpse of the man with the long box. "Let's get in out of the cold wind. We can make plans about what to do."

* * *

In the Palace Saloon Billy Chadwell sat morosely at a table in the back. His eager smile had completely disappeared. He was chewing on his thumbnail. When he saw them coming, he rose hastily and pulled out a chair for Mary Carolyn. His sympathetic eyes noted the remains of tears on her cheeks.

Jim Pool rudely ignored them. He sat across from Billy reading the second page of the *Herald* article one word at a time, his lips moving as he sounded each word out in a low monotone.

"Did they get off?" Billy asked unnecessarily.

"Gone north," Clell told him solemnly.

The saloon was empty except for a couple of swampers trying to straighten up and repair Jesse's rampage of the night before. The noontime drinkers had not arrived for the free lunch. It looked as forlorn as Mary Carolyn felt. She caught sight of herself in the mirror over the bar and wanted to die of mortification.

In dime novels a heroine wept beautifully with sparkling eyes and silver traces down her pale cheeks. Her quiet sobbing wrenched the hero's heart. But she had wept noisily and messily. If anything she looked worse than she imagined.

But her grief was real. Not pretended. She looked at Clell. He had called for beer and was staring moodily after the retreating barmaid. Mary Carolyn pulled her hat down low over her face.

Jim Pool raised his head and scowled across the table. "It says here that there was fifty thousand dollars stolen from the Rock Island. We didn't see no fifty thousand dollars."

"Where?" Billy Chadwell reached for the paper. When Jim refused to give it up, he laughed and punched Clell in the ribs. "Jim can't read worth a hoot. He's probably readin' five thousand. Did you count the naughts, Jim?"

Pool barred his stained, crooked teeth and flung the newspaper at Billy's face. "Read it for yourself, yuh dern fool. I ain't lyin'."

Billy made a production of unfolding the paper and smoothing it before he brought it close to his face so his nearsighted eyes could focus the print.

Clell exchanged a meaningful stare with Mary Carolyn. She had straightened up in alarm at Jim Pool's information. Now she eased back down in the chair.

"I didn't see no fifty thousand dollars," he continued. "You suppose somebody's holding out? You pull something off that train that we don't know about, Miller?"

Clell shook his head. "Why don't you ask Cole about what he got out of the express car? Next time we see him, I'll tell him you wanted to know."

At the mention of Cole, Jim tucked his head back down.

Billy read the story. His eyes narrowed; then he laughed out loud. "Yep!" He held the paper over in front of Clell's face. "It sure does say that fifty-thousand dollars was stolen. It also says there was ten or eleven of us. And," he announced triumphantly, "it also has a picture of Jim with Clell's name under it. Whoever put this mess together was just putting down anything. I don't reckon he'd be too careful about how much. About the only thing he got right was that there was a train robbery."

"Anybody'd care about how much," Pool scoffed.

Clell took the paper and started to read. After the account of the raid on the Samuel farm, the reporter had written an article on the James gang's latest depredations including the train robbery north of Unionville and the bank in Ottumwa.

The paragraph about the loot from the train was as Jim had reported. Clell's stomach clenched. Beneath it was a description of the masked boy bandit. How could anyone reading it not recognize Mary Carolyn Ross? Evidently Jim Pool had not gotten that far. He phrased his next words carefully. "This sounds like the guy made a bunch of this story up. Or he talked to somebody who wanted people to believe he lost more than he did so he could collect from his insurance company."

Scowling at his tormentors, Jim grabbed his beer and gulped it down.

Billy chuckled softly. "You're wasting your breath, Clell.

Jim don't believe anything that anybody tells him. He's just looking for an excuse to tear into somebody.''

"Gimme that." Jim half-rose out of his chair and made a grab for it.

Billy jerked it away from Clell, who tightened his grip on it. The paper tore in half.

"God damn!" Pool kicked his chair across the room. "I paid a nickel for that paper."

Billy guffawed. He rolled his half into a ball and threw it at the other man. "You'd already wasted your money. You can't read it no way. Just settle down and get drunk."

"The hell I will." Jim Pool stomped out without looking back.

Mary Carolyn breathed a sigh of relief. Clell folded the remains of the paper and stowed it under his chair. Billy dropped back down grinning. He took a sip of his beer.

Clell cleared his throat. "I think we're going to be heading out in the morning."

"Great! We'll go with you," Billy said. "We don't need to spend any more time around here. Jim's going crazy not having someone to shoot at."

Clell glanced at the door, then leaned over and whispered in the young outlaw's ear.

"Oh!" Billy's eyes bugged. He smiled appreciatively at Mary Carolyn. Then he grinned. "Why sure! I sure do see! Good luck to you, old boy. I'll see you in Missouri."

Chapter Sixteen

"What did you tell Billy?" Mary Carolyn wanted to know. She trotted along beside Clell toward Belle Shirley's livery stable. A pale Texas sun was casting their shadows lightly on the sidewalk. A blue norther was blowing straight down Main Street. She thrust her hands into her pockets.

He didn't slow his stride to accommodate her. If anything he increased its length. She thought he wasn't going to answer her. Then over his shoulder he growled, "I told him we want to travel alone."

"Why?" She was truly puzzled.

"Because we're still newlyweds. I told him we were going to make it a honeymoon. Come on if you're coming. Otherwise, go back to the room and pack our things."

She stood stock-still, staring at his broad back as he strode ahead like a man with a mission. He was really serious about getting her back to the money without any wasted time. She should be glad about that. She should be glad about so many things. The money, the fact that she wasn't pregnant, the fact that he wasn't going to make love to her anymore, so she didn't need to worry. Instead she felt like bawling.

Just before he entered the stable, he shot Mary Carolyn a

black look. "I'm telling you, Buster, either way, get a move on."

"Why're you wanting to buy horses?" Belle Shirley shook her head. "The train's the way to go."

Mary Carolyn looked to Clell. His habitual expression for over a week now had been a scowl. "Do you want to sell me a couple?" he rapped out. "I can go down the street to Hudspeth's."

Belle laughed. She leaned back in her chair and laced her fingers at her slim waist. "And the horses you get from him won't take you a mile. Crow bait. Wind-broke. Cow-hocked." She cocked her head to one side. "Why?"

"None of your damn business." He walked over to her office door. "I picked out two. Do you want to sell them to me, or are you going to wait until they drop dead and sell them for glue?"

She never lost her smile. But she did throw his companion an interested look. "What do you say about all this?"

Mary Carolyn was surprised to be asked her opinion. "I didn't—that is, I don't think it makes any difference. I mean"—she faltered—"he's my husband."

"It makes a hell of a lot of difference." Belle ignored Clell's ominous scowl. "Five hundred miles in January could kill you. One good ice storm and you've both got pneumonia."

The older woman had made a good point. A warning bell rang in her mind. Was he planning to take her out somewhere and lose her? Mary Carolyn stared hard at her outlaw, waiting for his answer.

Clell hesitated. At last he decided Belle Shirley should know his suspicions. "I think I saw a Pinkerton come in on the train. It was across the tracks from the one Jesse and Frank went out on. They were that close to meeting face to face." He grinned a little. "Might have been real interesting if they had met up. My name's in the Dallas papers. Course, another guy's face is over it. But they'll get the straight of it eventually. They're looking for us. They're on the trains and everywhere. If we're going to get out of here, we need to go and go quick.''

"You could be right. But you could just as easily be wrong." His explanation had not convinced Belle Shirley. She surveyed them both with a calculating stare. At last she shrugged. "If you're dead set on going that route, I'll sell you the best horses I've got." She rose and led the way into the stable.

At her shoulder Clell was telling her, "You've got a big bay gelding. He looks like he could go all day. And the chestnut with the bald face. I want papers on them. If somebody stops me, I want to be able to convince him that he's wrong."

Mary Carolyn hurried behind them. They were outlaws. On the run from the law. She felt a thrill of pleasure mixed with fear. She hadn't noticed the man on the platform. She hadn't even thought to look for anything like that. But Clell had. Her stomach clenched. They both could have been arrested on the platform. If his name was in the paper, even though it was under Jim Pool's picture, he could still be caught.

"The gelding's good for you," Belle was saying, "but you need a smaller horse for Mary Carolyn."

"I need two to keep together," he objected.

"She needs Lady Grace."

Mary Carolyn caught up in time to hear the name. "Oh, no, Belle. That's your horse."

Belle smiled a catlike smile. "And she's going to cost him like the very devil."

"Now just a minute—"

The horse trader walked down the shedrow to the mare's stall. Lady Grace poked her head out and nickered eagerly. "I'm not holding you up," Belle insisted saucily. "At least not very much. A little maybe, but you can always rob another bank. Right?"

"That horse'll stand out like a peacock. People will know for sure that we stole her. She'll make us easy to trail," Clell objected.

Belle ignored that argument as if it had never been made. "The gelding's not too bad," she added. "I've got better, but if you're going to be bullheaded, I don't want to argue with you. Your wife has to have Lady Grace, though. She can carry her without her getting sore or having her teeth jolted out of her head. Don't worry. In case you get stopped, I'll give you a bill of sale. Come on, Clell. You're riding your wife north in the winter. Give her a chance to make it.''

Clell swung back to Mary Carolyn. He looked at her long and hard while she fidgeted uncomfortably. ''I can ride anything,'' she offered. ''A horse is just a horse.''

With a grunt, he opened the stall door and stepped inside. While his practiced hands ran over every inch of Lady Grace's body, Belle lit a cheroot. Seating herself on a bale of hay, she leaned back and blew a cloud of smoke into the rafters. ''That horse is really one of the best deals in the stable.'' She chuckled softly as she ran her Gypsy black eyes over Mary Carolyn in her rumpled, shabby clothing. ''You sure could use a haircut,'' she remarked. And then, ''I sure hate to think of any girl falling in love with an outlaw.''

Mary Carolyn blushed. ''I—I . . .'' She couldn't think of what to reply. The lie had been too long on her lips.

''I still think Cole loves me.'' Belle's voice carried a hint of defiance. ''But he's such a stubborn bastard. He'd never admit it in a hundred years.''

Privately, Mary Carolyn didn't think Cole Younger loved anybody but himself. She tried to think what to say to make Belle feel better about the whole thing. Her own past gave her no hope for Pearl Younger's future. Belle's daughter would probably know a life no different from Mary Carolyn's. And hers had brought her here to Dallas with an outlaw.

She fell back on the belief that had given her a mite of consolation. ''Your daughter's better off without him.'' The words tumbled out in a burst of emotion. ''He's never given her a thought. She would just be hurt if she knew him. Believe me, I know. The kids in the orphanage whose folks had left them there and ridden off were the saddest.''

Belle's eyes widened. She pulled long on the cheroot before dropping it on the ground and grinding it out beneath her boot. When she looked up, her expression was sympathetic. ''You really think so?''

"I know so."

Clell led the black mare out into the shedrow and ran her down toward the corral to check her action. Both women watched him. At last Belle laughed shortly. "You know, I think Clell Miller's finally met his match."

Mary Carolyn couldn't figure out why. One thing was sure, Belle Shirley seemed to think the whole process was very funny.

The hair on the back of Buster's neck rose. She imagined she could feel people staring at her. She twisted her head around, looking hard, trying to judge the men as they rode down the dusty Dallas street. People who had been ordinary cowboys, cattlemen, and businessmen now took on sinister aspects. Not a few had guns strapped to their hips. Were they paying special attention to Clell, thinking to shoot him in the back and collect a reward?

She shuddered.

At that moment, Clell clapped his heels against the gelding's sides. The big bay broke into an even rolling canter. Lady Grace followed without any effort on her rider's part. Within an hour, the horizon was empty in every direction.

With an ease that surprised him, Leon Box got the whole story of the James gang's stay in Dallas. The owner of the Palace Saloon gave them a bitter blow-by-blow description of Jesse's rage the night before and the explanation for it. He also pointed out two members of the gang seated at a table in the back. "Why don't you arrest them?" he demanded as he returned Box's identification card. "Get them the hell out of my place."

"No warrants for them in Texas," was the smooth reply.

"The hell you say. I'll swear out a warrant." Sweat beaded the man's red face.

"That's for the local law to handle," the Pinkerton agent

told him. "If I were you, I'd do it soon." With a tip of his hat, he took his leave.

He telegraphed to Pinkerton headquarters in Chicago and to Elsdon Crown, the agent in charge in Missouri, the news that the gang had split up. In Kansas City they should watch the trains.

The next morning bright and early, Leon Box bought a horse and gear and headed out northeast. He might not be able to arrest them in Texas, but the James gang was wanted in Arkansas. Besides, there was a garrison commander in Fort Smith that owed him a favor.

A strong crosswind had chilled Mary Carolyn's right side to the bone by the time they reached the Red River. A pair of cables swayed across the wide expanse of choppy gray-brown water. On the far bank the ferry was moored. Clell rang the bell, waited, and rang again.

The wind moaned around their ears. Sawyers in the river drifted by with unbelievable speed. The ferryman would be a fool to try to make another run tonight.

Clell's curses blistered the air, but Mary Carolyn was so tired, she paid no attention. They had ridden for three days now; a hundred and fifty miles were behind them. Now she sat numb in the saddle, a wool scarf tying the brim of her hat down over her ears. On the left side her throat was a raw, swollen lump that made swallowing difficult.

Clell rang the bell once more. When no one appeared, he looked around. "We've got to camp for the night."

At that Mary Carolyn raised her head. "We could go back to the farmhouse," she suggested. "It wasn't very far. I'll bet they'd let us stay in the barn if we asked them nicely."

He scowled at her. He had been scowling at her since they left Dallas. She had gone from being hurt to resenting him to ignoring him. If he wanted to act that way, she couldn't do a blessed thing about it.

"No. We need to camp here so we can get started first thing in the morning."

She looked around her at the darkening sky. Threatening clouds had been scudding down it all afternoon. She was sure the temperature was dropping toward freezing. Rain had splattered her cheek from time to time, but fortunately the clouds hadn't burst. Pine trees mixed with oaks and other hardwoods grew thick along the river banks. No doubt they could spread their rolls in the midst of them and be protected from the worst of the elements. But a nice dry barn would be better.

She also had no doubt that the people at the farmhouse a mile back would be willing to give them shelter. Probably they were used to people who had missed the ferry spending the night.

Clell turned the rangy gelding and loped him toward the trees. She made an imaginary gun with her fist, thumb, and index finger and aimed it at the center of his broad back. No man should be allowed to be so contrary. She could ride back to the farmhouse alone and probably spend a more comfortable night, but what would her outlaw do if she did?

If she let him get out of her sight for that long, he might try to swim the Red River and ride on ahead. If he beat her to the money, she could be sure she would never see him—or it— again. She holstered her index finger without ever pulling the imaginary trigger.

In the northwest thunder rumbled softly, a long ominous growl. She'd better get her bed made before the storm struck, otherwise she'd be wet to the skin all night long.

They lay side by side, sharing their blankets and tarpaulins, clinging together, shivering. The rain pelted them, the tree branches tossed and groaned above their heads. Then thunder boomed directly overhead drowning Mary Carolyn's scream of terror.

A heartbeat later came the crackling sound. Lightning struck a tree less that a dozen feet from where they had made their camp. Electricity tingled through their bodies. Clell threw the blankets aside in time to see fire streaking down the trunk of a loblolly pine. It split the tree and ignited the needles, turning the whole thing into a gigantic torch. The air was filled with ozone and then with burning wood.

Mary Carolyn screamed again. Her wet face reflected the flames. She tried to scramble to her feet, but the heavy rain was already extinguishing the fire. It pounded the white smoke to the ground before it could rise and it set the burning branches to hissing.

Clell held her down. "It's all right," he murmured. His own voice wavered as he stared at the white column of smoke, dying flames still leaping from the tree's trunk. "It's all right. See, the fire's going out."

"W-we should have g-gone back to the farmhouse."

He didn't answer. Instead he hugged her more tightly against his body. She was trembling like a small animal. He put a hand on her cheek to press her face into his shirt. Her skin was clammy. Probably everything she had on was damp and cold. She was right about the farmhouse. He cursed himself for a fool. If she got sick . . .

"Hindsight is always right," he said coldly.

He was pleased when she lashed back at him. "Only an idiot would have missed the signs." Anger steadied her voice. She stopped shivering as her blood began to heat. "I may be from Chicago, but I know when there's a storm coming. This tree we're under could've been the one that got struck by lightning."

He got busy rearranging the blankets. "The storm's already moving on. We'll get back under them and be warm in a few minutes."

"No, we won't." Her voice sounded hoarse. "We'll be cold and miserable because we're wet to the skin. Any clothes I had on that were just damp are now soaked."

"That's your own fault. You were the one who tried to get up and run." He covered them over and began to chafe her arms with his hands. Everything was so cold and wet. The inside of the tarp was wet. The blankets were wet. The ground water was beginning to seep in. And still the rain fell in sheets. They'd be lucky if the river didn't rise.

"I don't think that was a bad idea. I think you were just lucky that the rain put the fire out. If it hadn't, we might have been in the middle of a forest fire." She shivered again. "Which wouldn't have been a bad idea. At least we'd die warm instead of freezing slowly." Her teeth began to chatter again.

She was getting too cold. He had seen soldiers die from being wet and cold in their blankets. The next morning they'd be dead, blue and shriveled, their bodies crunched together in tight stiff balls.

"You did this on purpose," she accused. Her voice sounded a little slurred as if she were drunk. But she wasn't, she was cold. "You want me to learn that outlawing is worse than anything else in the world. Well, you wasted your time."

He began to unbutton his clothing.

She went on, her teeth chattering so that the words came out in little bites of sound. "I'd already decided that for myself when Jesse got the news about his little brother. I'd already decided that I never want to steal anything again." She tilted her head back on her neck, trying to see his face in the darkness. He looked down at her. "And right at this very minute, I hate outlaws."

He grunted and began to unbutton her clothing.

"What do you think you're doing?"

"I'm going to get you warm. I brought you out here. I'll be damned if I'll let you die."

She slapped at his hands and struggled weakly. Her wet head tossed back and forth in negation. Wet strands of hair flicked against his chest like droplets of ice. "You're not going to put your hands on me." Her shirt was easy, but when he began peeling her undergarments down, she started to kick. "Stop it! Just let me die. You don't love me. You don't care anything about me. Let me alone. Let me go."

"Shut up and be still."

"Ooo-oohh! I hate you! Let me alone!" She couldn't slap at him any longer because her long underwear was down to her elbows. "Stop it. Keep your hands off me. What do you think you're doing?"

He twisted her over, so her back was to him. Then he gathered her in against him. He was practically lying on top of her. Her clammy skin chilled him, but before he knew it, his hands were on her breasts.

"Stop it!" she cried. Suddenly, she went still. "Stop it," she whispered. "Oh, how I hate you." Her voice trailed away.

He could feel himself getting hard. His own body was reacting powerfully to her struggles and the feel of her breasts against his palms. They were hard as apples, the nipples hard too, the skin around them pebbly.

He closed his eyes and groaned. He wanted her more powerfully than he had ever wanted anything in his life. He had denied himself and now his body took over and paid no attention to his brain.

"I'm not cold anymore." Her voice came from a long way off, an awed whisper.

For the moment both of them forgot the rain and their wretched states.

Her clothing anchored her elbows tight to her sides, but her hands were free. She twisted them down between them, reached back, and pressed against the bulge inside his pants. He sucked in his breath as they shaped it, pulled at it. Her fingers tore at the buttons.

"Don't," he begged her. "Don't. Stop." Even as he said the words, he squeezed her breasts so hard she cried out.

The sweet pain made her hunch her shoulders. Her buttocks thrust back hard. He sucked in his breath. All his resolutions disappeared in a fierce wave of desire. This was the woman he wanted. Crazy as she was, a hopeless romantic, he still wanted her. Powerful emotion welled up from deep inside him. His hands moved over her breasts, pulling her straight.

She moaned. Her back arched. Her buttocks bumped against him. She worked his buttons open and pulled him free.

"For God's sake!" he hissed in her ear. "What are you trying to do?"

She didn't answer. Her fingers encircled him, squeezed him, and tugged at him. Rhythmically. He couldn't resist. Didn't want to. He caught her earlobe between his teeth as his hands slid down, down, down beneath her clothing. His left splayed over her flesh, now warm and pulsing with excitement. The questing fingers of his right found the curls at the base of her belly.

She sighed and moaned again. Her hips rotated, thrashed back against him. He felt the power of her desire, matching his own. He clasped her tightly, his fingers sliding into her steamy opening.

She cried out with pleasure as she sought the same pleasure for him.

He could feel his climax approaching. His blood pounded beneath her hands. Around them the storm thundered. The flashes of lightning sent blue light beneath the edges of the covers. Cold rain still beat down on them, but inside the cocoon a greater storm raged.

Emotions, sensations mounted higher and higher. Her fingernails scraped across the sensitive skin at the top of his staff.

"Don't do that," he snarled. "You're going to be sorry."

She was implacable. Her fingertips rasped across the narrow opening, trailed through hot liquid, spread it down. His own fingers were drenched in her desire.

Suddenly, she stiffened. Her hands clasped him harder than ever. Her back arched, tossing her head back against his shoulder. Her buttocks vibrated, satin skin with sleek muscles beneath caressing him.

He could actually feel her sheath sucking at his fingers. At the same time he exploded, pushing himself into her hands, crying out in pleasure.

Gradually, their muscles returned to normal. Their bodies slumped and they arranged themselves in a more comfortable position. He pulled his hands from beneath her clothing and ran them over her skin. She was warm now. Every vestige of the clammy chill was gone. He pulled her clothing back up onto her shoulders. She pulled her hands around in front of her.

He had become almost too warm. If he had been by himself, he might have stood up in the rain for half a minute. But she was already snuggling down against him, he could feel her limbs relaxing.

He rearranged himself too, composing his mind for sleep.

He smiled, discovering his face was a little stiff as if he hadn't smiled in a long time. The rain was still drumming overhead, but now they would be all right for the rest of the night.

He was almost asleep when her voice came softly to his ears. "What did we just do?"

He chuckled. "Just what men and women have been doing for centuries to get warm. It sure works, doesn't it?"

"We won't have a baby, will we?"

He didn't answer for a while. He didn't want a baby. He didn't want a wife. He didn't want her hanging on to him for the rest of his life. If he repeated those sentences to himself often enough, he would believe them. "Not for that."

"Good." Why did he feel personally affronted at her comment? A baby would compel him to marry her and take care of her for the rest of his life. He certainly didn't want that, did he? Within minutes he heard her even breathing. It was faintly raspy. That was a bad sign. He didn't need a sick woman on his hands. He tucked her head underneath his chin and settled himself in the warm, richly scented cocoon that their bodies had created.

Thunder boomed farther away.

He prayed that tomorrow the sun would shine. That would help her to throw this off.

Mary Carolyn awoke with a scratchy throat and a headache. She swallowed experimentally. It hurt, but it was bearable. By concentrating very hard, she could put the pain in her forehead to the back of her mind.

When she opened her eyes, she could see only dimness. The air she breathed was stuffy. The tarps and blankets had done a good job of keeping her body warm and comfortable.

She tried to move, but Clell's weight was pressing down on her back. One arm passed under her neck. The hand clasped her shoulder. The other hand was . . . between her legs. Then she remembered what they had done last night.

A hot blush drove the headache quite out of her mind. What else did married people do? It seemed that she learned more every day. When she actually did get married, if she ever got married, she was going to have to watch her step. She possessed a lot of firsthand knowledge that might be hard to explain.

She listened for the patter of raindrops. Only blessed silence reached her ears through the layers of cloth above her. She stretched out a hand to test the temperature.

With a shiver, she drew it back. She wondered how long she could lie here ignoring her body's basic functions.

"Is it cold out?" His voice was a warm whisper in her ear.

"Uh-huh."

"But not raining." His beard scratched her cheek.

She didn't answer. He could hear that the storm had passed. In a minute he could throw back the blankets and let all the delicious warmth escape to the skies. And she would need to scramble up and run for the bushes before she had an accident that would make for a most uncomfortable ride for the rest of the day. She stuck her feet into the tops of her boots. He was doing the same. Her headache was back with a vengeance.

"Ready?"

She nodded.

He tossed the covers back. The day was gray and bleak with a stiff wind blowing out of the north. She drew a shallow breath as she reached down to pull up her boots. As she dashed behind a convenient tree, she began to cough. Her throat was really sore.

No use complaining. When they got some hot coffee, she would be right as rain.

Leon Box saw them board the ferry. He thought about riding up and taking it with them. Then decided against doing it.

The girl wouldn't pay any attention to him, what with the farmer's wagon and team, but the man would notice him. Through his binoculars, he noted the outlaw looking around, scanning the trees and the skyline. For the space of several seconds, that piercing gaze concentrated on the trees where the agent had concealed himself.

Through the binoculars he could see the man's face, look

into his eyes. He had the alarming idea that the man was actually looking at him. He blinked and lowered the glasses. The outlaw didn't move. In the tree above the agent's head a crow cawed hoarsely. The outlaw's head tilted.

The agent raised his binoculars and caught the hint of a smile and the slightest of nods. Again Box had the uncanny feeling that he'd been spotted. He tensed. Then the man led the horses onto the shifting deck. The girl followed, her shoulders hunched against the cold.

Better wait for the next crossing. He could see a buckboard pulling onto the landing across the river. They couldn't get too much of a start in the next few minutes.

Chapter Seventeen

Clell pushed them both as hard as he dared. Anticipating trouble, he watched the progress of the horses he had bought from Belle Shirley. The uphill slopes and looping climbs of the Ouachita Mountains took their toll on even the best mounts.

To his surprise and secret chagrin, the gelding he had picked began to flag after the first day. Its head drooped low, its hooves scraped along the rocky trail. The black mare Lady Grace, the horse he had scorned, tripped along at a good pace.

He was man enough to admit all this to Mary Carolyn, but with much grumbling. Lady Grace's rider weighed less than he did, so that was part of it. When she pointed out the difference in size of the horses, he admitted offhandedly that he might have made a mistake in judging the mare.

By this time Mary Carolyn was too ill to care about his excuses. She clung to Lady Grace's saddle. In the afternoon her cough was better. She would think she was going to be well by morning. In the morning, it seemed infinitely worse. On the third day, she could barely climb into the saddle.

Coming up behind her, Clell put his hands around her waist. ''Make it just for today. I promise you. After we get to Fort

Smith, we'll get a hotel room and take a day to rest. No sense killing ourselves.''

She nodded grimly. When he lifted her, her left foot slipped out of the stirrup. If he hadn't had hold of her, she knew she would have fallen. Once down, she doubted she could have climbed into the saddle.

"Hey, Buster, are you all right?"

Through burning eyes she looked down to find him still standing beside her, staring up at her, taking her measure. He was squinting against the weak January sun that shone full on his face.

He looked like he'd been through hell. If he could keep going, so could she. A heroine wouldn't give up so easily. But Buster didn't have to act like she liked it.

"Hell, no, I'm not all right. I feel like I've been dragged across three hundred miles of open country in the dead of winter. It's been a week since I've slept in a bed or been warm." She crossed her arms over the saddle horn and braced herself to wait while her head stopped swimming and the black spots cleared out of her vision. She coughed once, then cleared her throat.

He managed a faint grin. "We've hit it lucky. It could be worse."

She hated him with all her heart, and she'd tell him so if it didn't take so much effort. He no longer looked like an illustration from a dime novel. Instead, he looked like the photographs and sketches of real outlaws tacked on the post office wall in Dallas. His face was dirty and chapped red from the cold wind. His mustache and beard looked matted and scraggly. He had dark circles under his eyes.

She grunted. "If I look half as bad as you do, I'm surprised you can stare at me."

His grin widened. He held up the reins for her to take. "Well, I'll admit I'm having a time, but I'm tough. Outlaws get used to seeing people at their worst."

"Then I'd say we've both hit rock bottom."

"Uh-huh." He swung up onto the gelding's back. "There's not a damn thing romantic about this life."

She glared at his back as he clicked his tongue and urged the gelding into a lope. Sore and miserable as she was, she had no choice but to follow.

After an enormous steak and a bath hot enough to shrivel her skin and turn it bright pink, Mary Carolyn climbed into bed while Clell watched. Tired as he was, he could feel the quickening in his loins. He had it bad.

In his eyes she was beautiful. She had dried her short blond hair with a towel and combed it with her fingers. It lay on her cheeks in fishhooks and curled upward in spiky points. It might be unfashionable, but it suited her spiky personality. Involuntarily, he adjusted the bulge in his pants. He wanted her so badly that he ached, and he'd sworn not to take her again.

He cleared his throat. "Do you want anything?"

She lay on her side, her eyes glistening in the lamplight. "No. What more is there to want?"

He snorted. "You're mighty easy to please."

She turned over on her back and patted the quilts on his side. He was standing with one hand wrapped around the bedpost. His mind told him to get the hell out of there, but his feet wouldn't move. Still staring at her, he cautiously sat down. The springs squeaked and the mattress sagged.

She folded her hands across her chest. "I know you think I'm crazy."

She sure had the right of that. "Yep."

"But you've never been completely alone."

He frowned and stirred uneasily. She wanted to tell him something, and he wasn't sure he was ready to hear it. He'd heard a lot of stories in the past. Some were told by dying comrades in the hope that he might somehow find their families or sweethearts and set the record straight. Some were more lies than truth, wafting out with the whiskey fumes, about the sins of a misspent youth. He sincerely hoped it wasn't one of those long sad stories whores told in an effort to get extra money.

He chided himself. Mary Carolyn was no whore. Of that, he was absolutely certain.

Her eyes were fixed on the ceiling. "I don't tell people about myself. Never. I've too much to be ashamed of."

He frowned. This was a different way to begin.

"My mother and I lived in a cottage with trees and flowers. Everything was clean and new. I had two dolls and a doll carriage to roll them around in. I didn't have anyone to play with, but my mother played with me and told me stories and sang to me. And a man came to see her every week and took her driving in his big carriage. Sometimes she'd wave her handkerchief out the window to me as she drove away."

Suddenly she turned her head to stare into his face. A hot blush rose in her cheeks. "I'm telling the truth. Believe me or not. I'm just tired of you thinking I'm a complete idiot."

He tried to wipe the cynical expression off his face.

Her voice turned belligerent. Her eyes flashed. "I know what you're thinking. And you're right. But I didn't know anything about that. I didn't know anything except that a teacher came every day and taught me to read and write and play the piano."

He had the picture right enough. He didn't want to feel sorry for her. The picture she painted sounded so easy when he compared it to his own life on a dirt farm. His father had worked him and his brothers from morning till night. He wouldn't feel sorry for her. "I thought you said you couldn't play the piano," he drawled. "If you had all that, you could take turns with Belle in the Palace anytime."

"No, I couldn't," she flashed him a wry grin. "I was hopeless. I couldn't tell one note from the other. I can't carry a tune to this day."

"So what happened?" He was pretty sure that he knew exactly what happened, but he'd let her finish.

Her grin disappeared. She tightened her lips as if she wouldn't finish the story. Then she shrugged. "One day my mother sat me down and told me that I was going to go to a school where I would learn all sorts of wonderful things. She smiled a lot and looked over her shoulder at the man who took her driving. I'd look at him too, but my mother would pull me back around to face her. I knew something was wrong. But I didn't know what it was."

Clell could feel himself getting angry in spite of his determination not to care about her story. He knew exactly what was coming. He could spot it a mile off. "I'll bet you got the picture pretty quick."

"It was an orphanage." Her lips thinned tight over the word. "Oh, they called it a girl's school. And the nuns ran it. But it was an orphanage. The girls there didn't have any mothers or fathers. I'd been there for months before I found out the truth. I was scared at first."

She looked aside at him. "Don't ever let anyone tell you that nuns are kind, gentle people. Most of them were just plain mean. Finally, I got enough nerve to go to Sister Faustina and tell her there'd been a mistake. She had to send for my mother to come and get me because I didn't belong there."

He rested his back against the bedpost. In his mind's eye he could see her facing the nun. She wouldn't have paid any heed when the sister tried to reason with her. She'd have ignored any good advice. She'd gotten started early. No wonder she was so good at being Buster. "I'll bet they just jumped right up and sent a message right off."

Her memories were too bitter for her to appreciate his humor. "Sister told me that I was wrong. And when I argued, she whipped me."

"With a ruler?"

"A strap." Mary Carolyn's voice sounded thick.

He eyed her suspiciously. He'd been whipped with a strap by his father, but his mother hadn't let his sisters get a whipping. He couldn't imagine anybody hitting a little girl. The picture made him uncomfortable.

"So I ran away."

He nodded. "Sure thing."

"And they found me and brought me back."

He nodded again. "And you kept on acting like a fool."

She nodded her head. "Until Sister Faustina took me into her office and told me that my mother had died." Her voice lost all emotion. "They gave me some of her things, a locket and a little gold ring. I didn't cry."

He hoped she wasn't going to tell him they'd been stolen by some jealous person who hated her.

"After that I stayed at the orphanage. There wasn't any place for me to go. Then, when I was fifteen, I decided to take a look at my records. I was having trouble remembering my mother's name. I'd forgotten what she looked like long ago, but I'd discovered I was forgetting her name. I opened the drawer, and there it was. I couldn't believe it."

He straightened his back and smothered a yawn. "You were a long-lost princess."

She frowned. "I'll be through in a minute. There's a point to all this. It was a sheet with a list of payments on it. Someone had been paying for me to stay in that awful place. I wasn't a charity child, even though I was dressed like one and I ate with them. The name of the man who was paying for me was written there on the top of the sheet. A man named DeGraffen Somervell wrote a bank draft of thirty dollars every month for my room and board. DeGraffen Somervell. The bank draft was from the Citizens Mercantile and Industrial Bank of Chicago."

"Maybe your mother—"

"There was a letter too. It told how Mrs. Madeleine Somervell was deceased and to inform her daughter Mary Carolyn. I started to cry then. I didn't cry when she died because I didn't believe it. But now I knew that she really was dead. I wasn't supposed to be snooping around in the files, so the next dark night I tied up what I had in a blanket and left. Just walked out the door and nobody came after me."

He thought about Buster Ross leaving in the dead of night. They were probably glad to see the end of her. "You were old enough to make it on your own by then. As far as they were concerned, you'd made your choice."

"I thought the very same thing. I tried to find work. I couldn't. I sold the ring and the locket, and then I decided to get enough money to eat. I decided to rob a train."

"Just like that. You're crazy," he exclaimed incredulously.

"I'd been reading dime novels since I came to the convent. The janitor at school spent everything he made on them. He kept stacks of them in his room in the basement. I'd switch them back and forth.''

He gave a thin whistle through his teeth. ''You must have been all over that place. Didn't anybody ever catch you?''

She smiled a little secret smile. ''They only whipped me the one time. I don't think anyone paid any attention. I was different from the rest because someone was paying for me. Or maybe Sister Faustina told them not to. I don't think she did, though. She didn't like me much.''

''But I read in the Chicago paper how DeGraffen Somervell was buying banks all over the country. I read all about his trips. So—''

''How'd you get from Chicago to the water stop in Iowa that night?'' He couldn't believe what he was hearing. She had done all this to steal from the rich man who'd paid for her.

''Hid in a boxcar on an outbound train.'' She grinned at the memory. ''That part was easy. The waiting was hard. I got hungry.''

He nodded, his expression wry. ''That should have warned you off. But you stole his money anyway.''

''And met you. And became an outlaw,'' she finished with a lift of her chin. ''Just like Jesse James.'' She looked at him. ''I told you all about this because I want you to know that I'm not doing this for thrills. Or for romance. Oh, maybe I did at first, but not anymore. I want that money. I think DeGraffen Somervell took my mother away from me. He made her put me in an orphanage. I didn't understand. I still don't understand, but I'll never forgive him for that. That money belongs to me. It's what he owes me in exchange for my mother.''

He turned down the lamp and left her lying in the dark, her face set, her eyes staring. He couldn't see the sense of arguing with her. She was a crazy girl who'd been turned into an outlaw because the people with all the power didn't play fair. The banker had wanted the woman, but not the daughter. He'd made a rotten deal, and the mother had fallen for it. After she was dead, he was probably glad to stop paying that thirty dollars a month.

His own life after the War was an example of the same thing. And so were Frank's and Jesse's lives. They refused to let their mother and stepfather lose the farm because of people in power who grabbed up the lands of innocent folks. Clell hadn't wanted his father and mother to lose their farm, but the taxes were due and the money they had was Confederate. So Jesse James showed him how to steal.

He shook his head. He needed the solace of a couple—or three—serious drinks to calm him and ease the ache of his sore muscles. Fierce regrets and sudden longings swept over him. He wanted a wife and a home.

He wanted to bury himself in the little thief upstairs, his pretend wife. He wanted to forget that the War had ever happened and that it had turned him down the outlaw trail almost before he knew what was going on.

Stony-faced, he looked around the nearly empty saloon. The drummer at the end of the solid slab of walnut finished his drink and left. Clell moved down to the man's place, where he could survey the room and see anyone who came in. Again he felt the overwhelming regret that he couldn't sit down at a table with his back to the door and think about nothing more important than the weather and his crops.

His eyes closed briefly, then opened on the alert. Self-preservation was a wonderful thing. From this point he could see anyone who walked down the main street and passed by the boarding-house door. Ordering a whiskey, Clell tossed it off swiftly. He then ordered another set before him and sipped slowly.

Assuring himself that the rest of the men in the room were local customers, he leaned his elbows on the bar and concentrated on the door.

He was trying to decide whether to order a third whiskey when the man came in. So far as clothing was concerned, he was not too different from an ordinary drifter with a week's growth of beard. He wore a long yellow slicker, mud-spattered to mid thigh. Muddy boots showed underneath it. Only his expensive hat, pulled down low over his eyes, sounded the alarm. It shouted big city as surely as the simple felts and straws of the other customers whispered their status.

From the crook of the stranger's arm a bedroll extended down, held stiff by what was obviously a rifle or shotgun wrapped somewhere in its center. Neither of those weapons was out of the ordinary. A man traveling would be armed and would carry his guns into his hotel with him.

What was unusual was his behavior when he stepped inside the door. Instead of coming directly to the bar, he stepped to one side. His back was to the wall. His eyes slid around the room taking the measure of every man. Clell watched him tick off the customers, the drunks, the cardplayers, the men like himself who were there for a little relaxation before heading home to bed.

Eventually, his stare found Clell at the end of the bar. But Clell was looking downward at his whiskey. Out of the corner of his eye, he watched the stranger's reflection in the mirror. The man's right hand pushed the slicker back over the hilt of his pistol. Keeping his hat low over his eyes, he walked quickly to the opposite end of the bar which ran almost the length of the saloon. There the mirror wouldn't reflect his image.

Clell took a deep breath and raised his head. At that moment he looked into the face of the newcomer. And he knew without a doubt that he was looking at a Pinkerton agent, who was looking for him.

The broad shoulders of the bartender moved between them. The customer ordered a beer. While it was being drawn, he became intent on arranging his bedroll on the bar. The fine hat concealed his face completely. A thrill of alarm skittered down Clell's back. The business end of whatever weapon was concealed in that bedroll was pointed straight at his chest. The stranger's hand had disappeared inside the folds of cloth.

Clell calculated the chances of drawing his own gun before the man facing him got off a shot. He could drop behind the bar. The solid walnut would take anything less than a buffalo gun. But then where would he go? He was still boxed into a corner with no door or window to dive through.

With a perfectly steady hand, he lifted the glass and held the whiskey to his lips. Again he calculated the odds. A shoot-out in the saloon would end in death for someone—maybe even for two or three. He hated that. Innocent people often were cut down by stray bullets. He let his eyes slide down the bar. Three men stood directly in the line of fire. They were grinning, their eyes alight as they exchanged stories. Their faces were weathered; their clothing, well washed and neatly mended. They were family men undoubtedly with wives and children who depended on them. The War had created enough widows and orphans without outlaws adding to the number.

At that moment the Pinkerton man brought his hand out of the blanket to reach into his vest pocket. A silver dollar hit the bar with a musical clink. The bartender swept it up and made change. While he bent over the cash drawer, the agent turned his head so he surveyed the room through the mirror. His eyes moved over the rim of the glass while he drank his beer.

Remembering the sketch in the newspaper, Clell could feel sweat prickling between his shoulder blades. A big wood stove was going full blast somewhere behind his left shoulder. He had picked the wrong spot in every way. Jesse would get a laugh out of this.

The agent finished his beer. With another swift glance around the room, he called the bartender over. "Got any rooms upstairs?"

"Last time I heard, Marvin hadn't let 'em all," came the reply.

"Where'll I find him?"

Clell looked down at his hand. Suddenly, the whiskey had begun to vibrate in the glass. He was trembling. He set the glass down instantly and gripped the bar hard with both hands.

The agent settled the bedroll in the crook of his arm. He took another look around the room, being careful to look no longer at Clell than at any other person. Then he crossed the room and vanished through the swinging doors to find the night clerk.

* * *

Clell lay beside Mary Carolyn staring up into the darkness. A cold wind blasted the windows and rattled them in their frames. It was a hell of a night with no sign of letting up. The only salvation for them both was that so far the cold was a dry cold. A wet spell would mean sleet and snow. He couldn't take her out in anything like that.

The wind again gusted against the windows. He could feel the icy blast sliding in between the sash and the sill. He opened his mouth and watched his breath whoosh out in a white fog. Mary Carolyn murmured something and crowded in against his side. One hand clutched at his shirt. He wrapped an arm around her. She was hunting for someone to keep her warm. But she felt too warm, almost hot.

Damn it! Belle Shirley should have shot him in the butt when he bought the horses. Mary Carolyn's fever could turn into pneumonia in a couple of hours riding in this weather. The window rattled again. The tattered window curtains stirred.

His mind whirled. They were being tailed. He had been on the wrong side of the law too long not to know when he had been spotted. The only reason the agent had walked out instead of arresting him immediately was that he was searching for Jesse James. He was using Clell and Mary Carolyn to lead him to the outlaw.

In all likelihood, Allan Pinkerton would be getting a telegram in Chicago first thing in the morning.

Clell caressed Mary Carolyn's shoulder absently. The only thing to do was clear out in the dead of night. He had promised her that they could spend tomorrow resting, but the situation had changed. If they sneaked out now, they could get miles up the road before the agent knew they were gone. With any luck he might hang around watching until someone came in to roust them out.

Clell eased himself out of bed and crossed to the window. The three-quarter moon had a ring of ice crystals. He shivered as the cold seeped through his socks.

"Clell?"

He looked back over his shoulder. Her face was a white blur in the darkness. He took a deep breath. "I'm glad you woke up. We have to leave."

She sat up. "What? Why?"

"We got a Pinkerton agent on our tail."

"Oh, no." She threw the covers back and scrambled up on her knees.

She was so damn gallant. He could feel a wave of shame that he had put her in this position by trying to teach her how hard the outlaw trail was. He came across the room in a couple of long strides and caught her hard by the shoulders. "Why aren't you complaining?"

She lifted her face. He was near enough to see something of her surprised expression. "We have to get out of here in the middle of the night? Right?"

"Right." The word exploded from his mouth. "But why are you being so nice about this? You should be pitching a holy fit."

She sank back on her heels. "That's what you wanted to drive me to, isn't it? That's what this whole terrible trip had been about, isn't it? You wanted me to suffer. Well, you've succeeded. I have suffered. And I'm going to suffer more if that wind blowing around outside is any example of what we're heading into."

She swung her feet over the side of the bed and stood up. Her silhouette was a thin pale column in the dark room. His hands on her shoulders had clasped fine bones. With a pang he remembered how thin she was. She reached for her clothing hanging in dark drapes from the wall pegs. It rustled as she pulled it on.

"Well, I'm sorry, Mr. Clell Miller, outlaw. I'm not going to pitch a fit. I don't complain about my lot in life. If that disappoints you, that's too damn bad. If you're regretting what you put yourself through, that's too damn bad. But pitching a fit doesn't do any good, so I don't do that anymore. I just play out the hand."

He could hear her panting. She had to go through various

contortions as she pulled on her second pair of pants. In a couple of minutes, she was dressed in every garment she owned except the skirt that was torn in the bank robbery. Pulling both blankets from the bed, she folded them over her arm and went to stand by the door. "Leave money to pay for them," she commanded. "And leave money to pay for our room. We don't want these people to come after us. The Pinkerton man will be enough."

Her honesty and consideration infuriated Clell. He pulled a ten-dollar bill from his pocket and tossed it on the rumpled bed. His anger kindled because she thought he would sneak out without paying, he stalked after her. "Damn you, Buster Ross. I was going to do that anyway."

Boston Mountain was over fifteen hundred feet high. The trek north from Fort Smith was a nightmare for two people whose endurance had already been sorely taxed. Although the mountain shielded them from the worst of the wind, they suffered from exposure to temperatures below freezing. Their horses, born and bred on the Texas prairies, did well enough on the comparatively level stretches. Unfortunately, partway up the ascent, their lungs began pumping like bellows.

Clell didn't blame them. He himself was having the same trouble. At any minute the Pinkerton agent might appear on the horizon, and he might need to call on the animals to run. For that reason he didn't dare ride for more than a mile without spelling the mounts and walking a mile. He pulled his spyglass from beneath his slicker and surveyed the horizon. His own heart pounded against his ribs. Sweat poured from his body.

Mary Carolyn had protested that she could walk when the horses started laboring; but within a couple of hundred yards, she was lagging so far behind that he couldn't hear her. He realized her body wasn't equal to her will. He thought of tying a rope from the saddle horn to her waist, but her face was pale as death in the weak morning light. So he shifted her from Lady Grace to the gelding and back again for nearly twenty miles.

As they reached the crest, the sun came up on the right and a warm wind blew at their backs. Clell lifted his head and thanked God more fervently than he ever had before.

"We can ride now for a while, Mary Carolyn," he told her. "We're over the top. The horses can take it easy going downhill."

She merely nodded. Her face was set, her mouth pinched tight, her head tucked down against the sunlight as if it hurt her eyes. Two spots of high color rode her cheeks. He glanced at her worriedly. "How about a drink of water?"

He opened the canteen and held it out to her. She tilted it back and drank it down. Her throat worked as she swallowed thirstily. When she gave it back to him, he caught it as it slipped from her weak fingers.

"Sorry." She sighed and closed her eyes.

"Are you sleepy?"

She nodded. "A little. No. A lot."

He looked down the road ahead of him. It was a perfect looping trail not too steep, easy pacing. "Come here."

She heeled the mare forward until they were abreast on the narrow trail. He shifted himself up over the back of the saddle and reached out for her.

"What? What are you doing?" She tried to push his arms away, but he hauled her into the seat in front of him. "You don't have to do that."

"Yes, I do." He settled her comfortably against him. Then he surreptitiously wiped the sweat that had popped out on his forehead. The amount of effort involved surprised him. Of course, she had the hotel blankets wrapped around each leg. Still, he hadn't realized that he was so nearly done in. He guessed his body was telling him he wasn't a kid anymore. "Now just settle down and take a nap."

He had expected her to sit stiffly, to protest, to try to tell him how she was able to go on. He was surprised. She put one arm around his waist and leaned against his chest. The gelding had not gone a quarter of a mile before her breathing evened out.

Limp as a child, her arms dangling on either side of his body, she nestled down against him. Clouds appeared and the wind reversed itself and blew cold from the north, but she didn't move and her heat kept him warm.

Chapter Eighteen

"Wake up! Wake up! We've got to ride."

Mary Carolyn started awake. Her head ached, her back ached, and she couldn't remember where she was. A powerful heartbeat thrummed beneath her ear. Her lungs bellowed out.

Someone pushed at her shoulder. Clell!

She sat up. His left arm anchored her waist, bracing her at the same time that he held the reins. His right hand and arm were in the process of depressing his spyglass against his thigh. "He's coming."

"Who?" She looked around her, trying to orient herself. They were deep in the mountains. In a valley between mountains actually. Clell had turned the horses across the road to look back the way they had come. But which was the way they had come?

If she had had to move on down the trail, she wouldn't have known which way to go. "Where are we?"

"We're in the Ozarks, but we need to get off this trail. If we can, we'll let him ride by. We can detour over into Indian Territory or circle east and then turn north for the Missouri border." As he talked, almost to himself, his voice hoarse, his face dark and intense, he dismounted and held up his arms.

Still numb and half-asleep, she slid down into them. He transferred her weight and lifted her bodily onto Lady Grace's back. The cold wind hit her and she began to shiver.

After being in the circle of his arm inside his slicker, she was forced to sit upright. One of her blankets came unwrapped from her leg. She protested as the cold wind blasted her. He threw her one swift look. His face was unreadable. Was he disgusted? Was he agonized?

He tucked the blanket back around her leg, then swung into the saddle. "Hang on!"

He spurred the gelding. The big bay leaped forward. Lady Grace had no choice but to follow. Clell had ahold of her reins. Down the road they galloped.

Mary Carolyn wrapped her hands around the horn and hung on. The wind stung her face. She would swear there was ice in it.

Around a bend in the trail they came to a rill of water that ran across the road at an angle. Clell threw a look over his shoulder. He guided the gelding to the side of the road and turned him and the mare around and around in a circle until the road was thoroughly trampled. Then he guided them into the brush. Fifty yards in, he led them out over a slate shingle. From there he turned back and led them back to the trail.

Excitement and fear in equal parts temporarily drove all the tiredness from Mary Carolyn's mind. She merely sat her horse, ducking under tree limbs and fending off the pine and spruce branches that smacked at her face, as her outlaw led her into the forest. She marveled at how he led their pursuer on false trails and then doubled back.

As they wove and twisted through the thickets, she caught glimpses of his face. Intent. His eyes, deep-set from exhaustion, appeared almost black. They swept past her into the forest behind them. Twice, he stopped the horses dead still and cautioned her to silence. While she looked around in awe and back at him in fascination, he sat like a statue, listening. His head was turned, presenting his profile. Stripped bare of softness, dark against dim light, his mustache ruffled, and several days' growth of beard roughening his chin, he sent a shudder of desire through her.

He was just like the outlaws in the books. She fell in love with him all over again.

When he led them onward, she stared at his broad back, a little shaken by what she felt for him. Then she tried to remember if she had ever read anything this complicated about how a real outlaw threw his pursuers off the trail. She decided that she had not. Ned Buntline and Frederick Whittaker ought to have a talk with Clell Miller before they wrote their next novels.

They burst out onto the trail, and the wild ride in the icy wind began again. Where before he had nursed the gelding and mare, now he did not spare them. Nor their riders. Mary Carolyn bent low over the horn and tucked her head down so that her hat shielded her face and neck. Unable to watch where she was going, she closed her eyes.

To her horror she could hear the mare laboring. In books the horses ran for miles at top speed, their manes and tails rippling in the sunlight. But now, beneath her, Lady Grace's breath bellowed in and out in great wheezing grunts, the saddle leather creaked, the hooves reached out and slashed the earth, gathered and slashed again.

Mary Carolyn's eyes flew open. How could something so slender, so delicate withstand this awful pace? She raised her head, frantic to call a halt, to rest the mare. He was killing her. The wind whipped into her face. Instant tears streamed down her cheeks. Their paths turned to ice.

"Stop! Stop!" The wind whipped the words out of her mouth and carried them back down the road.

He lashed the reins across the gelding's withers. Around another bend he led them, down into a draw whose bottom was a dry stream bed. This time he turned west into it. The mare followed as best she could, but then, a broad patch of red sandstone, polished from years of spring thaws and flash floods was her undoing. Her iron shoes slipped. Her feet went out from under her.

Mary Carolyn screamed as she felt the horse go. She threw

herself in the opposite direction, but her weight wasn't enough of a counterbalance.

Lady Grace crashed to the ground. Only Mary Carolyn's effort to prevent the fall saved her leg from being crushed. As it was she ended up between the mares thrashing hooves. The fall stunned her, the breath whooshed from her body. For a minute the world went black.

She was unconscious for no more than a few seconds. She could feel Clell's hands on her shoulders, feel herself being dragged across the ground. She should be moving. But she couldn't.

He didn't drag her far, only so far as to get her out of the way of the hooves. He held her tight against him, his face pressed to hers.

"Mary Carolyn. Mary Carolyn. Ah, Buster. For God's sake! Say something. Goddam! Oh, Goddam. Mary Carolyn. Say something, sweetheart. Love. Say something. Damn, damn, damn."

His hands caressed her cheeks, pushed her hair back from her temples. She could feel his lips, moving over her face.

"Clell." She opened her eyes. His face was inches away. She stared into his eyes. They were wild with fear, searching her face, frantically, while he hugged her hard against him.

"Clell." She raised a hand. It was bruised and covered with dirt. She knew it trembled and stung, but she ignored it. Her fingers traced his cheek, touched his lips. He caught her hand in his and kissed it.

"I'm so sorry."

"I—I fell. Lady Grace fell. Is she hurt?"

He closed his eyes. She could hear the beating of his heart. When he opened them, he looked at the horse.

She followed his eyes. The black mare had climbed to her feet and stood shivering. With a sinking heart she saw how the beautiful creature favored her left hind leg. "Oh, no," she whispered. "She's hurt."

His own face was grim. If the horse had broken her hip, the Pinkerton would catch them for sure. His chest heaved. Still, he smiled and nodded reassuringly. "I think she's just shaken up."

Mary Carolyn managed to smile back. She could feel the numbness leaving her body to be replaced by pain in every joint. She drew a shallow breath and let it out slowly. "Let me lie here just a minute more. Then you can help me to my feet."

"Take as long as you want." He pressed her head against his chest.

She could hear the frantic beating of his heart. He must really care about her. "While I'm getting my breath back, you can call me 'love' again."

He stiffened. Then slowly he relaxed. "I don't know what you're talking about."

She punched him lightly in the stomach.

Leon Box was absolutely certain that he'd been spotted. As his sharp eyes scanned the trail, his thoughts revisited the scene in the Fort Smith saloon. He had come in like any ordinary drifter, bought a beer, paid no more attention to his quarry than to any other man. He shook his head. What had tipped the outlaw off?

As he came over a ridge, a freshening wind struck him in the face. He cursed mildly. One minute there was no wind at all and the day was almost warm. Then, like magic, a sudden blast was filled with ice crystals. The day was turning bad. He reached for his slicker. In a matter of hours, even minutes, he was going to get mighty uncomfortable. He might even lose his quarry and whoever was riding with him. And with them a sure lead to Jesse James.

At the bottom of a deep draw, he spotted a silvery ribbon of water. He halted his mount at its edge. Less than a yard wide, it would be the test. He studied it carefully. Sure enough. The hoofprints led to the right. The clay was badly churned at the point where the water disappeared in the dry undergrowth.

He crossed his arms over his saddle horn and stared at the clay in disgust. It was so badly churned that he would bet money the big fellow with the yellow handlebar mustache had thought this up. The outlaw wanted him to follow.

Ambush!

A cold sweat popped out on Box's forehead. An itch sprang up between his shoulder blades. Twisting right and left in the saddle, he scanned the trees, the thickets of brown leaves and grasses with evergreens standing out among them. He was a sitting duck.

His first impulse was to get the hell back down the road and raise a posse.

He rejected that idea reluctantly. He'd lose the outlaws for sure. No. That was what they wanted him to do. His second choice was to follow the men into the woods and wander around wasting valuable time until he lost the trail or they shot him from ambush and left his body to rot.

Or he could ride on ahead to the nearest town. With a resigned sigh, he pulled out his map. Up ahead lay West Fork close to Devil's Den where the James gang was rumored to have a hideout. A few miles farther on was Prairie Grove, site of a minor battle during the War. One or the other of these little burgs was bound to have a telegraph office.

He grinned. Telegraph for reinforcements, gather a posse, and meet the smart outlaw and his pardner as they rode north. Drops of rain spattered on his slicker. He pulled his hat down tight over his forehead and heeled his horse across the rill. If he pushed hard, he could be in West Fork in an hour, have a hot meal, and surprise the two when they came riding in.

"Have we lost him?" Mary Carolyn asked anxiously. They had ridden for hours in the brush. They had crossed and recrossed the road, doubled back on their trail, and twice waited in hiding while Clell listened.

Now he shrugged. "We might have."

"Might have?" She looked around, aghast. She was cold and exhausted. "You mean you don't know?"

He shook his head. "No. Not really. He was supposed to follow us into the brush and lose us. If he didn't fall for that,

we were supposed to drive him crazy. Spook him so he'd turn
around and go back for help.''

"But we haven't even seen him.''

Clells wiped a hand across his mouth; his hat only partially
protected him from the icy mist. He hated to tell her this because
she had been so good about all the hard riding. Still, he couldn't
lie to her. "Yeah, I know. I'm kind of beginning to think we've
been outfoxed.''

She slumped in the saddle. "How? He couldn't possibly
have followed us all this distance.''

"I don't think he did. I think he must have decided a while
back to go on ahead.'' He climbed down off the gelding and
unbuckled the cheekstrap to take the bit out of its mouth. With
an air of unconcern, he led the big horse to a nearby fall of
water. It trickled down out of solid rock into a clear pool that
overflowed and disappeared again. Filling his own canteen, he
stepped away to allow the horse to drink. Even though the day
was wet, the high cold of the mountains dried a body out fast.
"Here.''

She took the canteen numbly. He had to urge her to drink.
All she could think of was how tired they were and how hard
they'd ridden. And how it all might be for nothing.

She handed the canteen back to him and shifted in the saddle.
About the only thing to be said for this awful ride was that
she had finally stopped hurting. Her muscles and tendons had
stretched until they no longer suffered. She rode like Clell.

He tilted the canteen to his own lips, his eyes never leaving
her face. "I'm sorry. You ought to be cussing me instead of
sitting there so quiet and patient.''

She stared at him without really seeing. "I'm too tired to
cuss.''

He led Lady Grace to the pool and pulled the bit out of her
mouth. While the mare drank, he pushed the gelding away.
Standing between the horses' heads, he tossed a comment over
his shoulder. "Well, if it's any consolation to you, I'm just
about worn slick too.''

She stared at his back. At last she allowed herself a small
smile. "If I say you've convinced me that being an outlaw is

a hard life, can we go somewhere and get a hot meal and a bath?''

He slipped the bits back into the horses' mouths and buckled the cheekstraps. ''It's a hard ride, but I think we can make it.''

But they didn't.

On top of the hill above West Fork, he spotted the posse. Quickly he reined the bay into Lady Grace, crowding the little mare off the trail.

Mary Carolyn had been hanging on to the horn as they had come up the steep slope. She gave a little cry as her horse staggered. ''Have you lost your mind?''

''Hold him!'' Clell slapped the gelding's reins into her hand at the same time he whipped his spyglass out of his saddlebags. Then he flung himself off his mount and cautiously moved back to the crest. When he had the glass focused, he began to cuss. ''He didn't fall for any of it. Damn! All that time wasted and he didn't even try to find us.''

The icy rain dripped off her hat, but she sat her horse with the patience of exhaustion. He looked back over his shoulder. Her eyes had dark shadows under them. Her lips were blue with cold. He looked again at the men. The man in the fancy Chicago hat was directing them to hide along the trail.

He could see with half an eye that they were setting up an ambush. If he hadn't pushed her so hard, they would have ridden right into it.

Behind him, she threw her leg over the horse's hindquarters and let herself slide to the ground. Her legs wouldn't hold her at first, but she kept herself from falling by holding onto the horn and cantle. He came back to her.

''Don't get down,'' he ordered gruffly.

''I have to. I . . . er . . . need to find a bush.''

He steadied her. ''Don't worry about it. I'll turn my back.''

''My legs are cramping, I need to walk around a little,'' she insisted.

While she limped off the trail, he crept back to the brow of the hill. The posse had disappeared. Only the man in the black hat remained at the edge of the trees. He had his binoculars out and was scanning the ridgeline.

Clell consigned the agent to hell. Hunkered down there, he felt a desperation he had never felt before. This was all his fault. Every damn bit of it. He watched her come back to the road. She was picking her way, steadying herself against the trunks of the trees. If she had to ride much farther, he'd have to tie her in the saddle.

Moving clumsily, he hauled himself to his feet. The north wind blew tiny slivers of ice against his cheek, stinging his face. How much more uncomfortable must they be on her fine skin. While he watched, she tightened the wool scarf that tied her hat down over her ears.

Desperately, he swung his head from side to side. They were in the midst of the mountains. They couldn't turn back. They couldn't go forward. She clasped her saddle horn and leaned against the mare's flank. Water dripped off the brim of her hat. The mare's head drooped. Water ran down her mane and dripped on the ground. He had two miserable and exhausted gals.

He writhed inwardly, as he came to the inevitable conclusion. Anger boiled in him, but he tamped it down. This was his fault. He was going to have to pay the piper. He was going to have to give himself up. There was no way out but surrender.

So long as she was in the way to stop a bullet, he couldn't fight. He couldn't take her back the way they'd come. Neither they nor the horses had the stamina to climb Boston Mountain again.

With a violent curse, he jerked his hat off. Stepping up on top of the ridge, he began to wave it in long sweeping arcs.

"Clell! What are you doing?" She blundered to his side and caught hold of his arm. Her weight dragged him back. His boots slid in the greasy red clay, and they both fell on their stomachs.

"What are you doing?" she cried.

He set his teeth. "I'm surrendering."

She stared at him, her mouth agape. "What?"

''I'm surrendering,'' he snarled. ''They're waiting in ambush in the draw below.''

She blinked, then heaved a tired sigh. ''You don't have to surrender. You can't surrender. We'll go around them.''

''No.''

She got her elbow and her knee under her. ''You think I can't do it. I can.'' She made it up on her knees, planted her foot, braced her arms. She might have been heaving herself out of quicksand. His arm snaked out. ''Don't . . .''

Without the least effort, he pulled her over on top of him. His arms closed around her and he pressed his cheek to hers. ''No, Buster Ross. Hell, no. Neither one of you can do it.'' ''He gestured to the mare. You can't even stand up. This is all my fault and I've got to make it right.''

She twisted and pushed at him. ''Don't be stupid. I don't want to go to jail any more than you do.'' Tears started in her eyes. ''They might hang us. I don't want to hang.''

He put a hand around the back of her head and hauled her down to his chest. ''Listen.'' He slipped the hand beneath her scarf to rub the back of her neck. ''Listen. They're not going to hang you. You're just some poor little girl that I kidnapped. I needed a hostage. I was going to use you to buy my way out.''

''Then do it.'' She tried to raise her head, but he held it firmly. She was so exhausted that the tension was draining out of her body even as she argued. ''That's a good idea.''

He sat up and shifted her until she lay across his lap. Her cheek was smeared with red clay. Her eyes were sunken in her head. Her lips were blue with cold. She was just an inch short of being ugly. And there was no one else in the world that he cared more about. Looking down into her tired face, he read the love that made him ashamed of himself. She had fallen in love with him and didn't have the strength to hide it.

He hugged her close and rocked back and forth. ''They'll take you back to West Fork. I'll confess, and we'll both get in out of this weather. You can get a room at the hotel.''

''How would I pay for it?'' She laid both hands on his chest and pushed. ''Damn you, Clell Miller. I know why you're doing this. And it won't work. You want to keep from giving me my share of the loot from the train.''

He was so startled that he let go of her. She tumbled out of his arms and scooted away from him. ''Mary Carolyn, damn it—''

''You know a way out of these mountains. You do! You just want to get rid of me.''

''I swear . . .''

She clambered to her feet. The wool blankets wrapped around her legs were heavy with water and mud. Her boots slipped and slid, but she caught herself and finally managed to stand upright. From that small advantage she dug her fists into her hips. ''You'd break jail in the morning. Tomorrow night at the latest. All the outlaws do in the novels.''

He hung his head. A solid stream of cusswords flowed out. He cussed her. He cussed the dime novels. He cussed Jesse and Cole. He cussed the Pinkerton agency and the weather. He called her a damn fool and worse. Still cussing, he heaved himself to his feet. He retrieved his hat and slapped it against his slicker to get the worst of the mud off. Then he clapped it on his head. ''Damn you, Buster Ross. You get the hell on that horse.''

She lifted her chin. ''I'm not going with you if you surrender.''

''I'm not going to surrender.'' He stalked to the gelding and caught up the reins. ''I'm going to take us at a run down this mountain and then we're turning east. There's a farm a ways from here, if I remember how to get there. They were good people. If she's still there, she'll take us in.''

He mounted the gelding and walked the mare over to Mary Carolyn. ''Can you get up by yourself?''

''Yes.'' She wrapped both hands around the horn and tried to lift her left foot. Even the little mare's stirrup was too tall for her. She let go and tried to lift her leg. No luck.

He sat there with his teeth bared, determined not to help the little fool.

She looked over the saddle bow at him. Eyes flashing, she caught the saddle horn and stepped back. With an effort that wrung a grunt from between her teeth, she managed to swing her leg high enough to hang her ankle on the mare's hind-quarters. She pulled and strained.

He was sweating watching her efforts. His left hand clenched the reins.

With a sharp squeak of pure determination, she pushed the leg over the mare's back. She worked until her waist lay across the seat. Another wiggle, a squirm, a couple of grunts. Finally, she shifted herself upright. Her color was high. The smile she threw him was one of pure triumph.

He nodded shortly as if she'd delayed them both. Then he reined the gelding off the trail and into the short scrub. "Keep your head down. If you thought we had hard going this morning, you're going to find out you don't know what hard means."

The hell with you too. Mary Carolyn sat stock-still watching Clell ride away. Then she pointed her index finger at his disappearing back and thumbed back an imaginary hammer. Lady Grace tossed her head and pulled at the bridle. She had followed the gelding so long now she knew they needed to be going.

Mary Carolyn leaned over and patted the mare's sodden neck beneath the mane. "Go on, girl," she murmured. "But take it easy. We both need to save ourselves."

For the first few minutes, she couldn't lean forward over her horse's neck because the trail was too steep. Instead, she had to hang back for counterbalance. She couldn't figure out whether the trail wasn't nearly so bad as he had claimed, or whether she was just getting used to being thrown from side to side in the saddle and whipped in the face by branches.

She wondered where they were going. Wondered who "she" was. She hoped "she" was some dear old lady like Violie Bishop.

The gelding came to the bottom of the slope and Clell slashed his reins across its withers. It broke into a heavy gallop that took it over a brown meadow. A minute later Lady Grace came out of the trees and followed gamely.

Above them the storm broke loose. A clap of thunder caused the mare to shy and almost unseated Mary Carolyn. The rain fell in great slashing drops that stung because they were mixed with ice. She gasped for breath and then leaned low. The horn prodded her empty belly. It flashed through her mind that she could freeze, starve, fall from her horse, or be struck by lightning. She managed a weak smile. Right now a lightning strike sounded pretty good to her.

He had vowed he would never return to Cutter's Knob. Their unit of Quantrill's Raiders had been fleeing for their lives. They'd managed to shake a Union troop at the Missouri line, but they couldn't expect to fool the boys in blue forever. They were cold and hungry and scared out of their minds.

Chased out of Missouri, Jesse and Frank had led them south to the homestead of one of their mother's relatives in the little Ozark community. They hadn't meant to tell anybody they were there. They were just going to slip into the barn and sprawl in the hay, but the hounds had set up a howl to wake the dead.

Jesse's cousin Noah Woodson had come out and found them. He'd been afraid with good reason. In 1864 after Bloody Bill Anderson's raid at Centralia, Missouri, the Yankees were hanging anyone who gave aid and comfort to the enemy. But he'd let them stay the night.

The next morning Woodson's wife Rebecca had ordered them off the property. She was a hellfire and damnation preacher of some offbeat sect. She didn't hold with their sinful ways. The rest of the troop had been for leaving right then, but Jesse and Frank maintained that Noah should be the one to send them on their way. His daughter Esther had come out later with food and bandages. And Noah hadn't said anything about their leaving.

Clell shivered at the memories. A good man, a good friend, generous and kind. He couldn't bear to think about it. Some of them were shot up. He himself had a crease on his shoulder and a hole through his forearm. The daughter had bandaged it. He remembered Esther. Oh, how he remembered her. He shivered again. He'd gotten to know her better than he should while they'd lain around at Noah's for almost two weeks.

Then they'd ridden on into Indian Territory.

Later Frank had cursed and Jesse had said it was nobody's fault. But it had been. The Yankees had descended on the farm. They'd searched the premises, terrorized Woodson's wife, his young son, and his pretty daughter. And they'd hanged Noah Woodson from the rafters over his front porch.

The gelding had slowed as the killing pace told on its strength. Clell looked over his left shoulder. Mary Carolyn was there, her face grim, her hands wrapped around the horn. The little mare adjusted her pace to the gelding's.

Into the trees they trotted. Clell began to pick his way through the brush. The day was done in the valley. They couldn't go any farther. He looked over his shoulder in time to see his companion slide bonelessly from the saddle.

Chapter Nineteen

Sleet and rain fell, then ceased, then fell again. The going was miserable. Over and over, Clell told himself he was getting too old for this. It had been bad enough when he was a seventeen-year-old kid trying to win a war that couldn't be won. Young bodies could recover from riding all day and all night in an Arkansas version of a blizzard. This year he'd see his twenty-ninth birthday.

An especially strong gust stung his eyes. He ducked his head. Icy water from his hat brim trickled down on Mary Carolyn's cheek. She didn't stir. Cursing, he raised his head, squinting from the force of the gale.

Where in hell were they? On a wild-goose chase for sure. His memory had probably failed him. More than ten years had passed since he had ridden down this road. If this even was the road. When he'd come to the fork he couldn't remember whether to go right or left. The gelding had chosen for him, plodding wearily along, driven likely as not by some deep-seated sense of self-preservation that would keep it moving until its strength was gone rather than stopping to freeze in its tracks.

Clell's arms were so numb with cold and with holding Mary

Carolyn that he had long since ceased to guide the horse. He'd managed to button his slicker around his burden. Where their bodies pressed together, she was warm. But how much damage frostbite had done to her feet, he had no idea. His own feet were numb in his boots.

The wind moaned. Tree branches clacked together, shedding ice onto his slicker in soft little splats. He was just about at the end of his strength. He stopped cursing to pray.

The shape of a house rose out of the darkness. The gelding turned into the yard and plodded up to the hitching post.

Clell stared at the structure from under snow-crusted brows. Whether or not it was the Woodson place, it would have to do. If the people tried to refuse them shelter, he would take it at the point of a gun. Mary Carolyn had to get warm. He tried to summon the strength to throw his leg over the horse's neck. From the knees down, he was numb. He sent the message, but muscles and tendons didn't obey.

Trusting that the slicker would hold her, he reached down and hooked his numbed hand under his thigh. It was like hooking a log. He had to heave for all he was worth. Once he had his thigh up on the horn, he could guide it over without too much trouble. From there he started his slide. His contact with the ground sent agonies shooting all the way to his hips. He dropped to his knees and nearly fell face down on top of her body.

One more try, he kept telling himself. Just one. You can do it. You've come this far. Just a little bit more and you can rest.

He struggled up the steps. His boot heels were muffled by the snow on the porch. He didn't dare let her go to knock. Bracing himself against the jamb, he kicked at the door.

He had to kick a couple of times before he heard people stirring. A couple of dark shapes appeared at the window. He heard voices.

The door opened. A pistol came out first, leveled at his chest.

"Esther." He tried to say the word but his voice wouldn't work. He cleared his throat and tried again. "Esther."

The gun muzzle never wavered. A man's voice growled, "Who are you?"

"Miller's m' name." He couldn't feel his feet and legs.

Couldn't feel the porch. His head seemed to be spinning off in space.

"Clell?" A woman's voice asked, shrill with disbelief.

"Esther?"

The buttons of his slicker popped open. He held out the unconscious girl. "Take her please. She's near frozen."

The man let the gun swing downward in his hand. Turning it sideways, he reached for Mary Carolyn.

Clell wasn't able to stay awake any longer. Exhaustion, like a great black cloud, welled up around him. He slumped forward, pushing the door open with the weight of his body.

The last words he could hear and understand were a woman's. "My God! Jesse told me you were dead."

Mary Carolyn woke to an aching warmth. Every part of her hurt, most particularly her feet. They didn't just ache. They throbbed. If she hadn't been so tired, she would have sat up and grabbed hold of them. She had been frostbitten. Nerving herself, she made an attempt to wriggle her toes. The pain made her squeak. But she could count all five on each foot. Good news. They were all there, and they burned like fire.

She smiled grimly. Funny how she was glad that she was in pain. She decided that the outlaw trail had mixed up good and evil. Slowly, she opened her eyes. The sun streamed in through white curtains embroidered with bluebirds. Whether it was the morning or the afternoon, she couldn't tell. But the brightness testified that the storm that had almost killed them was over.

She lay there taking in her surroundings. She'd been in a room something like this only once before. The Reverend and Mrs. Samuel's bedroom where she and Clell had spent their wedding night had looked like this the next morning. The same cleanliness. The same homeliness of old furniture, well used, well kept, and gleaming through its protective coating of satiny beeswax. She turned her head. The pillowcase was embroidered with bluebirds too. They were the traditional bluebirds of happiness. They spread their wings among delicate flowers composed entirely of pink French knots.

A faint click reached her ears and a short creak. She raised her head. The door opened slowly. A girl stuck her head around the edge. A couple of long blond curls swung gently forward. "Oh, you're awake."

She straightened and stepped inside carrying a tray carefully before her. "Would you like some coffee?"

Mary Carolyn's stomach clenched as hunger pangs tore at her. The smell of the coffee made her mouth water. She pushed herself up on her elbows. "Oh, yes."

The girl smiled. She looked to be about ten or twelve. Although she was tall, her chest was still flat as a boy's. Likewise, the blond curls were caught up at the back of her head by a big pink bow. She set the tray down carefully and then straightened with a grin. "Didn't spill a drop."

Mary Carolyn grinned back. "Nobody could have done it better."

The little blond poured coffee into the cup and lifted the lid of the sugar bowl. "One spoonful?"

Mary Carolyn reached for the spoon. "I'll do it. Thank you so much." The spoon rattled against the cup as her hands shook in her eagerness. Her first swallow warmed her all the way down. She closed her eyes in pleasure. Even her feet didn't hurt so badly for a few minutes.

The girl was watching her closely. "Tastes good?"

Mary Carolyn nodded, forcing herself not to drink it all down and pour more. She took another swallow and set the cup and saucer down. "I'm Mary Carolyn Miller."

The girl rolled her eyes. "Oh, lordy, I'm so rude. Mama says I got a slow start on manners and I'm just creeping along now." She held out her hand. "I'm Sarah Sue Bradburn."

Mary Carolyn frowned ever so slightly. Something about the beautiful young face struck a familiar chord. Why? She had certainly never been in Central Arkansas before. She looked at the proffered hand. The fingers were long and delicate, the back of the hand lightly tanned, the skin thin enough that a faint tracery of blue veins showed. The hand was scrupulously clean.

It reminded Mary Carolyn that she was probably dirtier than she had ever been in her life. She glanced at her own hand before she extended it. Fortunately, the palm was clean. Thank heaven someone had given her a sponge before she had been put to bed. She clasped her young nurse's hand.

Sarah Sue smiled an enchanting smile. She was a beautiful child with flawless skin and regular features. Her most outstanding feature were very dark brown eyes. Now they crinkled at the corners. Mary Carolyn had never expected to see another person with eyes near the same color as hers. Blond hair usually went with blue eyes. "Mama says to ask you what you'd like to eat for breakfast."

Mary Carolyn returned to her own problems. "Would half a hog be too much to ask for?"

The girl laughed. "Probably, but I'll ask anyway. I imagine you'll get the same as everybody else. Mama scrambles eggs with bacon and onions in them. We like them. And she's already made biscuits."

"Sounds perfect."

Before she left, the girl added hot coffee to the cup. "Would you like to go down the hall?" she asked shyly. "Papa built Mama a real bathroom with everything fancy like he had when he was a boy in Philadelphia." Her pride was obvious. "It even has a special rack to keep the towels and washrags warm."

"Lead me to it." Mary Carolyn tugged the covers back and eased her legs over the side. Her feet were bundled in loose wool socks. The way her toes hurt she was glad she couldn't see them.

Sarah Sue came to her side. "Do you need to lean on me?"

Catching her lip between her teeth, Mary Carolyn hobbled forward. The strained muscles of her back and legs protested, but she made it all the way across the room. "It hurts. But I think I can make it on my own."

"Good for you." Sarah Sue opened the door. "I'll show you the way."

Once inside the bathroom, Mary Carolyn dropped down on

the commode. Body aching, feet throbbing, she had worked up
a sweat. Drawing a deep breath, she could hear her young nurse
hurrying away.

The bathroom was just as lovely as the bedroom, but in a
different way. It looked as if it had been transported complete
from some great house. The fixtures were new and shining.
A picture made of silk flowers hung on the wall above the
aforementioned towel rack. The embroidered towels had cro-
cheted lace on their hems. The basin rested in a marble-topped
washstand. The tub was porcelain, claw footed, and big enough
to bathe an entire family in. Coals glowed through the grate
of a Dutch tile stove.

Her mouth slightly open, Mary Carolyn turned in a circle to
take it all in. Sarah Sue was lucky to have a place like this.
Mary Carolyn experienced a moment of envy. Even though
she knew it wasn't true, she believed with her heart that all
girls who had fathers were lucky.

Beneath half-closed lids Clell watched Esther Elizabeth
Woodson—Bradburn now—move around the kitchen. Even
though he had no right to his resentment, it smoldered inside
him. From time to time, tiny flames leaped up from the ashes
of his memories to sear him.

Like now, when Esther was going to grind the coffee beans
to make a fresh pot. Without even bothering to ask, her husband
had taken the job right out of her hands. And she'd let him
with a smile. The smile was the worst part of the whole act.
Clell remembered that smile. She'd smiled at him like that a
long time ago.

How could Esther have married a Yankee? Yankees had
killed her father.

Despite the War's being over for ten years, Clell knew he
couldn't be that forgiving. Too much water had flowed under
the bridge to let him forget. From beneath his brows he glowered
at them both.

And their happy family. It drove him almost to madness to
see the sturdy boy in the high chair, industriously filling himself

full of oatmeal. Little Noah was awkward with his spoon, getting more on his face that in his mouth, but he was single-minded.

The girl came in. Much older, a young lady, the image of Esther with long blond curls and dark brown eyes. Esther's eyes. He had forgotten the color of her eyes. How had he forgotten? Mary Carolyn's eyes were that color too. He shouldn't be so upset, but his feelings for her had nothing to do with this. Clell felt a surge of pure murderous rage before he recognized it for what it was. Jealousy.

"Mary Carolyn's taking a bath, Mama. She said she'd like half a hog for breakfast." The little girl's smile was enchanting. "But she'll eat eggs and bacon and biscuits if that's all you have."

Esther nodded. Her eyes flitted to Clell's face and then back to her daughter. He couldn't believe it, but she looked like she was frightened.

The look stabbed him again. What did she expect he'd do, for heaven's sake? He was an outlaw, not a murderer. He'd never harm anyone she cared about.

York Bradburn exchanged a glance with his wife. "We'll get the hounds fed," he said decisively. "Give me a hand, Miller."

"Sure thing." Clell rose willingly enough. He wanted to speak to Esther alone, but he acknowledged that he'd missed his chance for now. He couldn't say what he wanted to with the daughter listening to every word.

The two men walked down the frosty hill together, eyes squinted against the icy brightness that coated every blade of grass, every leaf, every stone. The day was frigid. Ice crystals twinkled in the air.

"Esther asked me to speak to you." York Bradburn stood back for Clell to enter the storage shed.

Reluctantly, Clell entered. A chill scudded down his spine that had nothing to do with the temperature. "Esther can say anything she wants to say to me," he declared. "I'd never hurt her."

"I'd say you've done more than any other man ever has to hurt her," York snapped.

Clell lifted his chin. "I heard about her father. Yellowlegs hung him. Just like you. It wasn't my fault that Yankees butchered innocent citizens."

"There were bad things done on both sides ten years ago," York agreed. "Lots of innocent citizens died in Lawrence and Centralia."

Clell grunted. He hunched his shoulders and doubled up his fists.

York didn't back down an inch. "Esther's a wonderful woman. A wise woman. She's a woman who's got better sense than to blame me for what happened because some jayhawkers came out of Kansas and hid out on the place. You knew what you were doing when you did it. You knew what the orders were. The James boys just didn't care about anything or anybody but themselves. And if my guess is correct, they still don't."

"I didn't know," Clell protested lamely. It was only half the truth. They had all known. They just hadn't believed such a thing could happen.

"You're running from the law right now."

Clell grunted as York guessed correctly. Slowly, the belligerence went out of him. He couldn't deny that he was. He felt a hundred years old and so tired he wanted to lie down and die.

York swept his arm wide. "Esther's worked hard to keep this place and turn it into a successful kennel and farm. What would happen if we let you stay here for a week or two? Would a posse surround the place? Shoot it up? Would you and your woman make a break for it and leave us to face the consequences?"

"No!" Clell hadn't even considered the possibility of that when he came. The memory of Jesse's face when he'd learned his brother was dead rolled over Clell like a black tide. "I'm pretty sure nobody knows . . . that is—"

York's expression was dark with contempt. "Listen to me,"

he interrupted. "You can stay today, to rest the horses and your girlfriend—"

Stung, Clell interrupted. "She's not a girlfriend. She's my wife."

York laughed mirthlessly. "Oh, sure. I guess she sold her wedding ring to get you out of jail."

"Listen—"

"No. You listen. Esther wants you off this place within twenty-four hours. And she particularly wants you to keep away from Sarah Susannah."

"The girl—"

"Yes, my daughter. She's happy as a lark now. But it's taken Esther and me five years to undo what was done to her. You leave her strictly alone. Don't speak to her, don't smile at her, don't go near her."

Clell frowned. He couldn't understand what was being said to him. The War had done bad things to everybody, but the child didn't look old enough to remember much of it. Esther knew he was no rapist. He could barely remember the sweetness of their one time together, but he knew he hadn't forced her. They'd been kids, scared kids, their passions raging. He'd been more than half sure that he wouldn't survive the War. "I don't understand."

"Esther and Sarah have both paid for what you did."

Clell stared at him. "I never saw that girl before today."

A dark flush stained York's face. His eyes glittered with anger. "Then keep it the hell that way or answer to me."

Mary Carolyn hobbled into the kitchen. Sarah Sue introduced her mother, Esther, and her baby brother, Noah "the Beast."

"Sarah Susannah, that's a terrible thing to say," Esther chided. "Two children are so much fun," she remarked in an aside to Mary Carolyn. "They can play together. Whoever said that didn't know what she was talking about."

"Of course, Mama thinks he's a perfect angel," Sarah complained. "She tells me I should be thrilled to death because he's such a happy baby. Then, when he shows how happy he is, he makes a mess. I get to clean it up.''

''The Beast'' slammed his spoon down beside his bowl and announced himself, ''Froo.'' His black hair curled in a profusion of tight ringlets that fell over his forehead. His dark brown eyes snapped with excitement. ''Froo. Froo. Froo.''

Her hands sticky with biscuit dough, Esther exchanged a meaningful look with her daughter.

''Oh, let me take care of him.'' Mary Carolyn hastened to offer. ''I used to take care of some of the babies in the . . . er. . . . I'm used to taking care of babies. Will you come to me, Noah?''

Noah looked around at the three women, his dirty little face a study in baby joy. When Mary Carolyn held out her arms, he went into them crowing gleefully. Sarah dipped a washcloth into warm water and wrung it out over the sink. ''At least I'll get one day off.''

When the men entered, Mary Carolyn had him all cleaned up and sitting on her lap. He squealed with delight as she played horsey with him on her knee.

''Got that chore done,'' York announced heartily. He came to his wife's side and hugged her against him. His lips moved next to her ear.

Mary Carolyn frowned faintly. Had he sent word for the sheriff? She shook her head at herself. Being an outlaw made her uneasy. Another reason for quitting. Besides, Clell had been with him. He could hardly have sent a message unobserved.

She looked with interest at the man who made a point of caressing his wife and then sent a warning look to his guest. Mary Carolyn had not seen him before. The word ''handsome'' didn't do justice to Esther's husband. He had raven black hair and dark brown eyes beneath long black eyelashes. His skin was so dark it was almost swarthy. By contrast his teeth looked even whiter. He reminded her of an actor she had seen on a theater poster in Chicago.

The little boy Noah was the picture of his papa. Indeed, when Papa came in, the little one struggled to get out of her arms. When she set him on the floor, he took off at a headlong run that ended with a thump against his father's leg, where he clung, squealing in pure joy. Instantly, York picked him up.

A lump rose in her throat. What a perfect family!

Clell came to her side and put a hand possessively on her shoulder. She looked up in surprise. He hadn't touched her like that in a long time. He himself had bathed and shaved. When he bent to her, she caught the clean scent of soap. "How are your feet?"

She lifted one and wiggled it to demonstrate. "Good. They look like they've been pounded with hammers, but they feel fine."

"Are you sure? You're not just saying that?"

"No. Not at all."

"The weather's already warming up," York put in meaningfully. "By tomorrow all this stuff will be melted."

Clell shot him a poisonous look. "Then first light tomorrow we'll go."

"You mustn't go until Mary Carolyn's fit to travel." Esther placed a hand on her husband's arm. A look passed between them that caused him to shrug and walk to his place at the head of the table. Then she opened the oven and took out the biscuits. "Everybody sit down. Sarah, please put out the plates for everyone."

"I'll pour the coffee." Mary Carolyn rose a little creakily. She had said she was fine when in truth, her bones ached. By tomorrow she would be better she told herself. Moving a little slower than usual she forced herself to walk without hobbling.

While her daughter set warm plates at their places, Esther dished up a huge platter of scrambled eggs and thick-sliced bacon. Then she opened the oven and took out the pan of inch-high baking powder biscuits. A gust of hot air redolent of fresh-baked bread mixed with the mouth-watering smells. Mary Carolyn had to clasp her hands tight together and choke back tears. Never in her whole life had she seen people so happy and so blessed.

York seated himself at the head of the table, Noah on his knee. With his chubby hand the baby accepted a strip of bacon, which he waved about while he looked expectantly at his mother. Clell and Mary Carolyn sat side by side across from Sarah.

Esther set the biscuits on the table and seated herself beside Clell. In a moment of silence, she bowed her head. "Dear Lord, we thank Thee for this food. We thank Thee for the strength of our bodies that we use in ways that are pleasing in Thy sight." She paused fractionally. "And for the storm which spared the travelers and brought them safely to us as friends. Amen."

At the final word, the baby let out a crow of delight. The bacon crumbled in his hand as he tried to stuff it all into his mouth at once.

"He eats everything in sight." Esther apologized for her son as York patiently bent to pick up the pieces. "We've just got him to the point where he'll wait until he hears me say 'Amen.' Then he acts as if he's just been pulled back from the brink of starvation."

"Mama's mother was a preacher," Sarah felt she should add. "That's why we get the long prayers."

Esther's brows snapped together in a frown. "Three sentences hardly makes a long prayer."

"Oh, Mama. Most families just do with 'God is great, God is good, Let us thank Him for this food.' "

The inconsequential talk went back and forth among father, daughter, and mother. Mary Carolyn basked in its warmth. For the first time she felt a great need welling up inside her. She wanted to be married. She wanted to have a husband like York Bradburn and a daughter like Sarah and a squirming, wriggling bundle of energy like Noah for a son. She wanted it so much that she ached with the need.

She cast her eyes sideways at Clell. He pushed his food around on his plate while he stared sideways at Esther. Mary Carolyn's romantic imagination took fire and with that came a spurt of jealousy. Esther must have been his love before the War. She must have married another man. But Clell still loved her. Why did that hurt so much?

Suddenly she was very tired. The pain from her feet that she had resolutely pushed aside turned to an insistent throbbing.

She took another bite of the delicious biscuit slathered with butter and covered with blackberry preserves. It tasted like ashes. She chewed and swallowed with difficulty.

She swayed beneath a wave of dizziness. "I think I'd better go back to my room."

Even as the last words came out, she reached for Clell, who dropped his fork. Throwing an arm around her he steadied her.

"Poor thing." Esther rose. "We should have brought you a tray."

"I offered, Mama," Sarah said quickly.

Clell rose and lifted Mary Carolyn in his arms. "She's always this way," he declared. It seemed to Mary Carolyn that he clutched her to him a bit more tightly. Her eyelashes swept up. He looked down into her face. "Keeps going when anybody else would fall by the wayside." He looked into Esther's eyes. Did a sort of prideful defiance ring in his tone? "She doesn't know when to quit."

A faint flush appeared on Esther's cheeks.

York cleared his throat. Passing Noah to Sarah, he opened the kitchen door. "Take her back to her room."

"We need to get on out of here." Clell crossed his arms in front of his chest and stared around him tight-lipped. Even though Mary Carolyn could scarcely walk, anger and jealousy set his blood to boiling.

He and Esther stood in the parlor in front of the fire. He looked around him, taking everything in. Even as he did, he could feel his temper rising. The old house had never looked so fine in Noah Woodson's day. The floors had been sanded and revarnished. The walls had new paper. Apart from a few familiar pieces, the furniture looked expensive, not like the plain things that he was used to seeing in Missouri homes.

"You mustn't go if Mary Carolyn's not fit," Esther protested.

"She's fit enough," Clell declared stonily. "She can ride a ways and then I can carry her. One way or another, she'll make it across the Missouri line into Carthage."

"But . . ."

He looked her up and down, wondering how she had come to this. She had been reared to be loyal, to care for her family. She shouldn't have cared for all this stuff. He supposed women did when they got to be older. No doubt about it, Esther had matured. The slender girl he remembered had become a beautiful woman, glowing with health and happiness. Her breasts were fuller. The blond braid was coiled up into a couple of loops that hung halfway down her back. He knew he shouldn't ask, but he couldn't completely stifle his curiosity. "How long's your hair?"

She touched it self-consciously. "To my knees."

He shook his head and looked aside into the heart of the fire. It threw a red light onto his face. "York Bradburn's got it all."

She hesitated. "I'm very lucky."

He couldn't let it go. He should be thankful that he'd been welcomed here. Mary Carolyn might have died in the storm. But how could Esther marry a Yankee? He thrust his hands into his back pockets. It had the effect of throwing his chest forward. With his height, his posture was bound to be intimidating. "That Yankee must have been in the hanging party that did for your father."

She turned white to the lips. Her eyes snapped to the ancient rifle on the wall above the fireplace. "God damn you, Clell Miller. I'll forget you said that because your wife's not strong enough to travel."

He should have left it alone, but he couldn't bear to. Old hatreds ran deep. He made no attempt to conceal the bitterness in his voice. "How could you do something like that, Esther? How could you marry a Yankee with Noah not cold in the ground?"

Her eyes sparked fire. Planting her fists on her hips, she rocked toward him. "Who and when I marry is none of your damn business, Clell Miller. You left me without so much as a good-bye kiss. You don't know—" Her mouth snapped to like a steel trap. She whirled around and stalked to the door.

He came after and caught up with her. Catching her by the arm, he spun her back to meet his fierce gaze. "What don't I know? I know he's a Yankee. He talks like he's from the North. That bathroom looks like it's straight out of some fancy Northern hotel.''

"How would you know? You've never been in the North. Oh, you hate it that I have the least bit of comfort. You jayhawkers wouldn't care if your babies had a roof over their heads.''

"Babies!''

She hesitated. Color that had raged in her cheeks faded suddenly. She looked frightened. "I—I meant . . . I didn't mean . . .''

"Babies!'' A black shadow passed across Clell's vision. Suddenly, he felt as if the ground had been pulled from under his feet. "How old is Sarah?''

"Ten . . . er . . . nine.'' Esther pushed at his hands. When he wouldn't let her go, she slapped at him, at his face, at his shoulders. "Let me go. Let go of me.''

He endured it, reacted no more than a stone statue. His eyes were burning. Surely, he couldn't be about to cry. "Whose child is she?''

"Let me go.''

"Tell me!''

If she had fought before, it was a prelude for what began now. She attacked him with fists and feet. Kicking and punching, sobbing and cursing, she flung herself at him.

Obdurate as he was, he couldn't resist her. He fell back across the room.

"I hate you. Hate you. Hate you.'' Instead of screaming the words at him, she groaned them, grunted them, growled them. Her hard left fist caught him in the eye. Her right punched him in the throat. He was choking. He couldn't move.

"Stop it, Esther!'' Suddenly, York Bradburn was in the room. Neither knew when he had come or how long he had waited to pull his wife off. He turned her in his arms.

Clell discovered he was braced against the wall, arms at his side, palms pressed flat. One eye was rapidly closing. He swallowed experimentally, not surprised to find his throat swelling.

Esther was sobbing hysterically in York's arms. Death and

hell looked out of his black eyes. "You!" His hands on his wife's back were infinitely gentle, infinitely supportive. "Clear off this place at first light. And next time, Clell Miller, stay dead!"

Chapter Twenty

Mary Carolyn asked no questions.

She took her meals in her room the rest of the day. Neither Esther nor her handsome husband came near her. When Sarah brought her tray at suppertime, she merely said that her mother had become ill and her father had taken her into town to the doctor. Now she was lying down. All Sarah's innocent friendliness of the morning was replaced by a wary stiffness.

Clell came in shortly after Mary Carolyn had finished eating. His right eye was bruised, a swollen purplish red shiner. His face was grim. Desperation had turned it to stone. His hair was a tousled mess as if he had raked his hands through and through it. He dropped their saddlebags on the floor. "We'll leave first thing in the morning."

She took in his expression. "Maybe we should leave tonight?"

His hands drove through his hair. His eyes were agonized. She could imagine his head was pounding. "Believe me, if it weren't colder than a well digger's toe out there, we'd be gone."

She threw back the quilts, but he caught them and covered her back to her chin. "No. You need your strength. One more night can't do any harm." He paced to the window. His eyes stared unseeing into the darkness beyond the glass. When he turned, his haunted expression tore at Mary Carolyn's heart. "I'll sleep in here if you don't mind. Just stretch out on the floor."

"You can sleep in the bed—"

"No." He swallowed as if his throat hurt him. "I'll just stretch out on the floor. First light, I'll get you up. I'll buy us some breakfast in Bentonville."

"For heaven's sake, Clell. What's happened?"

He threw a hand out to ward off her questions. With a shake of his head, he dropped down on the floor at the end of the bed.

Mary Carolyn heard him moving around. She leaned up to see that he had pulled the wool punch rug over his shoulders. Recognizing punishment when she saw it, she left him alone with his pain. She turned off the lamp and lay back down. Staring into the darkness, she remembered his face. He looked like a man who had aged a dozen years in a single afternoon.

"Sarah? Sarah Bradburn?" Mary Carolyn doubted her eyes. How had York and Esther's daughter come to be out here in the middle of the road to Bentonville before noon?

The girl sat the saddle of a mare whose color had never been described in the dime novels. Mane, tail, and all four stockings were black as ebony, but the haunches and long neck shone like blue steel. Likewise, Sarah's black velvet riding skirt shone in the sunlight. She wore a blue wool jacket piped with black and a low-crowned black hat tied under her chin by black veiling. The outfit was the sort that a rich and haughty heroine from the East might wear when the hero first spied her. Mary Carolyn had never seen anything so fine.

Like a young princess, Sarah had turned her mount across the road. Her young chin was set, her lips pressed tightly together as if they might never smile again.

Clell appeared just as thunderstruck. His color faded. He hunched his shoulders and then urged the gelding forward. He leaned toward the girl. "You shouldn't be out here alone. It's too dangerous."

"I came after you," she answered coldly. "I know these mountains like the back of my hand. My mama and papa've taken me all over them while they train the hounds. I took a shortcut."

"Then you'd better ride back as fast as you can," Clell growled. "They sure wouldn't be happy to know that you're out here."

"No, they sure wouldn't," she agreed, her voice just as angry. She sat stiffly in the saddle, fairly bristling with defiance. The light of battle shone in her eyes.

Mary Carolyn urged Lady Grace up to them. The mares nuzzled in greeting. "Is something wrong?"

"Not really." Sarah's stare never left Clell's face. "Are you my father?"

Mary Carolyn gasped. Clell grunted and reeled in the saddle as if he had been shot. For what seemed like hours but was really only a couple of minutes, no one said a thing. Clell crossed his hands over the saddle horn and hunched his shoulders. At last he managed to ask, "What does your mother say?"

"Oh, she doesn't say a thing. She'd never say a thing. As far as she's concerned it was all over and done with. Everyone said you were dead. Until you showed up here. But you weren't dead. And for five years I was a female bastard because you didn't come back and marry my mother."

Clell's face went gray. His fists were clenched so tightly that the knuckles looked as if they would split.

Hardly able to believe her senses, Mary Carolyn looked from father to daughter and back again. Now she recalled the strange sense of familiarity she had noticed when she had first seen the girl. Sarah's brown eyes might be like her mother's, but her chin and mouth and nose were shaped like Clell's. A wave of pity swept her. She knew exactly how Sarah felt.

And then a wave of triumph struck her. Hit him again! she cheered silently. Harder! Give it to him good! Tell him exactly how you feel! Don't let him ride away without knowing. Don't let him get away with it any longer.

Clell's face was screwed up as tightly as his fists. In a hoarse voice he said, ''I didn't know.''

''And you never came back to find out.'' The accusation was all the more damning because the childish voice quavered.

Eyes on the ground, he shook his head.

''My grandmother took me away from my mother because of what you did to her,'' Sarah informed him sternly. ''I didn't have a mother or a father for five long years. No mother. No father. I might as well have been an orphan. And the whole town—every single person in Cutter's Knob—knew that I was a female bastard.''

''Don't . . . don't say that.'' No entreaty to a merciless god ever was more desperate.

''Female bastard!'' Her voice regained its strength on a shout. ''Female bastard!'' With a terrible smile, she uttered the next words in a whisper. ''Female bastard. They called me that every time my grandmother's back was turned. I'd hear them talking about me on the streets. They whispered about me behind their hands and stared at me and pointed.''

''Goddam!'' Clell's whisper was like an invocation. ''Oh, Goddam!''

''Are you my father? I was born nine months to the day after they hanged my grandfather.''

Mary Carolyn shook her head. She put a hand over her mouth to stifle the exclamation of horror.

Clell seemed shrunken in the saddle, his body curled down over the horn as if he bowed beneath a hailstorm or a rain of fire and brimstone. He nodded. ''I must be.''

''And do you ride with my cousin Jesse James?''

''Yes.''

Mary Carolyn had it in her heart to feel sorry for him. Nothing and no one seemed willing to spare him. As far as Sarah Susannah Bradburn was concerned, he didn't deserve to be spared.

The little girl gathered her reins. The steeldust mare stirred and pawed the ground. She had stood too long and now was eager to be on her way. "Well, I wanted to ride with Jesse James once. I wanted to be worse than Jesse James. I was going to be an outlaw and rob banks and hurt people and shoot them for all the terrible things they said about me."

Clell gave a groan. For the first time he shot a shamed glance at Mary Carolyn.

At last, she thought. At last he can understand.

"But then my father, York Bradburn, adopted me. I'm Sarah Susannah Bradburn now. And I don't need you. That's what I came to tell you. I never want to see you again. Don't you *ever* come back and bother my mother and father again."

With that, she guided the mare between the two horses. When the road lay bare before her, she slapped the reins across the steeldust's flank. "Yee-haw!"

The mare took off like a shot. The dust of the road rose behind them and hid her from them even before she rounded the bend. Above the thunder of the hooves came her voice again, in a wild rebel yell. "Yeeee-haw!"

They rode on in absolute silence. Clell led the way, his head bowed over his saddle horn, his shoulders hunched. Once he lifted his arm to call a halt. Climbing down, he disappeared into the trees beside the road. When he came back, he was wiping his mouth. Without looking at her, he climbed back into the saddle.

At Bentonville he took her into a small cafe and bought her breakfast. He drank several cups of strong coffee and stared at the wall. When she finished eating, he paid the check. "Are you feeling all right?"

She had been feeling weak and ill, but breakfast had given her strength. "I am. What about you?"

For the first time since his daughter had ridden away, he looked her in the face, but he didn't answer her question. Instead, he said, "We can stop here if you're not fit. There's no reason to hurry."

"What about the Pinkerton agent?"

He gave the barest of shrugs. "What about him?"

All the energy seemed to have drained out of him. His outlaw eyes that had roamed over the room, taking the measure of everyone who came through the door, now stared at nothing. Men went in and out without his paying them the slightest heed. The waiter refilled his coffee. He wrapped his hands around the steaming cup, as if in hopes that he could draw warmth from it.

She probed again. "Do you think he's still on our tail?"

"Probably."

"Oh, for heaven's sake!" She slammed a hand down on the table, the jolt slopping hot coffee over his hand. "We need to get out of here."

He jerked his hand away and looked at her in surprise.

She rose and bent over until she was inches from his face. "Let's get out of here. We don't want to hang around if it's not safe."

He wiped a hand on his pantleg. Otherwise, he didn't move. "It's safe enough. Sit back down. Finish your breakfast. He doesn't know where we are because he doesn't know where we disappeared to. We could have gone back south to Fort Smith. We could have gone west into Indian Territory. We could have gone east to Little Rock. If we went north to the Missouri border, then why haven't we gotten there? He's worried now. In fact, he's just about given up."

"You don't know that." He could have been discussing someone else's choices. She sat back down. She couldn't leave him because she still intended to have at least half of the money.

She looked at him coldly. The girl who had spent almost ten years of her life in an orphanage reminded herself that he would get over this. Just as Cole Younger had. Just as her own father must have done. Clell had said he was bad. He had been an outlaw a long time. Living outside society, breaking the law, always moving from one place to another, he would forget. Esther and Sarah's images would fade. He would reason that York was taking care of them better than he ever could. He would comfort himself with that. Then he would go get the banker's money and disappear.

He swallowed some of the coffee and picked at a splinter on the tabletop. Then he cleared his throat. "I've been thinking."

She looked at him inquiringly.

"I think we ought to get married."

She gaped at him. How could he possibly think she would want to marry him? Especially since he knew that she also was a female bastard. Such a terrible phrase. Righteous, Christian people were the cruelest of all sometimes. The nuns had taught Mary Carolyn that lesson above all others. Little Sarah Susannah must have heard it over and over until it was branded on her memory.

As for marriage to Clell, once upon a time Mary Carolyn had wanted it more than life. She still did in some small romantic portion of her heart where outlaws were heroes and rescued sheriffs' daughters or ranchers' young and beautiful widows. Fortunately, that was all behind her—or mostly so. She leaned across the table. "It's not necessary. I'm not going to have a baby."

His gaze flicked up to lock with hers. "I was reared to be a gentleman. You'd never know it by what you just learned about me. I guess I forgot it for a while. But now I remember. I want to marry you."

She looked around her uneasily. His voice was deep and resonant. The cafe was almost empty, but a declaration like that could draw attention to them. She rose again. "Well, I don't want to marry you."

He caught her wrist. She looked down into his eyes. The chill of steel was gone. He was pleading with her. "You can have the money. You can do what you want to with it. We'll go to California. I can work and earn a living for you. I can—"

She sat back down again. She was so insulted. Did he even have an inkling of how much he was insulting her? How could she make him see the light? "You didn't act very surprised when Sarah asked you if she was your daughter," she said coldly. "Had Esther already told you?"

He loosened his grip on her wrist, but he still searched her face warily. "Yes."

"And you want to marry me to make up for what you did to them ten years ago?"

"No!" He shook his head adamantly. But he could not meet her angry stare. He looked away and dropped her wrist to pick at the splinter again. "Not really."

"You haven't suddenly fallen head over heels in love with me, have you?" Her voice dripped sarcasm.

He didn't react. Silence grew between them. Finally, he said, "You need someone to take care of you. You're an orphan." He choked a little over the word. "You told me you don't have any way to make a living. I can make a good one. I can take care of you. I want to take care of you."

She barely suppressed the urge to throw the hot coffee in his face. "Because you feel sorry for me. Well, I don't want your sympathy. I don't want your pity. What I want is my money."

He cleared his throat. "I thought we might send at least some of that—at least my share—back to Esther for Sarah."

At that point Mary Carolyn saw red. Hooking her thumbs into her waistband, she stood up. "Oh. I can't believe you said that." Unable to contain herself, she ran out of the cafe.

He threw some money of the table and followed her outside. "Mary Carolyn—"

She tried to shake him off. When she couldn't, she spun around to face him. She sucked in her breath so hard, her nostrils pinched together. "Damn you! You're terrible. Goddam you! You've been working this whole thing out, riding along pretending to be so grief stricken. You weren't grieving. You weren't sorry for all the suffering you've caused. You've been trying to work out a way to make yourself feel better about it."

Suddenly, she couldn't stand the sight of him any longer. "Oh! Stay away from me!"

Clell watched her untie Lady Grace and swing up. He made a grab for the bridle, but missed. As she backed the mare away from the gelding, Clell blocked the street, spreading out his arms to stop her. "Listen to me."

"Get out of my way!"

"No. Just wait a minute."

Spitting out a vile word she had learned from Cole Younger, she whirled the mare and galloped down the street the way they had come.

He looked around him a little warily. Caution was too long a part of his makeup. They had attracted too much attention. People in the general store were looking at them. A man had stepped off the boardwalk and was walking toward him, probably with the idea of rendering aid to the lady. He backed off when Clell threw him a fierce look of warning. Then Clell mounted the gelding and galloped after Mary Carolyn.

From the shadow of a grove of pine, she watched him ride by. Furious, she aimed her index finger at him. Her whispered "Bang" gave her no satisfaction at all. She acknowledged that she was more hurt than anything, and felt foolish. But damn it! He didn't love her. He wouldn't have even thought about marrying her if he hadn't messed up those other lives.

For two cents she would disappear right now and leave Mr. Clell Miller, outlaw, to stew in his own juice. Then he could send the whole thing back to Esther Bradburn with her handsome husband and her beautiful bathroom and . . . and . . .

A dry sob racked her throat. How she hated to be weak and helpless and unloved! She had been born and reared that way, but she would be damned if she was going to give up the chance to get ahold of the rest of her life.

Clell had run the gelding for half a mile before he realized she couldn't have come this far. She had tricked him at his own game, the game he had taught her. He headed back, watching the ground on either side of the road. Around the bend he found her waiting for him.

"I could have shot you from ambush," she called out.

"But you wouldn't have," he replied. "You don't know where the money's hidden."

She waited for him. "No. And I'm smart enough to swallow my pride. At least on this business." When he caught up to her, she leaned as close as she dared and brandished a fist at him. "Now listen to me, Clell Miller. *I* stole that money. I. I. *I* stole it. I'm the one. All this stuff about the James gang and share and share alike is just that. It's stuff.

"I'll have to divide with you—you're bigger and stronger. And what you do with your share is strictly up to you. But I'd think twice about sending it all back to those people in Arkansas. They struck me as honest Christian people. They wouldn't use stolen money. In fact, they'd probably throw it in the fire."

"Damn it, Mary Carolyn." He hadn't thought of that, but she was probably right. In fact he was sure she was. Esther Elizabeth wouldn't accept stolen money even if she needed it. And from the looks of that house, she sure didn't.

Mary Carolyn turned the mare and headed back toward the town. "I'm going north. That's the only thing we can do. You buried those saddlebags somewhere up there close to the Iowa border. That's a hell of a long ride in January."

He caught up to her. "We can sell the horses and buy some train tickets when we get to Carthage."

The wind gusted in her face. She shivered. "Then let's do it. If you truly pity me, remember what I told you about how I didn't want to be a whore. You have the power to keep me safe from that. Now do it."

Leon Box leaned back in a rocking chair on the wide porch of the drummer's hotel across the street from the depot in Carthage, Missouri. He had telegraphed the Pinkerton Agency in Chicago and the agent in charge in Kansas City, relaying his progress. He had paid the livery-stable men good money to come running if a couple of fellows came in trying to sell a bay gelding and a black mare. But he had no real hope. The outlaws had vanished into the Ozarks.

Suddenly, his mouth dropped open and he sprang to his feet, setting the chair to rocking. As quietly as he could, he stepped back against the wall, hoping that the shade would hide him. He could scarcely believe that his patience had paid off. The big blond outlaw had just walked into the depot.

The Pinkerton agent took no chances on being recognized.

He hadn't figured out what had tipped the man before. He eeled around the door into the dimness of the hotel lobby. The second rider, the boy on a little black mare, looked in the direction of the porch too late.

Through the lace curtain Box studied the boy. Pinkerton's hadn't given him any information on this particular member of the James gang, but new men were always joining. Box could feel his palms start to sweat. He needed to get to the sheriff's office and insure the cooperation of the local law as quickly as possible. If he could pull this arrest off, the boss would be sure to give him a promotion. A promotion meant more pay, more responsibility, and more respect, plus a squad of men to command. Box liked the idea of sitting behind a desk ordering others to do the dirty work.

All that would be his—if he could be the first man in Missouri to arrest a member of the James gang. No trains were due for the remainder of the day. The outlaws wouldn't be going anywhere. Still, he hurried through the lobby into the saloon and out onto a sidestreet.

In the lobby the clerk registered them without so much as a glance at Mary Carolyn. She managed a wry smile. She must look like she'd been struck by lightning. She was so weary she could barely mount the stairs. Now that she didn't have to ride horseback for a couple of days, she allowed herself to feel all the aches and pangs of her strained muscles.

Once in the room, she dropped down into the creaky rocking chair by the window and closed her eyes. Light, filtered by lace curtains warmed her face.

"Why don't you lie down and rest while I go sell the horses?" Clell laid their saddlebags down beside the door and then leaned back against it, his thumbs hooked in his gunbelt. With the tickets in his pocket he felt a sense of urgency. He wanted to marry her. Out of more than love. He needed her. Because she needed someone to take care of her. Because he needed someone to take care of.

He stared at her face. She looked thin, her cheeks hollowed

out. If he hadn't known her age, he would have had trouble believing that she was only seventeen years old. Without opening her eyes, she asked. "Do you have to sell Lady Grace?"

He hesitated. He had been thinking the same thing himself. The gelding was nothing special. From the first day, he had missed Ginger. The minute he got the money, he was going back to the place in Council Bluffs where they'd sold the horses and try to track his roan mare down.

He knew that Mary Carolyn's mount was exceptionally fine. She had given everything that was asked of her and kept right on moving. He didn't doubt that she was part of Belle's hand-raised stock. As such she might bring a pretty price in Carthage, but nothing like what she might sell for in Kansas City or St. Louis.

"I guess we could ship her if they've got room for her. I'll check with the ticketmaster."

"Good. I'd hate to lose her. I figure I'm going to need a good horse."

Still, he hesitated. He knew she'd be here when he got back, but he had the sense that he shouldn't let her out of his sight. That must be part and parcel of the feeling that she couldn't be allowed to go on without him. Some way or other he must convince her to marry him. He swallowed.

She opened her eyes. Their depths asked a question.

He ducked his head and swung around. "Back in an hour. Then we'll eat. Get some rest."

They had not passed through the lobby unobserved. As they walked toward the stairs, their boot heels disturbed a young man dozing in one of the overstuffed chairs. He opened his eyes, let them slowly drift to, then opened them again. He frowned. He jerked to attention, his eyes scrutinizing the pair. Then a faint grin twisted his handsome mouth, accompanied by a tiny shake of his head.

It had been a long shot this coming to Carthage, Missouri. The Pinkerton agent in Kansas City had told him about Leon Box's telegram. He had taken the train down the day before and prepared to wait. A couple of days more and he would have called the search off, returned to his father with the sad news that Mary Carolyn Ross had disappeared forever.

His hand was shaking. He still couldn't believe in this kind of luck.

Still watching them, he slipped a hand inside a pocket and pulled out a cardboard-backed photograph. Studying it, he compared it to the younger man. All the way across the lobby and up the stairs, he studied the figure intently.

No doubt about it. The smaller figure belonged to a girl. The curves were there even under the bulky clothing. The walk was not a man's walk. The face had never known a beard. The profile, the coloring, all bore a resemblance to his despised stepmother. It was too striking to be coincidental.

He slipped the photo back into his pocket and waited impatiently until the clerk left the desk. Then he crossed the lobby in long strides and spun the register around on its swivel. Jim and Bill Smith.

No help there. But he would bet even money that his stepsister had just walked into the hotel.

Clell booked a box stall in one of the cattle cars for Lady Grace. Then he rode the gelding to the nearest livery stable. The horse looked shaggy and tired from its trip through the mountains. It needed a bath and a currying and a couple of days of grain.

The owner saw it all and haggled desperately, but Clell knew the animal's value. If anything all that mountain climbing in the cold had proved the horse's mettle and increased his wind. The stable would be able to sell the bay for a fine profit.

In the end the owner upped his offer. While he led the way into his office, he complained loudly that he wouldn't be able to put meat on his children's table if he had to do business with Clell again.

Then when Clell unfolded the sale papers, the man's eyes bugged. "You bought this nag from Belle Shirley?"

Clell rolled his eyes. He might as well wear a sign around

his neck—OUTLAW. "Never met her. I bought this horse from the fella running a stable in Dallas. I don't know anything about Belle Shirley, except that her signature was on the bill of sale."

"Well, sure." The man sniggered. His expression said he didn't believe a word of it. He cocked his head and squinted up at Clell. "You ain't Cole Younger, are you?"

Clell shook his head. "Never heard of him."

The owner laughed and nodded sagely as if they shared a secret. "Say, if you'd told me who you were, I'd 'a given you more for the horse. I can sell Cole Younger's horse for double."

Clell heaved a sigh. The train left in the middle of the morning tomorrow. Until then he'd better be on the alert.

Outside in the street, he buttoned his coat over his lean middle. The wind had sprung up again. He looked forward to the bed in the hotel. He hoped Mary Carolyn wouldn't pitch a fit about his getting in bed with her. He was too tired to do more than lie there in a stupor. He didn't have any hopes of sleeping.

The memory of that little girl telling him she never wanted to see him again made his stomach clench.

So engrossed was he in his troubles, he hurried into the lobby of the drummer's hotel without giving the room a look.

Two men simultaneously stepped out from behind the doors and drove pistol barrels into his sides. "Hold it right there, Mr. Smith."

Chapter Twenty-One

He cursed himself bitterly. He knew better than to let down his guard. Only a few more days and he would have left the life forever. Now he'd made what would probably amount to a fatal mistake.

"Get your hands up." Leon Box's voice came out shrill and strained.

Clell raised them shoulder-high, his body poised. If either one of the lawmen made one mistake, relaxed his guard for so much as a breath, he'd make his break. He recognized the agent's expensive black hat as it ducked beneath his chin. Pinkerton men were well trained, but they tended to be green.

Clell sucked in his breath as the agent's hand tugged loose the buttons on his coat and pulled his gun out of its holster. The man stumbled back.

"Hey, I ain't done nothing." He put on his best country voice. "Swear t' God I got a bill o' sale fer that horse."

A gun barrel prodded him in the ribs. "Turn around real slow."

Obeying, he found the Pinkerton man facing him on the right side and a man with a sheriff's badge on his left. The agent looked young. He was grinning with triumph, his hands trembling with excitement. He might be easily distracted. A quick move, a feint, and Clell could wrestle the guns away from him—if he were alone.

Unfortunately, the man behind the sheriff's badge was a horse of a different color. His hand was rock steady. The muzzle of the .45 Colt Peacemaker was pointed directly at the center of Clell's chest. One false move and the outlaw was dead.

"He's Clell Miller all right," Box announced excitedly. "He's been with Jesse James since the early days."

The sheriff said nothing. One thin eyebrow rose in inquiry.

"You got the wrong fella." Clell willed his eyes to turn red and his hands to tremble. "My name's Jim Smith. You can check the hotel book. Me 'n' my brother Bill are on our way to Kansas City—"

The sheriff cut him off. He stepped aside and motioned with his gun. "Let's talk about this over to the office."

"We need to arrest the other one," Box objected. Two members of the James gang taken by one agent would add to his reputation enormously. "He might get wind of what's happening and escape."

"Bill's takin' a nap," Clell protested. "He's been sick. Real sick. Like to die. That's why we're takin' the train. Don't go near him."

The sheriff gave no sign he had heard the outlaw's protests. His gun arm might have been made of marble. "The longer you wait to put a man behind bars, son, the more dangerous he gets."

"But—"

His level stare shifted to the agent's excited face. Some people pointed their guns where they looked, but Clell noted that the sheriff didn't make that mistake. "Right now, he's a-scheming and a-planning how to get your gun away from you. The longer we hold him here, the more likely he's going to be to try something. Don't do it, fella." His warning now was for Clell. "You could make us both sorry. Except you're going to be sorrier, 'cause you'll have a hole in you."

"We need them both," Box insisted. He strode to the desk to get a spare key from the goggling desk clerk. "Room twelve."

The sheriff herded Clell to the foot of the stairs. "Put your hands on top of your head and lead the way, fella." He prodded the outlaw in the spine. "Don't try anything foolish like trying to throw yourself backwards down the stairs. It won't work. And you'll be the one that gets shot. That's a promise."

A procession of three, they made the climb. Clell's heart was pounding. If they tried to arrest Mary Carolyn, he would grab the Pinkerton and throw him into the sheriff's gun. He'd probably get shot, but maybe she could escape. Too bad about her damn money. Clell tried one more time. "You've got the wrong man. I ain't whoever you say I am. My name's Smith. I got my little brother in there. He's sick."

Box reached around him and tapped with his gun barrel on the door.

No answer.

He tapped again.

They heard the sound of someone stirring. Footsteps came to the door. It opened. Mary Carolyn had washed her face and pulled off her boots and belt. Her shirt was pulled out at the waist. Her eyes widened at the sight of Clell's anguished face, his hands raised slightly above shoulder level. On either side of his wide chest, she saw the two men with their pistols trained.

For the space of maybe five seconds she stood frozen.

"Oh, thank God! Thank God!" She burst into tears and brushed past him. Throwing her arms around the Pinkerton agent, she clasped him tightly. "Oh, sir. You've saved me. Oh, thank you, thank you. I prayed and prayed that someone would come."

"M-Ma'am!" Box let his gun drop and fell back several steps. He looked around wildly.

At the same time, the sheriff poked Clell in the back. "Don't you move. We'll take care of this."

In a flash Clell regretted that Mary Carolyn had grabbed the Pinkerton agent instead of the sheriff. The younger man would undoubtedly have dropped his guard. Clell would have been able to grab his gun and get the drop on them both. Moreover, they wouldn't have been likely to try anything if they believed that Mary Carolyn was an innocent hostage who might get shot. They could have escaped.

Clell swung around. The sheriff didn't seem the least bit interested in the scene going on only a few feet from him.

"Oh, thank Almighty God and His Son Jesus." Mary Carolyn was sobbing. Her arms were wrapped around the young man's shoulders. "I've been so afraid. It's been so awful. I hope you hang him. Hang him high."

"Yes, ma'am." The Pinkerton agent finally succeeded in freeing himself. He holstered his gun and put an arm around her shoulders. "Who are you, ma'am?"

"I'm Mrs. Oliver Appleton. Mary Appleton's my name. I've been held prisoner by this monster for nearly a month."

Even the sheriff gaped at that, although the gun barrel never wavered.

"A month, ma'am?"

She put her hands over her face and began to sob again. Noisily. "Oh, you don't believe me." She spun and faced Clell. "You monster. You've ruined me." She slapped his face. No playacting there. She rocked him back on his heels. Then she pushed past him into the room.

Fascinated the agent followed her. The sheriff met Clell's eyes, then motioned him inside with the gun. Mary Carolyn dropped down on her knees in front of the saddlebags. "Here!" she cried. "Here." She pulled out the wrinkled remains of the fashionable hat and petticoats. She shook them out in the men's faces. "Now do you believe me? Here's my dress. The one I was kidnapped in. Here's where he tore it when he threw me across his saddle. The bruises were terrible for the longest time. Here's where he tore the sleeve when he . . . when he . . ."

She looked at Clell as if she wanted to kill him. Then she wrapped her arms around the material and bowed her head. Her shoulders shook with silent weeping.

The lawmen looked at each other in a mixture of embarrassment and pity. Then they both fixed stares on Clell.

He backed away. "She's crazy with . . . er . . . grief." The best he could do was play along. "She's my wife, but—"

Mary Carolyn shrieked in a combination of anger and pain. "I'm not his wife. Oh, the monster! I'm Mrs. Oliver Appleton."

"She's not." Clell raised his voice.

"Best keep your mouth shut." The sheriff prodded him in the belly.

"Ma'am. Ma'am." The Pinkerton agent hunkered down in front of her. He tried to take hold of her wrists, but she shrieked again. He looked for guidance to the older lawman. "What are we going to do?"

The sheriff allowed his concentration to drop long enough to scratch his head, although he kept his gun trained on Clell. "Maybe we ought to get some of the ladies up here to help her. Mrs. Griff, the preacher's wife, and Lucy Bailey, the doctor's wife."

"Oh, no," Mary Carolyn moaned. "I can't bear for another woman to see me right now." She raised her face. Tears had matted her eyelashes together and stained her cheeks. Her mouth was swollen too. "He made me wear these p-pants."

Both men leaned forward, pictures of sympathy. She had won their hearts completely. Even Clell, who knew she was lying, found himself hating the monster who had frightened and humiliated her.

A minute later he realized he could have jumped the sheriff and gotten the drop on both men, but he was too fascinated with her performance.

As she climbed to her feet, she wobbled. The Pinkerton agent caught her arm and steadied her. She thanked him with a tearful smile. Her lips trembling, she held the dress against her like a shield.

"I've tried and tried to get away, but every time I'd think I'd escaped, he'd catch me and d-drag me back." She clenched her hands. Her face contorted in anguish. "Oh, my sweet Oliver. He must be beside himself with grief and worry."

She charged over to Clell. "You! I never want to see you again! Do you hear me? I hope you hang." She swung back to the lawmen. "Please. Please take him out of here."

"Yes, ma'am," the sheriff agreed wholeheartedly. "Get over by that door, you."

"I'll order a bath. He wouldn't let me wash." She shook her head mournfully. One hand touched her hair. To Box, she said, "He cut my hair. Oh, I must look awful. I had such long, long hair. I could sit on it. Long and blond and curly. Oh, I'm so ashamed."

The agent gulped. "You mustn't worry about that, ma'am. We've got him now. And I'm sure it'll all grow back and be just as beautiful as it was."

She smiled through her tears. "What is your name, sir? I want to know who my rescuer is."

Suddenly, he remembered he still had his hat on. He snatched it off and held it to his chest. "Leon, ma'am. Leon Box."

"Oh, Mr. Box. I'm so glad you've saved me."

"Let's get on out, fella." The sheriff prodded Clell's spine.

Clell started. One thing might solidify her performance. "Damn you, you hussy," he snarled. "I treated you like a lady. I was bringing you back to your family. Now you won't even testify for me."

The sheriff pushed him through the door.

Leon Box made sure that every care was to be given Mrs. Appleton in Room 12. Pinkerton's would pay for everything. He would receive a commendation. Rescues were gold as far as reputations were concerned. Visions of rewards from grateful families and stories in all the newspapers sparkled before him. He ordered a bath and a tray of food. "And send for a dress-maker," he told the clerk. "The poor kidnapped lady needs a new dress in the worst way."

Then he sprinted down the street to the telegraph office to send his messages around the country. As he waited, he thought about the lovely young woman he had rescued. Photographers could take pictures of them together. He needed a haircut, a shave, a fresh suit of clothes.

With his purpose clear, he sent telegrams to the *Kansas City Times* and the *Arkansas Gazette*. The capture of the first member of the James gang ought to bring the reporters flocking.

* * *

Roger Somervell came in too late to see the arrest, but for a quarter he learned some sketchy details from the desk clerk. The lady upstairs had been kidnapped and was now rescued. The outlaw was in jail.

Now, Roger watched with some amazement as a bath was taken up, along with a tray of food. A dressmaker came and went with a workbasket of sewing notions and swatches of cloth. A milliner brought a selection of hats. Was the woman really not Madeleine Somervell's daughter? He couldn't imagine a penniless orphan of no importance, perhaps a thief if his father's guess was correct, getting that kind of service.

Much later, he watched the lady walk out, garbed in a dress that fit her well, her hair washed and curled, a fashionable hat perched on her head. To the life she was a younger version of his beautiful stepmother. He had to clamp his teeth against the anger and resentment. She had seduced his father away from his true wife. She had ruined Roger's childhood with her simpering and posturing.

At long last his revenge was about to be realized. He would take the money that should have been spent on him. Madeleine's daughter had that money, which made his revenge all the sweeter. His father wouldn't know what had happened to either one of them. Dear God, but he hoped his father was right about her being the thief.

"I want to see your prisoner, Sheriff." Mary Carolyn noted with mounting confidence that the man rose hastily and came from behind the desk to take her hand. She smiled tremulously at him.

He had kind eyes that measured her. Immediately, she felt nervous. He was a good man who wouldn't be easy to fool. "Ma'am, I don't think that's a good idea."

"Oh, I can't help it," she cried, putting an emotional quaver in her voice. "It's the way I am." She held onto his rough paw when he would have let go and stepped back. "He told me I'd never get away. He said I might as well take up with him because my husband wouldn't want me back. Well, I want to show him that I have gotten away. Please. It's so important to me.''

"Ma'am, this here is a member of the James gang. I've got a picture to prove that he's Jim Pool. He says it's all a mistake, but seeing you here today all dressed like a lady sure shoots holes in that story.'' He put a hand under her arm and turned her toward the door. ''Just let justice take its course now. You can tell him all that from the witness stand when he comes to trial.''

Damn! He was going to herd her out. She needed to see Clell, even for a minute to make sure that he was all right. If she could have a few minutes alone with him, he could tell her what to do.

''Please. Please let me see him. Just let me see him locked behind bars where he can't get to me. I have the worst nightmares. I'll sleep better if I can see for myself that he's locked up. Oh, please, please.''

The sheriff looked about to refuse. Her eyes pleaded with him. She balked, not allowing him to move her another step. At last, he nodded slowly. ''Just for a minute. And I'm going to be watching. He can't get at you if you stand back out of arm's reach, but I'm not taking any chances. By the age of him, I collect he's probably been with Jesse since the beginning. There's nothing he wouldn't stoop to.''

After the long speech, the sheriff closed his mouth in a disapproving trap. Taking up the keys, he led her through a wooden door, up a flight of steps to a door with a barred window. To Mary Carolyn, who had never been in a jail before, the flight of steps surprised and depressed her. She had never heard of cells being upstairs.

At the top of the stairs, the sheriff opened a door with a barred window and led her into an office.

In novels, the back window, which frequently had rusted bars set in rotted wood, faced out onto nothing. An outlaw's partner or sweetheart could talk to him through the bars and then fasten a rope around them and pull them loose. The outlaw could climb out and leap onto a horse, then they would gallop away into the darkness.

Instead, at a little desk sat a guard, an elderly man wearing a deputy's badge and reading what was clearly a Bible. He nodded to the sheriff who opened another barred door into a block of four cells.

In the novels a single set of bars separated the lawman from his prisoner. Clearly, she could not *get the drop on the sheriff* and force him to open the cell.

Carthage, Missouri, had evidently invested considerable money to insure that no one escaped from their county jail.* She quickly discarded several ideas she had planned to choose from to rescue Clell.

"First cell, ma'am." The sheriff nodded her forward. "I'll stand right here."

The jail had the feeling of something closed off and buried. All light came from tiny windows about four inches square near the floor. The bars were mere black on black in the gloom. Moreover, the place was icy cold. No heat, no light. She could feel the tears starting from her eyes. She mustn't cry. "Clell," she whispered. "Clell Miller."

She heard a rustle of clothing. Then booted feet hit the floor. "Mary Carolyn?" Then, "Mrs. Appleton?"

"Yes."

She could barely see him. His body was sharply silhouetted with the light at his back, but his features were shadowy. She longed to touch him, to rush forward and put her hands on him to assure herself that he was all right. She was conscious of the sheriff at her back, watching her, hearing every word that passed between her and his prisoner.

She strengthened her voice. "I had to come to see you behind bars where you belong." She hesitated. How could she send him a message when she didn't have anything to tell him? "You'll never escape from here. N-Not by yourself," she stammered.

---

*For the purposes of fiction I have given Carthage, Missouri, a fine jail nineteen years before they actually built the one that stands today.

He cleared his throat. Did he sound more hoarse than usual? Was he getting sick in this awful cold and darkness? "I guess you're right, lady. I sure am in a fix."

"That's right, you monster. You'll know better than to kidnap a helpless woman again. Pulling her between you and the bank guards, dragging her out, throwing her on a horse. You can't break out now. Not by yourself. Only if one of your gang helps you. And there's not a one here. Not one. Only I know where you are." She paused and turned halfway, clasping her throat. *Please, God. Let the sheriff think she was choking on her fears.* "But you'll never get out. You'll never get out. And I'm free of you."

"They're all miles from here. I wouldn't want them to try to get me out. It's too dangerous. Way too dangerous!" He raised his voice as much as he dared. "I'll sure never kidnap a helpless woman again."

"Ma'am," the sheriff called from the door. "I think that's enough, ma'am."

She swung back around. One hand reached out to Clell. The distance separating them was only a few feet, but it might have been a canyon. "You monster," she whispered, caressing the syllables, sending the meaning by her tone. "Monster."

Her eyes were becoming accustomed to the dimness. She saw him grip the bars. She could look into his eyes. His mouth twitched in what might have been a smile, then contorted in a grimace. "I guess you'll get to go back to that fool husband, after all. Where was he? 'Bout two miles south of Unionville on that place with the three big oak trees alongside the road."

What was he talking about?

Then like a bolt of lightning, she knew. She closed her eyes while shivers went down her spine. He loved her. She knew it as surely as if he had shouted it aloud. Clell was saying good-bye to her and telling her where to find the money. He was sending her on her way and insuring that she would be safe. Tears began to trickle down her cheeks.

"That's where he is all right," she agreed. She wanted to say something else. "I wish you could have seen the light of goodness, sir. You could have taken me back as I begged you to. You wouldn't be in this fix right now."

He grinned. A genuine flash of his teeth beneath the thick mustache. "You're sure right about that. But maybe when I get out of jail, I'll come and visit you both."

"Ma'am. Mrs. Appleton." The sheriff was determined now. "I think you've about said your piece."

She turned around. "You're right, Sheriff. I know I'll sleep better now."

Back straight, she walked out and waited while the sheriff locked the door. The guard room had a potbellied stove behind the desk. Through its grate she could see coals glowing, and little tongues of blue flames curling from them. The room was delightfully warm.

And Clell was so cold. The temperature in the cells must be below freezing every night. She wanted to scream at them. She wanted to grab the sheriff's gun and force them back. She wanted Clell out of there.

But Clell hadn't been able to grab the sheriff's gun even when she'd thrown herself on the Pinkerton agent. She knew she hadn't a chance of making anything like that work.

As the sheriff escorted her back downstairs, her mind was working furiously. She was taking an inventory of the place, she told herself. Just as she had the bank in Ottumwa. How many people? How many locks? How many guns?

Back in the office, she pulled her handkerchief from her purse and mopped at the tears on her cheeks. "Thank you so much." She imitated her mother's accent, even though she hadn't heard it in almost ten years. "He really is in jail. He is suffering for his crimes."

"Yes, ma'am."

She put her handkerchief back in her purse, extending her hand. The sheriff took it a little awkwardly. She flashed him a tearful smile. "I know I shall sleep better tonight. And tomorrow I'll be on that train back to my husband."

Outside in the street, she walked around the square to the back of the building. She stared upward at the slits in the brick wall. Clell couldn't even see her through them. The walls were too thick and the holes too small. The man who loved her couldn't even look out and see her.

Clell slumped down on the bunk. The bone-chilling, mind-numbing cold was temporarily driven back. In its place was heat and longing. Luck had really run out for him. Unless she got them both killed trying to break him out.

He leaned back against the rough wall. The crude mortar between the bricks poked through his clothing. Likewise, he could feel a chill on his neck. He sat up and looked around him. The light was already fading. He was going to have to keep moving to keep from freezing tonight.

He knew she was planning an escape for him. She had said as much, and he had told her not to do it in the same off-center way. Thank God, the sheriff hadn't caught on.

Unless he was much mistaken, she had adopted Jesse's bank plan to break him out of jail. She was looking the place over, counting the guns and doors and guards. Idiot! Brave, stubborn idiot.

He wrapped his arms around his body. The thought of her made him warm all over. He had been so close. So close to getting away from the life forever. Just a few more miles, and he would have had the money and the woman he loved more than anything else in his misspent life.

She had walked a good distance in the wrong direction before realizing she was lost. All that time she had worried over how to take him with her on the morrow, because as surely as she lived, she wasn't going to leave town without her outlaw.

Unfortunately, she wasn't Zerelda Mimms, who could arrive with ''a party of the best citizens in the Cracker Neck neighborhood and some big officials who had come quite a distance to rescue Jesse James.'' No one would help her. She had to do it herself. Yet how could she break Clell out of the second story of a stone building with the sheriff and a guard blocking the way?

He was locked behind four doors with at least two men to guard him. When she broke him out, they would have to ride through town, through witnesses and potential posse members. They might even be shot while escaping. Of course, if she could get on the train . . . The jail was only a couple of blocks from the depot. If she could break him out and somehow get him on the train . . . He had already bought the tickets. She had them in her purse. They could sit in their seats and look innocent.

She could see it all. Except the most difficult part.

Head down, she walked back toward the hotel and the depot.

She was too distressed to notice that the door to Room 12 didn't feel quite right. The skeleton key turned too easily in the keyhole. The door swung inward even as she realized what was wrong.

Before she could back away, a hand closed over her wrist and jerked her into the room.

She gave a short cry, quickly stifled as a man dragged her in against his body and covered her mouth. ''Don't make any noise, Mary Carolyn Ross. Otherwise, I might have to tell the Pinkerton agent what really happened the night the Rock Island was robbed in Iowa last year.''

Chapter Twenty-Two

She froze for only an instant; then she began to fight. Her mouth, already opened to call for help, chomped down on his palm.

He yelled and tried to pull his hand back. She refused to let it go before both her upper and lower teeth had scored it. Cursing, he brought his fist down in the middle of her back and sent her flying across the room. She caught herself on the foot of the bed and swung round to face him.

Mouth open, breath sucked in to scream at the top of her lungs, she held her pose. He looked strangely familiar.

"You'd better keep your damn mouth shut, Mary Carolyn!" He clasped the wrist of his bleeding hand. His anger was a potent thing, slapping her in the face from where he stood. At the same time, he took a couple of steps to the right and kicked the door closed.

"Who are you?"

Blood dripped off his fingers. She could taste it in her own mouth. She had torn quite a chunk out of his hand. He pulled a handkerchief from his pocket and clumsily wrapped it around the injury.

"You'd better leave," she threatened. "Unless you want more of the same."

He tied a knot in the handkerchief's ends using his teeth and one hand. Then he cradled the injured member against his chest. She thought he looked a little pale. "I don't think you want me to leave, Mary Carolyn Ross. Not unless you want me to go straight to that Pinkerton agent, who has spent the day sending telegrams to newspapers and having himself fitted for a new suit. He intends to make the most of the capture of one member of the notorious James gang. Imagine how much more he could make if he knew he had captured two. One of them a woman. Lots of notoriety there."

"You don't know what you're talking about." She couldn't afford to give an inch here. Or make a mistake. "I'm Mrs. Oliver Appleton. I was kidnapped—"

"My card, Mrs. Appleton." The young man stepped forward. The index finger on his undamaged hand slid into the pocket of his vest and he passed the pasteboard over to her. She took it from him without taking her eyes off him.

He was about Clell's age, expensively dressed in a brown derby hat and a wool double-breasted suit of brown pinstripe. A maroon silk tie was knotted beneath the detachable starched collar. He looked like a lawyer or—the gooseflesh rose on her arms—a banker.

Her fear must have shone in her face, for he smiled and sketched a rough bow. "Dear, dear stepsister."

Her eyes flashed to the card. "Roger Somervell."

Only the foot of the bed kept her from falling to her knees. This was far, far worse than she had ever imagined. If her stepbrother were here, then DeGraffen Somervell must have recognized her. But how? She had been masked. The car had been dark.

Roger supplied the answer to her unspoken question. "You look rather like the bitch. I knew you when you came in; even dressed in those disgusting boy's clothes, you're still dear, dear Madeleine's daughter. Of course, I have a picture of you. But it was taken some years ago. Your mother's picture, however, is branded on my memory."

She had never heard so much hatred in a man's voice. She wanted to scream that she wasn't her mother, but she would be wasting her breath on Roger Somervell. She tried one more time.

Drawing herself up haughtily, she extended the card. "I still don't know what you're talking about. Your name means nothing to me. I am Mrs. Oliver Appleton. My first name happens to be Mary, but I assure you my mother lives in Cleveland. My father is, unfortunately, deceased."

The man she now realized must be her stepbrother took the card and put it back in his pocket. Making himself at home, he dropped into the chair by the door and pulled a cigar from his pocket. "You're going to have to light this for me, my dear. And you will do that, won't you? While I tell you what you're going to do. Your father—whoever that charming bounder might have been—may or may not be deceased. Nobody knows for the very simple reason that nobody knows who he is."

He bit the tip off the cigar. Placing it between his teeth, he pulled a silver matchbox from his pocket and held it out to her. "Light me, stepsister."

When she didn't move, he jabbed them at her. "Light me, or I'll march over to the sheriff and give him the information that there is no such person as Mrs. Oliver Appleton. Since you haven't a thing on you except your word, and I have credentials and a letter of credit from the Bank of Chicago, who do you think he'll believe?"

He leaned forward, smiling broadly around the cigar.

Slowly, she took the box. It was solid silver, with the face of a devil on one side and flames on the other. The lid flipped back. She pulled out a match and dragged it across the striker. The little stick flared up.

Hating him, knowing if she had been Jesse James she would have shoved it down his throat, she held it while he puffed diligently. When the cigar had caught, he leaned back and blew a cloud of odorous blue smoke into the air. "Thanks so much. You do that well. Just like a whore would for a client. Just like your mother perhaps."

"Get out." She could feel the hot blood rising behind her eyes. One more word about her mother and she would kill him if she died for it.

He must have seen the change in her expression. He shrugged. "You can get me out of here in a minute. All you have to do is tell me where you hid the money."

She should have known. The money. Fifty thousand dollars was more money than most men saw in a lifetime. Of course her stepfather wanted it back. Who would be the logical person to send to find it? His son, her stepbrother, who would be likely to recognize her from family resemblances. "I don't have it." She hoped the first sentence carried an undeniable ring of truth. Because the second was a lie. "It's all spent."

He looked around him significantly. At the shabby room, at the dress made by the Carthage, Missouri, dressmaker, at the saddlebags lying on the floor. "Try again."

"It's true. There wasn't much for me when the James gang got their share."

"It sure as hell better not be!" She shrank back against the bed as he darted toward her. His good hand flashed out and caught her by the chin, turning her face into the waning light. She had never known what murder looked like until Roger's face hung above her, his eyes glaring down.

He squeezed her jaw until she thought he would break it. Then he shook his head. "No." He gave her face another shake before he took his hand away, very slowly. "No. You're lying. You're lying now. If you were smart enough to steal it all by yourself, then you're smart enough to hide it before you took up with those outlaws."

She pulled herself off the bed and edged back to the wall. If she could hit him in the head . . . Heroines in novels did resourceful things like that, but the lamp was glass and half-full of kerosene. If wouldn't do any good except to make him more angry that he already was.

He turned his back and began to pace around the room. Clearly, he was as desperate as she was, but in a different way. She wondered about him. She wondered about his father. If she had a gun . . . But she had no gun. The sheriff had gone through Clell's saddlebags and taken the extra pistol.

She had nothing but her wits.

"Where is it?" His jaw was set, his eyes narrowed. He caught her with his good hand and, doubling the injured one into a fist, drew it back behind his head. "Tell me, or I'll start punching."

He would do it. He would beat her bloody. And she didn't dare scream, or he would tell the sheriff that she was a member of the gang. The fist had actually started forward.

"I don't know! I don't! I don't!"

He hesitated.

"Why do you think I'm hanging around here while that outlaw's in jail? Why do you think I went to the jail today?" She looked at him fearfully. "You do know I went to the jail today, don't you?"

He nodded. He flexed his fist. The place where she bit him must hurt worse than she'd imagined. She hoped he caught blood poisoning and died.

He was choking her. She could barely force the words past his hands. "I went to see him to beg him to tell me where *he* hid the money."

"He hid the money?" Roger let her go and stepped back. "How did he get the money?"

Her hands went to her throat and massaged the bruises. She would tell him the whole truth now. Except for the last sentence. In a flash, she knew how she would get Clell out of jail. The two of them could deal with Roger when Clell was free. "He took it away from me. When I jumped off the train, I jumped into him."

At his look of disgust, she excused herself resentfully. Now that she thought about it, it had been stupid to jump off on the same side of the train as the James gang. "It was dark. The train was moving. I couldn't see where I was falling."

"And he took the money?"

"He took me too. I got shot."

Roger's face was suddenly wreathed in smiles. He struck his fist into his palm and then instantly regretted it as his bitten hand pained him. "It *was* you! That confirms it. Father said he thought he'd shot the person who robbed him."

"I thought you'd already made up your mind that I was the one." She wanted to cry. If she survived this adventure, she would never again tell another lie. The outlaw life was a maze of hiding and running and escaping and being hunted some more.

Roger directed a malicious smile at her. "An old schoolmate of mine who's a lawyer says it's always nice to have the defendant confess to the crime. It makes the jury feel so much better about hanging him. Or her."

She thought of the look Cole Younger had given her just before he'd dragged her out of the bank. She thought of the expression in Jesse James's blue eyes when Clell had told him his brother was dead. With those thoughts in mind, she looked at Roger. "Well, if you want to get that fifty thousand dollars, you'd better see that Clell doesn't get hanged. In fact, you'd better sit down and help me figure out how to break him out of jail."

Leon Box took his hat off carefully and set it in the crook of his arm. With the other hand, he touched his hair to be sure the curls he'd spitted to either side of his forehead were still in place. Then he knocked. "Mrs. Appleton!" He listened. "Mrs. Appleton. It's Leon Box."

He waited a minute before tapping again. "Mrs. Appleton, I thought you'd like an escort for dinner tonight. A lady such as yourself shouldn't have to eat alone in a strange place."

Inside Room 12 Roger and Mary Carolyn froze. Co-conspirators caught in the act, they stared at each other. Then Mary Carolyn shrugged. "Just a minute, Mr. Box."

To her stepbrother she whispered, "That's a Pinkerton detective. He's come to ask me to dinner. Who do you think he'd believe if I told him my pitiful story? I'll tell him I'll meet him downstairs in an hour. That'll give us time to plan. At any rate, we don't want him suspicious of us." She looked at Roger sternly. "Did you ask a lot of questions, get people suspecting anything?"

He shook his head. "I swear—"

She slapped her hand over his mouth. "Sshh. He mustn't suspect that you're here." While Roger fumed silently, she looked at herself in the mirror, touched her hair, and moistened her lips. Motioning Roger down behind the bed, she opened the door just the width of her shoulders.

"Mr. Box." Her smile was genuine. "I really do appreciate your invitation."

He took in her new dress and the ringlets about her cheeks. She could see his interest spark. "I'll be honored, ma'am." He nodded at her dress. "If I may say so, you look like you're beginning to recover."

She ran a hand down the front of her skirt, smoothing it. "I thank you, sir. I had almost forgotten how clean, properly fitted clothing feels. I do thank you so much. Rest assured that Mr. Appleton will pay back everything that is owed." When he would have objected, she shook her head. "Since you ask me so nicely, I'll be happy to meet you downstairs in an hour."

He inclined his head and took a step back.

She closed the door. Leaning her ear against it, she waited until she could no longer hear his footsteps. Then she turned to her stepbrother. "Now," she said, "we have to make a plan."

"How do I know I can trust you? You flirted with that man and lied to him." He was looking at her again as if he couldn't stand the sight of her.

She seated herself on the edge of the bed and cocked her head to one side. Clell's words sprang from her lips. "I'm an outlaw. I have to do those things to stay alive. If I don't do a good job, I'll get caught and killed. You can trust me because we both want the same thing—to get Clell out of jail so he can lead us to the fifty thousand dollars."

Roger's mouth dropped open. His resentment changed to uncertainty. "You just admitted to being dishonest. I don't understand how you can do that."

In a moment of almost heady satisfaction, she realized she was the leader while her stepbrother felt like a fish out of water. He was probably ten years old than she was, but he would do what she told him. Silently, she thanked the outlaw Jesse James, the terrible Cole Younger, and most of all Clell Miller for the self-possession she felt now. If an outlaw she'd had to become, at least she'd had the best teachers in the world.

She looked at Roger critically, "If you don't have the stomach for this, why are you here?"

His color deepened as his expression showed he was furious and frustrated by turns. "Because my father sent me to get the money."

"But you aren't going to give it back to him," she guessed.

He spun around and strode to the window. "Of course, I'm going to give it back to him. What do you think I am?"

"The kind of man who'd threaten and blackmail a woman, his own stepsister," she replied promptly. "You're a thief too, but you need more practice."

He swung around, stammering, trying to protest.

She went on. "We need a good plan. There are four doors and at least two guns between Clell and freedom. We've got to get him out if we want that money." She held out a hand. "Do we split it between us—even?"

His eyes slid away, even as he took her hand. "Sure."

She compressed her mouth so her smile wouldn't betray her. He was a very poor liar. "Good. Now here's what we'll do. We need a distraction, someone to get the sheriff away to another part of town. Since you don't want to be seen, I suggest you start a fight—"

"Me!"

"It doesn't have to be a real fight. You could just go off to the edge of town and shoot off a gun."

"I don't have a gun."

She made a wry face. Was he just too green to be taught in time? "Then get one. Get two. The sheriff took mine. While I'm having dinner with the Pinkerton agent, you get us two guns and the ammunition to go with them. You also need to buy yourself a train ticket."

"Why? Aren't we going to ride off on horseback?"

"You wouldn't last five miles," she said coldly. "We take the train. The three of us. We'll be all dressed up in fine clothes. Clell can wear some of yours, can't he?"

He actually clutched the lapel of his suit. "Why should I give him any of my clothes?"

"Do you want him to escape and lead us to the money?" He hunched his shoulders and glared at her. She tried another tack. "Is there any particular reason why you want to steal this money from your father? Like he keeps you on an allowance or something?"

He growled and came at her with fists clenched.

She held up a hand. "Hit me and I'll scream bloody murder. When that Pinkerton agent gets here, my dress will be torn. I'll swear you tried to rob and rape me. Nobody will believe a word you say after that."

While he fumed uselessly, she thought about the distraction. "The train comes in at nine o'clock. We have to be ready to get Clell on it at that time. So we break him out at four o'clock in the morning. It'll be pitch dark. Probably everyone will be asleep. Shoot off a gun at the other end of town. That'll get the sheriff down there. I'll get Clell and lock up the old man. Come back to your hotel room and call for a bath."

"A bath?"

"Right. You're taking the early train, you need your bath."

He began backing away from her, shaking his head. "Wait a minute. I don't understand."

Really, he was so stupid. "While they're searching for the escaped outlaw, Clell takes a bath. You shave him—"

"Shave him!"

"—and cut his hair and dress him in your clothes. Put your glasses on him."

He came back toward her. "Now just a damn minute—"

She would not be stopped. "The two of you, all dressed up, get out on the platform the minute the train pulls into the station. Mingle with the other passengers. Look like you belong there. Get on and sit down in a hurry. Read the newspapers. Hold them in front of your faces. I'll get Lady Grace." She had a happy thought. "I'll even get the Pinkerton agent to help me load her."

"Who's Lady Grace?"

She could see it all so clearly that she knew nothing could go wrong. It was exactly the sort of daring thing Jesse James would have pulled. She could have hugged herself with glee. "My horse. The horse Clell bought for me. I'm not leaving her behind."

Her stepbrother grabbed fistfuls of his hair and pulled it. "I can't believe this. You're walking around with a Pinkerton agent while I'm supposed to get on board the train with an outlaw."

She nodded. "Preferably with your arm around his shoulder. Like you're the very best of friends."

"Oh, Lord. Anything else you want me to do?"

"While I'm eating, after you buy the guns and ammunition, you need to go by the livery stable and look around at the horses. Pick out Clell's. It's a big bay gelding."

"I don't know what that is." He looked aside in some embarrassment.

She was beginning to see why his father kept him on an allowance. "Tell them you understand that they just bought a big gelding that you've heard good things about. Tell them you heard Belle Shirley raised it."

"Who's Belle Shirley?"

She ignored the question. He was too ignorant for words. "Ask the price like you're interested. Then tell them it's too much. At four in the morning, I'll break Clell out of jail. At five minutes after four, you steal that horse and ride it out to shoot off your gun on the far end of town. Then you ride the horse around the town and tie it out on the south side where hopefully they won't find it until long, long after the train pulls out."

He looked at her in amazement. While she planned, she had moved to the washstand. She had washed her hands and face and combed her hair with the air of someone planning nothing more than the daily chores. Meeting his eyes in the mirror, she gave him a cool look. "This will work. Without a hitch. Trust me."

She took stock of herself in the mirror. At the same time chills trickled down her spine. She had a fleeting memory of the street in Ottumwa with the lanky deputy and the gunsmith shooting coolly, shooting to kill. Yet they had all gotten away with the money. She smiled. "I've planned with the best."

She tilted the mirror down and began to smooth her dress. Being an outlaw was hard on clothes. With a sigh, she flirted the corners of her lace collar.

When she turned, her smile was firmly in place. "Wait at least five minutes after I leave. Then be absolutely sure no one sees you coming out of my room. I'm Mrs. Oliver Appleton. I mustn't be suspected of anything."

Roger Somervell shook his head as she went out and closed the door behind her. He crossed to the window and stared mindlessly out at the dark street. Not once did it enter his head to disobey her.

Mary Carolyn had never been so cold as she was at four o'clock that morning. She had waited now for more than half an hour. What could Roger be doing? She had to have help in this. In her hand she clasped the gun he had stolen for her as well as a hammer and chisel to break the lock on the sheriff's office.

The night was black as pitch. The moon and stars were completely covered by a thick layer of clouds that bespoke snow. She hoped it snowed enough to cover any tracks. She hoped the sheriff would be convinced that Clell had escaped by horseback.

A pistol shot rang out, shattering the peaceful stillness of the Missouri night. She knew a moment of uncertainty. Had she made a mistake? Perhaps she would have been smarter to do the whole thing without disturbing anybody. Too late now. She braced the chisel against the door lock and struck it with all her might.

It was ridiculously easy. The thing burst open so swiftly that she dropped the chisel. Her tool made more noise clattering around than she had ever imagined. In the thick blackness she struck one of Roger's matches. The keys hung on the peg against the wall, just where the sheriff had left them.

Her hands were shaking as she snatched them up. She had never thought what she would do if he had taken them home with him. The thought rattled her still more.

Another shot and another, and then another farther away. "Good, Roger. Good."

She opened the inner door. No light showed through the barred door at the top of the stairs. As she pulled her bandanna up to her eyes, she uttered a fervent prayer that the old man had gone home for the night.

A light came on.

"Damn."

The guard had heard the noise and wakened. Hopefully, he would still be groggy. Fairly leaping up the flight, she clutched the key at the ready. She didn't have to fumble for the lock because the light showed through it faintly.

She was amazed that her hands were so steady, her breathing so calm. A cold had settled over her that had nothing to do with the chill of the stairwell. In that moment she knew she was an outlaw. She felt utterly ruthless. The man she loved was behind that door. She would break him out of jail. His rescue would go off without a hitch.

She turned the key. With her gun drawn, she pushed the door open. The old man was standing beside his cot, his nightshirt pulled up about his flabby shanks. Half-asleep, he was blinking in the light as he pissed into a chamber pot.

Mary Carolyn almost dropped the gun. The old man started and clutched at himself sending the stream spattering on the floor between his feet. Then he threw up his hands. "Don't shoot. Don't shoot."

In a couple of quick strides, she crossed the room and picked up his shotgun. His gunbelt lay on the desk. She swung that over her arm. "Face the wall!" she growled, pitching her voice as low as possible. "Keep your hands high."

He did as he was told, and she thanked whatever gods might

be on the side of outlaws. She fumbled through the keys, until she finally found the one that opened the door to the cells.

"Now," she ordered. "Turn around and march."

Obediently, he shuffled into the cell block.

"Clell!"

Her outlaw sprang to his feet in the darkness. "Goddam you!" The words were only whispered, but they carried a furious resonance that played along her nerves. "Goddam you."

She prodded the guard in the back. "Catch hold of those bars."

He didn't want to do it. "He'll kill me."

She prodded him some more. "He won't."

Clell said nothing. He merely waited until the guard reluctantly approached. Then Clell's arms shot out between the bars and caught the man's wrists. He jerked back and the old man was pinned against them. He began to whimper and plead. "Don't kill me. Don't kill me. I won't say a word. I won't."

Mary Carolyn turned the key and the cell door swung open. "Let him go."

Clell had already done so. He leaped past her and caught the old man by the back of his nightshirt. He pushed him into the cell and shut it. "Lock it."

"I'll freeze," the guard protested. "Don't leave me here. I'll freeze."

When Mary Carolyn hesitated, Clell pushed her hand aside and turned the key. Her hour of dominance was done. She was no longer the leader of the gang.

He dragged her across the floor and pushed her into the office, almost as ruthlessly as he had pushed the guard. He whirled to lock it.

"Wait," she protested. She grabbed the blanket from the cot, dashed back into the cell block, and flung it at the bars. "Here."

The old man didn't reply, but his white arm and hand caught the blanket.

She slipped back through and Clell slammed the door and

locked it. "Damn you," he said again. "Have you lost your mind?"

She pulled down her handkerchief and flashed him a cheeky smile as she handed him the gunbelt. "You're sure welcome, Mr. Miller. Let's go."

He buckled it on and blew out the light. In the absolute darkness he caught her at the door and swung her around. His hands were icy cold through the layers of her clothing. She could feel the chill of his clothing as well. He loomed above her, a dark face with glittering eyes. They would be angry, wondering, probably despairing. "Damn you."

His mouth came down on hers in the swiftest, hardest kiss she could imagine. Then he led her at breakneck speed down the stairs.

By the time they stepped out into the street, they had locked all the doors behind them and the sheriff's keys were safely in Clell's pocket. The night was totally silent.

Roger's shots from the north end of town had ceased altogether.

Chapter Twenty-Three

Mary Carolyn's arms encircled Clell's waist beneath his coat. Her hands locked together in a death grip. Reaction had set in with a vengeance. She was trembling violently, alternately cold and hot by turns, her teeth chattering. If she had been by herself, she knew her legs would have given way, and she would have collapsed in a heap.

Only his arm, warm and sustaining, across her shoulders propelled her down the street. At the door of the drummer's hotel, he leaned her against the wall. "I'll go in," he whispered.

"Why you?" She caught at his shoulders. "What if they see you?"

"Then they see me and I duck back out and run for it. If you go in and someone recognizes you, they'll want to know what you were doing out in the middle of the night dressed in men's clothes."

He was right. And she thanked God that he was there to take over when her brain seemed to have frozen. She didn't have to think about following a plan any longer. In fact, she had not planned how they would enter the hotel.

She remembered her first job, the train robbery. She had not planned how to get away from it either. Happily, now she could turn all this outlawry over to someone who really understood it. "All right. But be careful.

"Good luck," she whispered to the icy night. She hadn't heard any commotion. If the sheriff and the Pinkerton agent had heard Roger's shots and gotten out of their beds, they must be taking their time getting dressed. Why weren't they saddling their horses and galloping down the streets. At least they could have walked out and looked around. With these kinds of lawmen in town, no one would even find the old guard for another couple of hours.

Clell was back in a minute. "The clerk's asleep behind the desk, tipped back and snoring like a buzzsaw. You go first. I'll bring up the rear. If he wakes up"—he hesitated, then shrugged—"it's his funeral."

The sheer ruthlessness of his words sent shivers down her spine. Fear gave wings to her feet. She fled on tiptoe across the lobby and took the stairs three at a time. In the hall outside Room 12, she waited, panting, pressed against the wall, the doorknob in her hand.

Clell came charging up the stairs like a panther. His boots made almost no sound. For a big man he was amazingly light on his feet. She opened the door and he plunged through it. She followed, closing it behind her. Then her strength gave out. The black spots before her eyes obscured her vision. She never felt herself hit the floor.

She awoke on the bed. The lamp had been lit. Her coat and hat had been removed, and he was sitting beside her, cursing flatly. He had wet a cloth and was doing a poor job of mopping at her forehead and cheeks. She pushed it away and stared at him.

"You haven't got a lick of sense," he railed. "I thought for sure you'd learned something in the past three months, but no. Not you. Not a lick."

"You're free," she whispered.

"Sure I'm free, for about two hours. Then we'll both be caught."

She started to tell him that the hardest part of her plan was still ahead of her, but he was off on another tirade. She was actually feeling rather sleepy. Nervous exhaustion had communicated itself to every part of her body. The bed was soft and the hotel room relatively warm. She tried to smother a yawn.

He caught her at it. "Did you sleep at all this night?"

She smiled wanly. "Not a wink. I was afraid I wouldn't wake up at the proper time."

"Which was?" His eyes had their old blue steel glint back.

"Three-thirty."

"You sneaked out of this room at three-thirty in the morning. You could have been robbed or assaulted or—"

She really didn't want to hear any more of this. He hadn't even stopped bawling her out long enough to thank her. She put her fingers over his mouth. "Not on the streets of Carthage, Missouri. The sheriff's a real lawman."

Mention of the sheriff sent him off into another tirade.

She stared at the ceiling, remembering what she had gone through to listen to this. Suddenly, she giggled. "I've never seen a man . . . p-pissing before."

Her comment shut him up completely. Then he grinned. "When did you see a man pissing?"

"The old guard. He was . . . er . . . you know."

Suddenly, Clell laughed. He threw back his head and laughed out loud. She had to sit up and put a hand over his mouth again. "Ssh. Somebody'll hear you. And you're not supposed to be in here."

He flopped back on the bed and laughed to the ceiling, silently, his chest heaving, pulling one knee up and slapping it in his delight.

She leaned over him, giggling. "Another thing I've never seen. When he saw me with the gun, he missed the pot."

Tears spouted from Clell's eyes, he was laughing so hard. This time both knees came up, and he slapped them again. He wiped at the tears with his fist. Then he put both arms around her and hugged her against his chest. "You scared him so much he missed the pot?"

"Yes. He splattered the floor between his feet." She laughed too. The poor old man had been so terrified, he'd never even thought about going for his gun.

Clell dragged her down on the bed beside him and rolled over. His face hung above her. He stared down into her flushed face. A faint humming began in her brain. His eyes gentled as his lips caressed hers. She tasted a delicious happiness in her mouth. He lifted his head. "You must think I'm the most ungrateful so-and-so alive.

She smiled. "Yes."

"Thank you," he whispered against her lips. "Thank you. You rescued me. I still can't believe it." His own lips kissed the side of her mouth, her cheek, her chin. He ended up with his breath warming her ear. "Little outlaw."

When he raised his head, she felt warm all over, wanting to taste more. She opened her eyes, her heart in them. He dipped his head and slid his tongue into her mouth. He caressed its slick velvet interior until she couldn't suppress a moan of excitement. When he jerked his head up, he gave a soft groan of what must surely have been pure misery.

She followed his look to find his eyes had dropped to her breasts. Pushing against the soft fabric of her chambray shirt, her nipples were embarrassingly erect.

"God!" he gasped. "You take my breath away."

Memory tugged at a corner of her mind. She had sworn that she would never let him touch her again. He had refused her and hurt her in so many different ways. He wanted to marry her for the most insulting of reasons—because his first love, the mother of his daughter, was forever out of his reach.

Despite all this, she wanted him desperately.

His hands closed round her midriff. He slid his thumbs up over her ribs, over the lower curves of her breasts. The most sensitive part of a woman's entire body. Tormenting sensations lanced through her belly.

She gasped and twisted. Then his thumbs covered her nipples.

I'm dying. It was her last conscious thought as her body became its own master. The mass of nerves between her legs, the sensitive opening of her sheath, the walls of that sheath itself, the skin of her inner thighs, all swelled as hot blood coursed through them. She moaned mindlessly, stirring, opening her legs. *Please.* "Please."

"Yes. Oh, yes." He kissed her ear, tugging at it, blowing his hot breath into it.

She thought he would take her then. She was sure he would pull down her pants and push himself into her body. The heat and pressure became a fiendish ache that kept her writhing.

But he didn't stop. His thumbs circled and pressed, circled and pressed down as if punishing her nipples for hardening. The minutes went on and on, minutes of exquisite torment. Her whole body quaked and trembled. No longer able to control herself, she twisted her hips. Her thighs brushed against each other searching for but not finding relief.

"Stop," she moaned. She opened her eyes, pleading with him. "I can't stand any more. I really can't. Please, do it."

For answer he dropped a kiss onto her upturned mouth and then pulled her shirt aside. Not her pants, but her shirt. His hands dived beneath the camisole and ran over her bare skin. Every finger left a trail of fire. Then he found her breasts again.

"Monster," she whispered. "Oh, you monster."

"No, ma'am. Just an outlaw." He sucked in his breath. The steel was back in his eyes. In that moment he looked capable of anything. This time his fingers shaped her breast, cupping it in his hand, pressing the nipple between his thumb and forefinger. He pinched her. She arched desperately, whimpering, pleading.

Her skin was damp and hot. The perfume of her passion rose around them. She forgot about the people who might overhear, as she lifted her distress to the ceiling.

Perhaps he had pushed himself to the limit. Perhaps, a little beyond. His hands fumbled at her waist. Desire had made him clumsy.

Still kissing him, Mary Carolyn brushed his hands aside and opened her garments herself. No words could describe the pounding, swelling desire. She wanted him, wanted his body, wanted the ecstatic release that he'd denied her and that she'd denied herself since Dallas. Desperately eager, she worked her pants off one leg and returned her hands to his shirt.

In seconds they were both naked after a fashion. His pants, pushed down around his boot tops hampered him not at all.

Groaning, he lowered himself between her legs. His hard shaft found its way unerringly. With a moan of pleasure, she wrapped her arms around his neck and her legs around his waist. He shuddered. No need for a delicate probing. He slid into her, burying himself to the hilt. She locked her heels and arched her back.

An exquisite explosion wracked them, spasming their muscles, driving the breath from their lungs, stopping their hearts. Then he collapsed with his face against the side of her throat. They shuddered together in the aftermath.

For more than half a minute, the sensations went on. When they ceased, they remained joined together, their breathing imperceptible. Breast to breast, belly to belly, they savored the languour of the aftermath.

Mary Carolyn could feel the blood pulse through her, feel the bud of pleasure still throbbing between her legs. She could barely move, but it swelled again against the nest of hair at the base of Clell's torso. A shiver, a twist to ease the beginning of another hot ache, and she stiffened. This couldn't be happening. Yet it did. Her back arched, her head dropped back, this time lolling off the bed, so far had his thrust driven her. And she was falling, falling, spinning, spinning into darkness and whirling bands of white and blue light.

The room was still in full darkness when he stirred. "I've got to get up. I've got to leave."

"No. You mustn't." She flung an arm across his chest to hold him down on the bed.

"They can't find me here. Maybe I'll get lucky. I can get away if I can get to the livery stable."

She held him with all her strength, until he subsided with a helpless sigh. "Buster, I will say this. You are one hell of a lover. You've sure taken the ginger out of me."

She laughed. "You can't go to the livery stable. It's too late to steal your horse. It's already been stolen."

She felt him stiffen, but he didn't protest. Nor did he try to rise again. After a full minute, he asked in a resigned voice, "Why don't you tell me exactly what's going to happen next?"

She shifted uneasily. Until that minute she hadn't thought what might happen between Roger and Clell. She had told her outlaw that she was an orphan. How would he react to the news that she had a stepbrother and a stepfather?

If Roger's sudden entrance made Clell angry, he would have to keep his anger to himself. The shots north of town were the signal that Roger had done exactly what she'd asked of him.

"My stepbrother will be here in a little while," she said evenly.

"Stepbrother!" Clell sat up and looked at her.

"I know what you're thinking. I didn't think of the man my mother married as my stepfather. I didn't even know that I had a stepbrother. And I surely didn't know they knew that I existed. When I got older, I decided that my mother had shipped me off to that orphanage to hide me away, so her new husband wouldn't know about her shame. I thought the tuition checks probably came from her. I thought she'd signed his name without his knowing. Evidently, that wasn't what happened."

"Which makes him even worse than you thought. Your stepfather and his son knew about you and didn't do anything to help you," Clell growled. "Real nice people your mother picked."

She shrugged. "I don't blame them for that. After all, nobody wants to admit to a bastard in the family."

He flushed and looked away.

She shouldn't have hurt his feelings, but right now she was sick to death with discussion of fathers. "My stepfather sent Roger to find me because, according to him, I look like my mother. My stepfather thought he recognized me during the robbery."

The warmth of their love had faded from Clell's eyes. They had chilled again to their normal steel blue. He leaned back against the head of the bed. "It's not hard to figure out what he's here for. He wants the money."

Her outlaw was more perceptive than she had been. "Yes."

He laced his hands over his lean belly. "What'd you tell him?"

"That you were the only one who knew where it was," she replied promptly.

"So he helped you break me out of jail, and I'm supposed to lead him to it."

She nodded sadly. No need to explain any more. Her outlaw's natural cynicism had already worked out the rest of the story.

"Those shots," Clell guessed, "were a distraction, and he stole my horse, didn't he? So they think I've gotten away and ridden out of town."

She nodded. "Just like Jesse James."

Clell grinned at the reference, but the deep frown creased between his eyes. "So far it's a good plan. He'll come back here, and the three of us will escape together."

His eyes narrowed. "And ten miles up the line, I throw him off the train?"

She looked at him bleakly. "You'll have to make up your mind about that. But here's what he's going to do when he gets back. He's going to take you to his room. He'll order a bath, and then you'll cut your hair and shave off your mustache." She could have laughed when he touched his fingers to the heavy blond hair. She knew just how he felt. Last year she'd taken the scissors to her own hair which had never been cut in her life. The scissor blades coming together in it was a sensation she would feel to her dying day. "He'll loan you a suit and a derby and his spare pair of glasses."

"Glasses! Damn!"

"He's already bought a ticket for you. You'll get on the train together the minute the conductor lets down the step. If he says anything, Roger will tell him that you're feeling sick. I'll see that Lady Grace is loaded and then I'll get on another coach." She looked at him anxiously. She had thought it was a good plan, but her real outlaw could probably shoot it full of holes.

Instead, he looked at her in dawning wonderment. Then he twisted around in bed and kissed her hard, a salute. "Damn! The sheriff and the Pinkerton agent will be out trying to find the trail. No one will be watching the train at all. You've done it, sweetheart. The smartest, bravest outlaw of them all. Jesse'd be proud to hear the whole story. He'd figure you learned it all from him.'' He drew back. His smile was broad. ''You know. We might just make it.''

They lay together on the bed as the morning light stole through the curtains. Clell had dressed. Mary Carolyn had put on her nightgown.

Suddenly, the door burst open. The outlaw dived off the bed. The girl sat up with her sheet pulled to her breast.

''It's me, sister dear. Did you get him?'' Roger Somervell closed the door behind him.

Clell rose from behind the bed as Roger swung round the end of it. He looked fagged out and furious. His suit was torn and muddy to the knees. He wore no hat, and his hair was falling in his face. His shoes were covered with mud. He pointed an angry finger at the outlaw. ''I just rode a horse at breakneck speed through a freezing night for you. And then ran a couple of miles back. Miller's your name, isn't it?''

Mary Carolyn rose, reaching for her robe. ''But you did it, Roger. You did it, and the sheriff is probably off trying to find Clell north of town.''

''Unless all of that was a wild-goose chase.'' He swung on her furiously. ''I never saw a living soul. Not one. That whole thing was just an excuse to make a fool of me.'' He looked at her flannel nightgown and the rumpled covers. ''While you probably had him out in five minutes and home and snug into bed.'' His mouth curled in disdain. ''And I don't have to ask what you and your outlaw have been doing in the meantime, my whorish—''

''That's enough.'' Clell lunged across the room. His fist wrapped around Roger's tie and twisted. ''Your *step*sister is my wife. She may have married the wrong man, but she's still a lady.''

''She's a train robber. And you're an outlaw.'' Roger

laughed. "And I don't believe for one minute that you married her. Why should you? You're getting what you want for free."

Clell hit him. The short left chop to the jaw snapped Roger's head back on his shoulders. He cried out sharply as Clell prepared to hit him again.

"Oh, don't." Mary Carolyn ran forward to separate the two men. "Don't hit him. Stop fighting, you two. Roger, behave yourself."

Clell let her stepbrother go with a violent shove. The banker's son staggered back into a chair which fell with him. Mary Carolyn wrung her hands. "Stop it. You're going to wake the hotel. Roger, are you all right? Clell, you have to thank Roger. The sheriff won't be combing the town for you and watching the livery stable and the train station. Roger, if you want your share of this money, you're going to have to work for it."

"I can just kill him now." Clell drew his gun.

Roger came off the floor in a rush and caught Mary Carolyn around the waist. "Shoot me and you shoot her."

For answer, Clell braced his pistol over his left forearm and aimed the barrel directly between Roger's eyes.

The banker's son paled. He clutched at his stepsister as if she were a lifeline instead of a hostage. "Tell him to put that gun down." He squeezed her hard. "Tell him if he shoots me he'll bring everybody in the hotel in here in two minutes flat."

"Let me go. Let go, Roger." She extricated herself from his arms. Suddenly, she was very tired. The escape was getting more complicated by the minute. The hardest part lay ahead, yet they were fighting like bad boys.

Clell's gun never wavered. "You came into her room. She shot you when you tried to rob her."

"You wouldn't dare," Roger blustered. "She'd be in jail and you'd still be trying to get out of town."

"Stop it! Stop it, both of you," Mary Carolyn stamped her bare foot. Since it made almost no sound, it made no impression on them. "Put that gun down, Clell. Roger, stop acting like a jackass and tend to business. You want the money, don't you?"

He nodded.

"Then take him to your room. It'll be light soon and people will see you. You have to get him bathed and dressed like we planned."

At that point Roget remembered his part in the plan was important. He assumed a brave stance and crossed his arms over his chest. "I don't suppose he'd just tell us what we wanted to know if we threatened to shoot him."

Clell holstered his gun and crossed his arms over his chest as if to say the suggestion was ridiculous.

Mary Carolyn feared she might collapse. She barely made the bed in time to sink down on it. From there she waved a hand at them both. "Just get out of here. I've done all I can for both of you. Leave me alone, so I can sleep for a couple of hours."

They looked at each other and at her. Clell stalked across the room and peeked out. With a muffled exclamation he jerked his head back in and closed the door. Whirling, he motioned Roger back. "It's Box."

"Oh, no," Mary Carolyn moaned.

"Who?" Roger looked around wildly.

"The Pinkerton." Clell darted across the room to catch Roger by the shoulder and drag him to the wall beside the door.

"What . . . ?"

"Shut up."

"Mrs. Appleton! Mrs. Appleton!" Box knocked sharply.

"Not too soon." Clell held up his hand. "You're sound asleep."

She nodded. Her stomach burned. Her knees were trembling. She said a little prayer.

"Mrs. Appleton, are you in there? Are you all right?"

Clell nodded to her.

"Who's there?" Mary Carolyn tried to slur her words to sound only half-awake.

"It's Leon, Mrs. Appleton."

"Oh, Mr. Box. What's wrong?" Still she kept her voice muffled. "What time is it?"

"It's five-thirty, ma'am." He waited, seemed to be hesitating. "Are you all right?"

"Of course, I'm all right. Except that someone has wakened me out of sound sleep in the middle of the night." She had no trouble in sounding irritated. Under no circumstances would she let him in. In fact, she wouldn't even open the door.

"No one's disturbed you?"

"Not until now." Had he seen Clell at the door? She looked at Clell fearfully. He drew his gun. Roger's eyes bugged. His face was white.

"Mrs. Appleton, Clell Miller's escaped from jail."

"Oh, no!" she exclaimed. Suddenly, she knew her ground. Her voice rose to a hysterical peak. "Oh, no. How did he get out? Other members of the James gang must be in the vicinity. Oh, that dreadful Cole Younger. Oh, oh, oh."

"Mrs. Appleton. Mrs. Appleton. There's no need for you to be afraid. They've gone." His face must be pressed to the door. His voice resonated as if he were standing in the room. "We heard the shots they fired as they rode out of town."

"Are you sure? Oh, how can you be sure?" She raised her voice as any terrified woman would have done.

"The sheriff's going to organize a posse and leave at first light. I wanted you to know. I'm going with him, of course."

"Oh, do be careful." She stepped closer to the door. "He's very dangerous, you know. Ruthless. You can't imagine. They all are. Utterly ruthless."

He said nothing. Had she said too much? What was he thinking? She rubbed her hands down the sides of her gown.

Then his voice came through the door. "I expect I won't see you again."

Mary Carolyn's eyes flashed to Clell. He grinned faintly and used his gun barrel to push his hat back. "Oh, I do hope you won't get hurt. I thank you for all you've done for me. And, Mr. Box, I hope you catch him. No poor innocent woman should have to go through what I have."

"No, ma'am. You're right about that." There was a silence outside the door. They listened intently. Clell leveled his gun barrel. Then Box's voice came softly, "Good-bye, Mary. Godspeed."

His tone caught her by surprise. A tiny thrill went through her. Clell scowled. Someone else found her desirable. Someone else could have loved her. "Good-bye, Leon. Thank you again. Godspeed."

Chapter Twenty-Four

The train was late.

Mary Carolyn's stomach had been twisted in a tight knot for more than two hours. She had waited on the platform for three quarters of an hour, pacing back and forth, shivering in the cold, patting Lady Grace, and pretending she did not know Clell and Roger a few feet away.

Finally, the ticket agent had announced that the train would be late by another hour. A rock slide in the mountains had blocked the track and damaged one of the rails. A crew had had to come up from Van Buren to replace it.

All the passengers had then walked across the street to the drummer's hotel where they'd waited in the lobby.

From where she sat, Mary Carolyn had a chance to study Clell's face. While Roger paced the hotel lobby like a panther in a cage, Clell slumped in a corner of the settee. Instead of a hat, Roger had dressed him in a cap, pulled low over his forehead. It was the ideal thing to wear. Of black and tan hound's-tooth wool with earflaps and a bill, it all but covered his face. Moreover, it was a Northern garment. Very few Southerners wore them.

Jesse James himself would have had to look twice to recognize Clell. With a haircut and a shave and the business suit of a banker's son, his appearance was unbelievably changed. Even though Roger's suit was tight across his broad shoulders and the trousers had to ride low about his lean hips in order to look long enough, he looked very handsome, very important. No one would dare to question him, she assured herself at least a dozen times.

If only the train would arrive, so they could get on before the posse got discouraged.

She had schooled herself to keep her face turned away from Clell, but she couldn't stand it any longer. Looking around with elaborate casualness, she glanced at him. Their eyes met.

His expression was like a blow. Feeling like a child that had been scolded, she whipped her face about to face the rest of the room. She mustn't do that again, no matter how much she needed reassurance.

He must be as nervous as she was. In the midst of his enemies, where a betrayal, no matter how accidental, could end in his death, he had to remain alert. One arm lay limp along the back of the settee, the other lay across his stomach. A hand was unseen inside his coat. She had no doubt it was on his gun.

She had to clench her teeth to keep them from chattering. He would kill if cornered.

She put a gloved hand up to conceal her eyes. *Please. Please, dear God. Let them get the track fixed quickly.*

A jitney pulled up in front of the hotel. Four men came in talking loudly.

"—bet they didn't even have a member of the James gang," one was saying. "Probably wouldn't know one if they'd had him. We've made a wild-goose chase."

"No telling who they had, but he couldn't have been much. Any idiot could have broken out of that jail," a second one agreed. "Not even a story in that." He signed the register and then stepped aside to lean his elbow on the desk and survey the room.

"The train's late, sirs," the clerk told them. "Trouble on the line." He read their entries upside down. "Ah, *Kansas City Star*. Reporters, are you? Looking for Jesse James?"

They looked at each other and then at him. "Was he here?"

"Oh, yes. Not too long ago." The clerk assumed an air of self-importance. "He registered right here at this hotel, under an assumed name, of course."

They gathered around. Two pulled out notebooks.

"What'd he say?"

As the clerk began to thumb through the register, the long blast of a train whistle sounded in the far distance. Finally, it was approaching the station. The reporters turned away without so much as a backward glance at the frustrated clerk.

At long last, Mary Carolyn thought. *At long last.*

Clouds had drifted across the face of the quarter moon by the time the train stopped for water and fuel. Mary Carolyn sat bolt upright, unable to sleep on the hard wooden benches. Even though the lights had been turned out in the coaches, she could not stop worrying.

The all-day trip to Kansas City had lasted well into the night. Every time the train stopped, either for a small town or for water and fuel, she had wakened. Several times Clell had walked by her. She knew his gait. She recognized the hand that he laid on the bench in front of her. Even though she didn't dare glance up, his presence reassured her.

Once she had been looking out the window and had seen his reflection in the glass. She couldn't stop herself. She had looked up into his face. This time he had nodded politely, as a gentleman might do upon meeting a lady. She took comfort in that.

Soon. Soon.

Suddenly, the lights came on in the coach. "Hands up, ever'body!" a man's voice shouted. "Up on yore feet, gents!"

Clell rolled his eyes in disgust and frustration. They were amateurs. A gang of scraggly roadside hobos. Some didn't even have guns. But their clubs, made of hickory and studded with nails, could do frightful damage. Without a cent to his name, he knew he was in for trouble.

Beside him, Roger whispered. "Oh, my God. Are they friends of yours? Can you—?"

"Never saw them before," Clell whispered back. "Tell them I'm feebleminded."

"What?"

"When they want my money, tell them I'm your feeble-minded brother and you don't let me have any."

"Why? Awwk!" Roger staggered forward as a hard object drove into the middle of his back. He had to catch himself on the seat in front of him.

"Shet yore trap there. None o' thet whisperin' back 'n' forth."

Roger rolled over, his hips on the back of the seat. His eyes bugged out as the barrel of an Enfield poked him in the belly. Worse than the sight of the rifle was the gargoyle face above it. "No. Take that away. Get away. Stop it!"

"Shet your trap!" the hobo repeated angrily. To a city-bred young man, he was a fearsome creature. Muddy brown eyes, a bulbous nose, and faintly purple lips were all that showed out of a dense tangle of grizzled hair. He and the rest of his band wore drapes of ragged, filthy clothing under tattered oilskins. Clell guessed they were remnants of the many bands of bushwhackers and jayhawkers that had roamed Kansas and Missouri for the last ten years. "Fork it over."

"What?" Roger looked desperately at Clell. Disoriented and frightened, he shook his head. He looked back at the hobo.

"C'mon!" The man poked again.

"What? Just a minute—"

The gun exploded in Roger's stomach.

Clell heard Mary Carolyn's scream a second before it was drowned by the cries and curses from the other passengers.

The hobo reeled back, his eyes widened in surprise. He turned the rifle to stare at it.

Clell whipped his own gun out from beneath his coat. His thumb pulled the hammer back. It went off in the robber's face. The bulbous nose disappeared in a spray of red. The man's head snapped back as he toppled over into the aisle. The passengers dived between the seats. At the door of the coach, another robber fumbled with a sack to bring up his gun. Clell shot him where he stood. The screaming and crying thoroughly rattled the two thugs at the other end of the car. They dived out the door.

Roger's body slumped down onto the floor between the seats. Slowly, he toppled over into the aisle. Gun still drawn, Clell knelt beside him. One glance told him that Mary Carolyn's blackmailer didn't have long for the world. Blood gushed from a hole in his belly. The wool around the edge of the wound was charred, a fiber or two still glowing from the heat of the explosion. Smoke from the black powder stained a circle over his ribs and down across his hips.

His eyes were closed.

Clell reached down and took one of Roger's hands. It was flaccid, but the man's eyes blinked open.

Clell looked up to see Mary Carolyn crawling down the aisle toward him. "Keep your head down," he called. Then in a voice that brooked no arguments he shouted, "Turn off the lights!"

The thwarted robbers fired the first of a series of shots. Glass shattered.

"Don't give them any targets! Turn off the lights!" At the same time he whipped out his handkerchief and pushed it into the flood of red welling from Roger's belly.

More passengers screamed and cursed. Then men at each end of the car leaped to turn down the lamps. It was a signal for several of the more intrepid passengers to return fire.

"Roger," Mary Carolyn called. "Roger." After one quick glance she did not look at his body. Instead, she tenderly lifted her stepbrother's head into her lap. "Roger."

His eyes moved, searched, found hers. His lips moved. "Sister . . ."

Pity, pain, resentment all clawed at her insides. Now he could call her sister. "Be still," she cautioned. "They're driving them off. We'll get a doctor to you in just a minute."

His eyelids fluttered. "Don't feel anything. Just numb. Must not be too bad."

"No," she agreed with him. "It's not too bad." She looked at Clell. His handkerchief was soaked. He looked around helplessly. Mary Carolyn pulled the shawl off her shoulders and thrust it into his hands.

Roger tried to lift his head, but he couldn't. Fear showed in his eyes for the first time. When he tried to speak again, terror took all the timbre from his voice.

Mary Carolyn bowed her head to catch the sound.

"Tell Father I found you."

Bright red blood bubbled through the loose strands of the shawl. Clell sank back on his knees.

Roger's eyes widened. Then the irises relaxed. Mary Carolyn was left staring into black sightless holes.

She stood beside Lady Grace while Clell scraped aside the snow and wielded an infantryman's spade. Between the roots of the largest of the three oak trees, he turned the earth over only a few times, before he grunted.

"Find it?" she asked.

"Sure thing," he replied heartily. "I hid it where it'd be easy. Unless somebody uprooted this big old tree and carried it away. We'll be on our way in a couple of minutes."

"Very clever." She praised him and meant it.

He dropped on one knee and pulled the saddlebags out. The leather was dark with damp and touched in spots with blue mildew, but otherwise the prize was just as he had left it. Clell carried it to her and put it into her hands. "It's yours. Whatever you want to do is all right with me."

"You're sure?"

He bent and kissed her, his lips soft and warm with promise. "I've never been surer of anything."

DeGraffen Somervell sat in the darkness as the Rock Island from Kansas City to Chicago rolled north across the prairies.

At the other end of his private car, firmly anchored with ropes, was the casket of his son.

Somervell's loss had not impressed itself on his consciousness until he'd watched the box being unloaded from the hearse and put on board.

Now he stared at it, trying to imagine his son inside, trying to imagine what he would do without a son. Roger had never been the best of boys. He had been resentful and rebellious, but he had been his own blood. He could marry again, he supposed, but the very idea depressed him further. He was well into his fifties.

Moreover, one did not replace one's child like a broken piece of furniture or a family pet.

He thought about the boy's death. Shot by train robbers. There was irony there also. In a sense the first train robbery had sent Roger to his death. And the money had hardly mattered. Not much. Not at all.

He had lighted a cigar and poured himself a glass of brandy, but the cigar had gone out and he had barely tasted the brandy. He lifted it to his lips, then heaved a sigh and set it down. Roger had liked brandy. He had liked all the finer things of life. He'd loved being rich, but he had hated the idea of working for wealth, especially after Madeleine had become his stepmother.

The memory of his dead wife sent him deeper into depression. He buried his head in his hands. She had been his such a short time. He had told himself that she would win the boy over. Perhaps she would have. But Roger had been so angry that they had decided to send him away to school. And she had died before he could come home. So he'd left the boy there until he graduated.

God! His life sounded like a Shakespearean tragedy. He sucked in his breath hard and pressed his fingers into his eyes. He couldn't let himself weep. But where better to weep than in this dim solitude. No one would interrupt him. No one could see his weakness.

The train began to slow. Its mournful triadic whistle wailed up to the ice-ringed moon. The wheels squealed as steel met steel. Each car shuddered in turn as it fought its couplings. Roger's coffin vibrated and shifted.

Somervell shuddered too at the thought of his son's body being jostled. He tipped his head back and stared at the coffin, willing it to hold his son's body securely.

The train had scarcely come to a stop when he felt the cold air on the back of his neck. He rose slowly and turned to face the intruder. The single lamp shone down on the same slim figure as before.

The hat was pulled low, the face was obscured in shadow.

Rage exploded in his brain. "Damn you!" he cried. "There's nothing here for you to steal this time. This is a funeral coach."

The figure came closer. "I know. I'm the one who sent you the telegram. I'm sorry about your son."

Somervell had been right. It was a girl's voice. And it sounded familiar. Then she jerked off her hat. He shuddered. "Madeleine?"

"No," she said. "Not Madeleine."

"Mary Carolyn?"

She didn't answer. Instead, she stepped forward quickly and thrust a large leather object into his hands. "Here."

It was a pair of heavy saddlebags. He handled them clumsily until he could get them looped over his arm. "What's this?"

"It's the money that was taken from you."

So he had been right about it all. Madeleine's daughter. He asked the question, more to keep her there than anything because she was already backing away. "Did you steal it?"

She was almost to the door. "Yes. Now I'm returning it." She drew in a sharp breath. "Roger found me. He told me to tell you he did. I was with him when he got shot. We were coming back to Kansas City together."

Somervell dropped the heavy burden. It thudded to the floor and he stepped over it in his eagerness to catch her. "So he was bringing you back to me. That's good. That's good. He was right to do that. Wait. Don't go."

Behind her, in the doorway, another figure appeared. Much

taller, broader of shoulder, a formidable man. "Don't come any closer, mister. You got back what was *borrowed*." The big man emphasized the word. "We've got to be on our way."

"Who are you?" the banker demanded.

"An outlaw," was the cool answer. Men's voices rumbled from outside as they walked along the track. The crew was returning to the caboose. "We'd better go."

"Madeleine," Somervell called. "Don't go with him. Please don't leave me. You're all I've got now."

"I'm not Madeleine," the girl said softly. She had backed up against the man's chest. He put a big hand on her shoulder. In another instant the two would slip out the door and vanish into the night. If that happened, Somervell knew he would never see either of them again.

"Stay!" he begged. "Don't go. Madeleine would want us to be together. You're my stepdaughter."

The girl froze. Then she gave a little shake of her head. The train shivered. The engine was building up a head of steam. "Why didn't you think about that before?"

"I . . . I . . ." In his desperation he couldn't think.

The man stepped back onto the platform. "Come on," he insisted. "No sense jumping if we don't have to."

"I have to go," she murmured.

The heavy door shut behind them. He ran after them. The man had already sprung to the ground and now held up his arms. The girl paused with one leg over the railing.

"Mary Carolyn," DeGraffen Somervell called. He was begging now. He had never begged before. "Please let me know where to find you. There's so much to say. I loved your mother with all my heart."

The ice-bound moon found her face. As she shook her head, tears glistened on her lashes. And then she reached out and slid into the waiting arms of the man. The train jerked and then rolled forward. The banker clutched the icy rail as her outlaw swung her down. Without a backward glance they sprinted hand in hand into the darkness.

The whistle blew a strong imperious blast. Again. The train

lurched forward. The iron wheels began to roll, faster and faster, gathering speed, bound for Chicago.

Northfield, Minnesota
September 7, 1876

Elias Stacy raced out onto Division Street and fired at one of the five mounted lookouts in front of the First National Bank. In his excitement he'd loaded the shotgun with birdshot. The blast knocked the outlaw out of the saddle, but it didn't kill him. With his face bleeding from more than a dozen wounds, he pulled himself to his feet, mounted, and charged.

Stacy ran for his life. Lucky for him, a medical student on vacation from the University of Michigan had found his father's old Army carbine. From a vantage point upstairs in the window of the Dampier House next door, he drew a bead and fired. The outlaw fell backward out of the saddle.

"Jim!" Cole Younger sprang down and knelt beside him. "Jim, can you hear me?"

Jim Pool tried to push himself up. Then fell back and rolled over. Cole grabbed the dead man's cartridge belt and pistols and swung up into the saddle.

As Jesse and a couple of the boys erupted from the bank, they were greeted by a hail of gunfire from citizens all along the streets. A hardware merchant did for Billy Chadwell, who fell dead from a bullet through the heart. The same man then shot Cole through the shoulder. Frank James was hit in the leg. Cole's brother Jim was hit in the face and Bob had a shattered elbow.

In twenty minutes the James gang were fleeing for their lives, bleeding badly, shot to pieces.

When the smoke cleared and the two bodies had been cleaned up, one was identified as that of the young outlaw Billy Chadwell.

The second was harder because of the mess the birdshot had made of his face. Only a picture from a newspaper and the accompanying description made a satisfactory identification possible. The authorities announced they had killed one of Jesse James's oldest and most loyal friends—longtime gang member Clell Miller.

Cutter's Knob, Arkansas
December 20, 1876

"It's a letter for me." Sarah Susannah Bradburn could hardly contain her delight. "I never got a letter before."

"All the way from California." Esther turned the envelope over and over in her hands. Finally, she raised it to the light. "I can't imagine who it's from. I thought your Uncle Daniel was going to stop in Colorado for the winter months."

"Mother!" came the exasperated protest.

"I'm sorry." Esther surrendered the envelope with a smile. "I've never gotten a letter from California, Miss Smarty-pants. I just wanted to hold it for a minute."

Sarah Susannah cooed over it, looking at the profile of Andrew Jackson on the two-cents stamp and the postmark dated almost two weeks before. Then she opened it, with almost reverential awe. When she unfolded the paper, five brown-backed bills fell out. "Oh, Mother!"

Esther went down on her knees with her daughter to stare in awe at five twenty-dollar bills with the words National Currency and United States across the top. The battle of Lexington was depicted on the left and Columbia holding the flag on the right.

They stared at each other. Sarah handed her the letter and then picked them up, counting out loud. She held them out like a fan. "A hundred dollars!" Her mouth shaped the words but no sound came. She had never seen so much money in her life. "A hundred dollars."

Silently sinking back on her heels, Esther gave her back the letter.

Still holding the bills, Sarah flattened the letter on the floor and bent over to read it.

Sacramento, California
Christmas, 1876

My dearest daughter,

    I take pen in hand to send you my love and this gift in the hope that it will stand you in good stead. I have devoted myself to hard work for almost two years now and can testify that I have earned it honestly. I have completely reformed and left the outlaw trail forever.

    My good wife, Mary Carolyn Miller, tells me to say that you should use it for your trousseau or your education. But if God is willing and my health remains strong, I will send more before that faraway day.

    Your baby brother Lee is chubby and smiling. His hair is blond and his eyes are brown just like yours. We wish you could visit us and get to know him.

    I know you will grow into a beautiful young woman and I beg you to think kindly of your Johnny-come-lately father.

I remain,
Clell Miller

The Bradburn women looked at each in stunned silence. Sarah trailed her fingertips over and over the black flowing script. At last she whispered, "It is all right?"

Esther's eyes were filled with tears. *Clell Miller. Not dead,* she thought. *Ah, Clell.* To Sarah, she said, "It's all right."

Author's Note

Just as all wars do, the Civil War left a generation scarred. The young rebels of Missouri who fought for the Confederacy returned to find their homes about to be sold for taxes, their money worth nothing, their towns under martial law, their enemies in power. They used the skills the war had taught them to save what they could. Their efforts were especially tragic, for they spawned the infamous gangs of outlaws that ravaged the border states for many years.

Cole Younger, along with his brothers Bob and Jim, was captured and sentenced to life in prison because Minnesota did not have the death penalty. He was paroled after twenty-five years and returned to Missouri, where the young people of Lee's Summit called him "Uncle Cole." He built a second career lecturing on penitent themes until his death in 1916. He never married.

Jesse James escaped the law at Northfield, only to be shot in the back of the head at close range by a pearl-handled Colt .45 on April 3, 1882. Jesse's cousin Bob Ford was sentenced to be hanged by a Missouri jury, but was pardoned by the governor. Some say that Ford shot a drifter to collect the $10,000 reward and that Jesse died variously in Texas, in New

Mexico, and in California in the first half of the twentieth century. Frank James surrendered six months after Jesse's death and was tried in a packed opera house at Gallatin, Missouri. He was found innocent amongst cheers from the crowd. He died on the James homeplace in 1922.

Myra Belle Shirley married Sam Starr of the Cherokee Nation. She moved with him to Oklahoma, to a section of land she named Younger's Bend. She continued dealing in stolen goods for other outlaws as well as dabbling in horse rustling and bank robbing. She took four rounds of buckshot in the back and died instantly near her home on February 3, 1889. Her daughter, Pearl, whose birth certificate listed her last name as Younger, commissioned a fine tombstone. Belle's murderer was never caught, but American folklore and legend were waiting to embrace her. In the year of her death, the first of many dime novels about Belle appeared. In black velvet dresses and ostrich-plumed hats, she became *Belle Starr, the Bandit Queen.*

Americans have always loved their outlaws.

Rachel Davis

Dallas, Texas

DANGEROUS GAMES   (0-7860-0270-0, $4.99)
by Amanda Scott

When Nicholas Barrington, eldest son of the Earl of Ul-
combe, first met Melissa Seacort, the desperation he
sensed beneath her well-bred beauty haunted him. He
didn't realize how desperate Melissa really was . . . until
he found her again at a Newmarket gambling club—being auctioned off by her father to the highest bidder. So,
Nick bought himself a wife. With a villain hot on their
heels, and a fortune and their lives at stake, they would
gamble everything on the most dangerous game of all:
love.

A TOUCH OF PARADISE   (0-7860-0271-9, $4.99)
by Alexa Smart

As a confidence man and scam runner in 1880s America,
Malcolm Northrup has amassed a fortune. Now, posing
as the eminent Sir John Abbot—scholar, and possible
discoverer of the lost continent of Atlantis—he's taking
his act on the road with a lecture tour, seeking funds for
a scientific experiment he has no intention of making.
But scholar Halia Davenport is determined to accompany
Malcolm on his "expedition" . . . even if she must kidnap
him!